THE FORGOTTEN DEAD

Tove Alsterdal is an established and well respected Swedish journalist, novel dramaturge and script writer. For the last 25 years she has written for theatre as well as paper media, television, radio, and film. She is also known as the editor of Liza Marklund's best selling crime novels.

In 2009 Tove Alsterdal published her successful debut *The Forgotten Dead*. The second one, *Grave of Silence*, was published in January 2012 and has been equally praised for the suspense and language, as well as a story that extends the boundaries of the genre.

Tove Alsterdal was born in 1960 in Malmö. Her family has its roots in the very north of Sweden, a rural borderland where her second novel takes place.

She now lives in Stockholm with three daughters.

www.tovealsterdal.se/books/
f Facebook.com/tove.alsterdal

TOVE ALSTERDAL

THE FORGOTTEN DEAD

Translated from the Swedish
by Tiina Nunnally

HarperCollins*Publishers*

HarperCollins
PUBLISHERS
Since 1817

HarperCollins*Publishers* Ltd
1 London Bridge Street,
London SE1 9GF

www.harpercollins.co.uk

First published in Great Britain by HarperCollins*Publishers* 2017
1

Originally published in 2009 by Lind & Co, Sweden, as *Kvinnorna på stranden*

A catalogue record for this book is available from the British Library

ISBN: 978-0-00-815898-9

Set in Sabon LT Std by Palimpsest Book Production Ltd, Falkirk, Stirlingshire

Printed and bound in the UK by Clays Ltd, St Ives plc

Chapter 1

Tarifa
Monday, 22 September
3.34 a.m.

The boat heeled over and the view through the small port-hole changed. For a long while she could see only the masts of other boats and clouds, but now she glimpsed the town for a moment. All the windows were dark. If she waited any longer it would soon be dawn.

When she stood up a sharp pain shot through her left leg. The world swayed, or maybe it was the sea and the boat.

Before the man took off he had told her three or four o'clock. She had crept into the corner and sat as still as she could. '*A las tres, cuatro,*' he said. '*Esta noche,*' and she understood at last when he held up three, then four fingers and pointed at the sun, motioning that it was setting. Darkness. Night. That's when she would leave. Tonight.

She couldn't tell him that she had lost both her watch and her sense of time. That's what happened when you prepared yourself to die and sank down into the big black deep where time no longer existed.

1

He had left a rolled-up rug on the floor of the cabin. She didn't know what a rug was doing on a fishing boat. It was red, and woven in a beautiful pattern; it belonged on a tiled floor in an elegant room. If they have rugs like this in their boats, she thought as she unrolled it and curled up to wait, then I wonder what kind they have in their homes.

All sounds had ceased after that. The clatter of iron tossed onto asphalt, men's voices, cars that started up and drove off. As the sun set the clouds turned a pale pink until all the colours vanished and the sky looked black and heavy. No moon, no stars, not a single fixed point. Like a silent prayer, a certainty that the world remained the same.

Slowly she pressed down the handle on the steel door. The smell of gasoline and the sea washed over her. She stepped quickly over the high threshold, closed the door behind her, and huddled on the boat's deck.

The darkness she'd been waiting for had not arrived. The harbour was bathed in the yellow of sodium lights that were taller than church towers. She crouched there quietly and listened. A mooring line creaked when the boat moved. The rattle of a chain, the water sloshing gently against the quay. And the wind. Natural night-time sounds. That was all.

She grabbed the mooring line and slowly, very slowly, pulled the boat closer to the quay. With a dull thud the boat made contact.

She felt the rough surface of stone against her palms. Dry land. With her uninjured leg she kicked off and heaved herself up onto the dock. She rolled over and landed on her stomach behind a pile of rolled-up fishing nets. When she looked along the quay she saw a similar net with a rug covering it. So that's what the fisherman uses those rugs for, she thought, to protect his nets from the rain and

2

wind, or from animals that roam about, looking for fish scraps.

A few seconds passed, or maybe it was minutes. Everything was quiet, except for the wind and the beam pulsating on and off from the lighthouse.

She took a deep breath and then ran, stooping forward, moving as fast as her injured leg would allow, past a harbour warehouse. With his finger the man had drawn on the floor the way she should follow the wall out of the harbour, continue along the shore, and then go up through the town. To the bus station. From there she could catch a bus to Cádiz or Algeciras or Málaga. Cádiz was the name she recognized.

She stumbled over some pipes and heard the sound reverberate between the stone walls. Quickly she pressed herself close to a container.

There are guards, she thought as she listened intently. I can't let myself be fooled by the calm and the quiet, and besides it isn't really quiet. I can hear the surf striking the seawall, and the wind making the sheet metal clatter somewhere nearby, but I don't hear any footsteps, and no one can hear mine.

She looked down at her bare feet. Her shoes had been swept out to sea, along with her skirt and cardigan. Now she was dressed in a green jacket that she'd found draped over her when she awoke on the deck of the fishing boat. In the cabin she'd found a towel and tied it around her hips as a skirt.

She pulled the cap further down over her forehead, climbed carefully over a pile of rebar. Hunched over, she ran the last bit before sinking onto a heap of empty plastic bottles bound for recycling.

This was where the harbour ended. She was hemmed in. In one direction was the high wall, in front of her a stone grate two metres high, and beyond that more harbour warehouses. She could see a section of street through the gaps, and some flowering weeds had pushed up through the holes in the asphalt. In the distance the ruin of a huge fortress loomed like a stone skeleton against the sky.

Her eyes hurt. She felt the strain of trying to focus in the yellow light, which was neither bright nor dim — more like a never-ending dusk. If she closed her eyes she would plunge into emptiness. It had been a long time since she'd slept a whole night through.

She got onto her knees and paused. That was something she'd learned in the past few months: to look all around, take notice of everything, and carefully plan her route.

Then she heard the sound. A vehicle approaching, inside the harbour area. She flattened herself against the ground and held her breath. The beams of the headlamps struck the wall right next to her feet. Bottles and other rubbish glinted in the light. That was when she caught a glimpse of the stairs leading up over the wall, white steps carved into the stone only a few metres away. Then semi-darkness descended again. The vehicle had turned and was heading away. It hadn't stopped. Thank God it hadn't stopped. She saw the blue light on its roof before it vanished in the direction of the gates, and the noise of its engine died away. A police car.

She raced up the stone steps and scrambled over the wall. To her surprise she landed on something soft. So far everything she'd encountered in this country had been hard: asphalt, stone, and iron pipes. But now she had soft sand underfoot, and it was like being caressed by the ground.

An umbrella lay overturned on the beach. Just for a moment, she thought, I'll take shelter, I'll rest here for only one breath of God's eternity.

She picked up a fistful of the fine sand and let it run

through her fingers. Tilted her head back and looked straight up at the black sky. The wind blew into her face and tore off her cap.

When is this wind going to stop? she thought. When will the wind subside and the sea grow calm?

She stood up again and realized that her leg would no longer support her. Her foot felt like it wanted to leave her body, and she had to drag it behind her.

Crouching down she continued along another low wall that kept the sand from drifting across the road and turning the town into a desert. Sharp weeds cut her feet. She raised her bad foot to see if it was bleeding and discovered that she had stepped in dog shit. Her foot stank. She couldn't make her appearance in this country with such a foul smell clinging to her foot, but it was too far to hobble down to the sea and rinse it off. What sort of person had she become? She rubbed her sole on the sand to get rid of the stink, then wiped away her tears with her hand and got sand in her eyes. The sand was everywhere.

I could walk along the road instead, she thought. Like a normal person, not like a thief or a dog afraid of being beaten. The road was lit, and she knew it was dangerous. Yet she straightened up and soon the asphalt of the road was beneath her feet. For a moment she felt like a human being again. Someone who walks without fear.

As if such women walk barefoot through town in the middle of the night, she thought. And just then she caught sight of something lying on a slab of concrete, a resting place by the road.

I'm hallucinating, she thought, I can no longer trust my eyes. She went closer and found that her eyes hadn't deceived her. A pair of shoes. She reached out her hand, but hesitated and looked all around. Was it a trap? Was somebody trying to trick her? But who would think up such an odd idea?

5

It was nothing short of a miracle. A gift from God. She hesitantly touched the shoes lying there. They were real. And they were made of gold.

All right, she thought and picked them up. They were quite ordinary cloth shoes that had been dyed gold, but still. They almost fit. Just a little tight in the toes. She didn't intend to complain. Some divine power had placed these shoes in her path. Wearing these shoes she wouldn't have to step in dog shit.

For the first time since she had come ashore she turned around and gazed back. On the horizon, across the straits, Africa loomed like a gigantic shadow. How close it was. She could see the mountains and the scattered lights in the dark.

Then she walked on, and did not turn back again.

Please let this be a nightmare, thought Terese Wallner when she awoke, lying on the beach. Let me wake up again, but for real this time, and in my own bed.

Slowly she sat up, a terrible pounding inside her skull. The sea was in motion, darkly surging towards her. A flock of slumbering gulls stood in a pool left by the receding tide. Otherwise the shore was deserted.

She closed her eyes, then opened them again, trying to comprehend what had happened. There was nothing around her, that much was true. He was gone.

Her white capri trousers were filthy, and the sequinned camisole and cardigan offered no protection from the cold. The wind cut right through them. Her mouth was as dry as a desert and filled with sand. She spat, cleared her throat, and tried to rub away the sand with her fingers, but it had settled under her tongue and seeped way down her throat. She would need a giant bottle of water, at the very least, to rinse it all away. But where was her purse?

Terese dug her hands into the sand around her. It was hard to see in the dim light. A dark-greyish dusk intermittently pierced by flashes that hurt her eyes, coming from the lighthouse beam. She knew it was out there on an island. Isla de las Palomas, island of the doves. Off limits to tourists. A military area. Reached by a causeway, but with signs posted at the gates. The waves slammed against the rocks out there, spraying high into the air.

Then she caught sight of her purse, and her heart leaped. It was lying half-buried in the sand, less than a metre from the dent where her head had lain. She grabbed it. Everything was still inside: her wallet and hotel room key, her mobile and make-up bag, even her good-luck charm, which was a tiny frog on a keychain. And the bottle of water, thank God. She always carried water with her when she went out, since the tap water tasted so terrible in Spain. There was still a little left in the bottle. First she rinsed her mouth and spat out the water. Then she drank the rest of it, wishing there was much more. She picked up her wallet and opened it, her heart racing. The banknotes were gone. She'd had almost a hundred euros when she'd gone out for the evening. She couldn't possibly have spent that much on drinks. What about her passport? She rummaged through her bag, but it wasn't there. Terese was positive she'd brought her passport, as she always did, even though everyone said it wasn't necessary.

Her shoes were also gone. She stared at her feet. They were suntanned, but white around the edges, with sand clinging between her toes. She looked all around, but the ballet flats she'd worn were nowhere to be seen. When had she taken them off? Before or after? She rubbed the palms of her hands against her forehead to stop the uproar inside.

I need to think clearly. I need to remember.

Had she been barefoot as she ran across the sand with

him holding her hand, urging her down towards the sea, both of them laughing loudly into the wind, wondering if their laughter would be blown away?

She pictured his tousled, sun-bleached hair, his eyes gleaming as he looked at her. His arms were hard and sinewy, muscles taut from working out. His shirt fluttered open so she could see his brown abdomen, not a scrap of fat anywhere. She couldn't believe she was the one he'd taken by the hand as they closed up the Blue Heaven Bar. He'd whispered in her ear that they should move on to someplace else. 'You can't go home yet,' he'd said. 'Not when I've just found you.'

Terese ran her hand lightly over the sand next to her. It was cold. Was there a slight indentation, an impression that his body had left behind, a trace of warmth? But that might simply be her imagination, because the wind blew more steadily in Tarifa than anywhere else on earth, wiping away all tracks in an instant.

No one needs to know what happened, she thought. Nothing did happen. Not if I don't tell anyone.

She drew her cardigan tighter around her. Sand chafed inside her knickers. She felt sticky down there.

'But what if someone's here?' she'd said as he urged her towards the sea. 'What if someone's here, watching us?'

'You're thinking about the wrong things,' he said, kissing her, pressing his tongue deep inside her mouth. And his hands were everywhere, under her camisole and inside her knickers all at once. Then he unbuttoned her tight capris and slid them down and they tumbled onto the sand together. And she thought she might fall in love with him. She thought he was the most gorgeous guy she'd ever been with.

If only her friends could see her now!

You can't go to Tarifa without having sex on the beach,

he'd told her. It would be like not seeing the Eiffel Tower in Paris.

Then she'd felt the sand against her skin as he pressed her down. Grains of sand rose up between her buttocks and pushed between her legs as he guided his cock with his hand, not finding his way at once, rooting around. All she felt was a scraping as he seemed to pump her full of sand.

She shouldn't have fallen asleep afterwards. It had happened so fast.

From up in the mountains came the endless rumbling of the wind turbines, turning counter-clockwise. She had thought they looked like electric eggbeaters, whipping the air into cream. He laughed when she said that. Terese bit down on her fingertips to keep herself from crying.

He must have thought I was no good. Worthless. Otherwise he would have stayed and made love to me again and again.

Nausea rose up into her throat. She might have had two or three Cosmopolitans, and then a few Mojitos after that.

The whole beach swayed as she stood up. She leaned forward with her hands on her knees and stayed like that until things stopped moving, swallowing over and over to keep herself from throwing up and having to smell everything that spewed out of her. She couldn't bear to be so disgusting. That was why she staggered down to the water. It wasn't far, maybe twenty metres.

She moved slowly, setting her feet down carefully, so as not to step on anything unpleasant. The sand felt cold under her feet, and she was surprised when the first wave reached her. The water was almost lukewarm and silky smooth. She waded out a few steps to meet the next wave. When it broke, she caught the foamy water in her hands and splashed

9

it over her face. It was refreshing and made her think a little more clearly.

To her left a low, black ridge rose from the sea, a jetty of large rocks that extended at least ten metres out into the water. It looked like a big prehistoric animal resting on the shoreline, the spine of a slumbering brontosaurus. She waded towards it, thinking that she would climb up and sit on the rocks at the very end. Let the sea wash over her wrists for a while. That usually helped against nausea. If she did throw up, the vomit would vanish into the water in seconds and be forgotten.

The water surged over her ankles. The wind from the sea picked up force. She'd thought the jetty would be hard and sharp, but when she set her foot on the first rock to clamber up, it felt soft and slippery and slid away.

She shrieked and fell forwards onto the rocks, striking her shoulder. She hauled herself up onto the jetty, quickly drawing her feet out of the water. Then she leaned forward and peered down. She had to find out what sort of revolting fish she'd stepped on.

The waves receded and the sea prepared to send in the next onslaught. Terese stared, the roaring sound growing inside her head.

It wasn't a fish. A hand was sticking up out of the water, attached to an arm below the surface. For a long moment she stared at the place where the arm transitioned into a shoulder and then became an entire body. A person was lying there, wedged between the rocks. A black person.

She whimpered when she realized that was where she'd placed her foot. She'd stepped on a corpse. On the chest or stomach. She didn't want to know where. She sobbed and stammered and slid backwards up onto the ridge, scraping her soles hard against the rough surface, trying to get rid of that soft and slippery feeling on the bottom of her foot.

10

But she couldn't resist taking another look. It was a man lying down there. That much she could clearly see. His skin was black and shiny with water. Like a fish, an eel, something slimy that lived in the sea. He was naked. She thought she could make out an animal creeping along his shoulder, and against her better judgement, she leaned forward. The next wave struck the rocks and the shore, spraying up into her face and then receded, the water foaming and roiling around the body. It looked as if it were moving. For an instant she thought the black man would rise up, grab hold of her ankle, and pull her down into the water. What if he was alive?

At that moment the first traces of morning light appeared beyond the mountains, and the colour of the sea changed to green. She was looking directly into the face of the dead man. His eyes were closed, but his mouth was wide open, as if uttering an inaudible drowned scream, his teeth gleaming white and swaying under the water.

Dear God in heaven, thought Terese. Papa, please help me. I'm all alone here.

Then her stomach heaved, and she pressed her hand to her mouth as she made her way across the rocks and tumbled down the other side. She was still throwing up as she ran, staggering, away from the scene.

Chapter 2

New York
Monday, 22 September

According to the charts, I was probably in my seventh week. I'd put off taking a pregnancy test for as long as possible, hoping in my heart that Patrick would come home. Then we could have done it together. Not the actual peeing on the test stick, of course. There had to be a limit. But the waiting for the stripe to appear.

My pulse quickened as I took my cell phone out of my jacket pocket. I might have missed a call because of all the traffic noise.

I hadn't. The display was blank.

There had to be some perfectly natural explanation, I told myself. For Patrick, his work was everything, and it wouldn't be the first time that he'd become so immersed in some ugly and complicated story that he forgot about everything else. He wouldn't give up until he'd turned over every last stone. Once, three years ago, before we were married, I didn't hear from him for a whole week, and I was sure that he'd got cold feet and left me. It turned out that he'd latched onto some small-time gangsters in DC and had ended up sitting in jail down there, wanting to do in-depth research from the inside. He'd come home with a broken rib and a report that was nominated for a Pulitzer Prize.

I tapped in his speed-dial number for the eleventh time this morning.

If you answer, I promise we'll do whatever you want, I thought as the call went through. We'll leave Manhattan and buy that house in Norwood, New Jersey. If it has already been sold, we'll find one just like it. And then we'll have babies and invite the neighbours over for barbecues, and I'll quit the theatre and start sewing appliquéd baby hats. Whatever. If only you pick up.

I heard a click on the line signalling his voicemail. *Hi, you've reached Patrick Cornwall . . .*

The same message I'd heard when I woke up in the morning, all last week. It sounded emptier with each day that passed.

If I'm not answering my phone, I'm probably out on a job, so please leave a message after the beep.

It had been ten days since he'd called.

That was on a Friday.

I was in Boston with Benji, my assistant, to pick up a chair dating from the Czarist period in Russia. That piece of furniture was the last puzzle piece needed for the staging of Chekhov's *Three Sisters*. It had belonged to an ageing hairdresser's paternal grandmother, who had fled St Petersburg in 1917.

Patrick had phoned just after I finished the transaction. Benji and I had each taken hold of one side of the chair and were on our way down a narrow flight of stairs in a building that looked like it might collapse at any minute from sheer exhaustion.

13

'I just wanted to say goodnight,' said Patrick from across the Atlantic. 'I miss you so much.'

'This isn't the best time,' I said, propping the chair onto a step while Benji held on tightly so the precious object wouldn't tumble down the stairs.

The hairdresser stood in the doorway above us, watching nervously. I really wanted to get out of there before he changed his mind. He'd told us that this chair, which he'd inherited from his grandmother, was the dearest thing he owned, but he wanted to see Mother Russia before he died. Otherwise he would never have even considered selling it. If he had enough money, he wanted to buy a burial plot near the Alexander Nevsky church in St Petersburg, where the great men of his native country had been laid to rest.

'You won't believe what a story this is going to be,' Patrick went on. 'If it doesn't turn out to be the investigative story of the year, I don't know what—'

'Are you in a bar or something?' I glanced at my watch. It was 5.45 in Boston. Midnight in Paris. It warmed my heart to hear his voice.

He was audibly slurring his words. 'No, I'm back at the hotel,' he said. There were sounds in the background, a car honking, voices nearby. 'And you know what I'm looking at right now? The dome of the Panthéon, where Victor Hugo is buried. I can see straight into the garret windows of the Sorbonne too. Did you know people live up there under the eaves? But their lights are out now, and they've gone to bed. I wish you were here.'

'Well, I'm standing in a stairwell in Boston,' I said, as I heard the hairdresser start arguing with Benji. Apparently he was asking for more money.

'I'll be damned if human life is worth anything here,' Patrick went on. 'Nothing but objects that can be bought and sold.'

'I really have to go, Patrick. Let's talk tomorrow.'

I could hear him taking a swig of something.

'I can't talk about it over the phone,' he said, 'but I'm going to plaster this story all over the world. I'm not going to let them think they can silence me.'

'Who could possibly do that?' I replied with a sigh, grimacing at poor Benji, whose face was starting to turn an alarming shade of red. I had no idea how much it might cost to be buried next to Dostoevsky, but it had to be more than my budget could handle.

'And afterwards I went out for a while, over to Harry's New York Bar, just to find somebody to speak English with. Did you know that Hemingway went there whenever he was in Paris?'

'You're drunk.'

'I needed to clear my head and think about something other than death and destruction. You have no idea what this journey is like, I'm headed straight into the darkness.'

'Sweetheart, let's talk more in the morning. OK?' I was having a ridiculously hard time getting off the phone. A small part of me was afraid he'd disappear if I ended the call.

Then I heard a shrill ringtone somewhere near him.

'Just a sec,' said Patrick. 'Somebody's calling on the other phone.'

I heard him say his name with a French accent. It sounded funny, as if he were a stranger. Who would be phoning him in the middle of the night in a hotel room in Paris? Patrick raised his voice, shouting so loud that even the Russian standing above us must have heard him. He said something about a fire, and God.

'Mais qu'est-ce qui est en feu? Quoi? Maintenant? Mais dis-moi ce qui se passe, nom de Dieu!'

Then he was back on the line.

'I've got to run, sweetie. Shit.' I heard a bang, as if he'd knocked something over, or maybe stumbled. 'I'll call you tomorrow.'

We both clicked off, and that was the last I'd heard from him.

I cut across 8th Avenue, heading for the Joyce Theatre. Out of the corner of my eye I saw a whirling blue light at the next block, but the sirens seemed to be coming from far away, from another universe, where none of this was happening. The silent phone in my hand. The tiny speck growing inside me. Patrick, who didn't know he was going to be a father.

'Ally!'

That was the girl at the reception desk — Brenda something or other — calling to me as I entered the theatre. 'Your last name is Cornwall, right? Alena Cornwall? There's a letter for you.' She held up a fat envelope. 'From Paris.'

My heart leaped as I took the envelope.

It was addressed to Alena Cornwall, c/o The Joyce Theatre, 8th Avenue, Chelsea, New York.

There was no doubt it was his handwriting. Neat letters evenly printed, revealing that Patrick had once been a real mama's boy.

The envelope felt rough to the touch and seemed to contain more than just paper. According to the postmark, it had been sent from Paris a week earlier, on 16 September. Last Tuesday. The image on the stamp showed a woman wearing a liberty cap, her hair fluttering, in a cloud of stars. The symbol for France and liberty.

'When did this get here?' I asked, looking up at Brenda. 'How long has it been lying around?'

'I don't know,' she said, wiping her fingers on a paper napkin. Under the desk she always kept a stash of sticky

16

Mars bars, which she ate in secret. 'Maybe on Friday. I wasn't working that day. I guess they didn't know where to put it.'

I went down the corridor, which led to the offices and dressing rooms. Why the hell couldn't I even get my mail delivered on time? Certain people seemed to think I didn't exist because I didn't have a proper job contract or mailbox. But why on earth would Patrick send the envelope to the theatre and not to our apartment? That seemed incredibly impersonal. And he hadn't even managed to write the whole address. No street number and no zip code. That had to be significant.

He must have been in a hurry. Something had happened. Maybe he'd met somebody new and didn't dare come home to tell me. Maybe he was leaving me.

I stopped abruptly when a door crashed open, right in my face, and out rushed one of the dancers from the show.

'But I nearly killed myself!' Leia cried. 'Don't you get it? The wall practically reared up in front of me.'

I groaned loudly. Leia was a 22-year-old bundle of nerves who'd been singled out as the next big star on the New York dance scene, which had made her believe that the rest of the world revolved around her. She opened her eyes wide when she caught sight of me.

'You need to do something about it,' she said. 'Or else I'm not setting foot on that stage ever again.'

'I can't rebuild the whole place,' I told her. 'Everybody knows how cramped the space is off-stage. You need to ask someone to stand there and catch you. That's what they usually do.' I turned my back on her and kept on walking. I had no intention of grovelling before a girl who was named after the princess in *Star Wars*.

'You shouldn't even be doing this job,' she yelled after me. 'Because you don't care about other people.'

I turned around.

'And you're a spoiled little diva,' I said.

Leia ran into her dressing room, slamming the door behind her.

The envelope I was holding was making my hand sweat.

I went into the small, windowless cubbyhole that was the production office for visiting ensembles and shut the door, but not all the way. Then I tore open the envelope.

A little black notebook tumbled out, along with a small memory stick and a postcard of the Eiffel Tower. I felt a burst of joy as I read the brief message.

Don't worry, I'll be home soon. There's just one more thing I have to do. Love you always. P.

P.S. Keep this at the theatre until I get back.

I read the words over and over.

The air was getting stuffier in the cramped office. The walls were closing in on me, and I had to kick open the door to make the space seem bigger. I reminded myself what I'd memorized: Turning left, the corridor led to the loading dock on 19th Street. Turning right, I could reach the foyer, where the art deco stairs led up to street level. There were exits. It wouldn't take me more than thirty seconds to run outside.

I sank back onto the desk chair and studied the famous steel structure on the front of the postcard.

There's just one more thing I have to do, he'd written. The envelope had been postmarked a week ago. Shouldn't he be done with whatever it was by now?

I leafed through the notebook. Scattered words and sentences, names and phone numbers. Why had he sent this to me? And why keep it at the theatre instead of taking it home? I saw darkness gaping beneath the illusory cheerfulness of the postcard.

Don't worry meant that I had every reason to be nervous.

18

I'd worked in the theatre long enough to know that people don't say what they mean. The true meaning is hidden behind the words. *I'll be home soon* and *when I get back* sounded like simple, practical information, but the words could just as well mean that he was trying to fool me. Or himself.

I stuck the memory stick in my laptop. While I waited for the pictures to upload, I slipped into an emotional limbo, a neutral position between plus and minus. It was something I did on opening nights or in disastrous situations. When Mama had suffered an embolism and I'd found her dead in her apartment, I'd wandered about in that state for several weeks afterwards. I'd finished up the set design for a music video at the same time as making arrangements for the cremation and funeral. My friends began telling me to see a psychologist. Instead, when it was all over, I slept for two weeks, and then I was ready to go back to work.

A picture appeared on the screen. It was blurry, showing a man partially turned away from the camera. In the next photo I saw two men standing outside a door. It seemed to be night time, and this picture was also blurry. I scrolled through more images, but couldn't make any sense of them. Patrick was definitely not a great photographer. Words and language were his forte, but he was usually able to take decent pictures. These were awful. Nothing but hazy-looking men with disagreeable expressions. One of them appeared in several photos. A typical bureaucrat or banker, or maybe an advertising executive, with thin, rectangular glasses and light eyes, wearing an overcoat or suit. The pictures seemed to have been taken from some distance, in secret. The men could have been any anonymous strangers, in any city on earth. And they told me absolutely nothing about what sort of story Patrick was so immersed in over there.

I closed my eyes to think for a few minutes.

Then I opened the browser on my laptop and found the home page for *The Reporter*. I looked for the phone number of the editorial office.

'I'd like to speak to Richard Evans,' I said on the phone. He was the editor of the magazine that bought Patrick's freelance stories, and a legend in the publishing world.

'One moment, please.'

I was put on hold. An extended silence, while I waited to be put through. Then I heard that Richard Evans was not available. After half an hour of being rerouted to one person after another, I reached an editorial assistant, and I was able to trick her into telling me where he was. When I said that I had a story to deliver from Patrick, she told me that the editor would probably be back from the Press Café in an hour because he was due at a meeting. The assistant advised me to make an appointment. Instead, I slipped out of the theatre and took a cab to the corner of 8th Avenue and 57th Street. That was the location of the Universal Press Café, just across from the magazine offices.

Richard Evans was sitting next to the window, leaning over a table that was too low for his tall body. He was deeply immersed in a newspaper and gave me only a brief glance as I approached.

'There are more tables over there,' he said, motioning towards the other side of the café. Even though he was over sixty, his blond hair was thick and wavy.

'I need to talk to you,' I said. 'My name is Ally Cornwall, and I'm married to Patrick Cornwall.'

Evans put down his paper. Though his gaze was piercing, his eyes were the faded blue of washed-out jeans.

'Oh, right. Aren't you from somewhere in Hungary? It seems to me Patrick mentioned that.'

'I'm from the Lower East Side,' I said and boldly sat

down on the chair across from him. That was my standard reply whenever anyone wondered where I was *really* from. 'We met once, at the celebration for the magazine's fifteenth anniversary.'

'Sure, of course.' He managed a half-smile. 'That's also when Cornwall was nominated for the Pulitzer.'

'But he didn't get it,' I said, waving to the waiter, who came rushing over to wipe off the table. I ordered a glass of orange juice.

I had stood beside Patrick on that evening, squeezed into a beautiful emerald-green sheath dress that I'd borrowed from a costume supplier. I had clutched his hand as the mingling stopped and everyone turned to look at the TV screens. In Patrick's line of work there was no higher honour than the Pulitzer Prize. His series of articles about the Prince George police district in Maryland had aroused tremendous attention, and being nominated for the prize was the biggest thing that had ever happened to him. But in the end, his name was not the one announced. Instead, the prize for the best investigative reporting went to a couple of journalists from *The New York Times*, for uncovering insider trading on Wall Street. Patrick got good and drunk. The following year he'd spent four months, two of them without pay, reporting on who the losers were in the new economy. It was a blistering account that was given extensive coverage in *The Reporter* and had stirred vigorous debate. It was also cited by numerous politicians. But Patrick was not nominated again, and his self-esteem had suffered ever since.

'I need to ask you about the assignment that Patrick's on,' I said. 'About what he's doing in Paris.'

'Is he still over there? I thought he was supposed to deliver something soon.'

Evans frowned as he shovelled scrambled eggs onto his

21

fork. It was clear that he would have preferred to eat his breakfast in peace.

'I can't get hold of him,' I said. 'He hasn't answered his cell phone in over a week.'

'It's not always possible to call home when you're out in the field,' said Evans, peering at me over the rims of his glasses.

'I know that,' I said. 'But we're not exactly talking about the caves of Tora Bora. This is Paris. Europe. They have reception everywhere.'

Evans turned his fork to look at the piece of sausage he'd snared. It glistened with grease.

'Well, at any rate it looks like a hell of a good story he's working on over there. He was very insistent that I hold space for it in one of the October issues, front cover and all.'

'What's it about?' I asked. 'His article, I mean.'

Evans raised his eyebrows. I swallowed hard. It was embarrassing to admit how little I knew about my husband's work.

'Patrick is always careful to keep the magazine's secrets,' I added. 'He never talks about his articles in advance.'

I had done my best to remember what he'd said. When he was drunk, on the phone, he'd talked about death and destruction, and about human lives not being worth anything. He'd mentioned cafés he'd been to in Paris, but not who he'd interviewed.

'Selling human beings,' said Richard Evans.

'Selling human beings? You mean like trafficking? Prostitution?'

'No, not exactly.' He wiped his hands on a napkin. 'He's writing about immigrants who are exploited as labourers. Slave labour, pure and simple. And how the problem is growing as a result of globalization. Poor people who die inside containers when they're being smuggled across borders, suffocating to death, or drowning in the seas between Africa and Europe, their bodies washing onto the beaches. A few years ago a whole group of Chinese immigrants drowned in England when they were forced to harvest cockles. They were farmers from somewhere, and no one had warned them about the tides. A shitty way to die, if you ask me.'

'England? So what is Patrick doing in France?'

'Exactly. There's no clear angle.' Having finished his breakfast Evans waved to the waiter behind the counter and then pointed at his plate. 'When we buy foreign stories, there has to be a fresh perspective, a unique viewpoint. But that's something Cornwall should know by now. He's been working for us a long time. How many years is it? Five? Six?'

'Patrick usually says that journalists who know exactly what they're after are dangerous,' I told him. 'They merely confirm their own prejudices. They don't see reality because they've already decided how they want it to look.'

Evans's eyes gleamed as he smiled. Like glints of sunlight in ice-cold water.

'I actually see something of myself in Patrick, back when I was his age. Equally stubborn and obsessed with work. The belief that you'll always find the truth if you just dig deep enough. Not many people do that any more. These days journalists are running scared. Everybody's scared. They all want a secure pension. They want to take care of their own.'

He ordered an espresso. I shook my head at the waiter. The smell of scrambled eggs and greasy sausage was already turning my stomach.

'But why did he go to Europe?' I asked. 'All he had to do was go over to Queens to find that sort of thing going on.'

Evans shook his head and gave me a little lecture about why a story about the miseries in Queens wouldn't sell as well as a report from Paris and Europe. He claimed that adversity is more appealing from a distance.

I felt sweat gathering in my armpits. The café was getting crowded. The lunch rush had started, and it was filling up with businessmen and media people.

'And the whole point of hiring freelancers is that they're willing to go places where no one else will go. That's something all those marketing boys up there don't understand.' He pointed his finger at the top floors of the building across the street. 'The minute I buy a story that's the least bit controversial, they think I'm going to drag them back to 1968.'

I knew that *The Reporter* had been forced to shut down in '68 because management couldn't agree on how the Vietnam War should be depicted, but that wasn't what I'd come here to discuss.

'Are you saying he's gone undercover?' I asked.

'If so, it would have been smart to talk to me about it first, but you never know. Maybe he'll surprise us.'

Evans sighed heavily and ran his hand through his thick hair. According to Patrick, Evans would have been promoted to editor-in-chief, if only he'd been able to stay on budget. He understood the profession, unlike the marketing yokels who were in charge lately. They were people that Patrick despised as much as he worshipped old journalists like Bernstein, Woodward, and Evans.

'In the past I could spend hours with the reporters,' he said. 'We'd go over the story in advance, try out specific analyses, and toss around various angles to take. But there's no time for that any more.'

The tiny espresso cup had shrunk to the size of a doll's cup in his big hand.

'I was in Vietnam. I've seen Song My. I was in Phnom Penh right before the Khmer Rouge came in. Nowadays reporters come out of college thinking that journalism has to do with statistics. But if you really want to get into a story, you need to go out and smell reality.'

I glanced at my watch. It was 11.15 in New York. Almost dinnertime in Paris. I had to get back to the theatre.

'So if I'm reading you right,' I said, my voice chilly, 'you've sent Patrick to Europe and paid him an advance, but you know almost nothing about the story he's working on, and there's no definite delivery date. Is that usual?'

'No, no. We haven't paid him any advance.'

My blood stopped. Time stood still. People passed by in slow motion outside the window, munching on sandwiches. I stared at Evans, but couldn't think of anything to say.

'We're not allowed to pay out advances any more, not to freelancers. It's a policy set in stone. I can remember when I was going to propose to my first wife, and I called up the editor to ask for an advance so I could buy her a ring. They've discontinued everything that once made this job fun.'

He shoved his newspaper in his briefcase and stood up.

'I'm sure he'll get in touch soon. Cornwall always delivers.'

I got up too. The whole place seemed to sway. Patrick had lied to me. He'd never done that before. Or had he?

'What if he doesn't?' I said, and then cleared my throat. 'I mean, hypothetically speaking. What would the magazine do then?'

'He's not on any specific assignment, so the magazine has no official responsibility, if that's what you mean. As a freelancer, he's in charge of getting his own insurance coverage.'

I felt someone shove me in the back as two students took over the table where we'd been sitting. Talking loudly, they put down their books and latte cups.

'That's all part of being freelance. Right?' said Evans. 'If you want to be free, with nobody telling you when to get up in the morning or send you out on routine jobs. I really miss those days.'

He smiled as he wrapped his shiny woollen scarf one more time around his neck.

'When you hear from him, tell him hello and that I still have space in late November.'

I gritted my teeth. In his eyes I was merely a nervous wife in need of reassurance, so the boys could be kept out in the field. Phnom Penh? Kiss my ass.

Evans was busy putting his wallet away in his inside pocket, but then he stopped.

'There's a stringer in Paris that we sometimes use,' he said, shuffling through a bunch of business cards. 'If they decide to set fire to some suburb again, we give her a call.' He dropped a few cards, and I watched them sail to the floor. Pick them up yourself, I thought.

'She's a political journalist.' He bent down to gather up the scattered business cards. 'I think I gave Patrick her name too. Damn. I can't find it, but I've got it on my computer.' He handed me his own card. 'Send me an email if you want the info.'

'Sure.' I didn't bother with any final courtesies and left the café, walking ahead of him and turning right on 8th Avenue. It was thirty-eight blocks to the theatre in Chelsea, and I walked the whole way. At that moment I needed air more than anything else.

'There stands an oak on the shore, with golden chains around its trunk.' The dancer on stage made the words float, her voice as delicate as a spirit or a dream.

The others joined in, repeating the words in a rhythmic chorus as Masha danced her longing. On the stage stood

26

three substantial chairs from Russia's Czarist period. I'd leased two of them from a private museum in Little Odessa, and then I'd spent weeks searching half the East Coast until I found the third chair in Boston.

I sank silently onto the seat next to Benji in the auditorium, noting that it had been worth all the effort. I watched the bodies in motion around the solid chairs, which were a constant, something on which to rest and yearn to flee. They were also practical obstacles that stood in the way, preventing the dancers from moving freely, forcing detours and pauses in the choreography. Chekhov's play was about three sisters who spend the entire drama longing for Moscow without ever getting there, as the world around them changes. At first I'd imagined an empty stage, with the starry sky and space overhead, but then I realized that something solid was needed on stage, something that held the sisters there. Why didn't they just leave? Take the next train?

I touched Benji's arm to let him know I was back. His real name was Benedict, but I wasn't allowed to tell anyone.

'What is it?' he whispered. 'Where have you been?'

I shook my head. 'Not now.'

I hadn't told even Benji how worried I was. I'd gone about my job as usual, while thoughts of Patrick whirled through my mind.

'They're doing Masha now,' he whispered in my ear.

The light changed from yellow to blue, then switched off before coming on again. The light technician hadn't yet worked out all the cues.

'They were supposed to rehearse Irina, but Leia has locked herself in her dressing room. She swears she's never going to dance in this theatre again. She says there's evil in the air, and she can't express her innermost emotions.'

He gave me a sidelong glance and smiled sardonically.

'And she says it's all your fault.'

'Oh my God. What the hell . . .'

I got up, groaning loud enough to be heard in the whole auditorium. He was talking about that girl I'd called a spoiled diva a few hours ago. Duncan, the choreographer, glared at me from the edge of the stage, motioning with his hand for me to leave. Out. Go fix the situation. OK, OK. I understood the signal.

'I'll go talk to her,' I whispered to Benji. 'Or do you think that would make her commit suicide?'

The whites of his eyes gleamed blue in the wrongly placed light.

'I hear she actually tried that once, in all seriousness. It was Duncan who found her. Did you know they used to be an item?'

'Be right back,' I whispered.

A small group of people had gathered outside Leia's dressing room.

'She won't come out,' said Helen, who played the third sister, Olga. 'She says we should find someone else for the part of Irina. But she knows full well that's impossible.'

'Take it easy,' said Eliza, who was the theatre's marketing manager. She'd witnessed all sorts of neurotic behaviour. 'She'll come out when she starts to wonder if we miss her.'

I knocked on the door.

'Come on, Leia,' I called. 'I shouldn't have said that to you. This show can't manage without you. You *are* Irina. Nobody else can play her the way you do.'

The silence lasted thirteen seconds. I counted. Then the lock clicked. I opened the door and slipped inside the dressing room, shutting the door behind me. The dancer's face was streaked with make-up. She was still sniffling.

'I don't understand what I ever did to you,' she said. 'Why are you so mean?'

'I don't know what got into me. I guess I'm just stressed out because of the opening night,' I replied.

'You don't care how I feel,' said Leia. 'You only think about yourself. Everybody in this fucking business only thinks about themselves.'

'Everyone's nervous,' I said. 'It's an important show.'

Leia looked at me from behind her smeared mask. A mask of despair, I thought. Maybe that's what I should use. Streaked make-up, a person who's on the verge of falling apart. First the make-up runs, then the whole face gives way, and underneath is an entirely different face. Neither is who she seems to be. There's yet another face behind the mask, just as real or phony as the outer one.

'What are you nervous about?' asked Leia, who had now stopped crying. She cast a glance at herself in the mirror and reached for some cleansing cream. 'You don't have to stand on stage in front of an audience that might hate you.'

'I'm not nervous,' I tell her.

'Then why do you keep yelling at me? Why do you call me names if you don't mean it?'

'They don't hate you. They love you.' I picked up a dress that had been tossed on the floor and brushed it off. What a stupid girl. She couldn't even take care of her costumes. 'It just slipped out. I must be tired. That's all.'

'Are you having your period or something?'

'No, I'm not.' I put a bit too much emphasis on those words, but it was too late to change what I'd said. I saw Leia's eyes studying me in the mirror. Those sharp blue eyes of hers.

'So are you pregnant or what?'

The words hovered in the air. I couldn't think of a thing to say as I stared at the girl in the mirror. A small, insecure girl who barely weighed a hundred pounds. And then I saw a spark appear in her eyes. I'd been silent a second too long.

'My God, you're pregnant!' said Leia triumphantly.

I turned away from her annoying, make-up-smeared face.

'Do you know who the father is?'

'Of course I do,' I said, my voice barely audible even to me. It was a mere exhalation, a toneless whisper.

'Congratulations,' said Leia. 'Poor you.'

'Nobody else knows about this,' I said quietly. 'If you tell anyone, I'll kill you. No, sorry. I didn't mean that. But I don't want anybody to know. It's way too early. It hardly exists at all.'

'But it does exist,' said Leia. 'Of course it exists.'

I sank down on the chair next to her, meeting her eyes in the mirror above the make-up table. My face pale, with dark circles under my eyes. We'd worked until two in the morning, and afterwards I couldn't sleep. I'd lain in bed, sweating, as I thought about how Patrick was about to leave me, and my child would be born without seeing his father. I realized I was more exhausted than I'd thought.

'I was once pregnant too,' said Leia.

I fixed my gaze on the table. She was the last person I wanted as a confidante.

'I had an abortion,' she went on. 'I didn't want to ruin my career. It wasn't the right time to have a child. And the guy was a real jerk. He never would have helped out with the baby. But you're married, right?'

I nodded.

'He was too,' said Leia.

I slowly turned to look at her. The cleansing cream had spread the make-up into big splotches. Right now I really needed to see about getting her on stage, or else Duncan would never trust me again as the set designer.

'Do you ever regret what you did?' I asked.

'You mean that I'm not sitting in some suburb as a single mother? I never could have taken this job.'

She spun her chair around so she was facing me.

'So, does he want it?' she said. 'The father?'

I nodded. 'There's nothing he wants more. He'd like to have a whole baseball team.' My voice quavered. I could hear Patrick speaking so clearly, as if he were standing right next to me, whispering in my ear. 'A mixed team, both boys and girls.' Speaking in that gentle voice of his.

'Well, at least you don't have to go on stage,' said Leia. 'You only have to build things. It's OK for you to have a big belly. So what's the problem?'

I took a tissue from the box on the make-up table and blew my nose. I'd also had an abortion, when I was twenty, after a one-night stand. Back then it had seemed such a simple and matter-of-fact decision. This was something else altogether.

'It would have been born by now,' said Leia, tugging at the elastic band holding back her hair. 'I know I shouldn't think about that, but sometimes I do. Even though I didn't want it.'

I grabbed a towel from a hook and tossed it to her.

'Wash your face,' I said. 'Then go out there and dance. That's what matters.'

Leia put the towel under the tap to get it wet, then washed her face. Her smile became a grotesque grimace in the midst of the splotchy make-up.

'Good Lord, why must I be a human being?' she said as she rubbed her face hard and stood up. 'Rather an ox or an ordinary horse, as long as one is allowed to work.'

Irina's lines from her monologue in the first act. Leia was back on track, and I should have sighed with relief,

31

but my body was as tense as hers as she assumed the pose. She was all sinews and muscles and nearly transparent skin.

'Oh! I long to work the way one occasionally longs for a drink of water when it's very hot. If I don't start getting up early in the morning to work, you'll have to end your acquaintance with me, Ivan Romanovich!'

'Hurry up now,' I told her, and then went straight to the production office, shutting the door almost all the way, and burying my face in my hands.

Don't cry, don't show any sign of weakness. That was such a deep part of my psyche that I hardly knew how other people did it. Those people who cried.

'Have you heard anything from Patrick?'

Benji had opened the door. Now he stood there, giving me a searching look.

'I need to go through all this stuff,' I said, looking down at the desk. I picked up a pile of receipts that needed to be entered in the books. Props and nails and fabric.

'Are you starting to worry?' Benji persisted. 'Haven't you got hold of him yet?'

I slammed the stapler with my hand as I fastened the receipts to pieces of paper. Benji caught sight of the postcard and snatched it up.

'Aha! *Tour d'Eiffel*,' he said. 'If he was my husband, I would never have let him go off to Paris.'

'You don't have a husband,' I said.

'It says here you don't need to worry.' He waved the Eiffel Tower and smiled. 'He probably just wants you to miss him. That's why he hasn't called.'

I shook my head. 'That's not what this is about.'

'Isn't that what it's always about?' said Benji. 'About who does the calling and who does the waiting? And the person who doesn't call always has the upper hand. That's what's so unfair.'

Benji's perfect pronunciation of *Tour d'Eiffel* rang in my head.

'Do you speak French?' I asked him.

'*Oui, bien sur*,' he replied, smiling. 'I spent a year in Lyon as an exchange student. I love that country.'

'France is a shitty country,' I said, and I meant it. It occurred to me that I'd been feeling annoyed ever since Patrick had announced that he was going there. Maybe my antipathy had been all too evident. Maybe that was why he'd told me so little. And why I hadn't asked any questions. I had once lived in France, in a hovel out in the country, during several dark years of my childhood. I remembered almost nothing of the language.

'Listen to this.' I concentrated hard on recalling what Patrick had shouted on the phone while I was standing in that stairwell in Boston.

'*Mais qu'est-ce qui est en feu?*' I said the words slowly so as not to leave out a single syllable. The words meant nothing to me. '*Quoi? Maintenant? Mais dis-moi ce qui se passe, nom de Dieu!*'

'Who said that?'

'Do you know what it means?'

Benji ran his hand through his hair, black and styled in a blunt cut that made him look slightly Asian, which he was not. But he'd explained it was the current fad in the club world now that we were entering the Asian era. He asked me to repeat what I'd said.

'But what's burning?' he translated haltingly. 'What do you mean? Now? But tell me what's going on, in God's name!'

He scratched his hand, which was chapped from all the washing of delicate fabrics.

'Although actually we might say "for God's sake", or "what the hell is going on". What's this all about?'

'I don't know.'

'This has something to do with Patrick. Am I right?' Benji squatted down so he was looking me right in the eye as I sat at the desk. He put his hand on my knee. 'Has something happened? You can tell me. Come on, Ally. It's me. Benji.'

'Benedict,' I said, getting up.

Benji made a face.

'If he was my husband and I hadn't heard from him, I'd go find him in Paris,' he said. 'I'd walk through the streets and put up signs on the lamp posts all over town, searching for him.'

I pushed past him and went out into the hall.

'I know, I know,' said Benji. 'I don't have a husband.'

Gramercy was a bland district on the east side of Manhattan.

When we took our first walks together, Patrick had tried to make it seem more interesting than it was. He pointed out where Uma Thurman lived, in a corner building by Gramercy Park. He'd once run into her ex, Ethan Hawke, and the guy had actually said hello to him. Humphrey Bogart had been married in the nearby hotel, and Paulina Porizkova lived somewhere in the neighbourhood, but that was all. There was nothing more to brag about, no matter how much he wanted to impress me. Gramercy was mostly the home of office workers, doctors, and employees of the hospitals that were scattered about. It was an anonymous district without soul, and I thought of it as a blank slate.

The doorman was dozing as I came in, just past eleven p.m. The rehearsals had gone on late at the theatre.

'That husband of yours isn't home yet?' he said inquisitively, leaning over the counter so he could watch me walk past.

'Not yet,' I replied.

34

'Still in Europe?'

Patrick always talked with the doormen. He was on a first-name basis with all of the nine men who took turns working the shifts in the building. After three years of living there, I still wasn't used to the fact that somebody always noticed when I came and went.

'Goodnight,' I said, and slipped inside the elevator.

I didn't breathe easy until it passed the twelfth floor and then stopped at the fourteenth. There was no thirteenth floor. I was glad the builders were superstitious, because it meant one less floor, and the ride in the enclosed space was a few seconds shorter.

I unlocked the door and stepped into silence. In my fourteenth-floor apartment, there was no time and no reality. It was a void floating high above 23rd Street. Through the window I looked down at the cars racing past like bright little toys far below. To the north I could glimpse the top of the Chrysler Building lit up in white.

There were no windows facing south. Otherwise, I would have been able to see the Lower East Side, or Lo-i-saida, as the Puerto Rican kids had called it when I was growing up. It was only ten blocks away, but it was another world. That was where Mama and I had lived when I was nine years old, in our first rented one-room apartment in Alphabet City, where all the streets were letters instead of numbers. I learned to fight and to swear in Spanish before I could even speak English properly. Seven years later Mama thought she had realized the American dream when she was able to move across the street into a tiny, rundown, two-room place on First Avenue. Over there the baker was Polish and she had neighbours with whom she could speak Czech. By then I'd forgotten the language, or maybe I just didn't want to speak it. I don't know. When she died I took over the apartment and stayed there until I met Patrick.

My email was flashing when I sat down at my desk.

Eleven messages in the inbox. None of them from Patrick.

Instead I logged onto the website of our Internet bank. Richard Evans's words had been echoing in my head all night.

We haven't paid him any advance.

We had two joint accounts. That was Patrick's idea, in order to keep track of our finances. Personally I was used to living hand-to-mouth. I'd never shared a bank account with any man before. It almost seemed more intimate than sharing a bed.

There was a total of $240 in the account we used for daily expenses. Neither of us had deposited any money yet for the next month's bills. Everything was as it should be.

Then I looked at our joint savings account.

The baby money.

He was the one who had dubbed it that. I called it our savings capital. We regularly deposited funds, and Patrick's parents contributed at Christmas and on birthdays. At the moment we were up to just over $16,000. We hadn't touched the money, not even last autumn when Patrick had posted a negative income from the story he'd written about the new losers in the current economy.

I stared at the numbers that were dancing in the grey glow on the screen.

The total in the savings account was $6,282. On 17 August, a withdrawal of $10,000 had been posted. Transferred to Patrick's personal account.

I dropped the mouse and grabbed the armrest of my chair, rolling backward to create a distance of two metres between me and the screen. An air pocket. As if the deception wouldn't be able to reach me there.

I thought back to the day when he had packed for his trip. Six weeks ago, in the middle of the summer's worst heatwave, when the air was motionless and scorching, and the asphalt was melting outside. I had been lying on the sofa, wearing only a long, thin tank-top. 'It might take a little longer,' he'd said after closing up his laptop. 'We want to run the article as the cover story in October, so I need to be done in mid-September, or at least no later than the end of the month.' He gave me a light kiss on the cheek as he slipped past to go into the bedroom.

'Do you have money for the bills next month?' I'd called after him. I wish I'd said something more loving, but I knew he was having a hard time making ends meet financially. He'd had so few assignments, and the pay was worse than before. Paris sounded like an expensive expedition. I was annoyed that he was so enthusiastic about leaving me behind.

'It's fine,' he said. 'I got an advance from the magazine so I have enough for the next two months.' Another kiss. 'This story is going to turn everything around. I promise.'

I spun in my chair and looked at Patrick's corner of the workroom. His desk was dark and neat. Against the wall was the external keyboard, looking lonely and neglected with the cord dangling idly in the air.

What else had he lied about? Was he even in Paris at all?

He could just as well have gone to Palm Beach with a lover. I pictured our savings being frittered away on champagne. But I quickly dismissed such a stupid idea.

He had in fact sent me an envelope postmarked Paris. And he had written that he loved me.

I placed my hand on my stomach, thinking I could feel it growing inside. Only a tiny sausage, a worm, a growth. So far.

Of course he was in Paris.

The next second I pictured another woman, pretty and

chic and elegant, like the girl who played Amélie from Montmartre, or some other big-eyed, dark-haired, petite and secretive Frenchwoman.

I got up and walked through the apartment, pausing in the kitchen to drink a big glass of iced water. From there I looked at his side of the bed, which was neatly made. Mine was chaos, with the covers sagging partway onto the floor.

When I closed my eyes I could almost hear his footsteps as he came into the kitchen and opened the cupboard where we kept the coffee, and then the plop when the vacuum seal released its hold.

We had torn down the walls between the rooms when I moved in, opening up the place to make it into an airy and bright loft space for our life together. At first I was bothered by his presence whenever we sat and worked. The clattering of his keyboard behind me, the faint creaking of rubber against wood as he rolled back his chair, and his footsteps as he paced around the room, trying to come up with the right wording. Later I'd learned to block him out, to focus on my computer screen and not think about sex as soon as he came close enough for me to feel the eddying air when he moved, and the smell of him: wool, olive soap, and a light aftershave. I suppose that's what people call daily life.

The biggest problem had been to merge our record collections. He arranged everything alphabetically, while I put the most important ones first. In the end we bought two identical bookcases from IKEA in Newark, and I was allowed to keep my Doors albums in peace. '*Strange people, strange lyrics, strange drugs*' was all he had to say about them.

Behind the bed a glass door opened onto a small balcony. Out there, from a certain angle, I was able to see the Empire

State Building. I could also see that our three potted plants had withered. Patrick was the one who usually remembered to water them.

I opened the door, letting in air, the faint sounds of the city below, and a chilly streak of reality that passed through me.

Why the hell was I thinking of doubting his love? I'd made him a promise, back when I'd suffered one of my first attacks of jealousy, convinced that he was going to leave me. I was not the sort of person who could hold onto anyone. They always left me.

'But I love you,' he'd said. 'I'm the one who can't understand why you want to stay with me.'

I took in a deep breath. Crisp and fresh September air. The skies had cleared during the evening, the stars had faded and vanished in the lights of the city.

I couldn't believe my ears when he proposed to me. I stared at him while all sounds stopped abruptly and a chasm opened up beneath the floor of Little Veselka.

Little Veselka isn't exactly what most people would call a romantic setting. A smoky, noisy deli in the East Village that has stood on 9th Street since the 1950s. It has an open kitchen, so you can hear the Ukrainian cooks screaming at each other as they grill their steaks in full view of all the customers.

It was there we met for the first time.

I was with a bunch of people from La MaMa, one of the little theatres down on 4th Street, off-off-off-Broadway, where I was working at the time. My whole life took place in that neighbourhood. I ate take-out from the Indian restaurants on 6th Street, and I lived in my mother's old apartment on the corner of 4th. Rumour had it that the building was due to be torn down soon, to be replaced by twenty storeys of luxury apartments, but those sorts of rumours about old buildings were always rampant in the East Village.

I noticed him as soon as he came in. He was with Arthur Nersesian, an Irish-Armenian writer who knew everybody. They sat down and he introduced Patrick as a freelance journalist who was writing a story about the last Bohemian in the East Village, meaning Arthur. All the others had been driven away by the rising cost of housing. They now lived in Brooklyn.

If Bohemians even existed at all. A heated discussion ensued at the section of the table where I'd ended up with Patrick, and a director who was practically horizontal, his arm around an eighteen-year-old student actress. Wasn't there a better name for people who loafed about and did no work? Who were incapable of pulling their life together and feared responsibility? Or were the so-called Bohemians the vanguard of the future, the first truly free human beings?

From a purely statistical standpoint, Patrick said, it was possible to ascertain that in the Bohemian belt, which extended straight across Manhattan and eastward into Brooklyn, there were more of those types of people than anywhere else in the world. People who worked freelance and had no permanent jobs, who had chosen to live that particular lifestyle.

He explained that he was actually a reporter of social issues, and he believed that words could change the world. 'Words are more powerful than most people think,' he said, and looked me in the eye after we'd finished off the seventh or eighth or God knows how many bottles of wine at the table, while the director was in the process of drowning between the breasts of the student actress.

'Plenty of people have no idea what a responsibility it

is to be a writer. They think it's all about winning fame and respect, but for me it's about taking full responsibility for the world we live in.'

I was fascinated by his serious demeanour. He wasn't trying to show off; he actually believed what he was saying. There was also something so extraordinary about the way he was dressed. He wore chinos and a shirt and a blazer — which was extremely unusual in that district, where everyone worked so hard to present a unique style.

When he walked me home and took my hand, he did that too with the greatest seriousness. 'Never would I allow you to walk home alone in the middle of the night.'

'But I've walked this same route thousands of times and survived.'

'I wasn't here then.'

Outside the shabby entrance on First Avenue he kissed me gently, and after that I simply had to take him upstairs with me and roll around with him in the bedroom that was so small it held nothing but a bed within the four walls. I wanted to penetrate deeper into that alluring seriousness, all the way to its core to find out if it ever ended.

The next morning I didn't want to get out of bed. I couldn't remember that ever happening before. On similar mornings with other men, I'd made a point of fleeing as soon as possible. I didn't want them to start groping for my soul.

But lying next to Patrick, I stayed in bed. I ran my finger over his cheek. 'Are you always like this?' I asked.

'Like what?'

'So serious. Genuinely serious. Are you like that all the way through, or is that just your way of picking up girls?'

That made him laugh. 'I had no idea it would work so well.'

A year later he proposed. At Little Veselka.

He must be teasing me, I thought at first. Then: I'm not the sort of person anyone marries. Then: Help. This is really happening. What do people do when this happens?

I said yes. Then I said yes two more times. He leaned across the table and kissed me. 'Hell,' he swore as his lips touched mine. He jolted back in his chair.

'What's wrong? It's OK to change your mind, if you want.'

Patrick covered his face with his hand and groaned.

'The ring! I forgot about the ring. What an idiot I am.'

He'd been so preoccupied with mustering his courage that he'd forgotten that little, classic detail. Could I forgive him? Could I give him another chance to do it over, according to the rulebook?

I took his face in my hands. I ran my finger gently along his jaw line. I said that I didn't want any other proposal. This was the best one I could have imagined. If he was so nervous that he'd forgotten the ring, that meant something. It was something I could believe. It was far more important than any bit of metal that existed on earth.

'But if you insist,' I went on, 'the shops are still open on Canal Street.'

On the way we stopped to buy a bottle of champagne and paused to kiss in a doorway, taking so long that some bitch started yelling for the police. When we reached Chinatown, the jewellers on Canal Street had all closed up for the day. 'Why do I need a ring?' I said. 'Who decided that?' And as night fell, we staggered deeper into the red glow of Chinatown's knick-knack shops, tattoo parlours, and disreputable clubs. I had only a vague memory of how we made it back home that night.

One year later, to the day, we were married, but it was the evening of our engagement that meant the most. Because it was only the two of us, I thought. After that his parents and all the traditions and the wedding magazines and the whole bridal package came into the picture.

Patrick's desk chair softly moulded to my body, faintly redolent of leather. Oddly enough, I'd never sat in his chair before. I ran my hand over the dark surface of his desk. In front of me lay a desk calendar bound in leather, a Christmas present from his father, who shared Patrick's passion for intellectual luxuries.

The page for 17 August held only a brief note.

Newark 21.05. That was the departure time for his plane. No hotel name. We always used our cell phones to call each other, never the hotel phones. It hadn't seemed important to know where he was staying.

I took a deep breath before I pulled out the top drawer. I was reluctant to start rummaging through Patrick's things.

Everything was in meticulous order. There were stacks of receipts. Postage stamps, insurance policies.

In the next two drawers he kept articles that he'd written, along with background material neatly sorted by topic. I quickly leafed through the piles of papers. Nothing about human trafficking. At the very bottom were the articles that had almost won him a Pulitzer Prize. He'd changed after that. Worked harder, become practically obsessed with whatever he was writing. I thought about a woman he'd interviewed for the series about the new economy. He'd found her under a bridge in Brooklyn. She talked about how she was going to get back her job as chief accountant very soon, and then she'd bring home her three kids and move back into an apartment in Park Slope. Under all the layers of clothing she carried a cell phone so the company would be able to reach her. It had neither a SIM card nor a battery. Patrick had spent three nights out there. When he came home he tossed and turned in bed, talking in his sleep. 'You have to call Rose,' he said. 'You have to call Rose.' I had pictured Rose as some secret cutie until I saw the article and realized she was the woman who lived under the bridges in Brooklyn. That was what he dreamed about at night.

I shut the last drawer, and the desk resumed its closed, orderly guise.

Hadn't he ever mentioned the name of the hotel? Not even once?

I fixed my gaze on the row of books above his desk.

Hemingway.

Patrick had said something about Hemingway the last time he called. About the bar where he'd gone. I hadn't paid much attention because I didn't give a shit about Hemingway. I would never have gone to that bar, even if he'd still been alive. But Patrick had also mentioned Victor Hugo.

He was sitting at the window of the hotel and looking at . . . what? A grave? The place where Victor Hugo was buried.

I kicked my feet to make the chair roll across the floor to my own work area, and pressed the keyboard of my laptop. The screen woke out of sleep mode.

I'd seen *Les Misérables* and *The Hunchback of Notre-Dame*, both the musical and the films, but I had no idea where the author was buried.

I typed 'Victor Hugo' and 'grave' into Google and pressed search. From the first hit I recognized the name that Patrick had mentioned. The Panthéon. I clicked on Wikipedia. Panthéon was Greek for 'all gods'. It was originally a church, but after the French Revolution it was turned into a mausoleum for national heroes. In 1851 Foucault had hung a pendulum from the dome to prove that the earth rotates. Victor Hugo was buried in crypt number twenty-four.

Impatiently I scrolled down to the technical structural details.

Patrick had said that he could see the dome from his window. The building was eighty-three metres tall. I pictured how it must rise above the rooftops. There could be hundreds of hotels that boasted of such a view.

But Patrick could also see the university through the window. The Sorbonne. *Did you know people live up there under the eaves?* I typed 'Sorbonne' and 'Panthéon' and 'hotel' in the search box.

The first hit was for the Hôtel de la Sorbonne. I felt a shiver race through my body. A feeling that Patrick was getting closer. I was pulling him towards me.

A click from the door, his footsteps across the floor, and everything would return to normal again. Breakfast and work. Watching *American Idol* with half an eye in the evening. Days passing, nights when I was able to sleep. The sound of him breathing next to me.

The hotel's website appeared on the screen. 'Near the Panthéon, the Sorbonne, and the Luxembourg Gardens'. The clock in the upper right corner of the screen told me it was approaching one a.m., which meant six in the morning in Paris. I tapped in the phone number, picturing in my mind the sun rising above ponderous stone buildings with gleaming cupolas.

'*Hôtel Sorbonne. Bonjour.*'

The voice on the phone sounded slightly groggy, half-asleep.

'Good morning,' I said. 'I'm trying to get in touch with a guest who may be staying at your hotel.'

A lengthy and rapid reply followed.

'Do you speak English?' I asked. 'I'm looking for an American named Patrick Cornwall.'

A long silence on the phone. I watched the clock change from 00.53 to 00.54. Tuesday, 23 September.

'No Cornell.'

'Cornwall,' I said, enunciating carefully. 'He's an American journalist.'

But I heard only a buzzing sound in my ear. I wondered how Patrick could stand it over there. But he spoke fluent French, of course, so he didn't have to put up with being treated like something the cat had dragged in.

On the website of the next hotel on the list, the Cluny Sorbonne, they boasted about speaking English. The description further said: *in the heart of the Latin Quarter, within walking distance of Notre-Dame, the Panthéon, and the Louvre.*

'I'm looking for an American named Patrick Cornwall. I'm not really sure, but I think he's staying at your hotel.'

'No, he's not.'

I clicked back to the search list. Were there more Sorbonne hotels?

'I'm afraid he has checked out.'

'What did you say?'

'He has checked out.'

I grabbed the armrest and held on tightly.

'When was that?'

'And who, may I ask, is calling?'

I was just about to say 'his wife', but something stopped me. Shame. I felt my cheeks flush. I suddenly saw the situation from the other end of the phone line. France was a country in which even the president had secret lovers and got away with it. And I was the abandoned wife.

'We're colleagues at the magazine,' I said. 'And I'm sitting here with a travel invoice that I can't quite decipher. That's why I need to speak to him. So I can send him his money.'

I sounded like a real bureaucrat.

'Just a moment.' An eternity passed as the clerk paged through the information in a ledger or a database or what-

46

ever they used in the Old World. I heard a clattering somewhere in the background. Maybe they were setting the tables for breakfast.

'It was last Tuesday,' he said finally. 'September sixteenth.'

A week ago. The same day the envelope was mailed. I took a deep breath.

'Were you on duty when he left the hotel?'

'Yes, of course. He was happy to be going home to New York. He said he missed his wife. I told him that he should bring her with him next time he comes to Paris. It's the romance capital of the world, after all.'

'Are you sure about that? That he was going home to New York?'

I gripped the phone even harder.

'Yes. He said that quite clearly. We almost had a quarrel about the fact that he was so eager to leave us.'

'Did he say anything else?'

'Just that he would stay with us the next time he's in Paris.'

I ended the call. The silence pressed against my skull. At any second it would explode. Fragments of information would scatter across the floor. Checked out. Back home to New York. The baby money. The positive pregnancy test. We never pay advances.

Restlessly I paced the apartment. Took some juice out of the fridge and drank from the bottle.

Where had he gone? Why had he lied about where he was going? And if he was telling the truth, why hadn't he come home?

On the kitchen counter were the remains of the snacks I'd eaten over the past few days. Since the kitchen was just a corner of the bedroom, we always did the dishes before we went to bed so we wouldn't have to look at leftovers when we got up in the morning. But now there was a small pyramid of empty yogurt containers. And I thought I noticed that they were starting to smell. The smell grew. Dirty glasses and cutlery, salad packaging and pizza boxes. All signs of his absence.

I picked up the garbage can and with my arm swept the whole pile of trash off the counter and into the pail. Several forks and a glass fell in too. I closed the lid. Then I went back to my computer and logged into the Internet bank again. I transferred $6,282 from the savings account — the baby money, all that was left of it — to my own account. Then I typed words in the Google search box:

New York. Paris. Flights.

Chapter 3

Tarifa
Wednesday, 24 September

'He wants to know what you were doing on the beach in the middle of the night.'

Terese slid further down on the hard plastic chair they had provided for her. It felt as if they could read her mind, as if everything were clearly visible even though she had showered for hours and changed clothes and slept seventeen hours and then taken another shower after that.

The policeman sitting at the desk leaned forward, twirling a pen between his fingers. His nails were stubby and ugly, grimy with dirt underneath.

'Why does he want to know that?' she whispered to her father, who was sitting next to her. 'What difference does it make?'

'You have to answer his questions,' said Stefan Wallner. 'I'm sure you realize that.'

Terese rubbed her ear. He was talking to her as he had when she was a child. She regretted agreeing to have him act as her translator during the interrogation. 'But we don't

49

need to call it an interrogation,' he had said. 'They just want to know what you saw on the beach.' Maybe it would have been easier to be surrounded by strangers, she thought. People who wouldn't be ashamed of her, or disappointed.

'I just went for a walk,' she said.

'In the middle of the night? Before dawn?' The policeman gave her a thin-lipped smile. It looked like a straight line below his moustache. She noticed an upper tooth was missing. His eyes were fixed on her breasts.

'I was drunk,' Terese said in Swedish. 'I didn't feel good. I may have got lost.'

Stefan translated.

'Was she alone on the beach?' asked the officer.

'Yes, I was.' She swallowed hard. Her throat felt tight. 'I already told you that.'

'Alone on the beach, a young girl, in the middle of the night.' He shook his head. On the wall behind him hung a picture of the Virgin Mary and the infant Jesus. Her father didn't translate what he'd said, but she understood. She had studied Spanish for three years in high school, and she knew enough to order food in the restaurants. That was why her father had invited her along, so she could practise her Spanish. He wanted to show her the places he'd visited in his youth, when he was hitchhiking through Europe. She gave her father a sidelong look. His hair was blonder, so the grey was hardly visible, and his skin was suntanned. They'd been in Tarifa for a week when their holiday was disrupted.

'Why isn't he asking me anything about the body?' said Terese. 'Why is he only asking about me?'

The officer leaned back in his chair, his legs wide apart. He was tapping the pen against his lips.

'I know exactly what the likes of you get up to on the beach,' he said. 'You come here and hang about in the bars, ready to take off your clothes for anybody. My cousin has worked on the beaches. He had to pick up after people like you. You have no idea what he used to find on the sand in the morning.'

He leaned towards Terese, and she gave a start when his eyes again fastened on her breasts. She wished she had put on a sweater. A cardigan over the camisole that was so tight it revealed half her tits.

'That's enough,' said her father in Spanish, placing his hand, heavy and warm, on her bare shoulder. 'My daughter has been through a terrible ordeal. You need to realize that she's in shock.' He glanced at Terese and then back at the police officer. 'She told you that she was alone.'

The officer smiled wryly, again exposing the gap in his teeth. Terese lowered her eyes.

'Who was the dead man she found?' Stefan went on. 'Do you know anything more about what happened to him?'

'An immigrant. From the sub-Sahara,' said the officer, standing up. He went over to a map of Europe hanging on the wall. It also showed the northern part of Africa. Terese knew that boats went there from Tarifa. The crossing to Tangiers took thirty-five minutes and cost twenty-nine euros per person. Her father had picked up some brochures at the tourist office. Terese wasn't particularly interested, but she hadn't told him that. She didn't want to upset him. When he'd suggested the trip to southern Spain, she'd pictured Marbella and sunny beaches and nightclubs. In Tarifa the wind never stopped blowing. She'd tried swimming on their first days here, but ended up feeling panicked when she was tossed about by the waves as the rip current dragged her away from shore.

'When they come this way, they're mostly fleeing from the countries south of the Sahara,' said the officer. He pointed at the map that hung on the wall of painted brick.

'Mali, Nigeria, Sierra Leone. Several years ago we were bringing in overloaded boats every single day.' He moved his hand over the sea, out into the blue of the Atlantic. 'Later more people started taking this route, via Senegal to the Canary Islands, then through Libya, of course, it's a total chaos there, and then the Turkey route . . . The smugglers know we have coastguard boats patrolling the straits, with cameras and radar. But that still doesn't stop some people from trying.'

Stefan Wallner translated for Terese, who relaxed a bit. She was already familiar with some of these facts. When she was lying in bed yesterday, wanting only to fall asleep and die, her father had gone out to talk to the police and the Red Cross. He came into her room every couple of hours to ask whether she wanted anything to eat. He sat on the edge of her bed and stroked her hair and told her about all the unhappy people who were fleeing poverty and possibly war as well. The head of the Red Cross in Tarifa had shown him pictures of people who had died in the sound during the past few years. He'd had an entire binder full of photographs. Whenever Terese closed her eyes, she saw the body of the black man and thought to herself that she was looking at death. And then she'd felt the old sorrows well up, from her teenage years in high school when she'd realized how meaningless everything was, and that it didn't matter what she did because she was nobody. Could anyone love a nobody? No one would notice if a nobody died. 'There's nothing I want to do, Papa,' she'd said. 'I don't know if I even want to go on living.'

The policeman went over to one of the windows and used his whole hand to point outside. Terese shivered when she saw the barbed wire and seagulls. She looked at the island out there, the surging waves and the lighthouse. She never wanted to go down to the sea again.

'If we catch them, they end up on Isla de las Palomas,' he said. 'A few years ago the place was packed, but these days we keep them only twenty-four hours, at most. Then they're sent to the detention camps in Algeciras. If we can't get them to tell us where they came from, they're released out onto the streets after sixty days. After that, they'll be picking tomatoes.'

The officer came around his desk and picked up a document. A flimsy piece of paper.

'But I'm talking about the ones who make it here alive, of course.'

He sat down, again spreading his legs wide, and gave a sharp slap to the paper in his hand.

'This arrived by fax from Cádiz early this morning. They've found two more. A man and a woman. Pregnant.' He picked up another piece of paper and held it up. 'The Moroccan authorities have reports of a rubber dinghy that set off in the early hours of Sunday morning. It managed to slip past. Maybe somebody was bribed. Who knows? These smugglers will try anything.' He used two fingers to smooth his old-fashioned moustache, which turned up slightly at the ends. 'They tell the passengers to jump into the sea when they get close to land so the smugglers can turn the boat around before we catch them.'

'Have you identified them?' asked Stefan Wallner. His hand was still on Terese's shoulder, occasionally giving her a light pat. Protecting her. She was ashamed that she'd lied. She was ashamed that she'd been abandoned on the beach. It was horrible that people were dying in the sea.

The police officer grinned. 'How would we do that? So far we haven't found anyone alive.'

'But I told you he had a tattoo,' Terese said.

'They already know that,' said her father. Terese bit her lip. Reprimanded, just like a child. Yet she was twenty years old.

53

'If they're Moroccan, we contact the Moroccan authorities directly,' said the officer. 'And they're here within twenty-four hours. But if we're talking about sub-Saharans, there's not much we can do. They have no identity papers, and even if they were alive, we couldn't get them to tell us where they're from.' He shrugged. 'We take blood samples and fingerprints, of course. And keep them on file.'

He shuffled all the papers into a neat little stack. Terese looked down at her hands. She could feel his eyes on her. Her bottom felt sweaty against the plastic of the chair.

'And you didn't see anything else on the beach?' he asked.

She shook her head. 'It was totally deserted. Nothing but a few seagulls.'

The officer turned to Stefan. 'If she saw anything that might lead us to the smugglers, we want to know about it. These are criminals we're talking about here.'

Stefan turned to Terese. 'So you really didn't see anything? No boats? No people?'

She shook her head as she spun the ring she was wearing. It was gold, in the shape of a heart. A confirmation present from her father.

'Then all we need to do is write up your statement,' said the officer. He pressed a button on his desk and a buzzer sounded outside the door.

'My assistant will take care of it. We'll want the precise time and where the victim was found.'

He narrowed his eyes and leaned across his desk.

'And I also want the name of the person you were with. Or maybe there was more than one.' His gaze slid over Terese's body. She shuddered, thinking that she would need to take another shower when she got back to the hotel. That was how he made her feel. Dirty.

'Did you get paid for it, or do you let them do it for free?' he said.

At that point her father finally stood up and slammed his hand on the desk. 'Enough. Stop harassing my daughter. She's told you everything she knows.'

The door opened and another police officer came into the room. Terese recognized him. He was the one who had shown them in when they arrived. He looked nice. She got up and turned, about to leave.

'We also need to report that your passport was stolen,' said Stefan.

'No, don't, Papa,' said Terese, taking him by the arm, but it was too late. He had already started talking to the officer about her missing passport.

'Are you telling me it was stolen on the beach? But she said there wasn't anyone else there. That doesn't make sense. I don't understand.' The officer smiled broadly, the gap in his teeth like a black hole in his mouth. 'So which of them do you think took your passport? Or was it a form of payment?'

His gaze settled on her body, as if licking her up and down, and then back up again to force its way between her breasts.

Terese squirmed and tugged at her father's arm. She hated her arse and thighs, which were too fat, and her nose, which bent slightly in the middle. But her breasts were perfect. Round and naturally big. The only part of her body she was completely satisfied with.

'I probably just dropped it somewhere,' she said. 'Come on, Papa, let's go.'

'No matter what, we need to file a report,' said her father without budging.

'For that, you'll need to talk to the local police.'

'We have to talk to the local police,' Stefan Wallner translated for Terese, but she was already on her way out of the door.

'I want to go home,' she said when they were out in the corridor.

'But we have a whole week left of our holiday.'

'Didn't you see how he was staring at me? He's bloody disgusting.'

Her father looked over his shoulder at the door that had closed behind them. The officer's assistant stood next to them, shifting from one foot to the other, holding the official form in his hand.

'Somebody like that should be reported,' said Stefan, putting a protective arm around his daughter. 'Come on, sweetie, let's get this over with. Then we'll go out and have a really good lunch. Just you and me.' He gave her a poke in the side. 'And we'll sit in the sun and have a glass of white wine. I think we need it. Both of us do.'

Chapter 4

Paris
Wednesday, 24 September

With a shiver of anticipation, I turned the key in the lock of room 43. As if he would just be sitting there. And he'd get up and come towards me with open arms and a look of surprise, wondering what I was doing here, laughing at me. What an impulsive thing to do, flying to Paris.

But all I found was emptiness. And the faint scent of lavender soap.

The door closed behind me with a muted *click*. Eight days and eight nights had passed. All traces had been carefully cleaned away.

I threw open the window. A damp gust of wind against my face. Beyond the rooftops rose the dome of the Panthéon. In front of me the university buildings were spread over several blocks.

It was here that Patrick had stood when he had called, in this very spot. I remembered his voice on the phone. *I miss you so much . . . I'm headed straight into the darkness . . .*

The wind was fluttering the curtains, which billowed up and then sank back to the floor. I turned around and took in all the details. The big bed, the open-work white coverlet with a floral pattern. On the wall, a framed poster of a sidewalk café. The telephone on the nightstand. That was the phone I'd heard ringing in the background. Someone had called to tell Patrick that something was on fire. *But tell me what's going on, in God's name!*

The room was exactly four metres wide and five metres long. After all my years as a set designer, I automatically took measurements. Four times five metres, twenty square metres. Those were the physical dimensions of loss.

In the corner of the far wall stood a small desk. That's where he had sat to write, bending low over his computer. Patrick always sat that way, as if he wanted to smell the keyboard, breathe in the words. In reality he needed glasses, but he was too vain to get them.

In the bathroom I met my own face in the mirror. Pale, with blue shadows under my eyes. My skin creased with fatigue. I rinsed my face with ice-cold water. Splashed water under my arms, and rubbed my skin hard with a towel.

Then I got clean clothes out of my suitcase. I was going to turn over every single stone in this city if that's what it took.

The price of a slave. That's what it said at the top of one page. Followed by numbers, amounts that appeared to be sample calculations:

$90 - $1,000 (= $38,000 = 4,000 for the price of one.)
Mark up = 800% profit = 5%
30 million – 12 million / 400 = 30,000 per year. Total?

The last calculation had been crossed out. Next to it were also a few words scrawled across the page, underlined and circled:

Small investment – lifelong investment
The boats!

I kept paging through Patrick's notebook, which was filled with these truncated and basically incomprehensible scribblings. I was sitting upstairs in a Starbucks café, determined not to leave the table until I'd figured out at least some of these notes.

The café was three blocks from the hotel, on a wide boulevard lined with leafy trees, and newsstands that belonged in an old movie. Everything reinforced by a feeling of unreality. Jetlag was making me hover somewhere above myself.

The simplest thing, of course, would have been to go straight to the police and report him missing. But Patrick didn't trust the police. He would hate me if they came barging into his story. First I needed at least to find out what he was working on.

I ate the last bite of my chicken wrap and crumpled up the plastic. Then turned to look at his last note. That was how I usually approached a new play, by starting at the end — *Where is it all heading? How does it end?*

Patrick had jotted down a phone number. That was the very last thing he had written.

Above the number was a name: Josef K.

This is the endpoint, the turning point, I thought. After this he'd chosen to check out of the hotel, and he'd put this notebook in an envelope and sent it to me.

Keep this at the theatre.

I turned the page to the previous note. It was scrawled

59

across the page, as if he'd been in a hurry: *M aux puces, Clignancourt, Jean-Henri Fabre, the last stall — bags! Ask for Luc.*

I spread the map open on the table. Looked up the words in the index of my guidebook. Bingo! My heart skipped a beat. It was like solving a puzzle, and suddenly the answer appears.

I felt like I was on his trail.

Porte de Clignancourt was way up in the north, where the Paris city limits ended and the suburbs began. It was the end station for the number 4 *Métro* line. It was also the location of the world's biggest flea market, Marché aux Puces. Rue Jean-Henri Fabre was one of the streets in the market. Then I read the next line in the guidebook and my mood sank. The market was open only Saturday to Monday. Today was Wednesday.

Out of the window I could look straight into the crowns of the trees. The leaves had started to fade, turning a pale yellow. At least it was easier working here than at the hotel. Patrick's absence wasn't screaming at me in the same way.

I continued paging through the notebook, studying what he'd written. There were a lot of names, addresses, and phone numbers, but no explanation as to who the people might be. I marked the addresses, one after the other, on the map, and slowly a pattern emerged, an aerial view of Patrick's movements around the city.

When I looked up again, rain had begun to streak the windowpane, and people down on the street were opening their umbrellas. It was close to three in the afternoon, morning in New York. I massaged the back of my neck, which felt stiff and tight after spending the night in an aeroplane seat.

I got out my cell and started with the number on the very last page of the notebook. Later, when the rain stopped,

I would go to see the places marked on the map. Force my body into this upside-down day and night, not wanting to waste any time.

The call went through. I glanced at the name: Josef K. Two ringtones. Three. A girl was wiping off the nearby table. A couple of tourists were talking loudly in Italian.

Then I heard a click on the phone, but no voice answered. The line was simply open, and I could hear the sound of traffic, a siren far away.

'Hello?' I said quietly. 'Is there someone there named Josef? Hello?'

I was positive I could hear someone breathing.

'I'm actually looking for Patrick Cornwall, and I wonder if you could help me. I'm in Paris, and I think he called this number and—'

The traffic noise stopped. Whoever it was had ended the call.

With a tight grip on my cell, I moved on to the next number on the list.

After four attempts to speak to someone, I gave up. The most extensive answer I'd heard was '*no English*' and '*no, no, no*'.

I was seized with longing to call Benji instead. To hear how the opening night had gone. And whether Duncan had won the acclaim he'd wanted. But all of that seemed so distant, as if it had ceased to exist the moment I boarded the plane.

Benji was the only one who knew that I'd gone to Paris. I'd told him at lunch, when we were sitting on the steps of the loading dock on 19th Street, eating burritos with jalapeños from the deli across the street.

'You're out of your mind. I can't handle everything on my own,' said Benji, missing his mouth. A big dollop of meat fell onto his lap, along with some melted cheese and a limp slice of tomato. 'What if something happens? What do I do then?' He tried to rub the spot off his baggy designer jeans.

'Nothing's going to happen,' I said. 'The stage set is all done, and they're going to dance this same performance for three weeks. I'll be back long before then.' I stuffed my half-eaten burrito into the empty juice container and stood up.

'If anyone asks,' I said, 'just say that something has come up in my family, and I'm terribly sorry, et cetera. That's all anyone needs to know.'

An hour before the curtain-up, I left the theatre. By then all the paperwork was in order: the account books and the certificate from the fire department inspection, the list of props that had to be returned — all in neat folders. Like a final accounting of that part of my life.

'Kiss Patrick when you see him,' said Benji, giving me a hug. I pulled away and didn't reply, just waved as I ran out to the cab that would take me to Newark and the Air India flight to Paris, leaving at 21.05.

The pill was supposed to be taken no later than an hour before departure, but I'd sat with the blister pack of pills in my hand until the gate was ready for boarding. There was no way I was going to allow myself to be carried through the air in a closed tube without some sedative inside my body. I'd suffered from claustrophobia as long as I could remember, and it wasn't just rooms with the door closed, basement apartments, and elevators. Sitting captive in an aeroplane or a subway was even worse. It was impossible to escape. There was no way out. I was at the mercy of other people, with no power over my own fate. That was probably why I became a set designer. In the theatre I built my own rooms and decided where the exits would be. Usually I was able to deal with my claustrophobia. I always checked to see where the emergency exit was when I entered a building, and I never rode the subway. If I needed to travel any distance, I hired a car. Going back to Europe had never been part of my plans.

I read the warning label over and over. If pregnant, consult your doctor, it said. And 'there is a risk the foetus may be affected'. Forgive me, I thought as I swallowed the pill. Forgive me, but I have to do this.

The cab crept along the glittery Champs-Élysées and turned off right before the Arc de Triomphe. That's where all the hustle and bustle ended. Rue Lamennais was lined with businesses, and most of the employees seemed to have gone home for the day. I asked the cab driver to pull over before we reached number 15, which was one of the addresses in Patrick's notebook.

I stopped twenty metres away, ducking into the shadow of a doorway. A car slowly passed and slid to a halt in front of the entrance. Then another equally shiny vehicle arrived. The first was a Bentley, the second a Rolls Royce. Three men wearing dark suits came out of the building carrying briefcases. A doorman hurried forward to open the car doors, bowing and anticipating every step the men took in an obsequious dance. There was even a red carpet on the pavement. The cars started up and disappeared.

This was the second address I'd gone to see. The first had turned out to be an American bookshop. Typical Patrick. He loved to ferret out old editions of classic novels that cost a tenth of the price in paperback. I'd roamed around inside among millions of dusty books, up and down narrow stairways, past benches with cushions and blankets squeezed in between the aisles. When I sat down to take a brief rest, two hikers with backpacks came over to ask me if I was an author. 'We're authors too,' said the boy. 'But we publish our writing on the Internet. We think of ourselves as akin to the beat generation, but in a whole different context, of course.'

It was now six thirty, and dusk was hovering like a blue note in the air. Yet another shiny car glided past, this one a Jaguar. At that moment my cell rang in my shoulder bag. The doorman glanced in my direction. I looked at the display. Unknown caller.

'Ally,' I said.

'You called?' said a woman with a French accent. 'You're looking for Patrick Cornwall?'

Adrenaline coursed through my body. My knees felt weak.

'Do you know where he is?' I said. 'I need to get hold of him.'

A brief pause on the line. No background noise.

'We can't talk on the phone,' said the woman. 'Where are you right now?'

'On a street called rue Lamennais,' I said. 'Outside a restaurant.' I quickly moved closer so I could read the gold script on the visor of the doorman's cap.

'Taillevent,' I said.

'In the eighth?' said the woman.

'Excuse me?' I asked, thinking instantly of the baby. The eighth sounded like a month at the end of the pregnancy. 'What do you mean?'

'The eighth arrondissement,' she said. 'In half an hour. How will I recognize you?'

'I'm wearing a red jacket,' I said, and then she clicked off. I lowered my hand holding the cell and smiled at the doorman.

He smiled back.

'Good news?' he asked.

'I think so,' I said, and put my phone away in my bag, going over the conversation in my mind. Thinking about the tone of the woman's voice. Formal but not hostile. I strained to remember the fruitless phone calls I'd made earlier in the afternoon, but they all merged into one. It didn't matter. I'd soon find out.

I smiled at the doorman again.

'Is it possible to get a table for dinner?' I asked.

The doorman surveyed my clothes: jeans and the red anorak I'd found in the Salvation Army shop on 8th Avenue.

'I'm sorry but we're fully booked this evening.'

He moved away to open the door of the next car that had pulled in, and I took the opportunity to slip into the restaurant behind him.

Thick carpets muffled all sound inside. The entire foyer was done in beige and brown. It looked like the decor hadn't undergone any changes in the past fifty years. A staircase with an elaborate, gilded wrought-iron banister led up to the next floor. The maître d' blocked my way.

'Excuse me, I don't speak French,' I said, 'but I'd like to ask you about a customer. I think he was here a little over a week ago, and—'

'We do not give out information about our customers,' said the man. 'They rely on our discretion.'

'Of course. I understand that,' I said, smiling at him as I swiftly searched for a suitable lie, a role to play. I knew that Patrick would never go to a place like this merely to have dinner. He must have been meeting someone here, someone he was going to interview.

'This is so embarrassing,' I said, making my voice sultry and feminine. 'I represent a big American company in Paris, and one of our business partners has booked a table here, and I've had so much going on, my mother died recently, and now I'm afraid that I've mixed up the days and the weeks.'

The maître d' frowned and glanced around nervously. Two men in grey suits stood near the cloakroom, leaning close as they talked. A petite, energetic woman with a pageboy hairstyle briskly took their overcoats and hung them up.

'So if you wouldn't mind just checking to see which day he booked a table . . .' I put my hand on the maître d's arm. 'I'll be fired, you see, if I lose this contract.'

He wavered, casting a glance at a lectern made of polished hardwood on which a book lay open. The reservations calendar.

'What did you say your name was?' The maître d' again glanced off to the side and then hesitantly went over to the lectern.

'Cornwall,' I said. 'It's booked under the name of Cornwall. Patrick Cornwall. He's my business partner.'

'No, I'm afraid not. I don't see . . .' The man ran his index finger over past lunches and dinners.

'Oh, good Lord,' I said. 'I guess it couldn't have been last week.' I clapped my hand over my mouth. 'In that case, I really need to come up with a good excuse and contact him . . .'

The maître d' kept paging through the book, and then his finger stopped abruptly.

'A Mr Cornwall made a lunch reservation on the previous Thursday, September 11, but it was for only one person.' He glanced up hastily and then closed the book.

What the hell was Patrick doing all alone in a luxury restaurant? I thought. Squandering our money? My hand moved involuntarily to my stomach.

'One moment please,' said the maître d', and he went into the next room. I took a few steps in that direction. He stopped to speak to an older man wearing a red jacket.

'This lady is asking about Monsieur Cornwall. Patrick Cornwall,' he said in a low voice. 'But then I noticed . . .' The maître d' glanced over at me. I fixed my gaze on the wall.

'Cornwall? You mean that journalist? The American?'

The older man lowered his voice. 'He is no longer welcome here.'

'I know. But what do I tell the lady?'

And then they both headed towards me, with the older man in the lead.

In the few seconds before they reached me, I thought to myself that it couldn't be possible. The men had spoken in French. I shouldn't have been able to understand them, but the language from my childhood had resurfaced like a repressed memory. 'I'm afraid we're closed now, madame,' said the older man in English.

'What happened when Patrick Cornwall was here?' I asked.

'Under no circumstances do we give out any information about our customers.'

The maître d' put his hand on my back and discreetly ushered me to the door.

'It's best if you leave now.'

And the doorman closed the door behind me without saying a word. The street was almost completely dark.

What on earth could Patrick have done to be refused admittance to such a place? Did he talk too loud?

I moved a short distance away from the restaurant, pulled up the hood of my jacket, and leaned against the stone wall.

Well, I'll soon find out something, I thought. If only she shows up. That woman on the phone.

I glanced at my watch. Ten more minutes.

While I waited, I tried to conjure up some words in French. Shoe, foot, stone, street. I couldn't do it, even though the language clearly existed somewhere in my subconscious. Those years spent in a French village were not anything I wanted to remember. I was six when we arrived there. My mother became a different person. I had faint memories of a house that echoed with silence. A man who demanded I call him *Monsieur*. Doors that were locked at night. Loneliness. And fear when I woke up at night and didn't know where my mother was.

The car pulled over before I saw it. If I hadn't been so lost in my own thoughts I might have noticed there was something wrong, that it wasn't a Bentley or a Rolls, but a worn-out Peugeot with rust on the wheel rims. Suddenly a man was standing in front of me. He wore a hoodie and that's all I saw. Adrenaline shot through my body, all my instincts screaming at me to flee.

'Get in the car,' he snarled, speaking English with an accent. He grabbed my arm. I pulled away, but he blocked my path.

'I'm waiting for someone. They'll be here any minute,' I said. The street was deserted. Not a single Jaguar as far as the eye could see. Even the doorman had abandoned me. I was getting ready to kick the man in a sensitive spot and then take off running when I noticed someone sitting in the car behind him. It was dark, but I was almost certain I saw a woman in the driver's seat. She wore a headscarf. With my heart pounding, I went over to the car. The man followed close behind.

'Are you the one who called me?' I said, leaning forward. The back car door was open.

'Get in,' she said, motioning to the back seat. I complied. The man crowded in next to me and slammed the door shut. A second later the woman started up the car and drove off. Fear surged like a hot wave through my body.

'Where are we going?' I said. 'Who are you?'

'Why are you asking about Patrick Cornwall?' said the woman. 'What do you know about Josef K?'

'Nothing. I don't know anything about Josef K. That's why I called.'

I saw her looking at me in the rear-view mirror. Brown eyes with heavy eyeliner. The rest of her face was hidden by the scarf.

'Where is Patrick?' I said. 'Do you know where he's staying? Is that where we're going?'

She turned onto yet another dark back street, again changing direction.

'First I want to know who gave you my number.' She had a deep voice with a melodic lilt to it. Aside from her accent, she spoke fluent English. 'Who's been talking about Josef K? Who do you work for?'

'Who do *you* work for?'

The woman made a sharp turn and braked. We were on the outskirts of a park. Not a soul in sight. I was starting to feel truly scared.

She turned halfway around.

'Was it Alain Thery who sent you?'

'Alain who?' I said, confused.

My instincts told me to lie. Then I'd have the upper hand, even though there were two of them.

'I work for the same magazine as Patrick,' I said. 'The editor hasn't been able to get hold of him. He was supposed to turn in a story, and the deadline is coming up. They go nuts if we don't stick to the deadline.'

'Let me see your press credentials,' said the woman.

'I'm not a journalist,' I told her. 'I work in the office.'

'What's your name?'

I don't know where it came from, whether it was fear that cast me back to the person I used to be, or whether it was a rational decision not to tell them who I was. A lie, and yet not a lie. As close to the truth as possible.

'My name is Alena Sarkanova,' I said, forcing a smile. 'What's your name?'

But the woman didn't return the courtesy. She lit a cigarette.

The smell of cheap tobacco stirred up hazy memories from my childhood. At that instant my cell rang, chirruping merrily in my bag, like an old acquaintance. I leaned down and fished it out.

'Don't answer,' said the woman. The man grabbed my wrist. I managed to see Benji's name on the display before I switched it off. It hurt to cut him off like that. Sweet little Benji, who right now was the only link to my normal life.

'You need to stop poking around,' said the woman. 'Do you hear me? You need to go back home to New York.' She met my eye in the rear-view mirror again. I swallowed hard. I hadn't said anything about coming from New York. So she must know where Patrick lived and worked.

'Where is he?' I asked.

'Go home,' said the woman, and then she motioned to the man. He leaned across me to open the car door on my side, signalling that the conversation was over.

'And don't tell a fucking soul about any of this.'

The man gave me a shove and I climbed out. I drew the evening air deep into my lungs, feeling vaguely euphoric at being outside again. The car door slammed shut, and with a lurch they were gone.

I walked quickly away, heading in the direction where the city lights were brightest.

'Good evening,' said the desk clerk as I entered the hotel. He gave me a welcoming look through his rectangular designer glasses. There had been a shift change since I had left around lunchtime, an eternity ago.

'Is it possible to get something to drink at this time of the evening?' I said, running my hand through my hair. I had a feeling that I looked awful. 'Nothing alcoholic, but anything else. Water.'

'Of course,' said the clerk, quickly getting to his feet. He came around the counter and disappeared up a small staircase to the dining room.

'I'd be grateful for something to eat too,' I called after him, and then sank down onto a sagging armchair. I'd walked at least three miles before I found a taxi. I hadn't eaten a thing since lunch at Starbucks, and my stomach was churning with hunger. Or maybe it was the baby. My legs still felt shaky after the episode inside the car.

Facts, I told myself. That's all that matters. The essentials.

The people in the car: a woman and a man. Age: somewhere between thirty and fifty. Definitely French.

The woman was the one in charge. Her English was grammatically correct. Well-educated. Her phone number was the last thing in Patrick's notebook. She'd had a dual agenda: to find out who I was and what I knew, plus make sure that I left Paris.

I rubbed my forehead. Jetlag was still clamped like a helmet around my head. No matter how many times I replayed the conversation in my mind, I didn't feel any wiser.

'Pardon me for asking, but aren't you Patrick Cornwall's wife?'

The desk clerk placed a small tray in front of me. Salami and cheese. Water, and a glass of juice. It looked heavenly.

'You don't happen to have another one of these, do you?' I said, my mouth full of bread roll.

I quickly drank all the juice. Then leaned my head back against the soft upholstery of the armchair.

Going home was not an option. I could always contact the police and the American embassy, get them to look for Patrick. Wait for him to get in touch.

I have a bigger responsibility now, I thought, placing my hand on my stomach. A real mother would go home. Not take any more risks. Eat regular meals and go jogging at

71

a sensible pace, start crocheting. Put together the baby's wardrobe. Buy a crib and buggy.

But my next thought was: the child will grow up, and one day ask about his father. And I'll have to say: 'He disappeared. I don't know where. I don't know why. I was too cowardly to stay and find out.'

'Patrick Cornwall was a much appreciated guest when he stayed here with us,' said the desk clerk, setting another roll on the tray. 'He's the first American in the last decade who didn't think the Louvre was a murder scene.'

The clerk laughed a bit at his own joke. He spoke excellent English. According to the name badge he wore on his breast pocket, his name was Olivier.

'Do you know the Taillevent restaurant?' I asked between bites.

'Absolutely,' he said, perching on the arm of the sofa across from me. 'It's one of the finest. Not as well known as La Tour d'Argent, but undoubtedly better. They lost their third star in the *Guide Michelin* this year, but their loyal customers continue to dine there. I think the restaurant opened just after the war.'

'Who are their customers? Who goes there?'

'Politicians, businessmen. People who attended the right schools. The elite. It's not a trendy place. If you're interested in places that are hot at the moment, I would recommend Spoon. Alain Ducasse's place.'

'Did Patrick ever mention that he'd been to Taillevent?'

'He asked where it was located. I remember because I had to look up the address. I've never been there personally. But I don't know if he actually went there.'

Olivier straightened his glasses. He was stylishly dressed. Grey jeans, and a shirt in a darker colour. Reminiscent of Patrick's clothing choices.

'Did you talk much with him?' I leaned back in the chair,

trying to pretend this was an ordinary conversation about casual topics. My husband's completely normal visit to Paris. I didn't dare tell the clerk the truth — that Patrick had disappeared.

'We argued a lot, mostly about the poet Rimbaud,' said Olivier with a smile. 'Patrick thought we should take down the plaque out there.' He motioned towards the street.

I knew what he was talking about. I'd read on the hotel's web page that Arthur Rimbaud had lived here during the wild year of 1872. Olivier leaned down and picked up a big book bound in red leather from a side table. Out tumbled a postcard with a greeting from Melbourne.

'Never trust a poet,' he read from the guestbook, which he then handed to me. My heart turned a somersault when I recognized Patrick's handwriting. *Never trust a poet.* He'd added a thank-you for a marvellous stay. Dated 16 September, the day he left the hotel.

'Were you working that day?' I asked. 'When he checked out?'

'No, unfortunately I wasn't.' He stood up. Two women about my age came down the stairs and placed their room key on the counter. Olivier wished them a pleasant evening, and they tottered out into the night on their high heels.

'Patrick had bought a biography of Rimbaud at one of the antiquarian bookshops down by the river,' he went on. '*The man with soles of wind*, as Verlaine wrote. Rimbaud largely stopped writing poetry at the age of twenty, and settled in Ethiopia. He devoted himself to business instead, selling weapons and slaves.'

'He became a slave trader?' I was on the verge of dozing off. I really ought to go up to my room, I thought. Take a shower and go to sleep, but I was afraid of the thoughts that would descend on me once I was alone.

Olivier laughed.

'Not everybody believes that, but Patrick thought it was logical. The slave trader was another side of the poet, a shadow, or some sort of innate soul that most people didn't want to acknowledge, though he did exist, believing in his own superiority.' He touched the little cross he wore around his neck, sliding it back and forth on its chain. 'I don't know if I'm explaining things very well.'

'You speak fantastic English,' I said, trying to picture Patrick sitting here having an intense discussion. Slave trade or slavery was clearly the red thread. But I realized that I was much too tired to think.

Olivier kept on talking about Patrick, praising his French pronunciation, which was unusually good for an American. Patrick had studied French in high school and continued taking classes at Columbia University. He was practically in love with the language. Whenever he had the chance, he'd bring home DVDs of French films, but I'd always fall asleep watching them.

'Did he have any visitors while he was staying here?' I asked.

'Yes. It's well known that he had a relationship with the poet Verlaine.'

'No. I mean Patrick.'

The clerk looked away, still fingering his silver cross. 'There are so many people coming and going . . .'

Suddenly I'd had enough of all this small talk. It was now or never.

'My husband didn't come back to New York,' I said. 'No one has heard from him since he checked out of this hotel. That's why I'm here.'

Olivier stood up abruptly and stared at me. I could feel my anxiety rising. By tomorrow word would have spread through the entire hotel, and then it was just a matter of time before something appeared in the newspapers too. And the man and woman in the Peugeot would be back.

'Please don't say anything to anyone. He's probably on the trail of some big story, and that's why we haven't heard from him.' I lowered my voice. 'Do you remember him getting a phone call, late at night, on a Friday, almost two weeks ago? Were you working that night?'

Olivier frowned and then nodded hesitantly. 'Yes, I was here. And I do remember it. The man who called sounded very upset. But I don't know what it was about. I just connected him to room 43. I thought it might have something to do with Monsieur Cornwall's job.' He smiled. 'I've always dreamed of writing.'

'Do you know where the man was calling from?' I asked. 'Could you find out?'

'No. To do that, we'd have to contact the phone company. And I think the police would have to be—'

'Never mind,' I said. Asking the police to trace a call from one of Patrick's sources was definitely out of the question.

'Could you help me make a reservation at the Taillevent for tomorrow?' I said. 'There are a few things I want to check on at the restaurant.'

'Certainly.' Olivier went behind the counter, tapped the keyboard to wake up his computer, and then found the home page of the restaurant. Photographs appeared on the screen. The price of dinner was 140 euros.

'That's crazy,' I said.

'Lunch is cheaper,' said Olivier. 'It's only 80 euros.'

Only, I thought. But I asked him to make a lunch reservation for the next day. On my way upstairs I happened to think of something, and turned around.

'By the way,' I said. 'Make the reservation under the name Alena Sarkanova.'

The desk clerk looked up.

'That was my maiden name,' I told him.

Alena Sarkanova had nothing to lose. She managed fine on her own. Didn't go begging for love. That's who I was before Patrick. After we got married I shed my old name like a snake sheds its skin.

I got into the shower and let the hot water run down my body. Sarkanova was my mother's surname. I had no idea what my father's name was. I didn't even know if he was alive. Mama had never wanted to talk about him, and by now she'd been dead for years.

On several occasions I'd rummaged through her papers, looking for a name, a photograph. Anything that might prove it was him I took after. I never found anything. She had erased him from her life. As a teenager I had fantasized that he was searching for me all over the world. One day a letter would arrive. Or I'd see a missing person notice on TV. One day he'd be standing at the front door, telling me how he'd risked his life to escape the Iron Curtain and find his beloved daughter.

'Stop those stupid fantasies of yours,' shouted my mother. I could still hear her voice ringing in my head. 'He ran off. Don't you get it? Because he didn't want to take care of a fucking kid.'

'That's not true!' I screamed back at her. 'He ended up in prison. You told me that yourself.'

'Lies,' she muttered. 'Lies, all lies.'

'At least tell me his name,' I pleaded.

'Then you'll just try to find him,' she said.

'How could I do that if he died in prison?'

'We don't know if that's what happened.'

'But that's what you told me.'

'No, I didn't.'

We went around and around. I no longer knew what she'd said or what I'd imagined. I had only one clear memory from my childhood in Prague.

I'm sitting on the steps outside a door, and I'm three years old. It's evening. A single lamp is shining from a post, turning the yard a murky greyish yellow. There are no sharp contours. A few trash cans nearby, and an old bicycle leaning against the wall. My legs and hands are freezing. I'm just sitting there, wearing thin, light blue pyjamas and brown shoes with laces. Mama is calling me from the stairwell. 'Come in now, girl,' she shouts. 'If you don't come inside, I'm going to lock the door and you'll have to stay out there all night.'

But I don't go inside because I'm waiting for Papa.

Then I hear her footsteps. They're echoing, becoming an entire flock of footsteps, and the door behind me opens and Mama grabs my arm hard, lifting me up. I'm dangling in the air like a rag. 'Come inside this minute,' she yells.

I kick and squirm to get free, crying '*Ne, ne.*' I shout, 'I have to wait for Papa. He'll be here soon.'

'Look at me,' she bellows, but I squeeze my eyes shut. 'He's not coming back,' she says. 'Don't you understand?' And then she drags me up the steps, making my legs thump against the stone floor. The sound of the door slamming reverberates in the stairwell.

And that's all I remember.

I'd never told what little I knew about my father to anyone, not until I met Patrick. He kept asking me about him. Those sorts of things were important to him. He always wanted to know where someone came from, who that person was.

'I want to know everything about you,' he said, pulling me close. 'Everything.'

'And I want more wine,' I said. We were at his place on

77

the evening I started telling my story, sitting on a small sofa squeezed in between the kitchen and the bed. That was before we tore down the wall between the rooms and I moved in. During that first, enchanted time.

'What do you know about the Prague Spring?' I asked.

Patrick opened a bottle of red wine.

'They were trying to democratize the country, open it up, release all the political prisoners, and so on,' he said. 'A kind of glasnost twenty years too soon, and it ended in '68 when the Soviet tanks rolled in.'

'The political aspect was just a small part of it,' I said. 'Otherwise it was the same as in Paris and the States and everywhere else in 1968. Hippies and rock music and free love. Smoking whatever you wanted, fucking whoever you liked.'

Patrick filled our wine glasses and sat down next to me again.

'And it didn't stop because the Russians moved in,' I went on. 'They kept on playing rock and doing all those other things whenever the bureaucrats weren't watching. You might say I'm the product of a basement concert and a whole lot of marijuana.'

'Was your father a musician?'

'He played in a band that nobody remembers any more, but I once heard Mama say that one time he jumped in as a substitute for the Primitives. Have you ever heard of them?'

'I don't think so.'

'One of Prague's many bands in the sixties. Some of its members later formed Plastic People of the Universe.'

'That's a band I know,' said Patrick, his face lighting up. Like all journalists, he took pride in knowing a little about almost everything.

Plastic People of the Universe became legendary in the

Czech underground in the '70s. They had lost their licence to play officially, so they continued in secret, converting radios into loudspeakers and giving concerts in barns out in the country. Inspired by Zappa and The Doors, they used to play under a banner with the words: *Jim Morrison is our father*. That was reason enough for me, during one period, to buy all The Doors' records, imagining that the music somehow connected me to my father, that in the lyrics I could find traces of his thoughts. That particular detail I didn't mention to Patrick.

'When they were finally arrested, there were violent protests,' I said. 'Václav Havel and other intellectuals wrote Charta 77, proclaiming that everybody had the right to express themselves, that people couldn't be imprisoned for playing music, and so on. A few years later, he disappeared.'

'Your father? What happened? Was he arrested?' Patrick took my hand.

'I don't know. He never came back.'

'What did you do?'

'I was three years old. What do you think I could do?'

'But your mother, friends of the family, didn't they protest?'

'She had a child to support,' I said, looking away. 'She couldn't get a job in the field she had trained for, thanks to him. She had to sew clothes and clean houses. Of course she was furious.'

I couldn't look at Patrick. Those eyes of his that wanted more and more from me.

'But haven't you ever gone back and tried to find him?'

I shook my head.

In November 1989 I was eleven. The Berlin Wall had fallen, and on TV I watched the crowds swarming Wenceslas Square in Prague, people rattling keys, joined by more and more, hundreds of thousands. And I thought I would recognize him if only I could see his face. I remembered the camera zooming in on a grey shed made of corrugated metal, with big black letters scrawled on the side: *It's over — Czechs are free!*

Then I read in the newspaper that the secret files kept by the police were going to be opened. Mama refused to discuss the matter. She certainly had no intention of ever going back. And besides, she said, I wouldn't find anything in those files.

'But they spied on everybody,' I said. 'There must be tons of information in those files.'

'Nothing but lies,' she said.

'How do you know that before you've even read what they say?'

'I just know.'

I could still smell the scent of her perfume as she came closer. I thought she was ugly. I wanted to be like my father.

'And do you know why I know?' she hissed in my ear. 'Because that sweet little father of yours lied. He lied about where he'd been. "Love is free," he'd said, and he wasn't going to let anyone take away his freedom. He had no interest in politics, he just wanted to play guitar, and fuck whenever he felt like it. In all those years he would go running across the courtyard to that other woman, and everyone knew about it except me. He didn't want to be bothered with a kid in dirty diapers who cried every night.'

'Then why did you tell me he was in prison?' I shouted. 'You said he was a prisoner.'

I pulled away and threw myself onto the bed, shaking as my whole world split apart.

'He ran off,' said Mama. 'He left us. And I was the one who had to pay the price. I was the one who couldn't get a job and was left behind in that rat hole with a kid.'

After that I didn't ask any more questions.

Patrick put his hand on my cheek. Pulled me into his arms. He smelled of olive soap and aftershave.

No matter what, she's dead now, I thought. And nothing that happened in the past plays any role. It doesn't exist. Time leaves everything behind. Only the present moment exists, and Patrick, who had asked me to move in with him. This is year zero.

That he was in my life at all constantly surprised me. And the fact that he didn't leave when he got to know me better.

'I would have gone back to look for him,' he said. 'I would have been totally obsessed with finding out where I came from.'

'It was too far, and we couldn't afford it. She didn't want to. And besides, she lost her memory during those last years.' I took a sip of wine. 'And no matter what, she's dead now.'

Patrick brushed a few strands of hair out of my face, and I wished he wouldn't give me such an insistent look. The look that made me want to be completely truthful.

'Right before the Communist regime fell, Plastic People was allowed to start playing again,' I said. 'But only on the condition that they changed their name.'

'Don't tell me they agreed.'

'Why shouldn't they? They never asked to be heroes. They just wanted to play music.'

I'd read that the band members had quarrelled about it, but in the end they'd taken the name Pulnoc, which means midnight. Because around midnight the misfits come out, those who refused to be captured and governed, a bureaucrat's worst nightmare of free people who go their own way or push all the boundaries, those who refuse to obey or be shamed or adjust to the norms, the insane and the fantastical. They are the 'plastic people'.

'But after the Velvet Revolution, they took back their old name, of course, and went on tour, making the most of their legendary reputation. They even played at the Knitting Factory.'

'Were you there?'

I shook my head. I was nineteen at the time. All dressed up and wearing make-up. With a beer in my hand and a pounding heart, I'd sat at home on my bed, trying to think of what I would say when I went up to them after the gig. The only thing I knew was that two of the band members had played with my father. Maybe. Thirty years ago.

'I didn't go.'

'Why not?'

'Because I didn't know my father's name,' I said, looking down at my hands and swallowing hard. 'I didn't know who to ask about.'

Chapter 5

Paris
Thursday, 25 September

The wind seized hold of the map, practically tearing it out of my hands. I stuffed it back in my bag, walking as quickly as I could in my new shoes. It was a district lacking in any urban planning whatsoever, with old buildings ready for demolition and a few high-rises pointing like grey fingers into the air, at God and the whole world. Men idly leaned against the walls, and I had to dodge past a pusher who came towards me, mumbling an offer to sell me drugs.

Under normal circumstances I would have worn sneakers and a hoodie if I was venturing into this type of neighbourhood. I would have leaned forward, taking big strides, and no one would have been able to tell whether I was male or female. But right now I was dressed as Madame Alena Sarkanova, who was going to eat lunch at Taillevent in two hours, wearing pumps and a light coat. I'd spent the morning shopping for clothes in the cheapest boutiques I could find close to the hotel. It was almost like being back on the job and having to create a role. After I'd bought everything I needed, there were still several hours left, so I decided to explore the northernmost addresses on my list.

I assumed that number 61 had to be located a bit further along, on the second side street. I hunched my shoulders and leaned into the wind as I cut across boulevard Michelet. That was why I didn't see the building before I reached it.

My mind abruptly stood still.

In front of me was a black ruin, a phantom. The windows were holes giving way to darkness. I could see the sky right through the seventh floor where the roof had fallen in, taking the wall down with it. On the fourth floor was the skeleton of a charred bed. The smell of smoke still hovered like a nasty irritant in the air.

It burned down, I thought, as I felt fear tighten in my chest. It burned down on that night. Patrick had yelled something in French on the phone, and then he had left, and this was what had burned. And he didn't come back.

Slowly I walked along the fence that had been put up around the site of the fire. It was already scrawled with graffiti. Next to the scorched building on one side was a vacant lot. On the other it leaned towards a low building. At the back someone had made a hole in the fence. I bent down and climbed through. All was quiet. In the middle of the yard lay the remains of a baby buggy. The fabric had been burned away. Only the steel frame, twisted and soot-covered, was left. A row of storerooms or sheds had also burned to the ground.

I went through a hole that had once been a doorway, paying no attention to the danger. I climbed over glass and rubbish. Put my hand on a wall, turning my palm black. I saw a pile of bags and clothes that must have been set there later, because they were too clean to have survived the fire. Along the wall, double rows of mailboxes dangled close to the floor. I counted them all. Twenty-four. One for each apartment that had burned. The whole place stank of charred plaster and garbage, and I pulled my coat up over my mouth and nose as I climbed over the rubble from the stairway that had collapsed, then headed for the hole of the doorway on the other side.

A restaurant had been located on the ground floor facing the street. The bar was still intact, while the rest was nothing but cold, black walls. The sign had fallen down outside and lay on the ground, partially obscured by ash and debris. I could make out the first letters: 'Resta . . .'

I checked to see that the ground was free of glass. Then I carefully knelt down and rubbed the sign with the sleeve of my coat until the words were visible. Restaurant Hôtel Royal.

And all I heard in my head was Patrick's voice, saying over and over: *'But what's burning? But tell me what's going on, in God's name!'*

On the door of the café hung a hand-lettered sign: *We speak English.* I ordered coffee and a baguette with cheese.

'What happened over there?' I asked the guy behind the bar, pointing towards the ruin that stood a few hundred metres away, across the street.

The young man shook his head as he filled a glass of beer from the tap.

'Terrible,' he said. 'A big fire, big scandal.'

He gave my clothes an appreciative look. The café seemed to be a local hangout for construction workers, who sat at the tables eating omelettes and drinking beer, as they watched the lottery results on the TV screens. Some came over to the counter to cash in their tickets.

'Seventeen people died.'

'What did you say?' An icy chill spread from my feet up through my body. 'How many people did you say died?'

The young man nodded and held up his hands. 'Seventeen.' He set the full glass of beer on a tray and slid it along the bar to a man standing a short distance away.

The bitter taste of coffee seemed to swell inside my mouth as I let that number sink in.

'What happened?' I asked. 'Why did it burn?'

'Immigrants, you know. Africans. No emergency exits.' He shook his head and said something to a woman sitting next to me. She was bowed low over her tall glass of beer. She wore garish eye make-up, and her hair hung in long wisps over her shoulders.

'*Une tragédie*,' said the woman hoarsely, gesturing wildly. I couldn't understand the rest of her words.

'They were burned alive,' the bartender went on. 'What idiots. They don't understand a thing. Five, six, eight people living in one room, cooking food, everything.'

'I saw a sign that said the building was a hotel.'

'Hotel,' he said, using a dishtowel to wipe a glass, which he then held up to the light. 'Right. Five, six, ten in a single room. Bad place. Children too. Women and children.'

A man with splotches of paint on his clothes and drooping bags under his eyes approached the bar, holding out several lottery tickets. The bartender went over to cash them in. The old woman kept on talking to herself, muttering something about '*la grande tragédie, une catastrophe*', as she sank deeper into her beer glass.

The taste of old smoke settled in my mouth when I inhaled. Patrick had checked out of his hotel on Tuesday. The hotel had burned in the early morning hours of the previous Saturday. He must have jumped into a cab and raced across Paris, maybe because he thought he could save those poor people. But he was unquestionably alive the next day. Three days later he had checked out, according to the hotel staff.

I need to fill in the gaps, I thought. Figure out what happened in order to find out where he went. And why he didn't come home.

For a dazed moment I thought there could be other fires. Maybe this wasn't the same fire. Maybe this wasn't the one that he'd survived. I coughed, noticing the taste of smoke way down in my throat.

'When was it?' I said aloud to the bartender. 'When did this happen?'

'Only two weeks ago. Yes. On Friday.' He went through the doors into the kitchen.

I breathed a sigh of relief, but the next second I felt ashamed. Seventeen people had been burned alive. From my seat at the bar I could see part of the rickety black silhouette across the street. It was now 12.15.

'*Toilettes*?' I said to the old woman next to me. She raised her head slightly and pointed with a trembling finger. A corner of red fabric stuck up from the sleeve of her sweater. She was wearing at least three layers of clothing. Maybe she's no more than fifty, I thought. But she had no teeth, and a person without teeth looks lost.

In the ladies' room I washed a streak of soot off my forehead. Then I took out my make-up bag.

By the time the third course was served, I hadn't yet succeeded in getting the waiter to say anything more than 'does it taste good?' and 'is this your first time here?'

An entire swarm of staff flitted among the tables, following a strict hierarchy denoted by the colour of their jackets and whether they wore a tie or not. Lowest in the pecking order were several young guys wearing beige-coloured shirts. One of their jobs entailed discreetly approaching with a silver brush and small dust-pan to brush away the breadcrumbs that I'd spilled on the tablecloth.

'It must be nice working here,' I said to one of them, his face covered with pimples. He blushed.

'A friend of mine was here two weeks ago. Maybe you remember waiting on him?'

The boy smiled as he kept his eyes on the table, brushed away the last of the crumbs, and then disappeared. I took a sip of mineral water and tried to see what Patrick must have seen.

The dining room of the Taillevent restaurant wasn't much bigger than two ordinary living rooms lined up in a row. In the middle of the space stood an orange orchid enclosed in a glass dome. Otherwise the decor was entirely done in beige and brown. A sign of power, I thought. I had once used only brown hues in the set design for a production of *King Lear*. I'd had to fight for my interpretation. The cliché was to envelop Lear in gold and red velvet, but in my mind absolute power wore brown. Like in Nazi Germany. Like in the former Eastern Europe.

The thick wall-to-wall carpet swallowed most of the conversations at the other tables. If Patrick had come here to eavesdrop, he couldn't have heard very much.

'I've heard that a lot of politicians eat at this restaurant,' I ventured, speaking to a waiter wearing a red jacket who presented me with a sculpted pear sorbet for dessert. By that time I was so full that I would have preferred to go out and stick two fingers down my throat. I wasn't sure exactly what I'd eaten, but there were lots of courses with long names in French. 'Is it customary for them to give interviews here?'

'We have many loyal guests,' he said and then slunk off with a faint smile.

The elite. That was what Olivier at the hotel had said.

I let my gaze slide over the tables against the walls. One suit jacket after another, greying hair, bald heads. The only

88

women in the restaurant were two Japanese diners who were enthusiastically photographing every new course set before them.

I almost choked on a piece of poached pear when the older man from the day before came over to my table.

'Welcome. I hope you enjoyed the food. Is this your first time here?' he said, patting his stomach.

He didn't seem to recognize me, but of course I'd put on quite a lot of make-up. My dress was tight-fitting and could pass for elegant, and I'd bought a cheap silver necklace with gemstones that had to be fake. It was the perfect accessory for my décolletage. I managed a delighted smile.

'Yes, it's my first time here, but a colleague recommended your restaurant. An American journalist who was here two weeks ago.'

'How nice.'

His plump, red face didn't change expression. I had an urge to call him *monsieur*. That same tightly knotted necktie, and the tensed folds of his double chins. And suddenly I saw him in all the waiters moving about the room, in the strict hierarchy and polite fawning over the customers. The smiles I'd seen would change into something else when he got home and loosened his collar.

At that moment my cell rang. Everyone turned to look at me. I reached under the table and fumbled with my phone to switch it off. The call was from Benji. Only then did I remember that he'd phoned the day before, while I was sitting in a stranger's car. I'd completely forgotten to call him back.

'Would you care to take the chocolates home with you?' asked the first waiter after I'd had a cup of coffee, but left the truffles untouched.

I nodded.

'I'm going to tell Dan Brown about this place so he can put it in the next book he writes. Then a lot more Americans will be coming here to eat.'

My last attempt, but it prompted only a strained smile in reply.

'But I heard that you had some trouble with an American journalist a couple of weeks ago. Patrick Cornwall. What exactly happened?'

'We have many nice guests from America.'

'But apparently he's no longer welcome here. Did he disturb the other customers?'

'You'll have to talk to the head waiter about that.'

I was convinced that he and the other staff members knew what had happened. Scandalous gossip would spread quickly through any workplace, but here in the dining room no one was going to say a word.

When I picked up my new coat from the cloakroom, the woman with the pageboy hairstyle discreetly handed me a little bag containing four chocolate truffles.

While Google searched for hits after I'd entered the words 'fire', 'hotel', and 'Paris', I watched endless streams of tourists moving past. The traffic was stopped in all eight lanes. I'd found an Internet café on the Champs-Élysées and then waited in line for twenty minutes for an over-priced computer station with a view of the boulevard.

A long list of headlines appeared on the screen. Most of them were from French-language newspapers, but a lot had also been published on English news sites.

17 DEAD IN HOTEL FIRE IN PARIS

At least seventeen people died last night in a hotel fire in Paris.

Many of the guests staying at the budget Hôtel

Royal in Saint-Ouen in the northern part of Paris were
African immigrants. According to the radio station
France Info, four children were among the victims.
Identification of the dead was made more difficult by
the fact that the immigrants had probably entered the
country illegally. More people were staying in the
seven-storey building, but the police have not been
able to interview any survivors.

'There was only one stairway. The hotel was a death
trap,' says fire chief Jean-Marie Gilbert.

According to the police, there is evidence that the
fire may have been arson.

The blaze broke out just before midnight on Friday.
More than twenty fire engines were called to the scene.
Work was still going on early this morning.

In a later article, any suspicion of arson was dismissed. According to the police, the fire was caused by faulty electrical wiring, or possibly by negligence on the part of the hotel guests. However, the hotel owner would be cited for a lack of safety measures. He was also unable to provide credible accounts for the hotel's operating expenses.

It was not the first time something like this had happened. I clicked on other links.

Some years ago, twenty-four people had died in a fire at a budget hotel in north-eastern Paris. Most of the victims were African immigrants who had been given lodging there by social services. In August of the same year, nine children died in a dilapidated building.

'To get a rental agreement, you have to have papers,' said one of the immigrants named Said. He didn't want to give his last name to the reporter. 'Without papers you have to turn to the black market, and those landlords don't hesitate to offer housing that is falling apart and dangerous.

No one with the rights of a citizen would dream of setting foot in a place like that.'

The government authorities had devoted a great deal of energy to evicting residents from dilapidated buildings. For instance, they'd discovered seventy immigrants living in an abandoned printing factory. With only one working toilet to share.

I went back to Google and clicked on other related links, typing in variations on my search words: hotel fire Paris immigrant illegal undocumented Europe.

I imagined myself racing along behind Patrick as I jumped from one page to the next, as if I might catch a glimpse of his back as he moved on to the next site.

There were at least 400,000 undocumented immigrants in Paris alone. Up to eight million in all of Western Europe, and the flood of refugees increased at the same time as entry policies were getting stricter. By now the European border control stretched all the way down to Senegal and Mauritania. The Mediterranean was patrolled with boats and radar, and fences were being erected along the borders to the east. But new refugees and immigrants were still arriving on overloaded boats, on trains and long-distance trucks. And via airports, using phoney passports. Most borrowed money to pay the scandalous prices for their passage, while others were smuggled in and sold to the sex industry. Growing numbers were being exploited in what amounted to slavery.

I leaned back, trying to ease the muscles in my shoulders. Slavery was a word that kept cropping up. In Patrick's notebook, and in my conversation with the hotel desk clerk.

I typed the word in the search box and got a whole new series of hits.

There I found the Chinese who had collected cockles in a bay outside Liverpool. The story that Richard Evans had told me. Twenty-one people drowned when the tide came in. The survivors reported that they were paid seven euros for a full basket of cockles, but the *gang master* took most of their wages as rent for a cramped basement room and as repayment for the amount they owed for their travel to England. This incident had taken place several years earlier, and it had become the subject of a documentary film. Nothing new, in other words. I kept clicking on other articles, skimming the text.

In Tuscany, Italy, thousands of Chinese worked in secret textile factories. *Made in Italy*, said a little Chinese girl, proudly holding up a garment. The cheap clothing was sent on to be sold in street markets and tourist spots all over Europe. Their wages consisted of food and a place to sleep in the factory. The workers had accumulated debts as high as 20,000 euros, the amount required to pay off the *snake-heads* who had arranged their travel to Europe.

Great, I thought. A slave trade in which the slaves paid for their own travel. No wonder Patrick wanted to investigate the topic.

I glanced at articles about children who had disappeared from Romania and were then made to work as thieves in London, Paris, and Stockholm, or take dangerous construction jobs, or do nightshift cleaning. And girls who were sold as household slaves.

Then something caught my eye. My pulse quickened. I could hear a pounding in my eardrums.

It was a story about a fifteen-year-old girl from Togo who had been held as a slave by two families in Paris, until the neighbours finally reported what was going on. The court had sentenced the families to pay the girl a salary retroactively. A total of 30,000 euros for four years of slave labour, seven days a week, fifteen hours a day. That amounted to barely one euro per hour.

The attorney who represented the girl was named Sarah Rachid. I knew I'd seen that name before, printed in neat handwriting in Patrick's notebook.

'It's good that she's receiving restitution,' said Sarah Rachid. 'But there are many more like her, and most of them we'll never manage to reach.'

I got eleven hits on her name, and almost all of them had to do with the girl from Togo. One article mentioned the name of the firm where Rachid worked. On the firm's website I found an email address. I wrote to say that I had some questions regarding Patrick Cornwall, and I signed the email Alena Sarkanova without giving any further explanation.

My time on the Internet café computer was about to expire, so I went over to the cashier and paid for another hour. I also bought a Coke. My stomach was feeling a little lighter. I'd felt like an overstuffed goose when I left the Taillevent restaurant.

The case of the girl from Togo was three years old, so it couldn't be the centrepiece of Patrick's article.

I sat down in front of the screen again and massaged my temples.

Somewhere in all this, Patrick had found his story. A thread he'd unravelled to find something bigger, something that hadn't yet been told. *A fresh perspective, a unique viewpoint*, Richard Evans had said. *The investigative report of the year*, Patrick himself had mumbled on the phone, slurring his words.

I thought about the exclamation marks in his notebook, and all the numbers. The price of a slave.

There were more slaves in the world than ever, in spite of the fact that all nations had passed laws to ban slave labour. Actually, the price had never been as low as it was now, just $90 on average. It was even possible to get a good slave from Mali for only $40. The amounts corroborated Patrick's notes.

In the 1880s, during the transatlantic slave trade to America, a slave cost $1,000. In today's currency, that was equal to $38,000, which meant that now 4,000 slaves could be bought for the price of only one back then. And that was the period regarded as the darkest era in human history.

I scrolled down until I found an explanation for the other numbers in Patrick's examples.

The figure 30 million was an estimate of the number of slaves in the world today. He had compared this figure to the 12 million slaves transported across the Atlantic — and that was over a period of 300 years. In the 1800s, slavery was completely legal; now it was part of the black market, a criminal operation. But it did exist, and the authorities didn't seem to be doing much to stop it.

I closed my eyes for a moment and again pictured the pages of Patrick's notebook. I remembered seeing the words 'The boats!'

I added 'boats' to some variants of the previous search words and new articles appeared on the screen. There seemed to be an endless list, but I had several hours to waste, so I decided to take my time and go through them properly.

During the past few years tens of thousands of migrants had died at sea between Africa and Europe. Refugees or people in search of work. Recently, eleven people were found dead in a rubber boat off the Canary Islands. Apparently they had died from dehydration. A fishing boat had capsized off the coast of Libya, and at least 300 people were thought to have drowned. And 240 migrants were rescued from a sinking boat near the Italian island of Lampedusa. There were no passenger lists, but the survivors estimated that between fifty and seventy people had disappeared into the sea. One man mentioned a heavily pregnant woman who had fallen overboard right before his eyes. A related article reported that female migrants were often pregnant. Either they deliberately got pregnant because that would increase their chances of being allowed to stay in Europe, or else they were raped on the way.

Or maybe they left because they were pregnant, I thought. To make a better life for their child.

I clicked on another related document. A Swedish tourist had found the body of an African migrant on a beach in Tarifa in southern Spain. In an interview the girl said how awful it had been to see a dead body. He had looked almost alive in the water. He had a tattoo, but he was completely naked, and this was on a beach where people went swimming and surfing. It was such a shock! The girl's father was also interviewed, and he was upset that something like this could happen. They hadn't been given any information or assistance from the travel agency. A few days later more bodies were found outside Cádiz, not far away. The Spanish police thought it had to do with a capsized rubber dinghy. In the narrow straits between Morocco and Spain the waves could reach several metres in height.

I swallowed hard. The nausea was back. I'd Googled the word 'pregnancy' in the morning and read that it often helped to eat a small snack, like a carrot or a dry roll. Even though I was still feeling very full, I got up to buy two almond biscuits. It occurred to me that I'd ignored Benji's phone calls for two days in a row. I tapped in his number as I kept scrolling through more articles, looking for yet another name to turn up.

'Ally!' he exclaimed. 'Finally. How's it going? How are you? How's Paris?'

'Good,' I lied.

'Have you found—'

'How was opening night?' I interrupted him, feeling foolishly touched to hear his voice.

'What's going on? You sound strange. Are you sure you're OK?'

His concern made my throat tighten. Don't ask me about Patrick, I silently pleaded. Don't say a word about any of this.

'A slight cold, that's all,' I told him. 'But Paris is amazing. What did the newspapers say?'

It was like a rejuvenating shot in the arm to hear him babbling. Life was continuing over there. It was only me who was absent. The reviews in almost all the important New York papers had been great, Benji chirped. They talked about a new creative depth that was classic and yet reached beyond all conventions. Except for one critic who claimed the dance performance had murdered the narrative soul of Chekhov's drama. And at the after-party a drunken Leia had latched onto Duncan, whose interest by that time had shifted to the girl who played Masha.

'And so we come to the eternal question of which profession enjoys the most sex in relation to the amount of work put in,' Benji went on. 'Should you be a choreographer, or a singer, or should you become the leader of some sort of cult?'

I didn't hear the rest. A new article had appeared on the screen in front of me, and the text was eating at me like a corrosive acid.

'Hey, listen, I'll call you later,' I said, and ended the conversation.

I was reading about yet another boatload of immigrants who had reached the Canary Islands. On board were thirteen men and a woman who was dying. The woman had brought her infant, whom she was nursing. When the food and drinking water ran out, and the promised three days at sea turned into five, and six, and then a week, the men had turned to her, the only source of food on board. They had sucked the milk out of her body until there was nothing left of her. Like a limp hide, she was carried ashore by the Red Cross and declared dead in a hospital in Los Cristianos.

I logged out and turned off the computer, but the text lingered on the screen until the humming ceased and it finally went blank.

Twelve of the survivors had said that the infant was dead when it was tossed overboard. The thirteenth claimed it was alive.

The pimply young man was among the last to come out of the restaurant, along with one of the others who'd worn a beige shirt. Now they were dressed in their own clothes, and I would hardly have recognized them if I'd met them in town.

They walked down the hill and turned left onto avenue Friedland. I got up from the park bench where I'd been sitting, from which there was a good view of the entrance to the restaurant. The Arc de Triomphe gleamed up ahead as I followed them at a safe distance, heading towards the Champs-Élysées.

If only I could get the pimple-faced boy alone, I was sure I could get him to talk. Swiftly I crossed the street so as not to lose them in the crowds. I saw them disappear down an escalator into the subway.

People were swarming all around me. Everybody else can do this, I thought. They take the *Métro* every day.

I stepped onto the escalator, taking big breaths through both my mouth and nose, trying not to panic.

Only people with no imagination took the subway, in my opinion. Only those who couldn't picture what happens when the lights go out, the alarm sounds, and thousands of people try to get out of the tunnels at the same time.

The ceiling rose into a vault over my head. There were orange mosaic tiles on the walls, and advertising posters. People passed by me, but I saw only a green jacket and ash-blond hair that curled slightly on the back of his neck. He was walking about twenty metres ahead of me. More tunnels, white tiles. The city is perforated by underground passageways, I thought. The whole place is going to fall right in on itself.

I pulled out one of the tickets that I'd bought earlier. They were good for both the bus and subway, though I'd never intended to use them for anything but the bus. I stuck the ticket in the machine, silently offering up a prayer, and it popped up at the other end.

Pimple-face gave his companion a fist bump and then continued on alone towards line 6. I followed, hoping that my analysis of his character was correct. Young and shy and subject to severe acne. The archetype of an easily duped young guy with low self-esteem.

Down on the platform I was met with a warm breeze. It was stifling, with a scorched smell, as if someone had been burning rubber. The train pulled in with a clatter, and I got on just as a foghorn sounded somewhere and the doors closed.

'Hey, I recognize you,' I said, sitting down across from the boy in the window seat. 'You work at Taillevent. You were my waiter today!'

'I'm not a waiter,' he said, looking away, embarrassed. 'I'm just a busboy.'

'Well, I couldn't tell the difference,' I said. 'It must be amazing to work in such a fancy restaurant.'

I was forced to lean forward a bit to control the dizziness. My knees touched his because there was very little room. He was holding a bag of candy on his lap.

'It's actually really hard work,' he said, looking out of

the window. A black tunnel covered with graffiti, cables running along the walls.

'Could I have a piece?' I asked, pointing to the candy. His cheeks flushed pink. I made a point of brushing against his hand as I fished out a yellow marshmallow crocodile. 'That's just like New York,' I said. 'It's always the busboys who do the hard work.'

'It's even worse now because Michelin took away a star,' he said. 'Everything has to be perfect. As if it was our fault they lost the star.'

The subway careened and whistled and braked. There couldn't be more than a minute between stations.

'You speak really good English,' I said. 'There aren't many in Paris who do, but I suppose it's a requirement because of all the foreign customers and celebrities who come to the restaurant, and you have to wait on all of them.'

'Except that I'm not a waiter.'

The tunnel outside grew brighter and the subway car clattered out into the fresh air above ground. I saw the river and the Eiffel Tower, and suddenly I could breathe again.

'I heard there was an American journalist who caused a big ruckus last Thursday. Were you working that day?'

'I work every day. Well, we're not open on the weekends, but otherwise—'

'It makes me ashamed to be an American when something like that happens.'

'But it's not your fault.' He was smiling now, at least.

'No, but it feels like it is. It's the same thing with the war in Iraq. I wasn't the one who thought that up.' I laughed, and he did too, his voice sounding shrill and nervous.

'One of the guys who works in the restaurant told me that he wasn't allowed to come back. That journalist, I mean,' I went on, digging my hand into the bag of crocodile candies. 'I heard he behaved abominably. Hitting people, and who knows what else.'

'He didn't hit anyone.'

'No?' I said, breathlessly. 'So what did he do?'

The boy squirmed a bit in his seat, but that merely brought my legs up against his other thigh as well.

'I guess he was bothering one of our customers,' he said. 'It's important for them to be left in peace. They often have meetings at the same time, while they're eating. They're very busy, and that's why it caused so much trouble. Because he was a journalist. Monsieur Thery said we shouldn't let in any of those scandal reporters. Paparazzi, you know.'

We had crossed the river and were now roaring into the tunnel realm again. My armpits were wet with sweat. I'd heard that name before, but where?

'Monsieur Terri?' I said. 'He's a politician or something, right?' I automatically copied the boy's pronunciation. That was something I'd always been good at. Mimicry and the ability to adapt. Hiding in a crowd.

'No, no. Monsieur Thery is a businessman. He dines with us all the time.'

'Oh, right. You mean Maurice Terri.'

'No, Alain. Alain Thery.'

A hot wind rushed through the subway car at the next station, and all of a sudden I knew where I'd heard that name. A woman's voice saying: '*Was it Alain Thery who sent you?*'

'So what did he do?' I asked. 'The journalist, I mean.'

'I don't know. I was in the kitchen.' He stood up. 'The next stop is mine.'

I waved as he pushed his way through the car. The next instant, as the doors opened, I headed in the opposite

101

direction and managed to jump out just before they closed again.

I kicked off my shoes and took off my dress as soon as I was back in my room. I sat down in front of my computer wearing only a bra and panties. Olivier had told me how to connect to the Wi-Fi, and five seconds later I was able to pull up Google. I'd also asked the clerk how to spell a name pronounced Terri in French.

I got a hit at once. The easiest first step. Wikipedia had a short article about the businessman Alain Thery. It was written in French, but I still managed to glean a few things from the text.

Alain Thery was born in 1959 in Pas-de-Calais. Among other things, he worked as a consultant in finance and development. The words were the same in most languages. He owned several companies, and there was a link to one of them. There was also a list of numerous newspaper articles in which he was mentioned. The first eighteen were in French, but the nineteenth was on a multilingual news site.

Five years ago Alain Thery had been named Newcomer of the Year in the business world. His consulting firm had shown a 400 per cent increase in profit over three years. The next step was to expand into several other European countries, aiming for the global market.

I sent an email to Benji, attaching the links to the eighteen other articles about Thery written in French and asked him to translate them for me. Not word for word, I added. Just enough so I'd know if there was anything in them besides the usual hype.

I got up and went into the bathroom to fill my plastic cup with water. Then I realized I still had three truffles left from Taillevent in my bag. They had stuck together a bit, and tasted of bitter cacao and silky vanilla.

Back at the computer, I pulled up the home page for Lugus, Alain Thery's company. The whole page was in blue tones, with images of the sky and clouds, and a floating molecule to illustrate the company's business concept. In the column on the left were four tiny flags. I clicked on the Union Jack.

'To kill two birds with one stone is our motto in every situation,' it said at the top of the page.

And further: 'By combining technical know-how, strategic planning, and contextual analysis, we pave the way for a corporation to become rejuvenated, as required by an ever-changing world.'

What bullshit, I thought.

I surfed aimlessly through the home page without understanding why Patrick would be interested in this man. Or was he? Maybe it was like Pimple-face had said. They'd taken him for a paparazzo.

But the woman in the car had also mentioned Alain Thery's name.

I clicked on the company name, and a picture appeared of a sculpture with three faces. The caption explained that Lugus was the name of a Gallic god who reigned over trade and business. He was also the god of travel, and had created the arts. Typical consultants, I thought. They always took those sorts of names, which sounded so profound and yet didn't mean a damn thing.

'You can choose between creating a future or reacting to the past.'

I got up and stretched so hard my joints creaked.

Patrick had talked about similar things in his story about the new economy. It was mostly about the losers — workers whose jobs disappeared or were outsourced to India. The winners included various types of consultants, brokers, middlemen. People who really didn't produce anything.

They were intermediaries, conveying information and knowledge, money, services, goods and property. They didn't create anything of value, and yet that was where the big money was. Patrick had quoted an author — I thought his name was Robert Sennett, or maybe it was Richard. At any rate, the man had written a book about how the new economy had changed people's morals and way of thinking so that everything that had previously lasted a lifetime became short-term, and fixed values evaporated.

That was the sort of thing Patrick wrote about. I cursed that pimply boy. Sneak a few snapshots of celebrities? Patrick would never do anything like that. But what if they really had thought he was a paparazzo? That meant he must have taken a camera into the restaurant. But why? To snap a picture of Alain Thery!

I slammed my hand on the desk. Of course. The photographs. Those boring and blurry pictures that Patrick had sent home from Paris.

The memory stick was in a folder with various bills and sketches for stage sets that I'd thrown into my suitcase when I was packing. I stuck it into my laptop. While I waited for the pictures to load, I opened the French articles about Alain Thery, one after the other.

In the fifth article I found a photo of him.

I sat there for a long time, staring at the man on the screen. He had a big nose, and he wore wire-rimmed glasses. His pale eyes looked almost white, but that could also be due to the photo's exposure. The image was cut off just below the knot of his tie. He wasn't bad looking, but not especially attractive either. He was the boy-next-door, the man in the bank, a type to be found by the dozen around Wall Street.

And he looked awfully familiar.

Patrick's photos now showed up on the screen, one after the other, and there was no longer any doubt.

Alain Thery was one of the men he had photographed. His face appeared in picture after picture, until I'd viewed him from every possible angle. Patrick must have been obsessed with capturing his image.

The question was why?

I got up again and went over to the window. Lights were on in the garret rooms of the Sorbonne. It looked so nice and homely, with the lace curtains in the windows. Somebody actually lived there. A little boy was riding a tricycle between the rooms. He was maybe three or four years old. He shot past one window and disappeared, then popped into view in the next. I wondered whether he was the son of the caretaker or maybe even the chancellor. What became of someone who grew up living in the garret apartment of a university? Then it occurred to me that somebody might be studying me in the same way. Like an animal in a cage, a woman in an aquarium, wearing a bra and panties.

I moved away from the window and sat down, clicking on the Lugus home page again, and this time I happened to open the French version. It looked slightly different, with more references, more banners. In French the phrase 'to kill two birds with one stone' was *faire d'une pierre deux coups*. At the very bottom of the page, in minuscule type, was the word *contacts*. I clicked on that and got the address: 76 avenue Kléber. I tilted my chair so far back that it almost fell over.

What the fuck?

I had marked number 76 avenue Kléber on my map. It was one of Patrick's addresses.

The street was only a stone's throw from the Arc de Triomphe, a fashionable kilometre from the Taillevent restaurant, in the same neighbourhood where I'd spent an entire afternoon at an Internet café. I hadn't felt like wandering around in those uncomfortable shoes I was wearing. I thought I'd save that for the next day. It had seemed more important to find out more details about the fire.

I clicked on the email address listed on the company's contact page and started formulating a polite request for a meeting. I paused to give it some thought, and then wrote that I represented an American company, which was basically true (even though my company consisted of only myself and a poorly paid assistant without a real contract). Only after I'd read through the email for the third time and was just about to press 'Send' did I realize what an idiot I was.

Alain Thery hadn't quadrupled his profit because he was a fool.

He would recognize the name Cornwall in the email address and associate it with the journalist he'd wanted to get rid of.

I scratched my head, pondering what to do.

It was the simplest thing in the world to create an address. Benji did it every fifteen minutes when he was web dating. He had dozens of digital personas, each with its own digital love life. It was a miracle he never got them mixed up. He could easily have ended up trying to date one of the versions he'd created for himself.

That prompted another thought. Had I ever cancelled my old email address?

I opened the email programme and quickly sent a test message to *a.sarkanova@workmates.com*.

When I came back from the bathroom, the mail had landed in my inbox. It was pinging merrily, like a good friend who had stopped by to end my isolation. Alena Sarkanova actually did exist. In the digital realm she hadn't disappeared. I hadn't called myself Alena since my early teen years. I liked Ally, since it didn't provoke questions about my origin. It was the name in my passport, but Patrick was the only one who ever called me by my real name. He said it was too lovely not to use it. Like 'music and purity, something Botticelli might have painted'.

Workmates was a usable IP address. It didn't reveal anything. If anyone wanted to track it down, they'd find a loosely connected collective of freelancers who had once shared an office but now had only this domain name in common.

I sent my message using this email address.

Then I let my laptop power down into sleep mode. The screen faded to black and fell silent. I crept under the covers, not bothering to take off the bedspread. The boy across the way had stopped riding around on his trike.

Chapter 6

Paris
Friday, 26 September

Attorney Sarah Rachid quickly crossed the square, heading for the restaurant where I was waiting. I knew at once it had to be her. There was something about her haste and determined stride.

'I don't really have time for this,' she said when I waved her over to my table. She sat down and took off a pair of thin gloves. I noticed she was wearing a simple gold wedding band.

'It's terribly kind of you to meet with me,' I said.

Sarah Rachid gave me a suspicious look and then turned to glance at the daily menu, which was printed on a blackboard. She didn't look especially pleased with that either.

Her reply to my email had been chilly and formal. She wrote that she didn't have time. She couldn't discuss anything due to lawyer–client confidentiality. If necessary, she could explain this over lunch. She really couldn't take the time (she again wrote), but she did have to eat. She'd be at Patio's on place de la Sorbonne at one o'clock today. Friday. Please confirm receipt of this email.

I'd written back to say that I was a researcher with the magazine, and I was supposed to double-check some of the information. I thought it best to stick to the same story.

Sarah motioned to the waiter.

'I don't understand why Patrick gave out my name,' she said. 'I told him I didn't want to be quoted.'

'So you do know him?'

'Why do you ask that?'

The waiter brought over bottles of water and a basket of bread. Sarah ordered *Cassoulet Maison*, the daily special, and I did the same, though I had no clue what it might be. Silently we helped ourselves to the bread.

'I read about that case of the girl who was working as a household slave,' I then said, trying to soften her up a bit. 'It was great you were able to help her win restitution.'

'I never talk about my cases.'

'But I saw that you gave a statement to the newspaper. It must have been a big victory.'

'I didn't know they were going to quote me.'

Two steaming soup tureens were set on the table. Meat and vegetables swimming in a greasy broth.

'I'm a lawyer. I devote all my energy to the law,' said Sarah Rachid, dipping a piece of bread in the broth. 'I don't use the media as an arena for playing out my arguments. In my opinion, it's the courts of law that should administer justice in this country. Not the press, the radio, or TV.' She gave me a hostile look. 'Maybe you consider that an old-fashioned point of view?'

'Is that what Patrick thought? Did he want you to make a statement?'

'He understood when I told him I didn't want to do that. Besides, I merely helped him with a few facts. He said it would be completely off-the-record.'

'What would?'

'What do you mean?'

'What would be off-the-record?' I said. 'I'm sorry for bothering you with all these questions, but we haven't been able to get hold of Patrick.'

Sarah wiped her mouth with a napkin and glanced away. She had a long face, and the corners of her mouth turned down, giving her a slightly surly look, enhanced by the fact that she actually was in quite a surly mood.

I picked at the food in my bowl, then bit into something that looked like a tiny chicken thigh. It had a strong, bitter taste.

'What sort of bird is this?' I asked.

Sarah cast a quick glance at the bone, which was dripping with greasy broth.

'Rabbit,' she said.

I dropped the meat back into the soup bowl and stabbed a piece of carrot instead.

'Are most of your clients immigrants?' I went on, trying to get her to talk.

'Why do you ask? Because you think I'm an immigrant?'

Her eyes narrowed into slits. This was clearly the wrong tactic.

'I didn't know you were an immigrant,' I said.

'I may have an Arabic name, but I was born here in France. I'm a lawyer. I do my job. That's all.'

Sarah stared angrily at her stew as she ate.

'I know exactly what you mean,' I said. 'My last name is Sarkanova, and everybody used to ask me where I'm *really* from.'

Sarah studied me for a few seconds before she spoke. 'So they've stopped doing that?' she said.

'What do you mean?'

'You said they used to ask you.'

I coughed so hard the piece of rabbit meat threatened

to come up again. That was one of the advantages of being married. Whenever I introduced myself as Ally Cornwall, I got a whole new set of questions. People wanted to know what part of New York I'd grown up in, what kind of work I did, and so on.

'I suppose I just don't notice any more,' I said, turning to look through the big picture window. The square outside was clean and stylish, with rows of trickling fountains. Three rumpled pigeons were standing in one of the basins, washing their wings in the water.

There's a way to approach every individual, I thought. This woman was as closed off as a construction site in lower Manhattan. I tried picturing how Patrick must have got her to talk. With his serious demeanour, I thought, and his total focus, his ability to make the person sitting across from him feel important and understood. I felt my stomach clench.

'Patrick hasn't submitted any completed texts yet,' I said. 'But I promise to check everything and see that your name isn't mentioned. He always keeps his word about things like that.'

The waiter appeared at our table. I pushed aside the rabbit stew and asked for a double espresso. Sarah ordered tea.

'I helped him with a number of facts about how our legal system works in those types of cases. That's all,' she said after the waiter had left. 'The law is complicated when we're dealing with people who are undocumented.'

'In what way?'

She took a sip of mineral water.

'I can't give you a simple answer. That's the same thing I told Patrick. It all depends on the individual case, and under what conditions the person finds himself living here in France. Whether someone can guarantee his income and residence, and whether the person in question is guilty of any crimes, other than living here. And the laws keep changing, especially over the past few years.'

I took paper and pen from my bag and began taking notes, since I was pretending to be a researcher. When she started talking about the law, the words seemed to pour out of her. She told me that, generally speaking, deportation was the norm if someone was living in the country illegally. Previously, the police would seize undocumented immigrants, arrest them, and take them into custody like criminals, but now the laws were stricter. Anyone who had not committed a crime but simply lacked papers could be held at the police station for no more than sixteen hours. The individual had to prove that he was entitled to stay in France or else he would be deported. In that case he would be transferred to a special detention centre at the Palais de Justice on Île de la Cité and held there for a maximum of forty-five days, waiting to be transported out of the country. It was the eighth department of the *Préfecture de Police* that specialized in these matters.

'You could always try to talk to the police,' said Sarah, folding her napkin. 'But I doubt you'll get any answers.'

'Did Patrick tell you who he was writing about?' I asked, venturing a little smile. 'It may seem strange that we don't know any of the details. In the past we could spend hours discussing the various angles of a story, but there's no time for that any more. And Patrick Cornwall is a freelancer. He goes his own way.'

The attorney raised her eyebrows. She took a toothpick from a little case and meticulously dislodged a shred of meat from between her teeth.

'He contacted me almost four weeks ago,' she said at last. 'He asked whether I'd consider defending several people, but I'm not the one who decides which cases my firm takes on.'

I held my breath, not wanting to provoke anything that might cause her to erect the barbed wire again.

'He also had a lot of questions about what happens if an illegal immigrant testifies against a criminal organization. Would he get to stay here? I didn't see any reason not to answer those kinds of questions — provided he wouldn't quote me, of course.'

'And you didn't meet with Patrick again after that?' I asked.

'I don't understand why you're asking me these kinds of questions,' said Sarah, stirring her tea.

I feverishly tried to think of how to respond, and decided to make use of her own weapons. Laws and regulations.

'Your oath of confidentiality. Does it apply to everyone you represent?'

'Everyone the firm represents,' she corrected me.

'And you never took them on as your clients, the people that Patrick was talking about?'

'I told him that it would have to be handled along official lines.'

'So that means there's nothing to prevent you from talking about them,' I said, pouring a little milk into my coffee. 'Unless you happen to think that I'm a hopelessly stupid busybody.'

A trace of a smile appeared on her face. She sipped her tea.

'My brother was the one who gave Patrick my name,' she said. 'Even though he knows what I think about journalists. The media never take any responsibility. They think the legal system is too complicated and moves too slowly. They tend to oversimplify and rush forward, wanting to write the story before the process has even begun, passing judgement before a verdict is reached.'

'So your brother . . . what did you say his name is?'

'I didn't.'

'But he was also in contact with Patrick, is that right?'

'He works for an organization that helps undocumented immigrants and launches campaigns. Things like that. He has a hard time remembering that I'm a lawyer and not one of his activists.' She raised her eyebrows and glanced away. 'From what I understand, these men were prepared to testify, but I didn't want to know any details about them. I made that very clear.'

'Who were these men?'

'They had escaped from an employer who was holding them captive. Patrick claimed it was a matter of slave labour, which in purely legal terms is not a crime. Rather, it's classified as *un délit*. A legal violation that is punishable, but considered of a lesser degree. It can be compared with an *offense* in your legal system. But if the story is accurate, there could be grounds for bringing an indictment for abuse, deprivation of liberty, maybe even murder.'

I stared at her.

'Murder? Did Patrick really say that?'

'Of course I told him that he needed to go to the police if he had suspicions of that kind.'

'So did he? Did he go to the police?'

'I'm sure my brother advised him not to,' she said. 'He doesn't trust the French police. He considers them corrupt.'

'Are they?'

'You can't reject the system just because a few individuals abuse it. Society is based on law.' She used her teaspoon to point at the wedding ring I wore. 'Take marriage, for example. Above all else it's a legal construct.'

'A lot of people would say it has to do with love,' I replied.

Sarah Rachid motioned to the waiter and asked for the

check. Then she opened her briefcase. She wrote down a phone number on a notepad, then tore off the page and placed it on the table.

'I suggest you go to see my brother. I'm sure he'd be willing to talk to you. Arnaud is an idealist.' She made it sound like some sort of sexual perversion.

'Just one more thing,' I said. 'Did Patrick mention someone named Alain Thery?'

'Why are you asking me that?'

'What about a company named Lugus? Josef K? Did he say anything about a hotel that burned down a few weeks ago?'

She counted out some cash, adding on a ten per cent tip. Her half of the bill.

'Say hello to Arnaud for me,' she said, and left.

I watched her take a short cut through the outdoor seating area on the square and then disappear around the corner onto boulevard Saint-Michel. The sun had broken through the clouds, and people were taking off their jackets and draping them on the backs of their chairs.

On my way out of the restaurant I phoned Arnaud Rachid. Compared to his sister, he was remarkably forth-coming.

'How nice,' he said. 'How's Patrick doing? I haven't heard from him in a while.'

I was overjoyed. Finally someone who knew something and was willing to talk.

'When did you last speak to him?' I asked.

'Hmm. When was it? A couple of weeks ago? He's not still in Paris, is he?'

I swallowed hard and suggested we should meet. He gave me directions to his office on rue Charlot, which was in the Marais district. He said he'd be there after six o'clock.

I ended the call. The city suddenly seemed brighter, the

atmosphere genuinely friendly. The pigeons had climbed out of their bath to perch in a row on the edge of the fountain, drying their wings. It was only 2.15 in the afternoon. Almost four hours to kill.

The *Préfecture de Police* was located on the Île de la Cité in the middle of the Seine, which cleaved the city into two parts. The stone building was huge. Daylight barely reached the ground. It struck me that the street must have been swathed in partial darkness for several centuries. Twilight was woven into the very fabric of the city.

At least I'm not on my way to the guillotine, I thought, turning right at the iron gates of the Palais de Justice, which were thirty metres tall. Right next door were the dungeons in the Conciergerie, where the death sentences had rained down during the French Revolution.

In the morning I'd awakened with a dream still lingering in my mind. I was wandering along white corridors, searching for Patrick, but no one knew where he was.

The police ought to know if he was lying unconscious in a hospital somewhere. I wouldn't have to tell them anything about his work.

'Sorry, no English,' said the woman at the reception desk in police headquarters. Her hair was so stiff with hairspray that it could have been made of porcelain.

'All right. But surely someone here speaks English?'

But nobody did. I swore loudly. The police department was only a block from Notre-Dame. The whole area was crawling with tourists, and yet they couldn't hire anyone who spoke English. Finally a man stepped out of the queue and offered to translate. I explained that I was enquiring about someone who'd gone missing. He took a step forward, pressing close to my back as he translated. The woman at the desk handed me a piece of paper with a phone number. Behind me the man was breathing heavily in my ear. 'It must be difficult for you, all alone here in Paris.' I stomped hard on his foot, and I heard him shouting after me: 'Looking for your husband, are you? I can see why he left you!'

Out in the courtyard people were waiting in long lines to apply for visas. Some were sitting on the cobblestones, leaning wearily against the wall as they smoked. I smoothed out the piece of paper that I'd crumpled in my hand. It said: '*Recherche dans l'intérêt des familles*'. Apparently missing persons came under the jurisdiction of the department dealing with family matters. I tapped in the number on my cell as I walked. A woman answered on the first ring.

'I have some questions about a specific person,' I said. 'Someone who is missing.'

'*Votre nom, s'il vous plaît.*'

Nom had to mean name.

'My name is Ally Cornwall,' I said. 'I've just arrived in Paris, and I just want to—'

'*Adresse?*'

I told her the name of my hotel. Two police officers gave me a sleepy glance as I went through the gate and came out onto the street. In my ear I heard the woman rambling off a long list of words: *mari, fils* . . . It was more difficult to understand French when I couldn't see the person.

'I'm sorry, but is there anyone there who speaks English?' I said.

'*Vous êtes* English?'

'American.'

'Call embassy, please,' said the woman, and she was gone.

I'd come out on the other side of the police headquarters. I walked over to the stone wall near the quay. In front of me flowed the river, murky and green. I breathed in the musty air and suddenly had a feeling that I'd stood in this same place before. Long ago. A barge glided past, loaded with coal and asphalt. On the opposite bank the facades of the buildings lined the water. There was something so familiar about the scene, a déjà vu that wasn't entirely correct. The buildings had been darker and the river wider, with blacker water.

The Vltava. The river that ran through Prague.

I was very young. I was certain about that because I couldn't reach up to the top of the wall, so somebody had lifted me up. *Someone had put strong hands around my waist and lifted me up so I could see the boats gliding past on the river.* It was him. I was sure of it, even though I couldn't see him or hear his voice. A memory of my father. And someone had laughed, or else it was the echo of a laugh. I tried to remember if I had turned around, but the sensation of his hands holding my body disappeared, and I was no longer sure whether it had actually happened or not.

Several metres away I saw an opening in the wall, and stairs leading down to the river. I sat down on the steps and took the guidebook out of my bag, looking for the phone number of the American embassy. The smell of urine rose up from the quay below.

'Excuse me, what did you say your name was?'

The official in charge of missing Americans coughed on the phone.

'Alena Cornwall. I don't know whether anything has happened to my husband, but I'm just wondering whether you've received any report—'

'And how long has your husband been missing?'

I realized this was almost more complicated than talking

to the French police. Patrick's name might be known at the embassy. They might even read *The Reporter*.

I explained briefly, without saying anything about Patrick's work.

'Have you been married long?' he asked.

'What does that have to do with anything?'

'Personally, I've been married for thirteen years. Not everyone appreciates eating the same food every week, if you get my drift.'

He took a bite of something, and I heard him smacking his lips. I gripped the iron railing of the stairs to try to stay calm.

'The problem is that I don't speak much French, and that makes it hard to talk to the police. But you would know if anything happened to an American, right? An accident or anything like that?'

'Let me have a look. Wait just a minute. Here's something.'

My heart jumped and turned over, but then landed somewhere deep down in my stomach when he went on.

'We have a retiree from Illinois who lost his camera outside the Eiffel Tower on Friday. He set it down to hold his place in line while he went off to take a leak. He'd been standing in line for two hours and had no intention of losing his place.'

'Patrick is thirty-eight.' A riverboat that looked like a giant turtle was approaching, with the tourists holding up their cameras in the air. I bowed my head so my face wouldn't end up in the foreground of their photos of Notre-Dame.

'Listen to this: A couple went into the Père-Lachaise cemetery night before last. They had hidden inside the chapel until it closed. They wanted to honour Jim Morrison by drinking bourbon and doing nasty things on his grave in

119

the moonlight. The guy said, and I quote: "Jim's spirit would rise up at the moment of orgasm." I assume that's not your husband?'

'Patrick doesn't even like Jim Morrison.'

I heard a rattling on the phone. Then he coughed again. Or was he choking back laughter?

'If I were you, I'd go home and wait another week,' he said in an amused tone of voice. 'If a Mr Cornwall happens to show up, I'll tell him to call home asap. OK?'

As I got out of the taxi, I realized my money wasn't going to last very long if I kept taking cabs in this city.

At any rate, there was no doubt that Alain Théry was doing quite well for himself.

The building at 76 avenue Kléber was an old stone mansion that had been modernized with black-tinted glass along the entire ground floor. It was only a few blocks from the Arc de Triomphe, and right next to two embassies and a Ferrari dealership.

Since no one at the Lugus company had replied to my email, I thought I might as well try to see Théry before he left for the weekend. I'd had enough phone calls for the day. Besides, I wanted to see his face when I asked him about Patrick.

Lugus was not the sort of business that encouraged walk-in visitors. The door could be opened only from the inside or by using a code. There was no doorbell. I tried to peer through the dark panes, but I saw only a mirror image of myself and the street. When I looked up, a lion's head made of stone glared down at me from a parapet.

A steady stream of office workers sauntered out of the surrounding buildings, but the door to number 76 remained closed.

I was just about to give up when a motorcycle pulled

up at the kerb. The driver took a thick envelope out of his bag and went over to a pillar, where he tapped in a code. Seconds later the door opened, making the sound of a slow exhalation.

In a flash I was right behind him.

'We've been lucky with the weather today,' I said, following close on his heels into the building.

Inside, muted Caribbean-inspired pop music was playing, and my footsteps were muffled by a thick grey carpet. A young blond man sitting at the reception desk accepted the delivery. Alain Thery seemed to be very fond of black glass, because all the interior walls were just as shiny and impenetrable as the windows facing the street. Maybe someone was standing on the other side of the glass watching me, someone I could never see, no matter how hard I tried. On the other hand, I saw multiple images of the motorcycle messenger, one reflection on top of the other, as he headed back to the door, which closed after him with a quiet sigh.

'Good afternoon. I'd like to speak to Alain Thery,' I said, stepping over to the reception desk.

'Do you have an appointment?' The blond guy was busy trying to unscrew the lid of a small pink glass jar. Behind him a wide marble staircase led up to the next floor.

'No, but I'm sure he'll see me,' I replied. 'I represent an American company, and we're interested in developing our skills in terms of interacting with our business associates in a more effective manner.'

'He's not here,' said the young man as he began rubbing cream on his cuticles. I detected a scent of almonds and honey. A new tune began playing. A woman singing in French to an easy dance rhythm.

'Could I speak to Alain's secretary?' I said, glancing up at the stairs behind him. Another glass wall at the top.

'Send an email,' he said, taking a nail file out of a small case.

'I already did,' I told him, but he didn't even deign to look at me.

OK, I thought, taking two steps back. Then I set off for the stairs, quickly dashing around the reception desk and taking the steps two at a time.

'Wait a minute. Hello? You can't . . . Stop!'

I heard him switch to French behind me. *Merde* and *putain* were words I understood quite well. At the top of the stairs I pushed open a glass door and stepped inside a huge office space that occupied the entire floor. The building's past was evident in the massive stone walls and the stucco work on the ceiling, but everything else could have been clipped out of a decorating magazine for the modern office. Desks made of chrome and glass, computers with oversized flat screens, spotlights. I stopped in the middle of the room.

There wasn't a soul in sight. It was completely deserted. The computer screens were all black. The desks were bare. No folders, no piles of paperclips, no colourful pads of paper or anything else that belonged in a workplace. I went over to a wastepaper basket made of shiny metal and looked inside. Not a single crumpled note, not so much as an apple core.

It's a front, I thought. There's nothing here. It's a projection of a company, an image of the perfect office.

At that moment I felt a faint change in the air behind me, and the next second someone was grabbing my upper arm. I screamed and turned around, finding myself staring into a shirtfront. Short sleeves, bulging muscles. The man was a head taller than me, with a broad face and a nose that seemed too small for it. Pig-like eyes. Bald head.

'I'm looking for Alain Thery,' I said, feeling his grip

tighten. 'But apparently he's not in, so I'll be on my way . . . Let go, damn it.'

But the security guard, or whatever he was, didn't let go as he escorted me back downstairs to the reception desk.

'Who are you? Why are you really here? Who do you work for?' The blond guy translated the questions, since the guard apparently didn't speak English.

My thoughts whirled chaotically. 'I was looking for the ladies' room. I thought I was going to . . . throw up. If you understand me.' I made an effort to smile. 'I'm . . . pregnant.'

I shouldn't have said that, but it was the only thing I could think of. The blond guy translated. *Enceinte* was the French word for it. The guard finally let go of my arm and gave me a shove in the back. Then he used his whole hand to point to the door.

'You can call back on Monday,' said the blond guy.

The door slid open and closed up again like a clam when I was back out on the street.

'Are you the one meeting with Arnaud?'

The girl standing outside the door wore ragged jeans and sported a crew-cut. On the wall of the building someone had scrawled: *zone anti-patriotique*.

'He asked me to let you in,' she said, putting out her cigarette in a tin can that had been cut in half.

I introduced myself and then followed her inside. The light in the stairwell was broken, and only faint daylight seeped in through a dirty windowpane.

'Plenty of people would want to throw something through the window if we advertised our address,' said the girl, whose name was Sylvie, as she pulled open a heavy metal door. For the first time since arriving in Paris I felt like I was in the right place. Patrick had definitely been here. It smelled of paper and ink and energy and struggles, with posters on the walls showing clenched fists and various symbols. Even if Patrick was now a well-dressed journalist, the rebel from his university years was still very much part of him.

'So you work with illegal immigrants too?' I said.

'That's politician speak,' she said with a glare. 'No human being is illegal.'

We entered an old industrial space where pipes and cables criss-crossed the ceiling overhead. Computers and bookcases were everywhere, along with stacks of newspapers and books.

'I work to help promote Fair Trade,' said Sylvie, 'and greater diversity. Several organizations share the expenses here, but we're actually all working towards the same goals. Gender equality, and justice for all nations and for the oppressed people of the world.'

'Did you meet Patrick Cornwall when he was here?' I asked.

'Yes, of course,' she said. 'He came here to interview Arnaud.' She cast a glance at a tall young man with tousled hair who wore a colourful scarf around his neck. He made his way around all the boxes and piles of newspapers and came over to us.

'Hi. You must be Helena,' said Arnaud Rachid.

'Alena,' Sylvie corrected him. 'Arnaud is hopeless with names,' she added, giving him a radiant smile.

Arnaud's section of the big office space was at the very back. There was a row of dusty windows four metres up on the wall, but otherwise the only light came from a few fluorescent lights on the ceiling. They looked as if they'd been there since the heyday of industrialization.

'Welcome to the hypocrites' paradise,' he said, dropping onto a chair. 'This country wouldn't last a day without all the undocumented workers who do the shit work. Cleaners and builders and apple pickers. Our ageing population would die if there was no one to wipe their butts. Maybe then, if not before, Europe would have to smell its own shit.'

I moved a pile of mail aside and sat down on the edge of the desk.

'When did you last see Patrick Cornwall?' I asked.

'Two weeks ago, I think, maybe less.' He ran his hand through his hair. 'How's it going with the articles he's writing?'

'I haven't read them yet.'

'So he's back in New York now?'

'No, there was something else he needed to do first.'

I looked over at the double rows of books on the shelves, noting titles by Karl Marx, Malcolm X, and Che Guevara. Arnaud continued talking about politicians who wanted to nail shut the borders, and at the same time pick and choose from the world's populations. Get to the point, I told myself, or else we're going to get bogged down in rhetoric and propaganda.

'Patrick interviewed several guys who had escaped from what was blatant slave labour,' I said, taking out my notepad. 'Were you involved with that?'

'You can't write that. It's not an official part of our work.'

'I'm not going to write anything. I'm a researcher.'

Arnaud pulled his scarf loose and then wrapped it around his neck again.

'We hid them,' he said. 'I took Patrick to their hiding place.'

He leaned back, and I fixed my eyes on him as he talked. I thought he seemed nervous. He kept fiddling with his scarf, and his foot was drumming on the floor.

He told me three young men from Mali had been smuggled into France and were being exploited as slaves on a construction site, forced to do heavy lifting and loading, without receiving pay of any kind. When they weren't working, they were kept locked up in a *safe house*, an old warehouse, and physically threatened. Arnaud had been put in touch with the men after they managed to escape.

'So that's what Patrick was focusing on? Some sort of criminal network that smuggles people into France?'

He sighed loudly and propped his feet up on the desk.

'Don't get me wrong,' he said, running both hands through his hair and making it even more dishevelled. 'We're not against the smuggling of human beings. We're for a Europe with open borders. If immigration was freely allowed, there would be no market for smuggling people. They are merely providing a service that people want. There are plenty of crooks, of course, who charge scandalous prices and risk lives. But that's a whole other story.'

'Did this criminal network know about what Patrick was writing?'

'What do you mean? Has something happened to him?' Arnaud Rachid lowered his feet back down, knocking some of the mail onto the floor. He bent down and picked up the envelopes.

'Where was Patrick going when he left Paris?' I asked.

'I don't know.' He gave me a searching glance. 'Doesn't his editor know?'

I was spared from answering because at that moment Sylvie appeared behind me.

'Would you like some coffee?' she asked.

'I'll do it,' said Arnaud, quickly getting to his feet. I went with him.

The coffee-maker was in a cramped cubbyhole. Arnaud took several little colourful plastic packets out of a box, and chose a black one. He pushed down a lever and pressed a button. Nothing happened.

'Who is Josef K?' I asked.

He gave a start and turned to look at me.

'What do you mean by Josef K? Are you talking about Kafka, or something?'

'I don't know,' I said. 'It was Patrick who mentioned something . . .' The cubbyhole was so small that his hip brushed against mine when he moved. I swallowed hard and backed up until I was standing in the doorway. 'So what happened to those young men?' I went on. 'Are you still hiding them? Could I meet them?'

'*Merde*,' said Arnaud, banging on the coffee-maker. 'I don't understand why this thing never works. Just look at these!' He motioned to the little plastic packets that each contained one serving of coffee. 'Why all this waste of resources for a single cup of espresso?'

Arnaud pressed the button again, and water sprayed out.

'Let's go out instead,' he said, switching off the machine. 'I just need to make a pit-stop first.'

As he disappeared up a narrow flight of stairs, the girl with the torn jeans came over to me.

'Go easy on Arnaud,' she said, coming a little too close for comfort. 'He knew some of the people who died in the fire. Did you know that? He may not show it, but he's been taking it really hard.'

I felt an icy shiver race down my back.

'At the hotel, you mean? The one that burned down two weeks ago?'

Out of the corner of my eye I saw that Arnaud was on his way over to us, cutting across the room with a jacket slung over his shoulder.

'By the way, I heard you asking about Josef K,' said Sylvie in a low voice.

My heart skipped a beat.

'What can you tell me about him?' I asked.

'I thought you knew,' she said, giving me a searching glance. 'Josef K is a human-trafficker. It's a cover name, of course. He's an Eastern European gangster. From Ukraine. He used to be KGB, but then he became a capitalist like everybody else after glasnost. A real nasty guy.'

I clutched at the doorframe. The last name in Patrick's notebook. Was he the one Patrick had gone to meet? I pictured the clichéd image of an Eastern European gangster: clean-shaven and scar-faced, with dead eyes. *There's just one more thing I have to do . . . I'm headed straight into the darkness.*

No, I thought. Sweetheart, please no . . .

'I'll come too,' said Sylvie, 'if you're going out for coffee.'

But Arnaud shook his head at her.

'Not now,' he said and headed off. I gave Sylvie a smile. She was clearly hopelessly in love with her revolutionary comrade.

'If you're really interested, you can sign up on the web,' she said, handing me a flyer, which I crumpled up and dropped into a trash can as soon as we were out on the street.

'Sylvie is incredibly committed to the cause,' said Arnaud. 'I remember how it was when I was a newcomer and had just had my eyes opened. Back then I could work 24/7 too. She's always here.'

He took long strides, and I practically had to jog to keep up with him.

'She told me you knew some of the people who died in the fire,' I said. 'Was it the hotel fire over near boulevard Michelet?'

Arnaud stopped abruptly and looked at me.

'What do you know about the fire?' he asked.

'Seventeen people died,' I said. 'And I think Patrick was there that night.'

Arnaud continued on without replying.

'Was that where you were hiding them? At the hotel?' I said, suddenly realizing how it all fit together. And why Patrick had rushed out in the middle of the night. 'Those young men from Mali were among the dead, weren't they?'

Arnaud turned right onto rue Bretagne and made his way past the displays of produce and basins of live shellfish. I had to run to catch up. This was a residential neighbourhood where people bicycled and did their grocery shopping and sorted their trash into colourful plastic containers. It reminded me a little of the East Village.

'Let's go in here,' he said, holding open the door to a bar. 'What would you like?'

I ordered a sandwich and juice and then sat down in the corner. Most of the customers were gay. Arnaud placed his order and came over to join me. He took a packet of tobacco out of his jacket pocket and began rolling a cigarette.

'We thought it was safe,' he said. 'Otherwise we would never have used that place.'

I shivered at the memory of the burned-out building. Arnaud's hands shook, spilling some tobacco onto the table.

'They had to share a room,' he said. 'It wasn't much of a place, but at least they had a roof over their heads, and beds to sleep in. There was a bathroom down the hall with hot water.'

'It was a deathtrap,' I said.

'There aren't many places like that left in Paris. Places where they don't ask for papers. Nobody knew they were staying there except me and a few others.'

Arnaud picked up a lighter, but then put it down along with the cigarette. 'Shit. I keep forgetting. I never thought they'd manage to make France smoke-free.' He ran his hand through his hair and nervously glanced around.

'Patrick went over there several times to talk to them,' he went on. 'The last time was on the afternoon before it happened. Everything seemed perfectly calm. Otherwise we would have moved them instantly, of course.'

The waiter set a toasted sandwich in front of me. Melted cheese seeped out onto the plate.

'Someone phoned Patrick that night and told him the building was on fire,' I said. 'Was it you?'

'I'd switched off my cell. I was sleeping somewhere else.'

I wonder where, I thought, but it wasn't any of my business where Arnaud Rachid spent his nights. He took some chewing gum out of his pocket and stuck a piece in his mouth.

'We met on Saturday after the fire,' he went on. 'We went to look at the site, and Patrick talked to the police. He was convinced it was arson.'

'But in the newspaper it said there was no evidence of any criminal activity.'

'The police took his statement. Later they dropped the investigation.' He fixed his gaze on me. 'Those people have contacts everywhere.'

'But how did Patrick know it was arson? Did he know who did it?'

Arnaud touched the scarf around his neck.

'That's something I can't talk about,' he said. 'My first priority is the people we're trying to protect.'

Finally I picked up my sandwich and took a bite as I studied him. The melted cheese had congealed. Arnaud finished his beer.

'What did Sarah tell you, by the way?' he asked.

'She said you're an idealist,' I replied.

He grimaced. 'Sarah thinks that she's seeing justice done, that everyone is equal before the law. But almost half a million people who live in this city are undocumented. They

130

have no rights whatsoever. What the law does for them is to throw them out of the country.'

'Then why did you send Patrick to see her?'

Again he looked uneasy as he lowered his voice.

'Those young men were scared. Salif was really the only one who wanted to speak out. The others demanded guarantees — residence permits and protection. Otherwise they didn't want to appear in the magazine. I told Patrick about Sarah. She can seem harsh, but I know she cares. I even think my sister developed a bit of a crush.'

'On Patrick?'

I stared at him in astonishment. So that's the part that was off-the-record.

'But she's married,' I said, managing to keep my voice under control.

He laughed. 'No, she's not. She's never been married. The wedding ring is just for court appearances. It wins her more respect.'

I looked away, saw a man kissing another man, people hanging out, having a drink, talking about the weather.

'I've got to go now,' he said, standing up. 'But you can always call me if there's anything else. Where are you staying in Paris, by the way?'

'Near the Sorbonne,' I said. 'In the same hotel where Patrick was staying.'

I stayed sitting at the table and watched him leave. Out of everything he'd said, there was one comment that kept echoing through my head. *I even think my sister developed a bit of a crush.*

'Would you like anything else?'

Harry shook the bottle of Worcestershire sauce and poured a few drops into the umpteenth Bloody Mary of the evening.

I swirled my whisky glass. 'Another one, please. And a glass of water.'

I was drinking what I thought Patrick would have had on the night he called me that time, when he was drunk. The whisky tasted of ashes. Harry's New York Bar was packed, the heat making it feel damp and foggy. On the walls hung black-and-white photos, drawings of classic Parisian cabarets, and American sports pennants. It was very pre-war, a place living on its memories.

I slid a photograph over to the bartender.

'Do you recognize this guy?' I asked.

'Why do you ask?' He glanced at the picture.

'Because I miss him.'

Harry dried his hands and picked up the photo of Patrick, studying his face in the light of the art nouveau lamps on the wall.

'Wasn't he here a couple of weeks ago?' He frowned. 'Yes, I actually do remember him. He talked about his wife.'

I coughed so hard the whisky rose up and stung my nose.

'About his wife?'

'He said he had a wonderful wife.' Harry smiled, mashing slices of lime and mint leaves into a glass. He had a way of crushing ice by placing it in the palm of one hand and then hitting it with the pestle like a baseball bat. 'He was longing to go home to New York, said he was sick of travelling. He said they were hoping to have a baby. He longed to have a family of his own.' He added rum and soda, dropped in a few ice cubes, and set the glasses on the bar to be picked up by a waiter. 'I told him to go for it. Having a kid is the best thing that can happen to a man. Everything else pales in comparison. I have four of my own. The youngest are twins.'

He wiped his hands and slid the picture back across the bar.

'So you're out of luck, honey.'

I looked down and met Patrick's eye, letting a lock of my hair fall forward to form a curtain around us. It was time to stop. I couldn't keep chasing his shadow. It was all well and good for him to sit in a bar and talk about me, but if he really loved me, he wouldn't be risking everything for a story, would he? I wanted to go back home to my own life, building fictional worlds that were torn down after the last performance.

'I know,' I told him quietly, running my finger along his jaw line. 'I know that you've taken the most difficult path again, and you know how I know that?' I pounded my fist on the bar with each word. 'Because. You. Are. A. Difficult fucked up kind of person.'

I drained my glass. When I looked up, the bottles on the wall began to sway.

'What about this?' I said, leaning forward so I was practically lying across the bar. 'A man goes to Paris. He's longing for home. He says that he's coming home, and by home I mean New York. We're talking about New York City, in the US of A. You're married. So tell me this, why would a guy think up such a thing?'

'Hard to say,' replied Harry, reaching for the rum bottle.

Of course his name wasn't Harry. That was an absurd notion that came to me after the second or third whisky. The idea that Harry was immortal, just like the bar he'd opened almost a century ago. Europe's first cocktail bar. That's what it said on the back of a little red book lying on the counter, listing the drinks offered and boasting that it was here that the Bloody Mary had been invented.

'He said that he'd done something awful,' continued the bartender whose name was not Harry.

'I know, I know. That's why he came here, to dig up the

dirt on slave labour so he could save the whole fucking world. But he can't.'

The bartender was stirring another drink with a swizzle stick.

'I thought he'd been unfaithful or something like that. The guy looked really unhappy. But you know what he'd done?'

I shook my head, making the room sway even more. The bartender smiled.

'He'd borrowed the *baby money*. He said it was like stealing from the baby's future, and he needed to pay it back. He had to finish the job before he could go home again.'

Something got stuck in my throat and I coughed and swallowed while the words danced inside me. He had only borrowed the money. He was planning to come back. *He wasn't blowing me off.*

And then the rest sank in: That's why he hadn't come home. He couldn't look me in the eye and say that he'd squandered our child's money on a story that he'd never finished.

'I told him to take it easy,' said the bartender. 'It's not money that matters when it comes to those little tykes. It's love. You have to love them to death. That's the only thing that counts.'

I reached for my glass, but missed, and it crashed to the floor between the feet of several British football fans. 'Sshorry,' I said.

The bartender swept up the glass.

'You want some good advice?' He pointed at the picture of Patrick. 'Forget that guy. He's married. He's going to have kids. You're out of luck.'

I picked up the photo. My drink had spilled across Patrick's face, continued in a trickle across the dark wood, and then dripped onto my lap.

'I think it's time to get you a cab,' said the bartender whose name wasn't Harry.

The door was ajar, letting in a strip of light across the floor. I opened the door and entered a passageway that led to yet another room, much bigger than the small hotel room I now realized had merely been my waiting room. Daylight flooded in from a row of skylights. Patrick was sitting at a desk in the middle of the room, bending over his computer.

'Are we paying for all this?' I asked. 'Did you know all along that these rooms were here?'

'I had to have somewhere I could work,' said Patrick.

'Why didn't you tell me you were here?'

'They've found the child,' he said, and I knew he was talking about the infant whose mother had died in the hospital in Los Cristianos.

'Is it alive?' I wanted to ask, but then Patrick was gone. I went from room to room, looking for him, and the alarm began wailing because the building was about to sink into the river. I ran back upstairs because I'd forgotten something. Benji was there, and Duncan the choreographer. The work was going on, even though we were about to drown, and ice-cold water filled one floor after another as the alarm howled and wailed.

I woke with a start, tangled up in the sheet. The blanket had fallen to the floor, and the night was black outside the window. There was a feeling from the dream that I wanted to hold onto. Something I'd forgotten and needed to remember. The alarm was still sounding, and I realized it was my cell. It was flashing and screaming from the night-stand. The time on the display was 01.23 a.m.

'It's about time I got hold of one of you. But I don't understand why he hasn't called.' It was Patrick's mother.

135

'Is it something we did? Is it his father again? Why is it so difficult to make a few plans?'

'Hi. Is that you?' I said, sitting up straight.

Something must have happened for my mother-in-law to be calling in the middle of the night. Then I realized that it wasn't night where she was. I pictured the light-coloured leather sofa in the living room where they sat and ate all their meals when they were alone. The dining-room table was set only when they had dinner guests. Silver candelabras and floral napkins and four-course dinners. Eleanor Cornwall always tried a bit too hard.

'I have to know now because I don't have the energy to do all the cooking myself. I need to call the caterers, and they always need a lot of advance notice.'

I leaned forward to pick up the blanket from the floor and wrap it around me. My head was pounding, and my mouth tasted of rotten fish. Caterers? Then I remembered they were going to celebrate their anniversary in a few weeks. Was it their fortieth?

'Just because he and his father have different opinions, that doesn't mean he should abandon his family. That's not how we brought him up.'

'Of course we'll be there,' I said faintly.

'It's not like it's our golden anniversary, or anything like that.'

'How many years is it now?'

'Forty-seven. And now we're too old to get divorced.'

In a flash I pictured Patrick and me sitting on a sofa as we silently ate dinner, our eyes fixed on the TV as if we'd seen enough of each other. I'd dreaded that ever happening to us, but now I wished more than anything that I could believe in that scenario.

While Eleanor chattered on about the menu she was planning for the anniversary party — it was just going to be close family members and a simple affair, meaning about fourteen relatives plus a few neighbours and Robert's former colleagues from the hospital — I considered the possibility of telling her the truth. Patrick wouldn't have wanted me to do that. He might want to come home and show off his Pulitzer Prize, but he didn't want his parents hovering over him.

I pictured his father as he sat in his library reading medical books. He had almost 2,000 volumes. 'All this,' he said, 'is knowledge about life and death. It means something in the world.'

'As opposed to what I do, you mean?' replied Patrick, and then the two of them went at it.

I crawled out of bed and rushed to the bathroom, taking my cell with me.

'We'll be in touch as soon as Patrick is back from Paris,' I said and ended the call without waiting for a reply.

Then I threw up. For a long time I splashed my face with cold water. When I went back to bed, the echo of the phone conversation had faded. I moved closer to the blanket, which was bunched up in a big pile, and hugged it to my chest. I shut my eyes and thought about Patrick's body close to mine.

'You idiot,' I whispered. 'Don't you realize I don't give a shit about the money? I just want you here.'

And then I suddenly remembered something else from my dream. I'd been holding a baby in my arms. I'd left the baby somewhere in the building. And I didn't know where.

Chapter 7

Tarifa
Saturday, 27 September

The window in the room was covered with cardboard and a piece of heavy cloth. Daylight seeped in through a narrow slit, casting a strip of sunshine across her blanket. She lay in bed, listening to the church clock strike seven. Seven fifteen. Seven thirty.

With each stroke everything sank deeper towards the bottom. Time took with it her memories. Soon she would forget even her name. She pictured it in the water, maybe as a pearl inside a shell, or as a ring on the hand of the sea goddess Owu.

She sat up and grabbed her leg, tugging it over to the edge of the bed. Then she set her feet on the flat, cold floor.

The woman with the necklaces kept asking her the same questions.

What is your name?

Where do you come from?

And each time she looked down at the floor, as if mute. She picked up the thin dressing gown draped over the

138

chair next to the bed and put it on. It was Jillian's, and it carried her scent. Everything in the room smelled of the woman with the many necklaces. She had awakened in the dark on that first night, flushed with fever, and with the fragrance settling over her like a heavy blanket. Roses and musk. She'd thought it was the scent of paradise. She'd thought she was dead.

Then she'd heard the church clock striking. The creaking of footsteps outside. The door handle turning down with a squeak, and then the light appearing in the doorway behind the figure standing there, a fluttering shadow. And another. She moved closer to the wall, listening to them speaking quietly in a foreign language.

They've come to get me, she thought. But instead the scent in the room grew stronger, and someone sat down on the edge of the bed. She closed her eyes and the waves washed over her eyelids. In the darkness was the sea and the screams that never stopped. She opened her eyes again. She saw a green cotton blouse and seven necklaces, one on top of the other, made of beads and stones and silver pendants.

'I've brought you a cup of tea,' said the woman. Now she was speaking English. The tea tasted of smoke and ashes. It was bitter and sweet and hot, with milk and a little honey added.

The cup shook in her hands.

'My name is Jillian.' The woman's voice was hoarse. 'I don't know if you remember how you got here.' Jillian stood up and went over to the door and suddenly the light in the room went on.

She gave a start and spilled tea on her hands. The gash in the palm of her left hand stung. That was where the rope had slid through her fingers as she'd tried to hold on tightly when they dropped her over the side.

139

'Don't be scared,' said the woman's hoarse voice. 'You're among friends.' Then the light went out and she was alone.

The nights were different from the days. At night there was no streak of light from the window. In the daytime she could hear traffic outside, and voices that she didn't understand.

Don't say your name.

Give us your papers.

Don't talk about what god you believe in, who brought you here, or where you came from.

Sometimes they were in the room. The smugglers who hissed like snakes in the night. *Hurry, hurry*, and *shut up*. Shoving everyone forward along the stony path as they all stumbled down towards the sea. And for the first time she heard the roar of the sea. Raging and pounding and slamming against the rocks.

'You have a fever,' said Jillian. 'We need to ask someone to take a look at your leg. Do you understand what I'm saying?'

Please don't let it be the infection, she thought. This is the way it starts.

The first man had forced himself on her in the desert. My God, she'd thought, when he took her from the camp and dragged her into his car. Please protect me from the infection.

Her leg was now wrapped in a bandage. She ran her hand over the gauze. Three days had passed. The fever had broken.

'You are in my house,' Jillian had told her. That was on the second day. 'My neighbours mustn't know you're here. We can't trust them. So you won't be able to go outside. And they mustn't see you in the window. Then the police will come, and you'll be sent to the detention camps. Do you understand what I'm saying? *Detention camp*. I'll be in trouble if they find you in my house. Do you understand? *Big trouble.'*

For three days she had said nothing.

Just slept.

Whenever she closed her eyes everything solid disappeared, and once again the sea was washing over her. She was shaking with a raging fever, the boat was rising and falling in the waves, the stench of vomit on the wind.

She had stopped short when she caught her first glimpse of the vessel bobbing near the shore. It wasn't even a real boat. It was made of rubber, flat like a raft, with low sides. There were no seats. No roof they could crawl under for shelter. Nothing to hold onto but the ropes along the sides. Twelve people were going to make the trip that night. One of the smugglers jabbed her in the back with a stick. *Hurry, hurry.* They kept on hitting people until everyone had climbed on board and was sitting with their knees drawn up to their chins, packed together so closely that no one could move a muscle. Three men pushed and shoved the boat into the dark water. The sky was black, with no moon, no stars, only clouds hovering over the mountains.

She sat way in the back with her knees pressed against the spine of the boy in front of her. His name was Taye. It was forbidden to know his name. The wind tugged at the ropes. Her hands were already wet. The boat ploughed into the night. Two of the smugglers clung to the gunwale next to the motor in the stern. The third sat in the bow. They wore life vests that made them look as if their chests had been inflated, almost like rubber balls. Suddenly they began tearing off the clothes of the woman seated next to her. Your watch. Give me your jewellery. Your money. Your purse.

She didn't understand what was happening. They had all paid for the crossing in advance on the night before they were picked up and told to come closer to shore, to hide. Now one of the men raised his stick and struck her on the head. She tried to use her arms to protect herself. She had no more money left.

It doesn't matter, she thought as she took off her watch. And the chain around her neck. Handed over the cloth bag in which she had a few extra clothes, a bar of soap. Just let me reach there alive. Just let me get there.

One of the passengers couldn't restrain himself. He stood up in the boat and yelled at the smugglers in Yoruba. They shouted back in a language she didn't understand, and an oar whistled through the air, striking the man in the side so he fell. The smuggler climbed over the people sitting in his way, grabbed the man's leg, and tossed him overboard. Then he struck those sitting nearest. They huddled there, murmuring and praying while the man's screams faded and then disappeared in the darkness behind them.

She closed her eyes, wrapping her arms around her legs. Dear God in heaven, she prayed silently. Please calm these crazy people, quiet the sea, and let me live. Let Taye live, she added to placate God. Take me but let the boy live. He's no more than sixteen, and his parents' only son. Then she murmured to herself the names of all the others in the boat, one after the other, keeping her eyes fixed on the bottom of the raft where she could feel the sea rolling beneath her. The secret real names they had whispered to each other at night in the shed where they'd been told to keep quiet.

The woman next to her threw up into the dark, and all around her surged whimpers and prayers, a plaintive song that became one with the waves. She pressed her forehead against her knees and prayed to the sea goddess Owu as well, even though she didn't believe in any of the old gods or the spirits of the villagers and ancestors, the superstitions

142

and magic that held Africa helplessly locked in the past. Sefi was supposed to have been here, she thought, picturing her sister's face that evening when she spoke of her decision, saying that she should take Sefi's place. Someone had to send money home. Her brothers were already in the South-South zone, hunting for jobs in the oil industry, but no money was coming from there.

Then the miracle happened. The sea grew calm. When she looked up, she caught a glimpse of the opposite shore, and she thanked God and Owu, not knowing which of them had made the wind subside. Then the smugglers again began moving along the sides of the boat. They grabbed a man sitting nearest the edge. He screamed and flailed about, but they hit him on the head and yanked on his arms. 'Jump!' they shouted. 'Jump!'

Everything happened so fast in the dark. A man was suddenly thrashing about in the water next to the boat, screaming. Then he was gone. He was one of those who had never seen the sea before. He was from the land where the mud swallowed the river and turned to sand. 'Help him!' cried someone. 'Help him!' But the smugglers merely laughed and shouted. The waves rose up again, and the sea heaved towards them as another man was thrown out of the boat. And another. Dear God in heaven, they're killing us, she managed to think when she saw them lift up the boy Taye in front of her. 'He's only a boy!' she screamed, and the next instant she felt one of the men grab her arm, and she was dragged over to the low gunwale. She seized hold of a rope and hung on tight, but they yanked on her leg and hit her with the oars, and finally they tossed her overboard. The rope pulled loose and came with her. The sea tossed her away from the boat and in among arms that were struggling and flailing and lashing out at her. She kicked her way free. They wanted to drag her down into the deep. She screamed, but the salt water poured into her. She remembered closing her mouth and hanging onto the rope. She remembered sinking until there was no more air.

'I wonder whether you know any of these people,' said Jillian, bringing with her a newspaper on the third morning. Each morning when the clock struck eight, the woman came in with breakfast.

Her stomach growled at the thought of the bread and cheese and the small bowl of grain and almonds and milk. She got up and limped over to the window. The day before she had torn away a little corner of the cardboard so she could peek out. She saw low houses painted white, and flowers climbing a vine in a garden, dark red blossoms against the white. The sky was blue with white clouds. A moped leaned against one wall.

Jillian put the newspaper on the bed and then pushed over a little table. She set the tray on top.

'They found a dead African immigrant here in Tarifa, and two more outside Cádiz. The Moroccan coastguard has reported finding more bodies in the straits.'

She couldn't resist casting a glance at the newspaper. The headline read: *Immigrants Found Dead on Costa del Luz*. It was an English-language paper. She saw a photo of people standing on the beach, and a little map with the town of Tarifa circled. Her heart was pounding. It wasn't far from there to Cádiz.

'They think the immigrants tried to cross in a rubber dinghy that capsized in the sound in the early hours of Sunday,' said Jillian, picking up her own cup and stirring the tea.

Her eyes scanned the text. Someone had seen a rubber raft leaving a beach west of Tangiers in the night, but there was no indication that it had ever reached the opposite shore. Nor did the Moroccan coastguard have any reports that it had returned. She thought about the smugglers. Had they drowned too? She'd heard the motor start up, and then they were gone. She thought about Taye, and searched the article for anything that would tell her he was not among those who had drowned. The bodies of two men and one woman had been found. The woman had been pregnant. She closed her eyes. Heard the whispering all around her in the dark. Zaynab. Catherine. Toyin. Who decided who would live and who would die? Or that she would be the one to hold onto the rope? When she was sinking and had lost all hope, the rope had resisted. She pulled and pulled on it with all the remaining strength in her body, and came up to the surface to draw the night air into her lungs. The rope had got caught on a buoy. She must have pulled the rope off the boat when she was struggling to hold on. The buoy was rocking in the water, and she clung to it with all her might, bobbing in the black waves. She could no longer see the rubber raft. She couldn't see any of the other passengers. There was nothing but sea all around her. A light flashing somewhere. She could no longer feel her legs in the cold water. Using the rope, she managed to lash herself to the buoy. She didn't want to let go even if she died, because then she'd sink to the bottom and become food for the fish. Then her mother would never know what had happened to her next oldest daughter.

'I see you can read English, at least,' said Jillian. 'So I think you must understand what I'm saying.'

She poured a little milk into her tea.

'I can't hide you here for ever,' she said.

Later that day the man named Nico had brought a small TV into the room. He was younger than Jillian, really just a boy, with long hair and sandals on his feet. She thought maybe he was Jillian's son, though he didn't live in the house. Maybe he was her young lover.

Now the TV stood on top of a cabinet in the corner. She didn't dare turn it on until Jillian had brought her breakfast. She was able to get the BBC. Late at night she'd watched a film about a man who worked as a police inspector in a village in England. She had quietly repeated the dialogue to herself, trying to mimic the elegant melody of the language, but it was nearly impossible. She had allowed herself to dream, imagining that someday in the future she would be married and live in a village like that, even though it would probably seem quite dreary. The years she'd spent at the university in Nsukka had given her a taste for freedom. She no longer wanted to live in a village. She didn't want to get married, at least not for a long time. Sefi was the one who was going to marry. She thought it was lucky she'd taken her sister's place. Sefi could never have survived at sea. She was timid and weak and vain.

'You're already awake?' said Jillian, coming into the room carrying the tray. 'You look much better. Let me feel your forehead.'

Jillian's hand, adorned with many rings, felt cool on her forehead. One of the rings was in the shape of a snake curling around her finger.

'I think the fever is definitely gone.'

Chapter 8

Paris
Saturday, 27 September

I leaned against the sink, splashing cold water on my wrists and then taking several big gulps of water. Black streaks appeared on the towel when I rubbed my face hard, trying to wake up properly. My face in the mirror looked as pale as a dishrag, with mascara smeared into a black wing along one temple.

Come on, I thought, getting out a bottle of painkillers. Pull yourself together.

'And besides,' I said out loud to my mournful image in the mirror, 'if the baby ingested a percentage of what I drank yesterday, then it also needs a fraction of this pill too.'

I swallowed the tablet (which was not recommended for women who were pregnant or nursing) and placed my hand on my stomach. There was actually something inside there that was greedily sucking in everything I drank and ate. For the first time I had a profound sense that it was no longer just me, alone.

I went back into the room and threw the window wide open even though it was raining. I turned on my laptop and spread out my sketch paper on the floor. It wasn't even eight o'clock yet, but time was getting away from me out there.

In order to get a handle on what had happened during the days before Patrick disappeared, I'd drawn a timeline. And on it I'd entered what I knew about his movements and the people he'd met. A logical, coherent picture was starting to emerge.

On Thursday he'd been thrown out of Taillevent for pestering Alain Thery and his important friends. I'd drawn a line from Thery's name to my notes about slave labour. The consulting firm was nothing but a front. I was positive that he was a spider in a web, which was the focus of Patrick's investigations.

On Friday he had interviewed the young men at the hotel. After that, he'd spent the evening getting drunk and then phoned me, elated about the story he was writing.

Then the hotel burned down. Someone had called him that night. *Who?* I'd written, underlining the word and adding a big question mark.

On Saturday he'd met with Arnaud Rachid. He had also talked to the police, telling them that the fire had been deliberately set. Seventeen people had died, and he knew three of them. The police had subsequently dropped their investigation. I knew that must have infuriated Patrick. The question was, what did he do then? And where had he gone? Maybe he'd met one of the human traffickers called Josef K. When I'd asked about Josef K, I'd been threatened. Somebody wanted me to leave the city. Who?

More question marks.

I looked up and found myself staring at a pigeon. It was perched on the iron railing outside the window. Grey as the sky and the day. Grey as this whole fucking city.

I went over to my computer where the number seven was flashing red on my inbox. I thought about how sometimes Patrick would send me two emails in a row, one right after the other. '*By the way*' it might say in the subject line, and in the email I'd find three little words: I love you. That was all.

There was no email from Alain Thery, but there were two from Benji. 'Help!' it said in the subject line of the first one.

'Do I have to?' he wrote. He'd made his way through two of the seventeen articles about Alain Thery, understanding only half of what he'd read. Words like 'synergies' and 'strategic development' were terms that meant nothing to him even in English. 'The guy's very successful,' Benji wrote. 'A businessman of the new era who hobnobs with celebrities, and sponsors sailing competitions. Clearly, a mother-in-law's dream.' Benji wondered whether I really wanted to know what the rest of the articles said or whether he could devote his time to set design instead. We had a meeting booked with Cherry Lane Theatre on Monday at 2 p.m. 'Looks like they're expecting to see sketches,' he wrote.

I replied that he could forget the articles about Thery for the time being. And I'd get back to him about Cherry Lane.

The other emails were spam, plus an invitation to a Broadway premiere the following week. I deleted all of them and went into the bathroom to stand under the shower. I let the hot water sluice over my body as I thought about everything.

The man named Alain Thery seemed to keep slipping away as soon as I glanced in his direction. A shadow figure who refused to be caught. In my mind's eye I saw the blurry photographs of him. Maybe he's not what's important, I

149

thought. Maybe it's the other men in the pictures, the ones he was with. Politicians and celebrities, Benji had written. I knew nothing about either group, since I always fell asleep during Patrick's favourite French films. The president was the only French politician I might recognize in a photo, but only if his name appeared in the caption.

As I was stepping out of the shower I remembered Richard Evans saying something about a political reporter. He couldn't recall her name, and he'd lost her business card.

Quickly I dried off and got dressed, then entered the URL of *The Reporter*'s home page. *A stringer in Paris that we sometimes use*, Evans had said. *A political journalist . . . I think I gave Patrick her name too.*

It was the middle of the night in New York, plus it was the weekend, so it probably wouldn't do any good to email Evans.

I hesitated for a few seconds before typing the name of the French president into the search box on the page. Links to eleven articles came up. Two were anonymous wire stories from the AP, but the rest were lengthy commentaries about the fires in the suburbs around Paris that had occurred a few years back, the terrorist attacks on a restaurant and a concert hall, and the uproar on the border with England when refugees tried to make their way through the Channel Tunnel. I also scrolled past some political analysis about the rise of the extreme right of the *Front National* and the harsher policies on immigration ever since the former president started shouting about 'clearing the riff-raff from the streets'. The by-line on the articles was Caroline Kearny.

I clicked on her name and got a French email address. I wrote a brief, formal message, signing it Alena Sarkanova. Then I erased the whole thing and started over. I told her

I was Alena Cornwall and that Richard Evans had given me her name. I said that I needed to meet with her asap.

It felt odd to speak the truth, but Evans might have already mentioned me to the woman. Besides, the editor's name carried a certain weight. Kearny was probably also a freelancer, and she needed to stay on good terms with her clients.

I went downstairs to the breakfast room to get a bowl of cornflakes and some juice. The email icon was flashing on my screen when I got back to the room. Kearny wrote that she was busy all day, but she suggested meeting for drinks at Les Deux Magots around five o'clock.

I took the memory stick with the photos out of my laptop. Caroline Kearny might be able to help me identify those anonymous men.

Everything is here, I thought, looking down at my time-line spread out on the floor. I just need to figure out the chronology and fill in the remaining gaps. Then I'll understand.

There was an empty spot next to Monday, 15 September, the day before Patrick checked out of the hotel. 'The market?' I'd written above it. And then the names, as if they were parts in a play.

Luc — purse vendor
Josef K — human trafficker

I put on an extra sweater under my anorak and left the room.

The rain was blowing horizontally. Under the canopies the air was sultry from weed and smoke, with music swinging on the backbeat. I was walking along rue Jean Henri Fabre and had already passed seven vendors selling purses. The longest queue was in front of a stall advertising North African tea products.

When the market stalls thinned out and the wares became mostly second-hand goods, I went back to the last purse vendor.

'Is this a copy?' I picked up a purse purporting to be a Louis Vuitton.

'Oh yes, very good old new copy,' said a guy wearing a knitted Rasta cap who came sauntering over. 'For you, only forty-two euros.'

'Are you the one named Luc?'

The guy reached out to straighten a row of wallets. 'Who wants to know?'

I stepped forward so I was under the canopy and held up the photograph of Patrick.

'Do you recognize him?' I asked. 'He's American.'

He cast a quick glance at the photo and shook his head. Then he turned away and began rolling a cigarette. At the next stall two young girls were trying on second-hand army jackets.

'He was here two weeks ago,' I said. 'I think he was asking for someone named Luc.'

The guy shrugged and stuck the cigarette between his lips.

'You can have it for forty if you decide quickly.'

'The only reason he came here was to look for you,' I said. 'On Sunday or Monday two weeks ago. Try to remember.'

'OK, OK.' He pointed at the purse I was holding. 'Special price for you today. Only thirty-five euros.'

'No problem,' I said, taking out my cell. 'I'll call the police instead. I'm sure they can get the information out of you.'

'Hey, come on.'

'But first I'm sure they're going to be real interested in having a look at your papers. Isn't it the eighth department of the *Préfecture de Police* that's in charge of people like you?'

I began tapping in a random number.

'Put that away, *merde*. Stop.'

'Don't worry, Luc my friend. You'll get food and a roof over your head in a nice little detention centre on Île de la Cité before they throw you out of the country. Provided you don't have papers proving you're a legal citizen of the Republic of France, of course.'

'I don't even know what it was all about. I just did what they said.'

'Who's they?'

Luc pulled off his knitted cap and ran his hand through his hair. I let my index finger hover over my phone.

'Look on the bright side,' I said. 'You won't have to stand out here in the rain any more, trying to sell purses.'

'They paid me. OK? This guy said I'd get 200 euros if I talked to him when he showed up. That's all.' He tapped his foot on the off-beat to some West Indian music playing from the next stall. 'He was supposed to come here and ask for Luc. That was the signal.'

'And what were you supposed to tell him?'

I was still holding my cell, like a gun with the safety off.

'I was just supposed to give him a phone number and say something like "call this number and say this, and you'll get what you need".' Luc grinned. 'I thought it was a joke. It sounded like he'd get . . . well, you know.' He made a few bump-and-grind motions with his hips. I glared at him.

'The eighth department,' I said.

'It was crazy. It didn't mean anything.' He kicked at a pile of cigarette butts floating in the gutter. 'They told me to say: "I want to talk about Josef K".'

153

'And that's what he was supposed to say when he made the call?'

Luc shrugged. 'I told you it didn't make any sense.'

A mother and a teenage girl with bleached hair crowded in next to me and began picking up purses. They were speaking Russian to each other.

'Who paid you?' I asked.

'Come on. I've got a job to do here. It wasn't anybody I know.' Luc looked around.

'What did he look like? Black? White? Tall? Skinny? Fat? Rich?'

He gave the teenager a strained smile. 'You can have it for thirty,' he said, pointing at a cat purse. Then he turned back to me.

'He was white. Just a guy in a suit. Don't ask me anything else.'

'Did he have really pale eyes? Almost white?'

'Come on. Those guys all look alike.'

The Russians were on their way to the next stall. Luc shook his head and put his cap back on. 'I'm telling you, that's all I know.'

I crossed boulevard Michelet and continued east, into an industrial area. In my mind I was adding facts to the timeline.

Patrick had been given the information about Josef K. He'd checked out of the hotel on the following day. *There's just one more thing I have to do*, he'd written to me on the postcard. Was he going to meet the human trafficker?

I turned left and walked along a huge railroad yard with power lines criss-crossing overhead. The burned-down hotel was less than two kilometres away. In Patrick's notebook there was one other address in this area.

I paused to lean against a brick wall. The rain had stopped.

There was something about that night of the hotel fire that I couldn't figure out.

Patrick's sources, the young men from Mali, had died in the fire. Yet almost no one knew where they were hiding. Except for Arnaud Rachid. But he denied phoning Patrick and said that he'd turned off his phone for the night. Why would he lie about something like that? And it was highly unlikely that the person or persons who had set the fire would call a journalist to tell him about it. So who else knew the hotel was burning?

I took my cell out of my pocket and tapped in Arnaud's number. After seven rings, he finally answered. Time to wake up, I thought.

'Did you say his name was Salif?' I asked. 'The guy you were hiding in that deathtrap of a hotel?'

'Right. Why?' His voice was hoarse and groggy.

'Is he the one still alive? Or is it one of the others? Which of them called Patrick on the night of the fire?'

I heard Arnaud grunt, and I realized I'd guessed right.

'What did Patrick really tell the police?' I went on. 'How could he know that the fire had been deliberately set? The place must have been engulfed in flames by the time he got there.' I pictured Patrick riding in a cab and approaching the hotel, with flames shooting up against the night sky. It was the only logical explanation. Someone who was there when the fire started must have told Patrick what had happened.

'Why are you asking about this now?' said Arnaud.

'Are you still hiding him?'

There was a long silence on the other end of the line.

'As I told you, my first priority is to protect these people,' he said at last.

I sank down onto the sidewalk. A train was backing out of the yard. A container was being unloaded. I heard the sound of steel slamming against steel.

155

'I'm not here in Paris to do fact-checking,' I said reluctantly. 'I'm looking for Patrick. We don't know what's happened to him. He checked out of the hotel on Tuesday two weeks ago, and no one has heard from him since.'

'What? He's disappeared?' Arnaud's voice rose to a falsetto. He sounded scared.

'So maybe you know where he is?' I said.

'How would I know that? I haven't seen him since the fire.'

'I need to meet Salif,' I said. 'Or whoever it is you're hiding.'

Silence for a few seconds.

'I can't talk about this on the phone,' Arnaud then said. He gave me the address of a *Métro* station. 'Be there in two hours, near the stairs outside.'

Then he ended the conversation.

It was only a hundred metres to the address on my map. I decided I might as well stick to what I'd planned.

A road led behind a wall concealing an old industrial area from view. I saw a row of buildings made of brick and concrete, workshops, garages, and warehouses, along with some wrecked vehicles. I didn't see any people working there. The buildings were all labelled with letters and numbers, and I found my way to E3. It was a warehouse nearly a hundred metres long. I went over to a double wooden door and knocked. There was no doorbell. No sign of life.

I walked around the building. A garbage can had been overturned, and some animal had scattered the contents across the asphalt. At the corner of the warehouse, a red truck was parked with two trailers and the words MPL Express painted on the side. According to a small sign on the back doors, MPL stood for Marseille-Paris-Le Havre. I continued on around the building and at the very end I saw a door standing open. Two men were outside, having a smoke. I got out my map, pretending to be lost, and went over to them. One of the men swiftly shoved the door closed. The other had a dog on a leash, a powerful-looking animal built like a compact bulldozer.

'Excuse me, but I think I'm lost,' I said. 'What is this place?'

The man muttered something in French. The dog moved towards me, straining at the leash. I took a step back. Don't run, I thought to myself. Or that dog will think I'm his dinner.

'I'm looking for the market,' I said. 'But I must have gone the wrong way.'

The dog growled, glaring at me with its eyes running, its jaws open wide. Suddenly I didn't know what I was doing there. One building more or less wouldn't make any difference. These men were not about to tell me anything. Nor was the dog or the building.

'I'm sorry. I'm just an American tourist,' I said, and headed at a modest pace for the road that led out of the property. When I turned the corner, and the bulldozer dog was out of sight, I started running. I didn't stop until I saw a petite woman wearing a black headscarf shambling across the street with bags of food in both hands.

'Salif was like their leader,' said Arnaud Rachid in a low voice, glancing over his shoulder as the escalator slowly carried us downwards. 'It was his idea for them to escape.'

'And he was the only one to survive?'

Arnaud nodded.

'I'd given him a cell phone. He climbed out onto the roof. That was where he called Patrick Cornwall. He broke his leg when he jumped down onto the building next door.'

We reached the underground and continued through a

gloomy shopping mall with grey hallways and low ceilings. I tried to ignore the fact that we were heading for the *Métro*. Huddled behind a pillar I saw three people leaning close to each other. I caught a faint mumbling, saw goods changing hands.

'Nice place,' I said, nodding at the transaction taking place in the shadows.

'Les Halles has been a marketplace since the Middle Ages,' said Arnaud. 'Around here you can buy anything you want. Grass, heroin, passports . . .'

I took in a deep breath as we passed through the *Métro* ticket barriers, noticing again the scorched smell, the gusts of warm air.

'So this is where you can get a fake passport if you need one?' I said, just to get my mind off the enclosed space.

'It's not so easy to make a counterfeit passport any more.' Arnaud headed for another tunnel. 'But there are tens of thousands of genuine passports in circulation, maybe hundreds of thousands. It's always possible to find somebody who is similar in appearance.'

'Stolen passports?'

'Some of them. But some people sell their own passport. Then they report it stolen and get a new one.'

'Which they also sell?' I said. 'Sounds like a great business.'

'Migrants who are smuggled into the country often have their passports confiscated by the same people who brought them here. Then the passports are sold. Ten or twenty immigrants can be brought here in various ways, but all on the same passport.'

Only after we'd stepped inside a subway car and the doors closed, with the warning signals sounding over the loudspeakers and the train lurching forward, did he tell me where we were going.

158

'We'll change at Gare de l'Est,' he said, pointing at the *Métro* map posted above the window. Graffiti flickered past. Tags and slogans painted on the tunnel wall. 'Then we'll take line five to Bobigny.'

He looked at me.

'I don't know what you think you'll get out of this. Patrick hadn't seen Salif since we found him a new hiding place. He doesn't know anything.'

I didn't reply, since I had no idea what to expect. I just knew I had to meet him. Patrick had run out in the middle of the night to save this man. Maybe he could save me in return. Something like that.

After changing trains, the track climbed above ground, and it was easier for me to breathe. When we pulled into a station with the absurd name of Stalingrad, I couldn't help laughing. No doubt the tension was taking a toll on me.

'What's so funny?' asked Arnaud, looking insulted. He'd been in the midst of telling me how the European economy would collapse without immigration.

'Sorry,' I said, pointing out of the window at the sign showing the station's name. 'It's just that I didn't think Stalingrad existed any more. I thought Stalin had been obliterated from the face of the earth.'

'It was probably named to commemorate the battle of Stalingrad,' said Arnaud. 'It would seem odd if they changed it.' He fell silent and looked at me with interest. 'Is that where you're from?'

'From Stalingrad? Is that what you mean? No, not at all.'

'Your name, Sarkanova. It sounds Russian.'

'Good Lord. Why is everybody always so obsessed with where people come from?'

The warning signal sounded. Had Patrick said something about me? If he had, would it matter?

'I'm from Czechoslovakia,' I said. 'But don't ask me what it was like growing up under a Marxist-Leninist regime. I was only six when we left Prague.'

I saw a glint appear in Arnaud's eyes.

'But that speaks for itself,' he said.

'What do you mean?' I said curtly. 'There was nothing heroic about fleeing. Mama married a man who was twenty years older in order to escape to the west. We drove in a car across the border. Mama told me to keep quiet. I didn't open my mouth for several years after that. I was an obedient child.'

I looked at him. 'What about you?'

'Algeria,' he said. 'My paternal grandfather was recruited into the French army. They wanted soldiers from north Africa to be the first to enter the villages.'

'Sarah said that you were French.'

'Sarah thinks you can become French just because from a *legal* standpoint, you're considered French.' He grimaced and then studied me for several seconds in silence.

'Does your father still live there?'

'Where?'

'In Czechoslovakia.'

'Czechoslovakia doesn't exist any more,' I said, turning to look at his reflection in the windowpane. Buildings were rushing past over his face. Blocky grey structures, suburban houses. 'You react with aggression anytime someone gets close to you,' said a school psychologist that I was once forced to see. 'Were you mistreated when you were young?' I had laughed in her face. 'By the communists, you mean? What do you think they did? Filthy Leninist things? Is that what you mean?'

When we emerged from the *Métro*, the clouds had dispersed and the sky was mostly blue. I practically had to step over a beggar, a young girl clothed all in black and with her head covered. A dog was asleep in her lap.

'Welcome to *la banlieue*,' said Arnaud. A cluster of dirty yellow high-rises towered before us. I could hear the sound of heavy traffic from the nearby highway.

'Was it here they burned the cars?' I asked.

'It started in Clichy-sous-Bois,' said Arnaud, heading for the closest high-rise. 'But then it quickly spread to all of Seine-Saint-Denis and on to other cities in France. In a single night they destroyed 150 cars in Bobigny alone, by torching them or throwing fire bombs.'

He paused to look up at the gloomy facade.

'Anybody can make a torch or a bomb,' he said. 'All that's needed is sufficient anger.'

The balconies were bare, but satellite dishes were visible in a few windows. All the curtains were drawn on the lower floors. 'Here, at least, he's safe,' said Arnaud, pulling open the door. The lock was broken. The elevator wasn't working.

'It's nine floors up.'

I took the steps two at a time.

No one answered when we rang the bell. Arnaud unlocked the door and led the way inside.

The hallway was painted beige. Nail holes and patches on the wall spoke of people moving out and taking with them pictures and anything else that would have given the place a homely feeling. A few pieces of junk mail lay scattered on the floor. A blazer hung from the hat rack. That was all. A blue light flickered from a room further along the corridor. I could hear a TV, the sound of a soccer match.

Arnaud motioned for me to wait while he went in. After several minutes he reappeared, waving to say I should join him.

The man called Salif was reclining on a bed in front of a TV, fully dressed. One leg was in a plaster cast. His jeans

161

had been cut open to make room for it. Both hands were bandaged. French teams were playing a match on TV. Salif looked at me without saying a word, then turned to Arnaud. His French had a different melody to it. The words were softer and seemed to be spoken more forward in the mouth. He rubbed his bandaged hands together.

'He wants to know if you're going to help him,' said Arnaud. 'He says that Patrick promised to help him. He wants to know if you're going to take him to America.'

I leaned against the wall. Aside from the bed and a small table, there was no furniture in the room. The blinds were closed.

'Have you explained why I'm here?'

Arnaud sat down at the foot of the bed, running his hand through his hair. 'I told him that you're one of Patrick's colleagues. That's all.'

'Tell him that I need to know everything about Patrick's work. Tell him that Patrick has disappeared. Ask him whether Patrick was in contact with the people who threatened Salif and his friends.'

Arnaud raised his hands in a deprecating gesture. Salif kept his eyes on the TV. Arnaud picked up the remote and pushed the mute button. Then he translated what I'd said. Salif sat up straight and stared at me. I attempted a smile, but the man's gaze made my heart race. In his eyes I saw only fear.

'He says that Patrick Cornwall promised to help him. He says you have to take him to America.'

Arnaud leaned forward to put his hand on Salif's shoulder. Salif said something, then repeated the same words four or five times. And even though I had a hard time understanding his French, I knew what Arnaud was going to say before he translated.

'He says that otherwise he's a dead man.'

I took a few steps closer and crouched down, looking Salif in the eye. He was younger than I'd expected, in his early twenties. Twenty-five at most.

'Salif,' I said. 'I know that you've been through terrible experiences, but I really need your help.'

Arnaud translated.

'I know that Patrick Cornwall helped you, and now I'm asking you to help me. I don't know where he is, and I'm afraid something has happened to him.'

Salif's gaze wavered.

'I know that he interviewed you. I think that may be why he has disappeared. Please try to think. Is there somewhere he might have gone?'

Salif looked at Arnaud and began speaking very quickly.

'The others ran down the stairs,' Arnaud translated. 'I shouted to them not to go down there, into the flames. The fire was roaring. They were screaming. I couldn't stop them.' Salif was staring up at the ceiling.

'You survived,' I said. 'It's not your fault they died. You told Patrick that the fire had been deliberately set, right? How did you know that?'

'I shouted to them not to go down there. I shouted but they just kept running. They ran right into the fire.'

I changed my position and sat down on the floor. In utter silence a red-clad player kicked a corner shot. The ball ricocheted out of bounds. I turned to Arnaud.

'Is there anything to eat here?' I asked.

'Of course,' said Arnaud. He took a baguette and a cola out of his bag and handed them to Salif, who opened the bottle. I rummaged through my own bag and found a chocolate cookie, which I set on the bed.

'Ask him to tell me what he told Patrick.'

Salif took a big bite of bread. The baguette wasn't very fresh, because the crust was soggy. After Salif had eaten half of the sandwich, he began talking. Arnaud translated, speaking faster and faster as Salif got going.

'Have you ever heard of Salif Keita, the great singer with the golden voice? I told the American to buy one of his records. He's albino, so he was disowned by his people, even though he's a descendant of Sundiata Keita, the founder of my country. He's back in Bamako now and has built a fine recording studio there. He's a rich man. I was named Salif after him. I'm going to be a businessman. I'm good at maths, just like Checkna. He has a maths brain. Sambala didn't do well in school. All he can think of is football. Checkna was no good at football.'

Salif's expression darkened and his eyes went blank.

'They're the ones who died in the fire,' said Arnaud in a low voice. 'All three were from Mali, from the same village.'

'Not everyone is able to leave. There's not enough money. I was the only one of my family this time. They collected money to pay for my trip.'

Salif had started talking again, with a mechanical tone to his voice, as if he'd told this story many times before.

'The elders in the village also helped to collect money, mostly for Sambala, because his family is poorer. It's best to go to France. Everyone knows that. Senegal isn't so good. There you can get work picking cotton. But I want to be a businessman. My father went to the Ivory Coast, but it's not good there any more. They throw out Muslims.'

Salif fell silent and ate the rest of his sandwich. Arnaud took over.

'Mali is one of the countries that doesn't directly intervene against smuggling people,' he said. 'Why should they? During colonial times, the country belonged to France. They've been sending their sons here for decades, and in the past they were welcome. There are villages that have been able to build clinics and schools, install electricity, and dig wells to provide fresh water for the whole village — all because of the money that has been sent home from France.'

Salif interrupted Arnaud's brief lecture, gesticulating and raising his voice.

'I've failed them,' he said, and Arnaud translated. 'When we escaped and went to the mosque, the imam helped us to call home. We had to warn our families. They had threatened us and our younger siblings, saying they would kill everyone. Mama said that I should go back and work. Others had gone away and later returned home to build houses for their parents. But many never came home. After a few years people stop talking about them. They're considered quitters who have forgotten their families.' Salif rubbed his hands over his head, which had been shaved. I wondered whether he'd had hair before the fire.

'I'm a dead man,' he whimpered.

'He means that his relatives consider him dead,' Arnaud explained. 'No one must know that he's alive. If he's dead, nobody will come looking for him. Then maybe his family will be safe.'

'Does he know who they are?' I asked. 'Did he talk about this with Patrick?'

'You can't expect him to know,' said Arnaud. 'You need to understand what he's been through. The man is in shock.'

'Ask him, please,' I pleaded. 'Patrick's life could be in danger too.'

Salif kept on rubbing his head, but his voice sounded less mechanical. I was getting used to his peculiar accent. It sounded as if he was punching the words out of the sentences and blowing them out, like bubbles.

'They weren't the same as the people who came to pick us up. They changed several times on the way north. At the Algerian border the Tuaregs took over. Then our *trolley*, the leader, disappeared. That was the man who was related to Checkna's family, a cousin of a cousin. A new *trolley* came, a *connection man*. We had to hand over our passports and more money. They said it was to bribe the guards and the customs officials, and the gangs in the desert. We travelled in the back of a covered truck to Morocco. We stayed in Rabat for three weeks. I don't know what went wrong. One night the police raided the house where we were staying, and we were driven back to the Algerian border, to the desert near Oudja. Several hundred people were waiting there. Three days later we were taken to Tunisia. It costs more than Libya, but it's safer. They told us it was possible to make it to Italy from there, and then it wouldn't be hard to hide inside a truck and get to France. There are lots of people from northern Mali living in Paris. They would help us find work and apartments. Sambala said he wanted to get a job with Paris Saint-Germain, the football team.'

'Ask him what happened in Paris,' I said, wanting to hurry him along. Arnaud gestured for me to be patient, and Salif continued speaking, hardly pausing to breathe. Like Scheherazade in *A Thousand and One Nights*, he was keeping death at bay, I thought. By telling his story, he was able to stay among the living.

'She was called the *Ariadne*. It was a big freighter. I saw it from shore the day before we left. Our *connection man* pointed it out. We were luckier than we could ever have dreamed. The *Ariadne* was headed directly for France, bound for Marseille. We sneaked inside the container during the night. There were several children with us, but they were given sleeping pills so they'd sleep the whole way. We had a barrel for water and another one in which to relieve ourselves. One man was nervous. He started pounding on the wall after we climbed in and sat down. We grabbed hold of him to make him stop pounding because he might

166

give us away. We had only a small amount of food. They explained this was so we wouldn't need to relieve ourselves too much. It was for our own good. I counted forty-two people in the container. Then they closed the doors and everything went dark.'

I shifted position on the floor. On the TV the first half of the soccer match was over. They were showing commercials. Salif leaned back against the wall, his face changing colour from the flickering images on the screen.

'It was night time when they opened the doors. It was hard to breathe. I had a headache and felt very tired, even though I'd fallen asleep several times. Some people could not be roused. They were carried out. I don't know what happened to them. We were taken to a big truck. It said MPL Express on the side. It was red. A long-haul truck.'

I gave a start. I'd seen that name outside the warehouse earlier in the afternoon in Saint-Ouen.

'What happened when you got to Paris?' I asked.

Salif scratched his leg along the edge of the cast. I'd had my arm in a cast when I was fifteen, and I remembered how horribly it itched.

'When we were sitting in the container we whispered about organizing a party when we arrived,' he went on. 'Checkna has an uncle in Paris. We were going to find him and have a festive meal. We were going to borrow some money and pay it back later.'

Salif suddenly fell silent. A spasm rippled through his body.

'You can see he's not well,' said Arnaud, placing his hand on Salif's shoulder. Salif didn't react. Then he continued.

'We arrived early in the morning. The sun was just coming up. They opened the back doors of the truck and told us we were going to a safe house. It was like a huge warehouse, with workplaces inside. No people around outside.'

'I think I know where it is,' I said, picturing the ferocious dog in my mind.

'They told us to go inside,' Salif went on. 'It smelled terrible in there. It smelled like human waste. With crowds of people in every room. Big rooms with people lying on the floor in rows. What is this place? I thought. Where am I? Sambala said it looked like a football camp. That made us laugh. I thought it would just be a few nights until we'd be able to arrange a place to live. But they locked the doors. They shoved us into a room. It looked like an office, with tables and chairs and a picture of a girl in a bathing suit on the wall, a calendar from 2001. There we met a man they called Boss Maillaux. He said we had debts we needed to repay. The trip was expensive. And interest had been added on. We had to work to earn the money. That sounded OK. But one guy, not one of us, started protesting. He'd expected to be living with one of his uncle's friends. They hit him. They beat him with boards until he was silent. There were three of them. One used a metal pipe. They dragged the guy out of the room. I never saw him again. Then Boss Maillaux asked if anyone else had anything to say. No one did. If we tried to escape, he said we'd get the same treatment. They would take our parents' houses. Things would go very badly for our parents. They would take our younger siblings too. They would rape our little sisters.'

The air in the room was starting to feel stifling. I wondered why the blinds had to be closed, since we were up on the tenth floor. It seemed highly unlikely that anyone would be able to look in.

'Usually the threats are enough,' said Arnaud. 'After a while they don't even need to lock the doors. The entire operation is based on fear. If anyone successfully escaped, the whole bubble would burst.'

'But you managed to run away,' I said, turning to Salif. 'How did you do it?'

'We worked all day, every day. Moving freight and then working at a construction site, demolishing a building. One night there was trouble in the safe house. A guy from Senegal who'd been there long before we arrived. He was shouting that he'd been duped. He wanted his money. He wanted to get out of there. They hit him. He was bleeding. We bandaged his wounds, but he got sick. He had a high fever. He was raving in delirium. He said he was out wandering and his child couldn't walk. I said that we'd work harder, that we'd do his job too. I said that he needed a doctor. One night they came to get him. They said there was no room for anyone who didn't work. I asked if they were taking him to a hospital. They told me to shut up and forget about that man.'

I stood up, making my knees creak. 'Is it OK if I pull up the blinds?' I asked, reaching for the cord. Arnaud nodded.

As daylight fell into the room, I saw how gaunt Salif was. His elbows stuck out like sharp knobs above the bandages on his hands. I thought he must have been fit and healthy when he left home. A soccer player. I thought about how a person could fade away so completely that nothing was left but a shell of what he used to be.

I stood there, leaning against the windowsill.

'There were more than ten of us demolishing that building,' Salif went on. 'Plus several white foremen supervising. There was a guard stationed with us from the safe house. I thought to myself: he can't shoot in the middle of the day, not while other people are watching. And at some point he'll have to go and relieve himself. I watched him. I told Checkna and Sambala that when the right moment came, we were going to leave. I would give them a signal

169

and then we'd run, all three of us at once. We would phone our families and then we'd hide. Maybe go to the police. Or find somebody from home who would help us. We whispered to each other in the evenings, deciding that we'd help all these people who were being held prisoner, that Allah had sent us here for a reason, and then we'd earn money and send it home to our families.

'One day when the guard headed for the sheds where the toilets were, I whistled the signal. We ran as fast as we could. Sambala was the fastest. I followed, with Checkna close behind. We ran through the gate in the fence and out onto the street. We had never seen the street before because we were always driven there inside a delivery van with the windows painted black. They shouted after us, but we didn't turn around even for a second. We just kept on running. First we ran through an industrial area, then came the residential neighbourhood, with high-rises. After seven blocks we ran into a Muslim woman. I asked her the way to the nearest mosque. She stared at us like we were crazy. "We have to find the mosque!" I shouted, and she pointed. It wasn't far. The imam let us in. He gave us tea. We asked him to call Checkna's uncle, who owns a café. They have a phone. We asked him to tell our parents to be careful, to protect themselves. The imam made the phone call from the next room. He came back and said that he'd talked to them. That we were supposed to call again in two hours. Then we'd be able to speak to our mothers.'

Salif buried his face in his bandaged hands, then used the sheet to wipe his eyes. He cleared his throat before going on.

'He said that he'd also called someone who could help us.' He turned to look at Arnaud. 'Later on Arnaud came to pick us up. In the night, when it was dark. He took us to the hotel.'

'It was an emergency situation,' said Arnaud. 'There was no time to look for any place else.'

'And then Patrick Cornwall came there to interview you,' I said. We'd been in the apartment more than an hour, and I still hadn't found out anything new about Patrick. I was starting to feel inclined to agree with Arnaud. It was a mistake for me to have come here to meet Salif. To get dragged into his story.

'The American was supposed to help us. He was going to talk about us in the newspaper. Then he was going to get them arrested, those crooks. Boss Maillaux and the others.'

Salif punched the wall. That must have hurt because of the burns on his hand.

'Do you know who the others were? Did Patrick know?'

Salif nodded. 'He asked about the safe house. About the number on the building. About what it said on the side of the trucks. He asked about everything. Where the construction site was. I showed him on a map which way we had run. I remembered it exactly because I had counted the blocks. I wanted to know where I was.'

'When was this?'

Salif tapped his feet on the bed and looked at Arnaud for help.

He has lost all sense of time, I thought.

'About a month since the first time he talked to Patrick,' said Arnaud.

'And the last time? What did Patrick say then?'

'It was a good place. We had our own beds,' said Salif. He didn't seem to have heard the question. His story was taking its own, specific direction.

'I was lying in bed reading. The American had brought me some books. I heard doors slamming in the corridor and a loud bang. Then I noticed the smell and the heat.

171

Do you understand? Both at the same time. The fire exploded. I ran out into the hall and saw that the stairwell was full of flames. I screamed and ran back to the room to get the others. I ran out into the hall and started pounding on doors to wake up everyone who lived there. I couldn't run down the stairs. The fire was everywhere. Beyond the stairs was a ledge with big windows. I thought to myself: I'll go over there and break the glass and jump out, and the family that lives on the floor below can toss their children down to me and I will catch them. The little girl has just learned to walk, and the boy is six years old and pretends he's a famous footballer like Ronaldo. We've played football in the hall with him. Sambala and I.

'But I don't go over to the ledge and the window, because the flames are getting even bigger. It burns my hands. Piles of trash are burning, and boxes and chairs. I know that all those things weren't there before, because we sat on the ledge with the windows open and breathed in the smell of earth from the park as we talked about women. Sambala and Checkna and I. So I'm standing there looking at the chairs burning, and I realize that someone has started this fire on purpose. Then I feel them pushing past me. Sambala and Checkna are yelling and running down the stairs, straight into the flames.'

Salif slapped his hands to his cheeks. 'I shouted, but they didn't come back, and the fire was rising towards me. There was nothing I could do. I ran up the last set of stairs. I knew I could get out onto the roof.' He looked from Arnaud to me. 'I'd made sure of that. I don't like to be closed in. I don't sleep well. In the safe house I didn't sleep at all when the doors were locked.'

'I know exactly what you mean,' I said.

Salif went on talking with his eyes fixed on the TV, as if that was all he could look at any more, after spending weeks in the apartment in which there was nothing else to see.

'I didn't notice any fire engines down on the street. I had the cell that Arnaud had given me. I phoned him from the roof, but he didn't answer.' He glanced at Arnaud, who was looking down at his hands. 'Then I called Patrick Cornwall. He'd given me two numbers. They were programmed into the phone. The first was busy, but when I called the other number, he answered. I shouted that he had to come and help us. Then I jumped.' Salif grimaced, remembering the pain when he'd landed on the lower building next door and broken his leg.

'There was a ladder on the other building. I climbed down and hid in the back yard, between two sheds. The fire engines arrived. I lay there for a long time, not daring to move. Then I heard someone yelling my name. It was the American. When he got closer I called out, but not very loudly. I was afraid someone would see me. The police or those other men. The American heard me. He was upset. Tears were running down his face.'

I dug my fingernails into the palms of my hands.

'"I'm sorry. I'm so sorry", he kept saying, speaking first English and then French. I don't understand English. It wasn't his fault. He wasn't the one who started the fire. He said that he'd talk to the police. He said they weren't going to get away with this. He was crying. He was going to write about us, tell our story to the world. He helped me get away from there, and then he got hold of Arnaud. Arnaud came to get us. We went to see a doctor.'

'A doctor who works for us,' Arnaud interjected.

'What do you know about the people who started the fire?' I asked.

'Patrick Cornwall said that they did it to get us. It was our fault. It was because of us that the fire was started.'

173

'I'm sure he didn't say that,' I told him.

'That's what I think, at least.' Salif looked away, turning his gaze to the wall.

'Did Patrick mention the names of any of these crooks?'

Salif nodded. 'He showed me maps and photographs. He said that he was going after them, that they would pay for what they'd done.'

Arnaud translated what he'd just said as: 'He didn't know any of their names.'

I'd heard two versions of what Salif had said. It took a few seconds for me to realize that I'd actually understood Salif's French. Arnaud was trying to fool me. Why?

'What were their names?' I asked now, hearing as if from a distance Arnaud translating my question into French for Salif as: 'You don't need to say anything more.'

Then I stuck my hand into my bag and took out the envelope with the photographs. I'd had copies made in a photo shop near the market.

'What's that?' asked Arnaud, trying to take the pictures from me, but I refused to hand them over. Salif wasn't able to look through the photos himself because of his injured hands, so I did it for him.

'Do you recognize any of these men?' I asked.

He shook his head.

'You're not even looking,' I told him.

'I've already seen them,' he said. 'The American showed them to me on the day of the fire. I told him that I don't recognize the others. Only one of them.'

'One of them?' I repeated, stupefied, feeling the blood freeze in my veins. 'Which one?'

'He came twice to the safe house. He didn't talk to us. Only to Boss Maillaux. It was a blurry picture, bad camera. I don't know what his name is.'

I quickly shuffled through the photographs.

174

'There,' said Salif.

In the photograph the man was standing behind Alain Thery, off to one side. It was impossible to tell where the picture had been taken. The wall of a building in the background. Part of a window. A third man was standing there with them. Only now did I realize I knew him. Shaved head. His nose that seemed a little too small. It was the man who had thrown me out of the office on avenue Kléber.

'I think we should go now,' said Arnaud. 'You can see that's all he knows.'

I inhaled so deeply that it seemed like all the air in the room was drawn down into my lungs and there was no oxygen left.

'Did he mention the name Alain Thery?' I asked.

I didn't need to wait for Arnaud to translate. I saw Salif's reaction at the name. He nodded.

'Yes, yes. Patrick Cornwall said that he was the boss. I didn't recognize him.'

'What about Josef K?' I said. 'Did Patrick say anything about him?'

'Josef?' Salif shook his head and looked unhappy. 'No Josef.'

Arnaud got up from the bed and headed for the door.

'We need to go now,' he said.

'Why?' I asked. 'Are you afraid Salif will say something more that you don't want me to hear?'

'It's complicated. He doesn't know the whole picture,' said Arnaud, fidgeting with his scarf. I'd noticed he did that whenever he was stressed or nervous. The scarf was almost a sort of security blanket for him.

'I know that Patrick wouldn't give up,' I said. 'I know that he would do everything in his power to get those people. Ask Salif what Patrick said to him before he left that night.'

Arnaud stood in the doorway as he translated. Salif nodded hesitantly.

'He was going to talk to the police,' said Salif. 'He was going to tell them what I saw. Arnaud says that when the police catch them, I can leave here a free man.'

Arnaud didn't translate the last part, but I understood from the context. Salif hadn't been told that the police had dropped the investigation.

'Thank you for talking to me,' I said.

'When are you coming back?' asked Salif.

'I don't know,' I said. 'I don't know if I'm coming back.'

Salif seemed not to notice as I held out my hand. His eyes had shifted to survey the bare walls of the room.

'The boy pretended he was Ronaldo.'

'I'm not going back with you,' said Arnaud as we left the building. 'I'm worried about Salif.'

'Why don't you want to talk about Alain Thery?' I asked.

Arnaud refused to meet my eye.

'What do you mean?'

'You didn't translate everything Salif said. Why not?'

'I thought you didn't speak French,' said Arnaud.

'I lived here for several years when I was a child. Out in the country,' I told him. 'What do you have to do with Thery?'

'Nothing,' snapped Arnaud. 'I just don't want to drag you into something that could have consequences you don't understand.'

'Save your concern for your poor refugees.'

His dark eyes flashed.

'You don't know shit,' he said. 'You come barging in here and think that everybody is going to help you find your American colleague. People disappear every day. People who are never found.'

'So one more isn't important? Is that what you're saying?'

A woman approached, carrying two heavy shopping bags. Arnaud held the door open for her. The woman glared at him and went inside.

'I put Patrick in touch with the young men,' said Arnaud. 'I gave him the facts. That's all. Now if you'll excuse me, I'm going to help that poor woman go upstairs. The lift is broken, as you know.'

He went inside to the stairwell, and the door closed behind him. I kicked the door with all my might. Salif had to be protected at all costs, yet Patrick had been allowed to disappear without anyone seeming to care. Why was everybody else in the world more important? And of course old ladies needed help with their groceries.

I grabbed the door handle, which was hanging loose. I wanted to yank open the door, run up the stairs two at a time, and slam Arnaud Rachid against the wall. I wanted to tell him what a cowardly and petty person he was. He helped only those who were weaker than him, which made him feel good. I wanted to pound his head against the wall. But instead I let the door fall closed again. I was vaguely aware of three teenage boys sauntering past. I noticed only their baggy, drooping pants, and their sneakers, their shuffling gait. I glanced at my watch. Getting close to five o'clock.

At five I was supposed to meet Caroline Kearny.

'So what are you doing in Paris? Are you a reporter?'

'No,' I said as I sat down at the table in the glassed-in veranda. 'No. I actually work in the theatre.'

Caroline Kearny was almost sixty. She was clad entirely in purple, from her patent-leather shoes to her hair and the big scarf draped around her shoulders. I had expected a French woman, but she was from Boston, though she'd lived in Paris for more than thirty years.

'Well, then, of course you realize you're sitting on legendary chairs. They have all sat here: Verlaine, Oscar Wilde. Jean-Paul Sartre sat here and wrote for hours. He and Simone de Beauvoir came here every morning.'

I had recognized the café from the photo on the wall in my hotel room. The original decor had been refurbished so it seemed new. From the ceiling inside hovered two full-size Chinese figures. They must be *les deux magots*, I thought. Doomed to hang there for all eternity.

'I think I'll have some juice and something to eat,' I said. 'I don't drink alcohol.'

Caroline snapped open the menu.

'Just imagine if I'd been that wise at your age. Then I wouldn't be sitting here.' She motioned for the waiter and gave him our orders.

'Did you see Patrick when he was here?' I asked. 'Did he tell you about the story he was working on?'

'Of course,' she said, giving me a big smile that showed all her teeth. 'But I never answer questions if I'm not sure where they're leading. You know how reporters are. You're married to one.'

The waiter brought two glasses of freshly squeezed orange juice and numerous plates holding ham, salads, an omelette, foie gras, bread, and cheese.

'I don't drink either,' said Caroline. 'Not any more. So food is my indulgence.'

She broke off a piece of bread and spread on a dollop of ripe cheese.

'How's your husband doing? He's a real cutie, if you ask me.'

I started crying. I clenched my fists and tried hard to restrain myself, but it was like a dam had burst. I wiped my face with a napkin. My nose started running as I attempted to apologize to the woman seated across from me, but I couldn't stop the tears. It was a flood of sorrow and panic and everything I'd been holding back for the past few weeks, maybe my whole life, and I sobbed loudly as it all came tumbling out. Through a fog I saw that everyone in the café was staring at me. Caroline handed me her napkin.

'I'm sorry,' I said, when the flood had receded, turning into a quiet rippling. I blew my nose on the napkin. 'I haven't been able to talk to anyone about this.'

'Has he left you?' asked Caroline. 'I know it may feel terrible right now, but believe me, it'll get better.' She spread a thick layer of foie gras on another piece of bread. 'My husband left me after twenty-two years of marriage, and here I sat, all alone in Paris. That's when I started writing. I had to make a living, you know. Now I can't picture going back. The States have become so vulgar, lacking all finesse, but maybe it's just that I've become French over the years.'

I tried to smile through my tears. 'I don't think he's left me,' I said. 'I'm scared it's something much worse.'

And then I told her the whole story, from beginning to end. About Patrick's last phone call, and Richard Evans, about the envelope from Paris, and what I'd found out over the past three days. Actually, it was now almost four days that I'd been following his trail. Caroline ate her food with a hearty appetite, occasionally interjecting a question. When I got to the meeting with Salif, she put down her fork and knife and handed me a tissue. My tears had turned all the cloth napkins into soggy rags.

'Patrick contacted me almost three weeks ago,' she said, taking her pocket diary out of her bag. 'We met on Tuesday, 9 September, at one thirty in the afternoon.' She nodded at me. 'He was sitting right there where you're sitting now.'

'That was a week before he checked out of the hotel,' I said.

'He wanted me to look at some photographs,' she went on. 'He wondered whether I could help him identify some of the people in the pictures.'

I took out the envelope and handed it to her.

'Are these the photographs?'

Caroline put on a pair of gold-framed glasses. As she studied the pictures I quickly ate what was left of the food.

'Not all of them, but I do recognize several,' she said. 'Terrible quality. I told him he'd be worthless as a paparazzo.'

'I recognize Alain Thery,' I told her as I ate. 'But who are the others?'

She tapped a long, purple-painted fingernail on the photo on top.

'Marcel Defèvre. He's a politician and a member of the European parliament, where he hasn't done much of importance. But the person who interested Patrick the most was this man.' She placed another photo on top of the stack.

'Guy de Barreau,' she said.

'The name doesn't mean anything to me.' I took a closer look at the man she was talking about. He was in his sixties, with thick grey hair. He looked a little like a Hugh Grant who had aged with dignity.

'He's a lobbyist,' said Caroline. 'That alone makes him an odd duck in French politics. They don't have the same tradition of professional lobbyists, not like we have in the States.'

She pulled a book out of her bag, and I saw the author's name on the cover. Guy de Barreau.

'*L'art de convaincre*,' she read aloud from the cover. '*The Art of Persuasion*. My curiosity was piqued after I talked to Patrick, so I went out and bought the book.'

I riffled through the pages as she explained. Guy de Barreau had started the think-tank, *La Ligne Française* — the French Line — in the early '90s. He lobbied for reducing immigration, though without appearing to be openly racist. Instead, he talked about preserving French culture and French values. And he'd been extremely successful. La Ligne Française was thought to be behind several new laws instituted over the past few years. For instance, immigrant citizens were not allowed to bring their families to France unless all of them had full-time jobs, spoke fluent French, and could sing the 'Marseillaise' in their sleep. The group promoted the importation of workers, but only on a temporary basis. Obtaining citizenship was made more difficult. Those who came into the country and stayed without official permission were criminals and would be deported immediately.

'He has managed to market ideas that would have been impossible twenty years ago,' said Caroline. 'In spite of everything, the French used to take liberty, equality, and fraternity very seriously.'

She paused as the waiter came over to clear the table.

'We must have coffee and dessert,' she said.

I leaned back while she ordered. I looked through the glass wall that ran the entire length of the café's veranda. The crying jag had been like a cleansing bath. I felt more clear-headed than I had in a long time.

'Did Patrick say anything about what those two were up to?' I asked, taking out a photo in which de Barreau and Thery were sitting at a table in some café or restaurant. I realized it could be the Taillevent, given the brown background.

Caroline smiled and shook her head.

'No. Only that he was onto something big. He was poaching on my territory, so he was probably afraid I'd steal his story.'

'If I've understood correctly, this Alain Thery is mixed up in criminal activities in some way.' I didn't give a damn whether someone stole Patrick's story. 'It has to do with slavery, and even with murdering those who try to escape . . . But I don't understand how it relates to La Ligne Française.'

'Maybe they're just old friends,' said Caroline, taking out a lipstick and freshening her make-up. 'Although I doubt it. Thery is a climber. He's from Pas-de-Calais in northern France. A place that has been left behind by the textile factories and the metal industry and the rest of the world.'

'I'm impressed,' I said.

'He made his first hundred million in the IT business.'

'I don't mean him. I'm impressed by you. Do you know this much about everybody in business and politics?'

'No, but I decided to read up on things after meeting your husband.' Caroline laughed. 'I actually know much more about the love lives of celebrities. Gossip pays better than politics, but the two combined is unbeatable. The president's love affairs have made me financially independent for the rest of my life. Although I write those stories under a pseudonym, of course.'

She straightened up, making room for the waiter, who set coffee cups on the table, and two tall glasses of ice cream and sorbet in various colours, garnished with fruit, chocolate wafers, and almond slivers.

'By the way, Alain Thery usually shows up at high-profile gatherings,' Caroline went on. 'Every Sunday when the actors finish their performances, he holds court at his regular table in the Plaza Athénée, with champagne corks flying. When winter comes to Paris, he leaves on one of his yachts. He has two, according to the gossip bloggers. He keeps one in Saint-Tropez and one in Puerto Banus on the Spanish Costa del Sol. They're floating luxury palaces, with lots of parties and all sorts of delicacies on the menu, but they never go further than a few hundred metres from the harbour. And do you know why?'

My mouth was full of melting vanilla ice cream, so I couldn't reply.

'He can't swim!' exclaimed Caroline Kearny.

I smiled, but couldn't manage a laugh.

'There's a Plaza Athénée in New York too,' I said. 'Nice drinks, expensive people.'

Caroline tasted the yellowish-red sorbet. 'Passion fruit,' she said, smiling at me. 'It's their best.' She licked her spoon and closed her eyes for a few seconds before going on.

'If I've done my homework right, Alain Thery is obsessed with status. He doesn't want to be the boy from the coal heaps in Pas-de-Calais. But in France it's not enough to make money. You have to be from the right family and go to the right schools.'

She tapped her fingernail on the cover of the book. 'This man, on the other hand . . . He knows people at all levels of power — members of the government, public officials, supreme court justices. His family can be traced back to the 1700s. Royalists who served at the court of Louis XVI. He's gone to all the best schools.'

She sampled the other sorbets, the flavours mingling in her mouth, as she listed the schools that mattered. The political elite were all former classmates from Sciences-Po, the university for political science. A few years back, the admissions system was revamped so that talented students from even the worst suburbs could be admitted. That prompted an outcry from the upper classes. How were they supposed to tell people apart? It was also desirable to have a degree from ENA, École Nationale d'Administration, which was founded by de Gaulle. The previous president diverged drastically from tradition, since he had not graduated from that school. On the other hand, he did have a very attractive wife. Now order had been restored in the palace, since the president was a genuine *énarque*. Besides, despite his bland image, he had shown himself capable of keeping an actress as his mistress, which was practically a requirement in French politics.

At that point I lost interest.

'This isn't getting anywhere,' I said. 'I feel like I'm going in circles, picking up loose threads here and there, but nothing makes any sense. And time keeps moving along.' I placed my hand on my stomach and looked out of the window, seeing the square and an ugly church. A couple, arms around each other, stood there, studying a statue that portrayed a Cubist woman. The couple wasn't doing anything, just standing close together and looking at the statue. I felt sobs rise again, and I had to hold them back. I felt such an intense and painful longing to be with Patrick. Doing nothing. Just looking at something would be enough. It didn't have to be a Picasso statue. It could be the weather forecast.

'Over the past few years they've focused on the EU,' said Caroline Kearny.

She glanced at me as she slowly ate the last of the ice cream and sorbet, which had melted together.

'On the borders,' she went on. 'That's where the battle is being fought. If the immigrants keep on entering through Italy and Spain, not to mention Turkey, the French police will have a hard time throwing out everyone who continues on into France. Of course a lot of people come here legally, as tourists, and then they simply stay. But La Ligne Française and their friends prefer to talk about those who are pouring in by boat and hiding in trucks, because that's an image that frightens Dupont.'

'Dupont?'

'The average decent Frenchman, the worker who makes an average income, who is not a racist, but wants his children to grow up in a country that he recognizes from his own childhood.'

'Do you know whether Patrick interviewed any of these men?' I asked.

'He said that he'd met Alain Thery once, but it didn't go well. Thery ended the interview when Patrick got to the more interesting questions.'

'What kind of questions?'

'He didn't tell me. I'm a competitor, after all.'

'But you both work for the same magazine.'

Caroline laughed and slurped up the dregs of her ice cream.

'I offered to do an interview for him. Apparently Thery had made himself unavailable. He wasn't answering his emails, and Patrick's calls were all diverted to his secretary. Patrick thanked me for the offer and said he'd be in touch.'

'Did he get back to you?'

Caroline smiled regretfully and shook her head. I understood. Patrick would never have involved another reporter in his story.

'Could you try to do it now?' I said. 'Schedule an interview with Alain Thery?'

'Nothing new from your husband?' asked Olivier when I returned to the hotel that evening.

I shook my head.

'Have you thought of anything?' I asked. 'Anything at all? Someone he met, someone else who phoned?'

'I don't know whether this means anything, but . . .' Olivier refused to look me in the eye.

'What?' I said, leaning on the reception desk. 'Is it something you've remembered?'

'He said they were going to the Louvre, and I thought . . .'

'They? Who did he mean?' I stared at Olivier, who was

tugging nervously at his necktie. 'Why didn't you say anything before?' In a flash everything fell into place. 'It was a woman, wasn't it? He was going to the Louvre with her, and you haven't said anything to me because you thought she was his fucking mistress.' I pounded my fist on his damn reception desk. There he sat, being so discreet.

Olivier took off his glasses and then put them back on. 'It was on one of the last days. Actually it was the day before he checked out because he'd just come back from the market, and I asked him if he'd bought anything, but he didn't answer. Just went up to his room. And then, a little later, she arrived, this woman, and asked for him.'

I froze when I realized the connection.

In the market Luc had given Patrick a phone number to call. He was supposed to say: *I want to talk about Josef K.*

And then a woman had arrived to get him, the same way someone had picked me up outside the Taillevent restaurant. This woman had met Patrick on Monday, the day before he left, and she knew something about Josef K. I paced back and forth. That meant she must know where he'd gone.

'What did the woman look like?' I asked, hearing the quaver in my voice. 'Can you describe her?'

Olivier looked away as he ran his hand through his hair. 'Well, I mean, she was the kind of woman that a man would notice.'

'Attractive?'

'Dark, very short, big eyes.'

Her eyes were the only thing I'd seen. And her physique. The desk clerk was as tall as Patrick. Compared to both of them, the woman was obviously quite petite.

Olivier smiled a bit nervously. 'I thought she looked like

186

Juliette Binoche. I even told her so, but she didn't seem impressed. She probably hears that all the time.'

'Could you hear from her voice where she was from?'

'She was definitely Parisian, and not exactly from the streets.'

I took out my key and my cell, tapping in the number as I climbed the stairs. It was programmed into my phone under the name Josef K.

I heard the phone ring once. Twice. I unlocked my room and went inside.

On the fifth ring, the call was cut off.

When I tapped in the number again, I was connected to voicemail, an automated message from the telephone company. When I heard the beep, I began speaking.

'I want to talk to Patrick Cornwall,' I said. 'I know that he was supposed to interview Josef K.'

I ended the call and sat down in front of my laptop. I sat there for a long time in the glow of the screen, staring at a picture of a French actress as the city fell quiet outside. So that was how she looked.

Chapter 9

Paris
Sunday, 28 September

'Hello?'

It said 'unknown caller' on the display.

'Didn't I tell you to stay away?'

It was her. The woman in the car. I sat bolt upright in bed. I'd know that voice among millions of others.

'Who exactly are you?' I said. 'Where did Patrick Cornwall go when he left Paris?'

'You should go home,' she said.

'He was supposed to meet Josef K. Isn't that right? So where is he?'

I heard her take a breath, followed by a second of silence. My heart was pounding hard, as if it wanted to leap out of my chest and land like a pulsing blob in my lap.

'Yesterday you met a man named Salif,' said the woman on the phone.

'How do you know that?' I wrapped the blanket around me. The ringing of my phone had awakened me. 'What do you know about Salif?'

'He's dead,' said the woman. 'Shot once through the head. Are you satisfied now?'

Then she was gone.

The word was like a glaring headline in my mind.

Dead.

It wasn't possible. That couldn't be.

And then: It was my fault. I was the one who'd led them straight to Salif. I got out of bed with the blanket around me and went over to the window to look down at the street. No one there.

I turned to look at the digits on the clock radio. 9.15. Dazzling sun above the rooftops. Traffic noises.

I'm a dead man, he'd said. Salif. How old was he? Twenty-three, twenty-four?

I looked up the number for Arnaud Rachid. My hands were shaking. The phone rang. No one answered. Released from my paralysis, I got dressed. I grabbed my bag and jacket, ran downstairs to the breakfast room for a sandwich, quickly drank some juice and coffee, then hurried over to the river and across the bridges to the right bank. Three times I veered onto a side street and waited around the corner to see if anyone was following me, but I saw no one. I jogged the rest of the way through the Marais and stopped abruptly when I reached rue Charlot.

The entrance was cordoned off. I quickly retreated to a doorway, breathing hard.

There were two police vehicles and an ambulance parked on the street outside the building where Arnaud Rachid had his office. They had blocked the entire entrance to the courtyard. Bystanders had gathered outside the police tape. I caught sight of Sylvie, the activist girl, standing in another doorway with others wearing similar baggy clothing. I went over to her.

'What's going on here?' I asked.

'It was murder,' said Sylvie, wide-eyed. 'He was lying on the stairs outside the office this morning, shot in the head.'

'They shot him here?' I said dumbfounded. It didn't make sense. Salif wasn't supposed to leave the apartment in Bobigny.

'Arnaud was the one who found him. He was terribly shocked, of course. It's the man that Arnaud has been hiding. The one you were supposed to see yesterday. Because that's where the two of you went, wasn't it?'

She gave me a searching look. I glared at her. She had some nerve thinking about her own jealous feelings when Salif was dead.

'So where is Arnaud now?' I asked.

'I don't know. He panicked and ran off.'

'Do the police know what happened? Do they know who the dead man is?'

Sylvie looked at me with an expression that showed what an idiot I was.

'Of course not. He didn't have any papers on him. That's the whole problem. And Arnaud isn't about to run around saying that he was hiding the man. Then the police would be after him, and everything would go to hell.'

The medics slammed shut the back doors of the ambulance. They seemed about to leave. I considered going over to ask if I could see the dead man, but I decided not to. Instead I headed in the opposite direction. At the next street corner I paused to tap in Arnaud's phone number and left a message telling him he had to call me.

I'd gone only ten metres when my cell rang.

'Were you the one who leaked where he was hiding?' Arnaud said.

I denied it, and he seemed to believe me.

'How were they able to find him?' I asked. 'Do you think they followed us?'

190

I heard Arnaud moan.

'He was lying there when I arrived this morning, with a hole in his head. Do you understand? They shot him. What did he ever do to anyone?'

I managed to get Arnaud to tell me that he was outside the city, in *la banlieue*. 'Where we were yesterday,' he said.

'I'm coming over there.'

The door was ajar. Sitting on the bed where Salif had sat yesterday, Arnaud Rachid was staring at the wall. The bedclothes were in disarray.

'I wonder if they shot him here,' said Arnaud. 'Or if they dragged him down to rue Charlot first.' He buried his face in his hands. He was shaking.

'All he wanted was a good life, for God's sake.'

I sat down on the edge of the bed. The room was as dimly lit as it had been before. As if time had stood still. Except that Salif had been taken away.

But his smell still lingered in the air. The smell of sweat and fear and confinement.

'It was like he was staring up at me, but his eyes were completely blank, and then there was that hole in his forehead.' Arnaud slammed his fist against his own forehead. 'Then I noticed that the cast on his leg had been crushed, and the bandages on his hands had been torn off, and his body was twisted in such a strange way, as if . . . as if . . .'

'As if?' I said, though I didn't want to know.

'As if they'd broken both of his arms.'

Arnaud began to sob. A deep, keening sound that prevented me from thinking.

'Is it wise for you to be here?' I asked. 'They might come back.'

'The door was open. He must have opened it to let them in. Even though I told him not to open the door for anyone.'

191

Arnaud kept sobbing.

Stop crying, I thought. If you cry, you have no chance. They'll get you. And I realized it was my mother's voice speaking inside my head.

'How did they find him?' I asked, putting my hand on his shoulder.

'I've been trying to talk to some of the neighbours,' said Arnaud, fidgeting with the TV remote control, which he held in his hand.

'Isn't that the job of the police?' I said.

'The police don't know he was living here.'

I looked at him.

'You have to tell them. We're talking about murder now. Not a risk of being deported.'

Arnaud got up and went over to the window. He wiped his face with a corner of his scarf and then turned to look at me.

'The police aren't going to be investigating this case,' he said. 'Haven't you realized that yet?'

I went with Arnaud to speak to the rest of the neighbours. Salif's fate was somehow linked to Patrick's. I was certain about that.

The first doorbell we tried was broken. Arnaud knocked on the door. It opened a crack and a tiny woman wearing a headscarf peeked out at us.

Arnaud spoke Arabic to her. After a moment she opened the door another few centimetres. She eyed me suspiciously.

'The police were here yesterday,' Arnaud told me after the woman had shut the door and gone back inside. 'They were looking for an illegal immigrant.'

'But it couldn't have been the police who shot him, for God's sake.'

Arnaud strode over to the next apartment. No one opened

the door. The same at the next place. I thought I could hear sounds coming from inside.

'People are scared,' said Arnaud. 'They know it's bad news whenever the police show up.'

The next neighbour who came to the door was a man wearing long underwear. He spoke French and undressed me with his eyes as he talked to Arnaud.

'They showed ID,' he said. 'They asked about an illegal refugee they were looking for.'

'Did they say his name?' asked Arnaud.

'Yes, but I don't remember what it was,' said the man, scratching his crotch.

'Salif?' I said.

His face lit up. 'Yes, that was it. And then some long surname. I said this whole place is crawling with them. Impossible to keep track of them all.'

Back in the apartment, I pulled up the blinds, which instantly rolled back down halfway, but still let in a wide swathe of sunlight. Then I went over to the kitchenette, filled a cracked cup with water, and drank it down as I waited for Arnaud to come out of the bathroom.

'How did they know he'd be here?' I said when he reappeared. 'Do you think they're following me? Or you?'

'I don't know.'

He leaned against the counter, tugging at his hair.

'I can't understand why he opened the door. He wasn't supposed to let the police in. Or anybody else.'

'Do you think someone paid them off?'

'Or maybe they bought the police ID they were carrying. No one could have known his name except the people he'd run away from. I haven't told his surname to anybody.'

Arnaud fidgeted with a cell he was holding.

'I found this here,' he said. 'It was in the bathroom.'

'Is it Salif's?'

He nodded and said, 'There's something you'll want to know.'

He took a step closer and held up the cell. On the display I saw a name.

Patrick C.

A shiver raced through my body.

'Of course he would have Patrick's number,' I said, grabbing the phone and staring at the name. 'Salif called him before.'

'Sure,' said Arnaud. 'But this was the last number I got when I checked his incoming calls.'

I clutched the phone in my hand, and the world closed in around me. I had the feeling that I was now all alone with this small object.

'According to the phone, Patrick called Salif at ten o'clock last night,' Arnaud went on. 'That was an hour and a half before the so-called police began knocking on doors here.'

Gently I pressed the 'call' button.

And held my breath.

I heard the ringtone. It seemed to be echoing through the whole apartment. Four, five, six times. No voicemail. No one saying: *You've reached Patrick Cornwall.* Then a voice spoke. A man's voice. 'Hello?'

'Patrick,' I whispered. 'Is that you, Patrick?'

'Who is this?' said the voice on the phone, and it wasn't Patrick.

'Where is he?' I said. 'What have you done with him?'

Nothing but silence. I lowered the phone and looked at Arnaud.

'What does this mean?' I asked him. 'Where is Patrick?'

He touched my hand, which was still holding the phone, and I felt my body starting to shake. The tremors were billowing up from deep inside me.

194

Arnaud looked at me in surprise. 'Are you in love with him, or something?'

Quickly I turned away. Don't lose control, I thought, pinching myself hard on the arm.

Don't be a fucking cry-baby.

'I just want to know what's happened to him,' I said, still holding Salif's cell.

Someone had used Patrick's phone to make the call. They must have stolen it.

And at the same moment I realized what could have happened. They'd used Patrick's cell to locate Salif. If they'd been able to get police IDs, they could also have had access to the cell network to trace the call. That would also explain why Salif had opened the door. He thought it was Patrick coming to see him. Or someone who was friends with Patrick. Maybe they'd promised to take Salif to the States.

I took a tissue out of my pocket and blew my nose.

Then I explained my theory to Arnaud. He stared impassively out of the window where the grey suburbs extended on and on, as far as the eye could see.

'I can't make any sense of all this,' I said. 'These past few days . . . If only I knew what he was thinking.'

Arnaud slowly turned to look at me.

'Josef K had defected,' he said. 'He was ready to tell everything about how these businesses are run, and who's in charge. He was prepared to name names. Patrick was supposed to interview him.'

The words sank in and settled into place.

'Where?' I asked. 'Where were they supposed to meet?'

'I don't know. I only know that Patrick left Paris on Tuesday two weeks ago.' He fixed his eyes on the floor. 'I wasn't supposed to say anything. If word had got out that he was going to meet Josef K . . .'

'Did Patrick tell you that? That you weren't supposed to say anything?'

Arnaud didn't answer. He turned around and began rinsing off the plates stacked on the counter, doing a clumsy job of it.

'Salif is dead,' I said. 'So what the hell is so important now? There's nobody left for you to protect.'

'I wasn't the one hiding him.'

'Then who was? I don't see anyone else here.'

'I'm not talking about Salif. I mean Josef K. He'd gone underground. I didn't even know where he was. I wasn't involved in that.'

I sank down onto a rickety kitchen chair. It's like a hall of mirrors, I thought. Someone is always hiding behind the others, and there's no way to figure out where the exit is. I hated the hall of mirrors at the amusement park when I was a kid. Not knowing where everyone was positioned, or which version was real. And all those distorted faces.

'So you have no idea where Patrick went?' I asked.

'Afraid not,' said Arnaud.

Then both of us fell silent. A fly danced beneath the fan. The walls turned yellow.

'We need to leave,' he said at last.

'I think I know what she looks like,' I said.

'Who?'

'One of the people behind all this.'

And I told him about the woman who'd picked me up in the car. How she'd threatened me if I didn't go back home to New York. I said I was almost positive she was the same woman who had come to get Patrick the day before he disappeared. And it had something to do with Josef K.

'She was the one who phoned me this morning and told

196

me that Salif was dead,' I said. 'She has to be involved. Otherwise how would she know who he was?'

I met Arnaud's eye. The next second he looked away.

'Maybe she was right,' he said. 'Maybe you should have gone back home to New York. Maybe then Salif would still be alive.'

'Don't put the blame on me,' I shouted. 'You were the one who was supposed to be protecting him.'

'I know that,' yelled Arnaud. 'You don't have to tell me that, damn it.'

Then neither of us said another word. Maybe he was thinking the same thing I was.

That it no longer made any difference.

It was late afternoon by the time I got back to the hotel.

'You have a visitor,' said René, the desk clerk. He nodded towards the easychairs in the lobby.

For a nano-second my heart stood still. In the time it took for me to turn halfway around, I thought Patrick would be coming towards me with a smile. Instead, Sarah Rachid got up from where she was sitting.

'Who are you really?' she snapped as I approached. 'There's no Alena Sarkanova working for *The Reporter* in New York. Or staying here at the hotel either. So the question is: who are you?'

I sank like a stone onto the sofa. There was nothing to say. I retreated into a haze of fatigue, hearing her continue to talk in the distance.

Arnaud had phoned her after I'd gone to see him the first time. He had shouted and carried on, wanting to find out if Sarah knew what I was really after.

'So I called New York, the magazine where you claim to work. They've never heard of you.'

'Those switchboard operators are hopeless,' I said faintly.

197

From Arnaud she'd learned that I was staying at the same hotel where Patrick had stayed.

'So I come here. I ask for Madame Sarkanova, but they've never heard of her. When I repeat the name, and say Alena, he reacts. The clerk over there.' Sarah points at René, who is pretending to be preoccupied. '"Oh, Alena Cornwall," he says. "Is that who you're looking for?" As you can imagine, I was very surprised, but I introduced myself and told him I'm a lawyer, and then he said I could wait for you here in the lobby.' She raised her chin aggressively. 'Why did you lie?'

'Sarkanova is my maiden name.'

'And you're married to Patrick Cornwall?' Sarah sat down on the armchair across from me and shook her head. 'But you're going around telling everyone you're a reporter. That's sick.'

'I needed to ask questions,' I said. 'Your brother must have told you that Patrick has disappeared.'

'What?' said Sarah. 'Has something happened to him?'

I studied her face. Her surprise was genuine. Her expression changed to concern and she lowered her eyes.

'I didn't think you were interested in journalists,' I said coldly.

She looked at me. Didn't respond. I pointed at her left hand.

'Did you tell Patrick that the wedding ring you're wearing is just for show? That you bought it for yourself?'

Sarah quickly got up, but then stood there, looking confused. 'If I'd known that you were . . . his wife . . . then . . .'

'Then what?' I gave her a piercing look. 'If you'd known I was married to him, would you have told me you were attracted to him? Would you?' Anger surged inside me. For the first time in days I felt like myself again.

Sarah flicked the lock on her briefcase, making a nervous clicking sound.

'Is there somewhere we could talk?' she said in a low voice.

They'd met more than once. I got that out of her at last. We were sitting in my hotel room. Sarah had taken the desk chair, hunching over like a little girl with her legs pressed together and her hands in her lap. I didn't like seeing her sitting in Patrick's chair, but there was nowhere else except the bed, and that option was no better.

She said that she'd helped him with something that must never get out.

I didn't need to ask why she'd done it. I could hear it in her voice whenever she mentioned his name. A gentleness that wasn't there when she was rattling off legal terms.

Patrick had wanted help with two other matters. He had turned to her because she knew the French legal system and where to find the information. She knew people.

The first thing he wanted to know involved property records. He wanted her to find out who owned a building on avenue Kléber.

'Number 76,' I said. 'A company called Lugus owns it.'

Sarah raised her eyes to look at me and nodded.

'The other property was a warehouse up in Saint-Ouen, in the northern part of Paris,' she said, leaning down to take a small notebook from the outer pocket of her briefcase. 'Actually, I wasn't able to find out very much.' She leafed through her notes and then read aloud: 'The property at 76 avenue Kléber is owned by a real estate company named Epona, which is part of a corporation that also owns the consulting firm Lugus, which leases the premises. The entire firm is controlled, in turn, by a foundation registered on the island of Jersey.' Sarah Rachid looked up. 'It's impossible to get any information from Jersey.'

'Just give me the short version,' I said.

'The warehouse is owned by another real estate company, which is part of a corporation controlled by the foundation on Jersey.'

'The same foundation?'

Sarah nodded and again looked at her notebook. 'That's all I was able to find out.'

I got up and went over to the windows to open them. Connections. That's what Patrick was looking for. Something that could link Alain Thery to the imprisoned slave labourers in the warehouse. I wondered whether he'd collected enough information to publish the story. Salif had identified one of the men associated with Thery. But now Salif was dead. I thought of the deserted office space with the glass walls and thick carpets on avenue Kléber. Behind the stage set of a successful consulting firm was something else altogether.

I turned around.

'What was the other thing Patrick wanted help with?'

Sarah drew her jacket closer around her. 'Do you think you could close the window?'

'No,' I said.

She looked down at her notebook again.

'It had to do with a think tank, a lobbying group, or whatever it's called. *La Ligne Française*. He wanted to know where their funding comes from. Are you familiar with that organization?'

I nodded and sat back down on the bed. 'Did you find out?'

'Well, the information is not available in any public records.'

'But you did make an effort to find out, didn't you? For Patrick's sake?'

She blushed.

'Nothing happened,' she said.

'What do you mean? With La Ligne Française?'

200

'Between Patrick and me,' she said, the crimson spreading to the lobes of her ears. 'I want you to know that.'

I dug my fingers into the coverlet that the cleaning woman had put on the bed. That same invisible person who left the scent of lavender in her wake.

'Did you know that he was assaulted?' said Sarah.

I gave a start. The next second I flew into a rage.

'What else are you not telling me?' I said, standing up and taking a few steps towards her. 'You sit here hiding behind your fucking laws, thinking you have the right to keep quiet, but this is my husband we're talking about. Do you understand?' I leaned against the wall with my arms crossed. 'What the hell do you mean he was assaulted?'

Sarah wrung her hands.

Patrick had phoned her late at night on September 11.

'That's a date that always sticks in my mind. We talked about that too. About what it was like to be in New York on that day.'

Sarah shifted position on her chair.

'I was in bed reading a novel by Maryse Condé. I always go to bed at eleven. He said he needed help, and he didn't know who else to call. I said he could come over to my place. I live in Belleville. He took a cab.'

Sarah stood up and went over to the window. 'They dragged him into a doorway not far from here, a little further along rue Saint-Jacques.' She pointed to the left, towards the river.

'He wasn't bleeding, but he'd suffered a serious blow to the head and had vomited. He thought he might have a concussion.' She closed the windows and turned to look at me. 'It was a warning. They wanted him to go back home.'

'Who did?' That was all I could manage to say.

'He didn't tell me.'

I was sitting down on the bed again, feeling a mixture

of fear and bewilderment. And searing jealousy. The next day, on the twelfth of September, he'd phoned me. Why hadn't he told me about what had happened?

I'm not going to let them think they can silence me. That was what he'd said as I stood in that hopeless stairwell in Boston. And then something about not being able to talk about it on the phone.

Sarah Rachid had tried to persuade him to go to the hospital, but Patrick had refused. He just asked her for some aspirin and an ice pack for the back of his head.

'What an idiot,' I said aloud.

She gave a start.

'Not you,' I said. 'Patrick. That warning probably just egged him on. He was convinced he was on the right track. Believe me, I know him. He never gives up until he gets to the bottom of things and digs up all the shit he can find.'

She stared at me in silence before going on.

'In the morning he was up and dressed, ready to go out and land his story, as he said.'

'He slept at your place?'

'On the sofa.'

Sarah turned away. I looked out of the window at the dome of the Panthéon, picturing the pendulum inside, demonstrating the rotation of the earth and the passage of time. One day after another.

Thursday, September 11. Patrick eats lunch at Taillevent, and Alain Thery has him thrown out. That same evening, he's assaulted.

Friday morning, 12 September. Patrick leaves Sarah's apartment in Belleville.

I didn't know where that part of town was located, nor did I want to know. At any rate, later on Friday he goes to Hôtel Royal to talk to Salif and the others. And that night the hotel burns down.

He hadn't paid any attention to the warning.

'Don't be mad at Arnaud,' said Sarah, unable to look me in the eye. 'Sometimes he crosses the line in terms of what's legal, but it's only because he wants to help. Plus he has a weakness for Nedjma. She can get him to do anything.'

'Who's that?' I asked. I'd been thinking about Patrick and was hardly listening.

'She's the woman Arnaud has been seeing. I don't trust her.'

Sarah fidgeted, looking unhappy. I fixed my eyes on her. Arnaud's love affairs didn't interest me at all.

'Did you see my husband again?' I asked. With special emphasis on 'my husband'.

She shook her head. Tugged at the sleeves of her blouse. First one, then the other. Finally she told me that late on Sunday night she had called Patrick. She'd heard about the hotel fire on the news, and Arnaud had told her that Patrick was there that night.

'I just wanted to hear how he was doing,' said Sarah quietly.

'So how was he?'

'He said he was going to get them arrested. He yelled about the police burying the investigation. He was ranting, worse than Arnaud ever does. The politicians are in on it too, he said. I got worried. He was so angry. He was in a bar. I don't know whether he was drunk. I thought it was strange for him to go to a bar when so many horrible things had just happened.'

'Did he say which bar?'

'Plaza Athénée, somewhere near the Champs-Élysées. I don't go to those sorts of places.'

I recognized the name at once. Caroline Kearny had mentioned it. *Every Sunday he holds court at his regular table*, she'd said. And Patrick had been there on a Sunday, upset and angry. That was exactly two weeks ago, today.

'Thanks,' I said. 'Now I'd like you to leave.'

I got out of the cab and stepped into a world of boundless luxury, with Prada and Chanel competing for attention in the shop windows. The Plaza Athénée was a white palace that looked as if it was straight out of a fairy tale. A warm light enveloped me as I entered the gilded lobby, with crystal chandeliers sparkling high overhead. In the cloakroom I encountered a voluptuous blonde wearing a fur coat. She cast a patronizing glance at my clothing before she took the arm of her seventy-year-old escort and strode off in her stiletto heels.

I had changed into the black dress that I'd worn for my lunch at Taillevent. I'd spent twenty minutes looking for the cheap necklace that had glittered so nicely in my décolletage, and finally found it in my suitcase, stuffed inside a dirty stocking.

In the bar I headed for a rococo style stool. The counter itself was sand-blasted glass, as if sculpted from a block of ice. Candelabra seemed to float in mid-air, burning blue flames. The whole scene could have been a set from *Harry Potter*.

Twenty or so guests sat scattered about, mostly couples, plus a group of girls drinking colourful cocktails. None of the men matched the photo of Alain Thery. It was almost ten thirty. I ordered a non-alcoholic drink. The bartender placed a small bowl of nuts and olives in front of me.

At that moment a group of five men came in, accompanied by three young women wearing dresses that ended just below the panty line. Alain Thery was the man in the middle. I'd studied the pictures of him so many times that there could be no doubt. Those eyes that seemed almost white, but otherwise his appearance was so ordinary that it was hardly memorable. He wore an expensive Italian suit and a blood-red tie. *He doesn't want to be the boy from the coal heaps in Pas-de-Calais.*

The group sat down at a low table in the comfortable lounge area of the room. Their arrival had heightened the activity behind the bar, and two waiters were already on their way over with champagne. Thery was sitting so that I could see his face, on the sofa against the wall. The sofa back was a classical painting printed on fabric surrounded by a large frame, making the guests seem as if they were part of a work of art. Behind Thery a full rigger was pulling into a bustling and dimly lit dock on the Seine in the early 1800s. Reclining on a silver cushion next to him was one of the blondes who had stretched out her legs on the sofa.

The champagne frothed in the glasses, and Thery put his hand on the girl's thigh. They all raised their glasses in a toast. I thought about the god with the three faces that had been chosen for the name of Thery's company. What would it take for another face to appear? For the masks to fall? What had Patrick done when he was here? Aimed his camera at the man, or punched him in the jaw? Accused him of exploiting people as slaves? Of killing the seventeen who had died in the hotel fire? I wondered how the guests in this place would have reacted to such a scene. Maybe they'd think a movie was being filmed, or it was some sort of bizarre art happening. After all, they were in a place where the candelabra seemed to be floating in the air.

One of the men who sat with his back to me stood up, said something to Thery, and then turned around. My heart leaped into my throat when I saw his face. I coughed and quickly turned away.

I'd met that man before. A wide face with a nose that

seemed too small, and little pig-eyes. He was the one who had thrown me out of the office on avenue Kléber. I'd assumed he was a security guard, but if he was sitting here drinking champagne, he had to be a much closer associate to Thery.

I tried to look outside, but I couldn't see the street, only the black night sky. The fabric window drapes made the outdoors seem hazy and unreal, as if it existed in a different era, in a black-and-white film.

When I dared to turn my gaze back to the bar, the man with the pig-eyes was gone. Maybe he'd gone to the men's room, or maybe he'd left for home.

I realized this was my best chance, so I slid off the bar stool and, on trembling legs, headed for Alain Thery's party. Two more women had joined the group. They wore black-and-white dresses with bold graphic patterns and big, chunky jewellery. Maybe they were actresses, since Caroline Kearny had said Thery had a weakness for actresses. I thought of the picture of Juliette Binoche, and decided that these two bore no resemblance to her whatever.

Thery had removed his hand from the thigh of the blonde, and was pouring champagne into the glass of one of the black-and-white-clad girls. The champagne bubbled and sparkled. He didn't notice as I stepped close.

'Oh, Alain! How nice to see you,' I said loudly.

He looked up with an enquiring expression.

'I'm afraid you have me at a disadvantage,' he said with a wan smile. Nice white teeth, a slightly shrill voice.

'It was in Saint-Tropez. Don't you remember?' I said, slipping onto the chair next to him.

'No, but I meet a lot of people.' He smiled at the girl on his right. 'I have a yacht down there, you know. A sixty-nine-foot sloop.'

I reached out to nudge his knee with my hand.

'But you really must tell me about our mutual friend. How is he? I heard that you met here in Paris.'

Thery laughed and glanced impatiently at the other women. One of them gave a big sigh.

'Who do you mean?' he said.

'Patrick Cornwall, of course. The journalist.'

Thery's whole body tensed. I could feel the vibrations as his muscles tightened. He pushed the blonde away. 'I don't know what you're talking about.'

'I'm talking about Patrick Cornwall,' I said loudly, so everyone in his party would hear me. 'He was supposed to interview you about your companies, and now he's missing. Where is he?'

'How would I know? I have no idea who you're talking about.'

He motioned to the man sitting across from him. I refused to look away from Thery's pale eyes. I had my gaze fixed on him.

'He knew too much about you and your companies. Was that it? What have you done with him?'

Thery stood up.

'This bitch is crazy. Can someone get her out of here?' He looked in all directions, signalling to the men sitting nearby.

'Throw out this crazy whore. She's drunk.'

The next second strong hands lifted me up, locking around my arms and gripping the back of my neck.

'I know what you're doing,' I screamed, kicking my feet and sending two champagne glasses flying off the table. The girls on the sofa threw themselves aside to avoid getting drenched with the bubbly.

'She's fucking out of her mind,' one of them said in French. 'Do they let in just anybody these days?'

'Which of your men killed Salif?' I shouted as they

dragged me away. Out of the corner of my eye I noticed that one of the men strong-arming me was the same guy who'd thrown me out before. He narrowed his pig-eyes and snarled in French in my ear: 'I remember you, you little bitch.'

The last thing I saw was Alain Thery putting his arm around the girl sitting next to him on the sofa as they merged with the picture of the full rigger. His icy-grey eyes were fixed on me as I was hauled out of the room.

Chapter 10

Paris
Monday, 29 September

Fourteen metres away a beat-up old Peugeot was parked on the street. I recognized it at once the minute I came out of the hotel. A woman sat in the driver's seat, staring at me.

I went closer, my heart pounding.

Soon Olivier, the hotel clerk, would come out. He'd promised to accompany me to the police station to file a proper report. Sarah Rachid was right, I thought. Society is based on the judicial system, and if we don't put our trust in the law, then everything will fall apart.

I took the last few steps over to the car and leaned down to the window. Again I noticed the rust on the wheel rims and the door handle, which was slightly crooked.

Slowly, she rolled down the window. The woman was truly beautiful. Finely etched features and short dark hair. There was no doubt that she was the one who had come to get Patrick at the hotel. *She was the kind of woman that a man would notice*. She was elegantly attired in a blue coat, and she looked out of place inside that old car.

'Who are you?' I asked.

The time for polite phrases was definitely over.

'Get in.' She motioned towards the passenger seat.

'Not on your life,' I said. If she was somehow mixed up in what they'd done to Salif, I had no intention of going anywhere with her in a car.

She seemed to hesitate for a few seconds. Then she opened the door and got out. We stood on either side of the vehicle. Both of us the same height.

'Alena Cornwall,' she said with an indifferent tone of voice, giving the impression her words meant nothing at all. 'Married to Patrick Cornwall. Why didn't you say that right from the start?'

'And what's your name?'

No answer. We eyed each other, then glanced at the surrounding area, both of us waiting. How does she know that? I thought. Where has she been hiding to find out who I am and what I've been doing?

'I'd like to propose an exchange,' she said now.

'Meaning what?'

'We can talk on the way,' she said, and started walking. We passed Olivier, who had come out of the hotel. I murmured to him that I'd be right back. He pointed at the woman and gave me a meaningful look.

It's her.

Thanks, I'd already realized that.

I hurried to catch up.

'Do you know where Patrick is?' I asked.

The woman glanced at me, her expression devoid of all emotion.

'You should have gone back home to New York,' she said.

'I don't give a shit who you are,' I said. 'I just want to know what's happened to him.'

'You can call me Nedjma,' she said.

I stopped abruptly. I'd heard that name before. It took a few seconds before I remembered the connection. Sarah Rachid had mentioned Nedjma the night before. The woman Arnaud was seeing. A garbage truck braked, and the rattling of metal cans reverberated between the brick walls. My head was spinning. Had Arnaud told her everything? Why did she want me to leave Paris? What did she have to do with Josef K?

I saw her blue coat turn at the street corner, and I had to jog to keep her in sight as the crowds swelled.

'So it was Arnaud Rachid who told you about me.' I was breathing hard as I caught up with her at the intersection.

Nedjma gave me a crooked smile.

'Arnaud is naïve,' she said, crossing the street. 'He thinks that everything will be fine as long as you're nice to other people.'

'Whose side are you on, anyway?' I asked.

She didn't answer as she headed towards a park at the end of the street. People passed by me. Faces that were only a blur. I had to step aside to avoid running into a baby buggy. *If there's no baby in the buggy, what could there be?* That's what I used to think about. A doll? A puppy? Explosives?

'Why did you want me to go back to New York?' I asked.

'It was for your own good.' She walked through the tall gates, and the park closed around us with its lush vegetation. The leaves were turning yellow on the edges. There were statues among the trees. Nedjma stopped and looked at me.

'It was Patrick who contacted me. One day he phoned and wanted to talk about Josef K. Where did he get my number?'

'Why don't you ask him yourself?'

211

'Cornwall refused to divulge his source. But you're not a journalist, even though that's what you're pretending to be.'

I was thinking frantically. If the purse vendor ended up getting in hot water, that really wasn't my problem.

'A guy named Luc who sells purses at the market in Saint-Ouen,' I told her. 'He was paid to give Patrick the number.'

'*Merde*,' she said. She frowned and stared at the trees for a moment.

'It must have been a trap,' she said at last.

'What do you mean?'

'Let's sit down over there.' She pointed to chairs near a big pond where colourful little sailboats were bobbing in the water.

'What do you know about Josef K?' asked Nedjma, sitting down on one of the rickety chairs.

I sat down next to her.

'He's a human trafficker from the east,' I said. 'Apparently he decided to jump ship, and now he's hiding from his old cohorts.'

'Everybody has a weak spot,' said Nedjma, staring at some children using sticks to steer their toy boats. 'Josef K had a god-daughter who meant everything to him. She was his princess. Then she grew up and became a big girl. A year ago she travelled to the west to become a model, but she disappeared.'

I studied her profile as she told me how Josef K had gone mad with worry. He'd searched for the girl for months, in Amsterdam, London, Paris. All over Europe. Finally he'd discovered that his own network had lured her away.

'Not anyone who was close to him, of course. It was a branch that was operating alongside his own, using Bratislava as its base. That's how these kinds of organiza-

212

tions function. Like a bunch of islands that appear to be independent.'

Nedjma picked up a stick that one of the kids had left behind and drew a picture in the sand. A group of islands separated from each other.

'If the police seize one of them, the others aren't at risk. This group had no idea they'd sold the god-daughter of one of the bosses to a bordello in Cologne.'

'So that's when he suddenly became a good boy?' I said. 'He wanted to speak out in the press and be forgiven, or what?'

Nedjma gave me an annoyed look.

'Two human traffickers from Bratislava died a short time later, killed in an especially vicious way. Then Josef K went to the top boss and threatened to expose the whole operation if he wasn't given his god-daughter back.'

'And who is the top boss?'

She turned to look in all directions before answering.

'His name is Alain Thery,' she said in a low voice. 'A Frenchman who runs a successful consulting business, but it's just a front. His real business is carried out in the shadows. That's where the money comes from.'

I shivered at the memory of that deserted office.

'It's the perfect cover,' said Nedjma. 'No one reacts if the consultant invoices a million a week for nothing but air.'

She paused and looked at me.

'It was actually your husband who worked out how the whole thing was organized.'

'Tell me how he did it.' A bewildering sense of joy came over me in the midst of all this. It made me happy to hear that Patrick had done a good job. That was more important to him than anything else.

Patrick had followed people, she told me. He'd gone poking around. A construction company with undocumented workers who received no wages claimed to have hired the manpower from an employment agency. Patrick threatened to go to the police, and finally forced them to show him the account books.

'Lugus,' I said.

Nedjma nodded. She pointed the stick at the middle of the circle she'd drawn.

'This is where the money is,' she said. 'Imagine the profits from thousands of people working day after day, year after year, if you don't have to pay any wages or insurance.'

It struck me that the drawing in the sand looked like a flow chart for any modern enterprise. I recalled Patrick's articles about the new economy. It was the same structure, or lack of structure, that he had outlined. Companies were broken up and arranged around smaller islands, organized as project groups or normal small businesses. By all appearances they were free and independent entities, but they were actually governed from the centre by a new form of iron fist. Assignments were handed out with clear directives. Any group that didn't live up to the demands and deliver was simply cut away. None was irreplaceable.

'Human trafficking is an attractive type of crime,' said Nedjma, 'because it's so profitable, and is almost risk-free. There are always people looking for work at any price. The higher the walls are built, the greater the chance they'll keep quiet. Everyone wants cheap labour, but nobody wants to know where it comes from. And the traffickers never get caught because they have friends everywhere. Influential friends.'

'Guy de Barreau,' I said.

She nodded. 'Patrick suspected that Alain Thery is among those who finance his organization.' She fixed her gaze on an older couple doing t'ai chi together, moving in unison in a soundless dance.

She ran her boot over the circle she'd drawn, rubbing it out.

'Give me what Patrick sent you,' she said. 'We had a deal.'

'Only if you tell me where he went.'

Nedjma held out her hand. I took the notebook out of my bag. And the envelope with the photographs. Silently she looked through the material.

'Is this all?' she said. And then came the words that made everything stand still. 'Didn't he send you anything from Lisbon?'

Slowly I turned towards her. Lisbon? Had Patrick gone to Lisbon? Tears welled up in my eyes. Why hadn't anyone told me about that? Here I'd been, searching and searching all over Paris, and almost a whole week had passed.

'He went to Lisbon?' When I finally managed to speak, anger surged inside me, and I gave her a withering glare. Back in high school I'd learned how to reduce people like her to pulp with one look. 'And all of you have known this the whole time? You fucking bastards! Why the hell couldn't your lover-boy have given me a heads-up?'

She merely raised an eyebrow.

'Arnaud wasn't aware of this information,' she said.

'Oh. Right. In that case, at least *he* was telling the truth.'

Nedjma tossed the notebook back to me.

'I have no use for that,' she said, and then continued to study the photos of Alain Thery with Guy de Barreau. 'But I'm going to keep these,' she said, stuffing the pictures into her coat pocket.

'Tell me about Lisbon,' I said, swallowing hard.

She got out a little silver case and shook out a cigarette.

'That's where we hid Josef K. His network has no connections in that city.' She lit her cigarette and blew smoke up into the air. 'In the past Josef K was a meticulous KGB agent, and he continued to document everything — transactions, names, addresses. He'd kept records on all his friends, down to the smallest detail.'

'So Patrick went to Lisbon to interview him?'

Nedjma nodded.

It was true that Patrick had phoned her on Monday, two weeks ago. From Arnaud she knew that he was a journalist. She and Arnaud had known each other for a long time, but politically they'd gone in different directions. Arnaud wanted to help people as best he could, but Nedjma talked about blowing up the system from the inside. That was where Josef K came into the picture — and Patrick.

They had reached an agreement.

Patrick would get an exclusive interview. In return, he would compile Josef K's testimony and make the documents public. When everything was ready, Josef K would be given a ticket to Brazil. Together with Patrick's photographs and Salif's testimony, a magnificent info bomb would be detonated inside the judicial system and the media, blowing the network apart and causing so much damage to the political powers that change would be possible.

Her eyes blazed as she talked about explosions that would reverberate even inside the European parliament.

'So where is Patrick now?'

'I don't know,' said Nedjma, looking away. 'I haven't heard from him since he left.'

I froze.

'But that was two weeks ago,' I said. 'Something must have happened. Surely you can see that.'

Nedjma tossed away her cigarette butt. It lay smouldering in the sand.

'Tell me what the hell happened in Lisbon!' I cried. A little boy standing near the pond looked up in fright. His sailboat scudded away, out of control.

'We don't know,' said Nedjma. 'We don't know what happened in Lisbon.'

I stared at her.

'But at least you must be in contact with your wonderful defector. Is he still there?'

'Josef K is dead,' said Nedjma.

'What?' Something began wailing inside my head, a siren coming out of nowhere. 'When? How did he die?'

'Wednesday, two weeks ago,' she said. 'He fell from the terrace of a viewpoint. The police think it was suicide.' She raised her eyebrows to show what she thought of that theory. I looked at her in confusion, unable to say a word. That was the day after Patrick had gone to Lisbon.

'His old friends must have found out I was hiding him,' said Nedjma. 'And then they passed on the information to Patrick, so he'd lead them to Josef K. They probably counted on the fact that I'd trust an American journalist.' She got up, took a good look around, and then started walking, heading for the railings that surrounded the park. 'I haven't heard from him since he left Paris. Cornwall knew what he was getting into. He went there of his own free will.'

I strode to catch up and reached out to grab her coat. 'And you just decided to forget all about him? Is that it, you bitch?'

'So you've lost your husband,' she said quietly. 'People die every day in this business, and yet it's only your loss that matters. Why is that? Because you're a better person?'

She removed my hands from her coat.

'Don't you want to know what happened to the princess? He finally got her back. Two months later. In a coffin.'

I shivered and pulled my jacket closer around me.

'I need to go to Lisbon,' I said.

'You're booked on the morning flight, leaving at 6.25 from Charles de Gaulle,' she said. 'Someone will leave an

217

envelope with your itinerary at the front desk of your hotel. You have a reservation at the same hotel in Lisbon where Cornwall stayed.' She leaned closer. 'There's also a poste restante address you can use for sending the documents, if you find them. I assume that you will honour the agreement.'

Then she turned on her heel and walked away. A patch of blue that swiftly disappeared among the trees.

'Wait!' I shouted. 'We don't have an agreement, damn it!'

I ran after her and saw her go down some steps near a café. The sign said the stairs led to public toilets.

It was surprisingly neat and clean down there, with potted flowers set along the stairs. I waited five minutes, but Nedjma didn't come out, so I went over to the woman attendant who sat outside the doors. She was small and plump, with a black scarf wrapped around her head and a bowl of coins in front of her.

I dredged my memory for the words and finally managed to put together a sentence in French.

'Excuse me. I'm looking for a woman in a blue coat. Is she inside?' *Excuse-moi je cherche une femme . . .*

The toilet attendant shrugged. I placed a two-euro coin in the bowl and repeated my question.

No answer.

'Is there another exit?' I asked. *Une autre sortie?*

The woman shook her head.

'Not understand French,' she said.

The police tape was gone and everything seemed to have returned to normal outside the entrance on rue Charlot.

Not a trace of the man who had lain there in the morning, dead and abused. I wondered whether Salif's family would ever find out what had happened to him, whether he'd be identified.

Arnaud Rachid opened the door. I had phoned to say I was on my way over, so he was prepared.

'She told me not to say anything. What could I do? It was out of my control.'

I looked daggers at him and then went up the stairs with Arnaud contritely slinking behind me.

The receipt for my electronic plane ticket had been waiting for me at the front desk, as promised, along with the confirmation of my hotel reservation for two nights. Coming to see Arnaud was the last thing I wanted to take care of before leaving Paris for good.

'And by the way, you could have told me that you're married to Patrick Cornwall. How was I supposed to guess that?'

I stopped on the landing and turned to face him.

'You could have told me that it was your girlfriend who lured him to Lisbon.'

'She's not my girlfriend,' said Arnaud.

Once we reached the cluttered office area, he sank down onto his desk chair.

'And I didn't know he'd gone to Lisbon.' He ran his hands through his hair. 'She doesn't tell me everything. I've told her I don't want to know.'

'So who is she, really?' I asked.

Arnaud smiled, though a shadow passed over his face.

'A woman who is loved by many men, but none of them can have her,' he said slowly. 'She comes and goes, like the seasons of the year.'

'Spare me the poetry,' I said.

'It's a quote from *Nedjma*, a great Algerian novel. Nedjma is the heroine, but the name is also symbolic. It means "star".'

I perched on the edge of his desk, pushing aside a stack of newspapers, which crashed to the floor. I didn't care.

'So she's from Algeria too?'

'No, no. That's just the name she chose. An alias.' Arnaud fidgeted with a pen, tapping it on the desk. 'She grew up in Neuilly-sur-Seine. Do you know it? The former president lives there.' He smiled. 'But unlike him, Nedjma has graduated from Sciences-Po. Her father forced her to attend, and she says the only thing she learned was to hate everything that world stands for.'

'What's her real name?'

'It's better if you don't know. She has cut all ties. She never uses her real name. Lately she's gone underground. I don't even know where she's living any more.'

'Because of what happened in Lisbon?' I asked.

'The only thing I know is that she was hiding Josef K, and now he's dead. Somebody leaked information about her.' Arnaud looked around, his expression nervous and desperate. He lowered his voice. 'It's the same people who got Salif. They'll come and get her in the end too.'

'How do you know she's not playing both sides with you?'

'I don't agree with all of her methods, but I know who she is when no one is looking, when it's just her . . .' He met my eye. 'She's the most honest person I've ever met.'

'Was she the one you were with on the night of the fire?'

Arnaud looked unhappy. I wondered if it tormented him because he was in the wrong place that night, or whether what pained him most was loving a woman like Nedjma.

'Being with her,' he said, 'is like hovering on the border between heaven and hell. It's a place that most people will never know.'

I felt a burning in my chest. I looked away. I didn't want to hear any more about his love life, or about anyone's damned love life. All of a sudden it occurred to me that

220

the place where Sylvie usually sat was empty. Maybe she wasn't feeling so involved any more. She'd probably given up on Arnaud. There was obviously too much competition for his affections.

'So where's your other admirer?' I asked. 'I thought she was always hanging around here.'

'You mean Sylvie? I don't know. I haven't seen her since yesterday morning.'

We both fell silent, his words hanging in the air.

Yesterday morning. That was when he found Salif dead on the steps of the building.

But it wasn't Salif that I pictured in my mind right now. It was Sylvie. And an idea was slowly taking shape. Something I'd missed among all the puzzle pieces floating around.

The girl with the cropped hair and torn jeans who kept on popping up wherever Arnaud was. Who was so filled with jealousy.

What the hell? Could that be the connection?

I went over to the place where she normally sat, making my way past boxes of posters and other junk. I tried to remember what she'd said. She'd talked to me about Josef K and said that Arnaud knew the young men who had died in the fire. Nothing remarkable about that, and yet my suspicions were growing.

Several flyers were scattered on the desk. There were no dirty cups or personal possessions, no photos, no letters or anything with her name. Not so much as a calendar. Arnaud had said she was new to the struggle. I picked up a stack of newspapers and the usual books: Che Guevara and Malcolm X.

'What are you doing?' asked Arnaud from his desk. I glanced up and noted that from here I could see everything he did. It was also easy to hear whatever he said, even if he wasn't speaking very loudly. Further away a guy with a ponytail was playing a computer game. The space and the brick walls amplified every sound.

'What do you really know about Sylvie?' I pulled out the desk drawers. They were empty.

'I think she got scared by what happened to Salif,' said Arnaud. 'Otherwise she's always here.'

'Or else she felt she'd completed her assignment,' I said.

'Not a chance,' he said. 'It's going to take generations before the world is a just place and every human life has value.'

I went back and perched on his desk again. I remembered how she'd sneaked up behind my back when we were talking about Josef K.

'Do you know who she is? Where she lives? What she did before she came here?'

'What are you getting at? We don't actually check up on people who work here.' His voice took on a harder edge. 'We're fucking grateful for all the idealists we can find.'

'In other words, it would be very easy to plant somebody here,' I said quietly. 'If someone wanted to know what you're doing. Who you're hiding and where they are, for instance.'

'What do you mean?' He reached up to touch his scarf, unwinding it and then wrapping it around his neck again as he stared at me. 'Sylvie is a little annoying, but you're crazy if you're accusing her of—'

I interrupted him. 'How did they find out where Salif was staying?' I asked. 'Who leaked the information that Nedjma was hiding Josef K?'

'You can't be serious.' He stood up so fast that his chair rolled back and rammed into the wall. He went over to Sylvie's workstation and began tearing open desk drawers, turning over piles of newspapers. He stopped and looked at me, a hint of desperation in his eyes. 'Shit. I thought she was just—'

'In love with you?' I said. 'Well, one doesn't necessarily exclude the other.'

Arnaud ran his hand through his hair, looking unhappy. I glanced at my watch. There was still plenty of time before I had to go out to the airport.

'Did you tell her that Salif was alive?'

He shook his head.

One by one the puzzle pieces fell into place.

'Maybe they *did* think he was dead. Until the other day when I phoned you and demanded to know what had happened,' I said. 'Sylvie was eavesdropping, of course, and even if you didn't spell it out for her, she realized it had something to do with Salif.'

Arnaud sank back onto his chair.

'And then they managed to track him down,' he said. His face seemed to collapse, losing all force. 'I don't remember what I said to her. We'd always talk—'

'Do you think you might have mentioned that Nedjma was hiding Josef K?'

'I don't know,' said Arnaud, his voice on the verge of breaking. 'Maybe. Not specifically. I can't remember.' He buried his face in his hands, and I could hear the instant he recalled something. He began groaning, and I turned away, not wanting to see him fall apart.

'No,' he whimpered. 'No, no . . .'

It took several minutes before he managed to say anything coherent.

'She helped me take food over there,' he stammered. 'Sylvie knew I was hiding them at the hotel.'

'But there's one thing she didn't know,' I said. 'She couldn't have known where Josef K was hiding, because Nedjma hadn't told you. Right?'

He didn't look up. He was lost in his own feelings of guilt and regret. It didn't matter. I could figure out the rest for myself.

They had used Patrick to find Josef K. Paid off a guy at the market who then put him on the trail. Like buying purses, I thought. Everything can be bought.

But that wasn't true. Patrick had never allowed himself to be bought. Nor had they managed to scare him off. He'd kept on pestering Alain Thery, like an annoying fly that refuses to leave. He wasn't about to let them get away.

A French phrase popped into my head.

Faire d'une pierre deux coups. I was forced to grab hold of the banister when I stepped into the gloom of the stairwell. Another variant of the phrase was 'to kill two flies with one blow'. The saying existed in different forms in different languages, but they all meant the same thing. Two for the price of one.

Josef K, who was going to testify against his old cohorts.

Patrick, who was going to expose them in his report, who knew too much.

Daylight washed over me when I came out into the courtyard. A wave of sunshine. And I remembered that I'd seen a version of that phrase somewhere, in both English and French. On the Lugus website. *To kill two birds with one stone is our motto in all situations.*

Without thinking I ran out to the street and then along the much busier rue Bretagne, where I could easily find a cab.

As if there were some faster way for me to get to Lisbon.

Chapter 11

Tarifa
Monday, 29 September

They were playing reggae music in the Blue Heaven Bar, just like they'd done on that night.

Terese heard the music as she came around the corner and saw the sign further down in the narrow lane. Her skin felt hot from the sun and the anticipation. Her whole body was on fire at the thought that he might be there.

Dear God, let him please be there tonight.

It was her last night in Tarifa. Tomorrow they would go back home to Stockholm, and she'd never see him again. Alex from Ipswich.

If only she'd have a chance to see him one more time.

She stumbled and had to pay attention in order not to fall on the cobblestones. Her new shoes had high heels. They were a present from her father. Bought during one of their excursions, in a big department store in Puerto Banus, along with the yellow dress that made her look so slim and showed off her suntan. The whole outfit had cost 140 euros, but that was nothing compared to what clothes cost in the shops down by the harbour. Donna Karan and Versace. She'd never in her life seen so much luxury. And her father wanted her to have something nice. He would do anything to make her happy.

Terese felt almost beautiful as she stepped inside the Blue Heaven Bar. The place was cramped and hot, just as she remembered, and it smelled of pizza and suntan lotion and smoke. A faint scent of hash wafted towards her from one corner.

She stopped just inside the door, swaying a bit to the music and trying for a casual look. The bar in the middle of the room was packed with surfer dudes in baggy shorts or cut-off jeans, and girls wearing loose trousers and tops that left their midriffs bare. A few had on long skirts and rings in their navels. A bleached-blonde waitress with a lizard tattooed on her shoulder swept past, carrying a tray of red and turquoise cocktails. Terese craned her neck to look at the sofas in the far corner.

She didn't see him anywhere.

'Could I have a beer, please,' she said to the waitress behind the bar who had beads plaited into her hair. Her fringe was cut at a sharp angle.

The first few days after that horrible experience, all Terese had wanted to do was hide, to disappear from the face of the earth. Do as her mother had told her on the phone: get on the first plane back to Sweden, crawl into her old bed at home, have a good cry, and drink hot cocoa. But her father didn't think that was a good way to cope with a crisis, as he'd said.

Running away was not the solution. The world was a cruel place, but life had to go on. So he rented a car and took her out on excursions. They'd driven to Gibraltar, and to an old town way up in the mountains called Ronda. At night she'd cried a lot and thought about the two men:

Alex who had left her on the beach, and the dead man in the water. In her dreams they would sometimes merge into one and the same person.

The past few days she had started thinking that the whole thing with Alex was a misunderstanding. There could be all sorts of explanations for what had happened. For instance, maybe Alex had woken up in the night and felt ill, and he didn't want her to see him throwing up. Maybe he'd been so drunk that he couldn't remember what he'd done. Or he had another girlfriend, and felt guilty because he'd taken up with Terese before ending the other relationship.

The past few nights she'd fantasized that he was looking for her. He didn't have her phone number, nor did he know where she was staying, or even what her last name was. So night after night he went to the Blue Heaven, hoping to find her there.

Terese leaned her back against the bar and looked up at the TV screens hanging from the ceiling. They were showing films from beaches around the world — kitesurfers and windsurfers and ordinary surfers who were all world-class champions, riding the waves and flying through the air. It made her feel motion-sick. The waitress brought her beer. It was easier to stand there when she had something in her hand. She remembered that Alex had been drinking beer that night.

She'd felt a fluttering in her stomach and heat flooding through her body when he'd leaned towards her. They had been standing in exactly this spot. Alex from Ipswich. With tousled hair. Worldly and suntanned.

'Once you've experienced being lifted up by the wind, you'll never want to come down to earth again,' he'd said. 'Out there it's just you and the sea and the winds. No thoughts at all. You have to try it, Tess. It's total freedom. Can I call you Tess?'

She pictured his eyes. They were neither blue nor green. Like the sea, she'd thought. He was like the sea. So free. All summer long he'd hung about Tarifa and gone kite-surfing.

'In the winter I always go to Australia. I follow the winds. It's a whole lifestyle. But not to Sydney. The west coast, outside Perth. That's where the best winds are.'

'Ipswips,' she'd slurred later as they were sitting on one of the low sofas against the wall. She was very drunk by then. 'Isn't that where the serial killer was from?'

'Don't worry. It's not me,' Alex said, pretending to strangle her, but then leaving his hand on the back of her neck. Caressing her skin. She shivered at the memory. She felt a warm throbbing between her legs.

'Did you know the aboriginals never worked more than four hours a day?' he'd said, a big smile lighting up his face. His eyes sparkled. 'Then they'd sing and fuck and tell stories. And you know why?'

'No,' said Terese, feeling stupid. She had just told him she wanted to be a hair stylist. How ordinary and boring.

'Nobody ever told them they needed to have a house and two cars,' said Alex, leaning closer, whispering into her ear. 'And because it's more fun to do it under the stars.'

Now she sipped her beer, keeping her eyes fixed on the door so as not to miss him. A new bunch of people came in. Terese sucked in her stomach, tensing her abdominal muscles to make it look flatter. But he wasn't among them. She exhaled. Two Swedish girls had taken up position right next to her. One of them was wearing bright green harem trousers and a ring in her lip. The Blue Heaven Bar was filled with those sorts of supremely confident girls. 'And so they wash up onto the beaches, right in the middle of the charter tourist season. Isn't that awful? But everyone just

228

closes their eyes.' The bartender brought the girls their drinks. 'I didn't know they'd started bringing in charters here,' said the girl with the lip ring. 'I think we should go to Portugal tomorrow. This place is getting too overrun.' Her friend nodded. 'North of Lisbon there are still some genuine villages left.'

Terese headed for the toilet. She'd felt an urge to tell them that she was the one who had found the dead man on the beach, but she didn't want to risk standing next to two Swedish girls who were prettier than she was.

Just as she was passing the entrance, Alex came in. At precisely that moment. Terese quickly stepped away so she was hidden behind a pillar. He had on cotton trousers with the cuffs rolled up, a rope for a belt, and a turquoise T-shirt. Her heart was pounding. He was just as good-looking as she'd remembered. He paused at one of the tables to talk to a couple of guys. The waitress with the lizard tattoo walked past. Alex gave her a kiss on the forehead and ordered something. For a second Terese panicked. Maybe he'd found somebody new. She shouldn't have waited so long to come back here.

Terese was looking at his hair from the back, and her hands remembered what it felt like to touch his coarse locks, to grab his hair with her fists when he gave her the first real kiss, in a doorway along the main road in the middle of the night after the others had gone inside the Vampire.

It had meant something. It had to mean something.

She wondered what would be best. To go over to the bar and pretend to catch sight of him as she walked past, or to slip out from behind the pillar and let him see her first. At that instant he turned around. Terese pulled in her stomach and smiled, raising her glass of beer to him. Alex barely glanced at her. He turned back to his friend and said something. Terese felt her face flush. Her hand was shaking so hard that it made the beer slosh in her glass. Then he came over to her, grabbing a glass of beer from the lizard girl's tray in passing.

'Hi,' he said. 'So you're still here?'

'I leave tomorrow,' said Terese.

'Then it's your last night to party.' Alex laughed and tossed his head. There was something about guys with tousled hair. She always fell for them.

Terese pressed her glass against her chest to stop her hand from shaking. And so he'd notice her breasts.

'What about you?' she said lightly. 'When do you leave for Australia?'

'Soon. Unless the wind changes. This bloody *poniente* has been lingering for weeks now.' He shifted from one foot to the other. Terese realized that her presence was making him nervous.

'I'm getting tired of waiting for the *levante*,' he said, glancing around.

'Sure. Of course,' said Terese. 'It's been blowing really hard.'

He rolled his eyes and laughed a bit, glancing at someone standing nearby.

'What I mean,' he said, 'is that the *poniente* just blows inland, coming straight from the west, with the Atlantic at its back. It brings big waves with it, but it lacks finesse. The *levante* is a whole different story.'

He took a swig of beer, his gaze roaming. Several other people were listening.

'What we need is a high pressure area from Africa. When it collides with the low pressure over Andalusia, strong air currents are created that push down through the straits of Gibraltar and generate big waves that are higher than anywhere else.' He used his hands to demonstrate the high pressure and low pressure flying through the air and being forced through the straits. 'The *levante* is said to drive people mad.'

'Oh, come on,' said the guy standing next to him. 'That's only a myth.'

'Haven't you ever felt it? That dry, hot wind? It does something to people when it stays around for week after week, sometimes even for months during the summer. People kill themselves. More people commit suicide here on the Costa de la Luz than anywhere else in Spain. The number of schizophrenics is abnormally high in Tarifa. It's the *levante* that does it. It pushes people over the edge.'

Alex craned his neck and waved to someone standing behind Terese. She turned around. A bunch of people were sitting on the sofas.

'Are those your friends?' she asked.

'I know almost everybody here,' said Alex, raising his glass to them and signalling that he'd be right over.

'I found a dead man on the beach,' said Terese.

Alex turned to look at her again. 'What do you mean?' he said.

'That night. You know.'

'What night? Oh, right! You mean when you and I . . . ?'

'Uh-huh.'

'When was that, exactly?' He glanced up at the TV screen where a surfer did a triple somersault and landed on his board at the very top of the giant wave. 'I mean, I don't really know what happened. I was really loaded that night.'

'I know,' said Terese. She saw the colour shift in his gleaming eyes. Eyes she could drown in. He laughed.

'I hope I wasn't too drunk to . . .' He wiggled his hand.

'Not at all.' Terese leaned forward and ran her fingers lightly over his hip. 'It was great.'

Alex took a long swig of his beer and took a step back, leaving her hand dangling in the air.

'So what about this dead man?' he said. 'Don't tell me it was that same bloody night. I heard they'd found one. Was that you?'

Terese nodded. 'It was horrible. He was lying in the water. I was just going over to rinse off my face.'

'Oh, Christ. Jesus H Christ.'

He turned towards a guy who was standing a few metres behind Terese and raised his voice. 'Hey, Ben, did you hear that? This girl was the one who found him. That dead migrant in the water last week.'

Terese noticed how everyone's attention shifted to her. Faces turned to look at her, questions tumbled through the air and washed over her.

My, God. You poor thing. Wasn't it horrid? What did he look like? Where on the beach? Weren't you scared? I can't understand why they don't do something about it. What do you mean? The authorities. The EU. Those people just want what we have. And why shouldn't they be entitled to the same things? The borders are just something the politicians have made up. In the past people were free to come across from Morocco, but when Spain joined the EU, an iron curtain came down. Bam. I think everybody should be allowed to go wherever they want, and live wherever they want. But that would never work. But we do. We live here. You can't compare that with the fact that half of Africa wants to come here. I think we need to help them before they come here. Combat poverty. Then they won't have to leave. But people want to leave.

In the smoky haze she saw Alex slip away, going over to join the cool surfers and the backpackers at the table where his friends were sitting. He doesn't remember my name, she thought.

She downed the rest of her beer and set the glass down. Then she quietly followed him, her mouth dry, her heart pounding. They had kissed each other, they'd made love with each other. Surely they should be able to talk to each other.

Alex was sitting on a leather ottoman with his back turned, carrying on a lively conversation with one of the girls on the sofa. He had stretched out his long legs towards her, crossing his bare ankles. He was wearing canvas sneakers, with a silver chain around one ankle.

Terese touched his shoulder. He turned around.

'Could we go outside for a moment?' said Terese.

'Why?' Alex cast a glance at the girl, whose feet were close to his own. She was wearing tight cut-offs and had a gemstone in her navel.

'I need to talk to you,' said Terese.

Alex fidgeted with his glass. He leaned forward to say something to the girl. She looked up at Terese. 'Is that true? How awful! I would have died if I'd been the one to find him.'

Alex set down his glass and got up. He pushed Terese ahead of him towards the entrance.

'You're not going to make a scene, are you?' he said, once they'd come outside into the lane. He took her by the arm and drew her away from the door. 'We had fun that night, but that's all. Just think of it as a holiday fling.' He let go of her and leaned back against the wall, fishing a crumpled cigarette out of his T-shirt pocket.

Terese rubbed her upper arm where he'd grabbed her.

'You said you didn't remember anything,' she said.

'You were bloody terrific.' He plucked a shred of tobacco off his tongue. 'But that doesn't mean I'm in love with you.'

She swallowed hard and felt the chill of the night air on

233

her bare arms. She was freezing. Alex turned to look up the lane, taking a deep drag on his cigarette. He blew out the smoke, which quickly dispersed in the wind.

'I'm sorry about the dead guy. I really am. If I'd known that—'

'You wouldn't have left me there?'

He bent down to scratch his ankle. Terese stared at the silver chain he wore.

'My passport disappeared that night,' she said. 'Do you think somebody might have swiped it?'

'How would I know?'

'You were there.'

'What's the problem? You don't need a passport to go back home to Sweden. Not when you're a citizen of an EU country. Haven't you ever heard of the Schengen agreement?'

Terese stared at him, his parted lips, his crooked teeth. The words spilling out.

'Did you take it?' she said, fixing her eyes on the street. She waited for him to say no. She scraped the tip of her white shoe on a piece of gum stuck to the cobblestones.

Alex gave a little laugh. 'Relax. You can get a new passport when you're back home. You might even be able to get one here. They probably have a consulate in both Málaga and Seville.'

'Did you take my money too?' Terese stared at him, backing up until she could feel the wall behind her. 'Why did you do it? Did you go through my bag after I fell asleep? And here I'd just . . .' She pressed her hand to her mouth. Sobs were welling up inside her, and she had started shaking all over.

Now was the moment when he would put his arms around her and say it wasn't true.

'Hey, come on.' He ground out his cigarette butt with

his foot and then gave it a kick to send it flying into the gutter. 'How much was it, anyway? Twenty or thirty euros? You said you were here with your father. I'm sure he can give you more cash.' His turquoise T-shirt slid up as he scratched his stomach. He glanced in both directions, then leaned in close. 'Don't go running off blabbing about this. If you do, people are going to hear plenty about you too.' Behind him the lights in the bar dimmed and the reggae music stopped. Electronic techno rhythms started up, throbbing club music. A few people were already dancing.

'But that was my passport.' Terese forced herself to say the words. 'What were you going to do with it? And that was my money. Did you take my shoes too?'

'Quit your blubbering.' His face came closer. 'Do you know how many people need passports around here? People who are desperate to get hold of one? They can't go running to their daddy or to the consulate to ask for a passport. You're acting like a spoiled brat. You're so typically middle-class, so fucking narrow-minded and stingy. It doesn't even mean anything to you.'

'Did you give my passport to somebody else? That's illegal.'

Alex whooped with laughter. 'Sure, honey, but I didn't just give it away. If I did that, I'd never get to Australia. I don't have a rich father paying my way.'

He took two steps towards her, and she felt him grab the back of her neck. His lips close to her ear. 'Don't run home and tell Daddy about this or I'll tell the cops how you screamed for more. And how you paid me to do it over and over again.'

He's going to hit me, she thought, shrinking back. I don't want him to hit me.

'You got what you wanted,' he said, and pushed her away.

Just before he re-entered the bar, he turned to look over his shoulder. Terese was still standing against the wall on the other side of the lane, shaking all over.

'You're off your rocker,' said Alex, laughing loudly. 'Why the hell would I take your shoes?'

Chapter 12

Lisbon
Tuesday, 30 September

Seeing Lisbon in the pale morning light was like meeting a drunken old whore who'd been at it for far too long. Tiles had slid off the facades in places, windows gaped blankly, and electric wires dangled from the buildings. A faded beauty, enticing, with a scent of something sweet and long gone.

I had gone into the hotel, only to turn around and leave. The woman at the reception desk shook her head when I asked about Patrick. She referred me to the hotel manager, who was not in at the moment.

I went down the hill to Avenida da Liberdade, the fashionable street in the centre of town. The sidewalk rippled under my feet as I walked, as if the ground had buckled in protest when the pavement was laid. A burned smell wafted towards me on the smoke rising up from the little stalls selling roasted chestnuts.

This time I wasn't going to wait to notify the police. I was not going to vacillate or postpone or take Patrick's views into consideration. Josef K had plunged off a view-point terrace. Even if the police believed it was suicide, they must have conducted an investigation.

'I have information about a murder,' I said when it was my turn to speak to the receptionist at police headquarters. 'It's about a man from Ukraine who was killed two weeks ago, here in Lisbon.'

The receptionist raised her eyebrows and asked me a few routine questions, including my name and address. Then she picked up the phone, and seven minutes later a uniformed officer came to get me. He ushered me along five corridors, zigzagging through the building until I finally found myself three floors up in the opposite wing, with a view of the Tejo river.

The sign on the door said: Inspector Helder Ferreira. The man who received me was in his forties, wearing civilian clothes. A shirt and tie, with a stomach that bulged over the waistband of his trousers.

'So you have information about the death of Mikail Yechenko?' he said. He spoke excellent English and gave me a firm handshake.

'Oh, is that his name?' I replied.

The officer motioned towards a wooden chair with a leather upholstered seat and then sat down behind his desk.

'What do you know about Yechenko?' he asked.

I sat down and said, 'I know he was from Ukraine.' I had decided to tell him what I knew. It was not my problem what the evasive Nedjma might think about the matter. 'He was hiding in Lisbon because he'd defected from a criminal network that deals in human trafficking and slavery. He was preparing to be interviewed by an American journalist.'

The inspector picked up a ballpoint pen from his desk. He leaned back in his chair and tapped the pen against the palm of his hand.

'Yechenko didn't kill himself,' I said. 'He'd given up his old life. He wanted to start fresh. He was lured into a trap.'

'And how is it that you know all this?'

'It was my husband who was supposed to interview him.'

'Are you also a journalist?' he asked, pointing his pen at me.

'No, I'm not.' I looked out of the window at the ponderous stone buildings and a statue of a man on horseback, facing away from me. Off in the distance I saw the river, which was as wide as a small sea, and flowed into the Atlantic, the ocean that separated my old life from the unfamiliar surroundings where I now found myself.

'I'm a set designer,' I said. 'I create stage sets for the theatre.'

'Aha!' Inspector Ferreira gave me a big smile. 'I love the theatre. My mother was an actress.'

'What do the police know about what happened to Yechenko?' I said. 'Did you find any evidence? Were there any witnesses?'

Ferreira flicked his pen.

'We do have a suspect,' he said. 'But we haven't apprehended him yet.'

'Who is he?'

'We're looking for a black man.'

I stared at him.

'Why's that?'

He frowned and gave me a searching look. I felt my cheeks flush.

'Witnesses saw him at the scene,' said the inspector. 'Several are certain that he was the one who threw Yechenko off the terrace.'

Slowly I leaned down and opened my bag, taking out

the photograph. I met Patrick's eye before I reached out and placed the picture on the desk. Two of the corners were bent, and a big stain on the left above his chest was a reminder of that drunken night in Harry's Bar in Paris.

The inspector's expression shifted as he leaned forward to look at Patrick's face.

'Who is this?'

'Could he be the one?' I asked.

He picked up the photo, frowning.

'That's my husband,' I told him. 'Patrick Cornwall. Freelance journalist from New York.'

Ferreira studied the photo carefully, then looked at me and back at Patrick, as if comparing our faces, weighing one against the other.

'He didn't do it,' I said. 'They're after him too.'

I fixed my eyes on the inspector's face, forcing myself not to look away. A black man. Those witnesses were full of shit. They saw what they wanted to see.

But Patrick had been there. It was possible they did see him, even though they misinterpreted what he was doing. They must have misinterpreted.

Ferreira reached for his glasses and read from a document that was on his computer screen.

'Joana Rodrigues, twenty-seven years old. Sitting on the café terrace on Largo das Portas do Sol, reading a textbook.' He tapped his pen on the screen. 'She's studying psychology and often goes to a park or a café if the weather is nice. She shares a room with a classmate, but the room is cramped and there's no view, so . . .' He jumped down a few lines in the text. 'At approximately 3.10 p.m. she hears a commotion and somebody screaming, so she looks up from her book. A man is standing nearby, staring at her. She thinks he looks crazy. Here it comes.'

Ferreira peered at me over the rims of his glasses.

'The man is black,' he said.

I could feel my pulse racing. My mouth had gone dry. The inspector pushed up his glasses and continued to read: 'The black man was standing near the footbridge that leads up to the terrace look-out. The next second he was gone, according to Joana Rodrigues, psychology student.'

He leaned back, motioning towards the computer screen with his pen. 'Largo das Portas do Sol is a popular place in Alfama, filled with tourists admiring the view, with students and lovers. We have three more witnesses who claim to have seen a black man at the scene. One of them is positive that he was the person who threw Mikail Yechenko over the railing.'

'That's not true.'

I closed my eyes, then opened them again, but the nightmare was still there.

'António Nery, seventy-two years old, retired. Born and raised in Alfama, and still living there. He was out walking his dog and happened to be high up on the stairs near the look-out when Mikail Yechenko plunged twenty metres to the lane behind him. The black man then came running towards Nery, forcing him to step aside, right where his dog had . . .'

I got up abruptly from my chair.

'Patrick is a journalist, for God's sake. That's where he and Yechenko were supposed to meet. Go ahead and call his editor in New York if you don't believe me.'

Inspector Ferreira took off his glasses and folded them up. His eyes had taken on a stern look.

'Your husband must have hated a man like Yechenko. Isn't that right?' he said, leaning across his desk. 'We've found out a lot about him from Interpol. A ruthless white scumbag who bought and sold people. A slave trader. Doesn't your husband hate slave traders?'

I had no intention of showing any reaction. I kept my expression impassive. The inspector leaned back, studying me.

'Maybe Yechenko threatened him,' he went on. 'Maybe he called him a nigger. He wouldn't like that, would he?'

'They followed him,' I said. 'It was a trap. They beat him up on a street in Paris, trying to make him abandon the story. They were after both Yechenko and Patrick. Two flies with one blow. Because they were trying to ruin their trafficking business.'

'Perhaps,' said Ferreira. 'But it's my job to consider all the possibilities.'

He stood up. I looked out of the window at the clouds drifting across the sky.

'Could I make a copy of this?' he said, picking up the photograph of Patrick.

I nodded without saying a word. He left the room, leaving me alone. Tears filled my eyes. I kicked the desk, sending a sharp pain shooting up my leg.

Shit, shit, shit. It was always the same thing. All they saw was a black man. If there was one thing I never cared about when it came to Patrick, it was the colour of his skin. That he was black and I was white was a ludicrously irrelevant difference, a non-existent fact, as important as the length of a person's toenails. That was what I'd decided the minute I realized that I'd fallen in love with him.

The only thing that matters is you and me.

If you love me.

I love you.

Just as I am?

Just as you are.

I felt suddenly dizzy.

242

When the inspector returned, I was ready.

'This may sound absurd to your ears,' I said as he handed me the photograph and then went back to his desk to sit down. 'But there's one thing Patrick wanted more than anything else. He wanted to win the most prestigious prize that a journalist can get in the United States, because he wanted to prove he was just as good as — no, better than — those errand boys on Wall Street who make millions by writing phoney stock forecasts. Maybe it also has something to do with Patrick's paternal grandfather and great-grandfather. Maybe not. What's important for him is to show the magazine and his colleagues and his father and the whole world that it's possible, it has to be possible, to write stories that aren't solely for the sake of the advertisers or the magazine owners or the rich subscribers. To write simply for the sake of telling the truth.'

Helder Ferreira laughed.

'*Yes, we can*,' he said, raising his fist. 'So some of you actually still sound like Barack Obama.'

Then he leaned back and fell silent for a moment.

'I considered making it public that we were looking for this mysterious black man who was suspected of murder, but my boss vetoed the idea. We'd be drowning in infor-mation about well-dressed black men. Every decent, hard-working civil servant from the colonies would end up being suspected.'

A seagull flew past the window. I caught the movement out of the corner of my eye. At least they'd noticed that Patrick was well-dressed.

'So. Patrick Cornwall, American journalist.' The inspector jotted something down on a piece of paper on his desk. 'At least we now have a possible identification.'

'So he's not a suspect?'

243

I sank down on the chair, feeling worn out and drained.

'We have another witness.' Ferreira leaned closer to his screen. The computer was at least ten years old, and gave off a low humming sound.

'Marlene Hirtberger, fifty-two, a German tourist who had just stepped onto the terrace to have a look at the view. She says that two white men approached the look-out and a commotion ensued. Then she heard the screams.'

'It must have been them.' I leaned forward to get a partial view of the text. 'What else did she say?'

Ferreira squinted. He'd forgotten to put on his glasses, so he practically had to press his nose to the computer screen.

'Jorge Maurício, thirteen, who was skateboarding on the wall nearby, collided with a white man who was running towards the street. Jorge didn't see Yechenko fall, but he heard screams as he got back on his board, and then he lost his balance, forcing him to throw himself to the right in order not to plunge ten metres down in the other direction. Crazy kids, always trying to defy death. I hope he got a good scare so he never does that again. Jorge flew right into that man. He says the man, and I'm quoting here, "told me to get the fuck out of the way", and ran off across the street, heading for Mouraria. He was white and wearing a suit, according to young Jorge, whose parents are from Angola.'

I tried to picture the scene, the people moving about like actors, but I wasn't quite sure what the set looked like or exactly where Patrick had stood.

'The German woman, Ms Hirtberger, also says she saw a black man,' the inspector went on. 'But he was on his way out to the terrace right before all the commotion started up. She's positive about that because she'd been watching him. She says, and I quote, "He was a real tasty morsel".'

Ferreira gave me a wry smile. 'Do you know what your husband was wearing when he disappeared?'

I ran both hands through my hair. A real tasty morsel. What a bitch.

'He almost always wears a sport coat over his shirt,' I said. 'Dark colours. Nice slacks, maybe chinos. Hardly ever jeans.'

Ferreira pointed at me, pretending to be shooting a pistol. 'That's exactly what Marlene Hirtberger says. Grey sport coat and grey shirt, dark trousers. He was also wearing a tie, but he'd loosened it and unfastened the collar button. It was a hot day.'

'Well, there you are,' I said dully. 'Then you know that he didn't do it.'

'Time for coffee,' said Ferreira, reaching for his phone. He pressed a button and said something to whoever answered. Portuguese sounded like a cooler, slightly haughtier version of Spanish.

'Witness statements can be a somewhat unreliable source of proof,' he said after hanging up. 'People remember things incorrectly, they mix up the days. Some can't even tell the difference between black and white.'

'Have you found out who those two men were?'

He threw up his hands.

'We don't have the resources to comb Lisbon's streets for two ordinary-looking men wearing ordinary suits. That's how they were described. It's not a high priority case, and I find that annoying. I don't want these kinds of incidents happening on my streets.' He got up and went over to the door. 'According to the autopsy, Yechenko's death could have been suicide. The injuries he suffered when his body struck the cobblestones twenty metres below would have been the same.' He opened the door just as a bell rang, and accepted a small tray with coffee and a plate of pastries. I didn't see who had brought them. The inspector kicked the door shut and then set the tray in front of me.

'You said your husband has disappeared, is that right?' he asked.

I took a bite of pastry, which was unbearably sweet. Then I recounted the whole story as the inspector stuffed himself with jam-filled butter cookies.

'We haven't located him, at any rate,' he said, after I'd finished. 'All the districts know that we're looking for a black man who was at the scene of the crime, so if he'd shown up anywhere in Lisbon, I'd know about it.'

'Are you sure?' I said.

He brushed a few crumbs off his trousers.

'All suspicious deaths that occur outside the home come to my attention. When foreign citizens are involved, the case is assigned to me, without exception. I'm the only one in the department who speaks English.' Ferreira cast a glance at the picture of Patrick, which lay in front of him. 'And after Yechenko was murdered, we also made enquiries at all the hospitals.'

I leaned back, allowing his words to sink in, but I felt no sense of relief. The inspector wiped his hands on his trousers and motioned towards the pad of paper where he'd jotted down notes as I told him my story.

'I'll need to check up on this,' he said. 'But I doubt we'll make any progress. Unless Yechenko's widow shows up with new information, that is. A name or two, for example.'

'His widow?' I stared at Ferreira. It had never occurred to me that Josef K was married, or that anyone would miss him. 'Is she here in Lisbon?'

He nodded.

'She identified his body. She said they were embarking on a long trip. To Brazil. That's why they'd stopped here.

Her husband went up there to see the view. That's all we managed to get out of her.'

'Is she still here in the city?'

'As far as I know.' The inspector shrugged. 'She wanted to arrange for a funeral, but her husband's body is still in the morgue.'

'Do you know where she's staying?'

'Of course you realize I can't tell you that.'

'I just want to talk to her. Maybe she knows something about Patrick.'

He crossed his arms and shook his head.

I took a deep breath.

'I'm pregnant,' I said, and then looked away. I felt as if my stomach had assumed firmer contours. It will have a name, I thought. One day I will no longer be saying 'it'.

The man's expression softened and took on a fatherly look that made my skin crawl. I leaned down and grabbed my bag, slinging the strap over my shoulder as I got up to leave. I should have kept my mouth shut.

'Maybe you'd like to see the place where Yechenko died?' said Inspector Ferreira behind me.

I paused on my way to the door and turned around. He was aiming his pen north, from what I could gather. 'Take the number twenty-eight tram to Alfama and get off at Largo das Portas do Sol. If you go down the stairs from the look-out, you'll pass the spot where Yechenko's body struck the ground.' He looked down at his papers. 'Further along the lane you'll see a door marked number 62. There's no street name, and besides, it would be confusing to talk about streets in Alfama. They're not on any map.'

'Thank you,' I said.

'At the very top.' He pointed his pen in the air. 'And if she mentions any names . . .'

'Then I'll come and tell you,' I said.

'Tell Vera Yechenko that she'll soon be allowed to make funeral arrangements for her husband.'

'Patrick Cornwall?' The hotel manager got up from his chair. He'd been sitting at a computer, entering my check-in information. 'Do you mean the American?'

He's here, I thought. He must be here. My heart fluttered wildly. It was actually totally logical. This was where he'd been hiding all along, in a dingy third-class hotel in Lisbon, where the buildings perched on the steep slopes and the bars advertised peep shows.

'Yes,' I said, smiling. 'He's my husband.'

The hotel manager lowered his head and slowly came towards me, looking like a boxer ready to go on the attack.

'Are you here to pay his bill?' he asked.

I automatically stepped back.

'What? What do you mean?'

'He left without paying.' The man pointed at the key in my hand. 'I can't give you a room unless you pay his bill.'

I pressed my hand to my chest, taking in breath after breath without getting any air. It was a physical sensation. Hope being ripped out of me. Leaving behind only emptiness.

'We didn't realize at first that he'd left, so it was four nights in all.'

The man showed me a printout and pointed at the number at the bottom. One hundred and forty-four euros. I stared at the name at the top. Patrick Cornwall. And our address in New York. The length of stay was: Tuesday, 16 September until Friday, 19 September. The dates merged before my eyes.

'Or else we'll have to take up the matter with the police,' said the manager, drumming his fingers on the plywood veneer desk.

248

I turned away. From the reception area I had a good view of the bar. A painting covered an entire wall, showing cannons and ships in Lisbon harbour. The place was empty. No guests, no music, only a timeless silence as weighty as the furniture and the heavy drapes that had clearly never been cleaned. Spots on the ceiling. Dust. A great weariness hovered over the whole bar, a sense of bygone times.

Patrick would never have left a hotel bill unpaid. He was too much of a mama's boy to do that. Properly brought up and always careful to do the right thing. But that was the Patrick I knew, the man who had left New York, filled with anticipation. So much had happened since that moment, until he had checked in here, in this shitty hotel.

'Where are his belongings?' I managed to say. 'Did he take them with him or are they still here?'

The hotel manager didn't reply. He was still drumming his fingers on the front desk.

'I'll pay the bill, of course,' I told him. 'I'm sure Patrick intended to do that, but . . .'

I got out my wallet and put two one-hundred-euro bank-notes on the desk. At the airport I'd taken out a thousand euros. I had less than $3,500 left.

The manager took the money and my passport. It occurred to me that it was essential to have a passport, no matter where someone intended to go or what they intended to do.

'Do you still have Patrick's passport?'

'No, we gave it back. We keep it only long enough to verify the information in the computer.'

'What about his other things? His clothes and his laptop?'

The manager opened a drawer and took out a key ring. Then he raised the flap at the end of the counter and stepped

249

out. 'Follow me,' he said, letting the flap fall shut with a bang.

He led the way down a corridor, past a pile of empty crates, and then down some narrow stairs. At the bottom he unlocked a door.

'This is where we keep baggage that has been left behind.' He touched a wall switch and a bare bulb in the ceiling came on. It was a storage area for all sorts of things: broken chairs and paint cans. In one corner I saw a small pile of abandoned suitcases, a backpack, and several plastic bags with clothes sticking out of the tops. I recognized at once Patrick's brown suitcase with the metal fittings. My throat tightened.

'I need to get back to the front desk. Turn the light off when you leave.' The man's footsteps reverberated on the stone stairs as he left. The sound was then muted on the wall-to-wall carpet in the corridor, before it faded out entirely.

I stood there motionless, staring at the suitcase. I remembered it lying open in our apartment, with Patrick moving around it, putting his clothes inside and then closing the lid.

The suitcase wasn't locked. I placed it on the floor and opened the lid, and there were his clothes stuffed inside, all wrinkled. His grey chinos and a blue shirt, and the red cashmere designer sweater that I'd given him for his thirty-seventh birthday. Everything haphazardly jumbled together. I picked up the sweater and held it against my face, burrowing my nose in the soft wool that smelled of him. Olive soap and the faint scent of aftershave, with a slight tinge of sweat. I couldn't tell what I was really noticing and what was merely a memory of how he smelled. I was breathing cautiously to keep the traces from vanishing altogether. And an image appeared in my mind of Patrick when he'd left. I saw his back disappearing into a white haze in which only oblivion remained, and loneliness. Tears ran down my face and I made no attempt to stop them.

Patrick would never have left his things in such disarray. He was the kind of guy who arranged his socks by colour. It was clear that he hadn't left voluntarily. And he hadn't come back. I could no longer help thinking the worst. That he might be dead.

I had no idea how long I sat there, huddled on the cold stone floor, clutching his sweater in my arms. Five minutes, ten minutes, an hour? A lifetime passes and then it's over. It's a fucking lie that there's anything left but loneliness.

And Patrick's scent in every breath, his soft sweater against my face.

I just wanted to say good night . . . I miss you so much.

Finally I straightened up. Carefully I folded the sweater, and then lifted out all the other items, one by one. The travel guide for Paris. A book by the poet Rimbaud in the middle of the dirty underwear and socks that smelled sour when I picked them up. I took out one garment after another, and then put them back in the suitcase. Missing were a pair of black chinos that he almost always wore, a grey shirt, the grey sport coat. The clothes he was wearing when he disappeared. I saw that his laptop was also gone, and there was no research material. I closed the lid and locked it. Without the combination no one else was going to rummage through his things. Then I put the suitcase back in the corner, switched off the light, and closed the door behind me.

I went upstairs to my room.

I noticed a faint mouldy smell. The carpeting looked like

251

it had been there since the 1960s. The walls had the same dirty yellow colour as the rest of the hotel. I opened the glass French doors and stepped out onto a narrow balcony that faced the street. Over the railing hung a string of flags with washed-out borders and fields of colour. A wheeled suitcase rattled over the cobblestones below.

Somewhere out there is an explanation, I thought.

And some bastard is going to pay for all this. He's going to burn in hell.

'Where's his computer?' I asked when I went down to the lobby twenty minutes later. I had freshened up and changed into an almost clean shirt. 'He had a laptop with him, and it's not in the basement.'

The manager handed over a receipt, which I took without even glancing at the amount.

'Everything that was in his room is in the suitcase,' he said, giving my signature a suspicious look. 'It was a real mess in there, and the maid had to clean up after him.'

'I don't believe that,' I said. 'Who told you that?'

The manager narrowed his eyes.

'Everyone who works in this hotel is totally reliable.'

Somebody must have ransacked the place, I thought. Somebody other than Patrick.

'I know he had a computer. Did he take it with him when he left?'

'No, I didn't see it.'

'When was the last time you saw him?'

'I don't remember.'

'Listen to me,' I said, mimicking his stern expression, lowering my head and glaring like a bull or a boxer about to attack.

'You may be upset because you lost some money. How much was it? Let me see.' I picked up the receipt and looked

252

at the amount. 'One hundred and forty-four euros.' I crumpled the paper in my hand. 'But my husband has disappeared, and his laptop is missing. Tomorrow morning I'm going to the police. If you don't tell me everything, I will personally see to it that they turn your hotel upside down and that every single American TV company is here when they do it.'

He held up his hands.

'I'm telling you there was no laptop. I was there in person when we decided to enter the room and remove his belongings. He must have taken the key with him and slipped out.'

'Why do you say that?' Strange how the threat of media attention could make people talk. It was like the fairy tales I read as a child: Watch out or the wolf will get you. Or the Russians.

The manager explained in meticulous detail how the maid had cleaned the room as usual on Tuesday.

That's when Patrick had gone out to meet Yechenko, I thought.

The next day, on Wednesday, she'd found everything in the room scattered about, but she cleaned it all up, and that was that. Except that Mr Cornwall hadn't come back. The maid was positive that he hadn't slept in the bed. On Friday they had entered the room and emptied it.

'Could anyone else have been in the room?' I asked.

'There is always someone here at the front desk.'

'But you went with me into the basement. There was no one at the desk while you stepped away.'

'What I mean is that someone is always on duty.'

He pressed his lips together and straightened his tie. Then he turned his back and sat down at the computer. An electric clock on the wall told me it was 1.50 in the afternoon. I felt my stomach churning, and I realized with surprise that I was hungry. And that everything would just keep on going, as if nothing had happened.

I was clinging to a leather strap hanging from the ceiling. The tram was ancient, rumbling and whining and coughing and complaining like a live animal as it rounded the bends. We made it to the top of a ridge and the road levelled off and ended in a marketplace. I got off, along with three Scandinavian tourists, and a black-haired girl carrying an easel under her arm.

The view from up here extended for miles. The city climbed the mountainsides in a hodgepodge of little white buildings, worn-out roads, and curving red-tiled roofs. I saw verdant backyards with cats, and laundry hanging outside to dry. And far below me was the harbour and the river that widened as it spilled into the Atlantic.

A single café was open outside a small kiosk, and I bought a cup of coffee and sat down on a rickety chair. A couple in their twenties were making out over their beers, and the girl from the tram was setting up her easel. It was a scene that anyone but me would call romantic. Mikail Yechenko probably hadn't found it very romantic either as he plunged headlong down to the cobblestoned lane below.

I looked at my watch. It was 2.50. Twenty minutes left until the precise moment it had happened. The double hamburger from the Hard Rock Café on Avenida da Liberdade felt like a hard lump in my stomach.

I thought to myself: Here sits Joana Rodrigues, reading her psychology textbook. Over there, Marlene Hirtberger will soon come walking across the square, heading for the terrace to admire the view, but on the way she'll catch sight of something else that attracts her attention. *A real tasty morsel.*

I saw Marlene Hirtberger. I saw Joana Rodrigues. I saw

the thirteen-year-old skateboarder, who had come here to defy death. I placed them all in their positions. It was important for me to have arrived at the proper time, when the shadows fell as they had on that day. Only when everyone else was in place would I allow Patrick to make his entrance.

I finished my coffee and stood up to move closer. A footbridge, some eighteen metres in length, led out to the actual viewpoint, bordered by low, white walls on both sides. It was there the daredevil Jorge Maurício had been skateboarding. I cast a sidelong glance to my left. If he had veered to the wrong side, he would have either landed in a thicket of nettles ten metres down, or he would have been killed when he struck the stone steps.

The terrace itself was about twelve metres wide and twenty-two metres long, protected by a long balustrade.

It wouldn't take much to toss somebody over the railing, I decided as I walked across the paved surface to the south corner, where Yechenko had been standing. The railing was a metre tall, reaching to my navel.

Here I am, I thought. Mikail Yechenko. I'm waiting for an American journalist. He's my ticket to Brazil and freedom and my new life. I'm looking forward to his arrival, but I'm not looking in the direction he might appear because in this place you feel compelled to turn towards the river, towards the magnificent view across the channel of Lisbon harbour where the conquerors and colonizers sailed for America. And if I take in a deep breath I can sense the Atlantic, carrying an eternal scent of salt and dreams.

I leaned over the railing, and there was the lane, twenty metres below. And the cobblestones. I shuddered and took a step back.

He didn't even notice them coming, I thought. They must have stood here, no more than a metre away from him.

Yechenko, they say, and he turns around. Do they tell him hello from the boss? Do they say that Monsieur Thery sends his greetings before they heave him over the railing?

What does Patrick see, on his way at that very moment to meet the man he calls Josef K?

I quickly retreated to the outdoor café. How had Patrick arrived here? Presumably he'd taken the tram, wanting to hide in the crowd. But he had to be careful, so he gets off at the stop before this one. He walks the last short distance along the narrow pavement that runs past the whitewashed facades of the buildings. Excitement throbs in his body, all his senses are on high alert. He breathes in the air, and listens intently as he approaches. The screeching of the tram and the smell of grilled fish, cool shadows and music issuing from a bar somewhere. He is close to his goal now. But does he turn to look over his shoulder? Does he sense that he's being followed?

I looked down the slope as yet another tram appeared and then passed me. A stooped old man was trudging his way up.

If they were following Patrick here, he should have managed to reach the terrace before the assault occurred.

So they must have been waiting up here for him instead.

Somehow they must have found out where Patrick was supposed to meet Yechenko. The Ukrainian had been trapped like an animal in a cage on the terrace, but they couldn't wait until Patrick arrived. Tossing one man over the railing was simple. Throwing two men over the side was too big a risk.

I went over to where the bridge ended, to the place where Jorge had hopped on his skateboard. This was where Patrick had stood when the men had pitched Yechenko off the terrace. He must have seen it happen. I imagined the shock-wave striking him. He must have been frozen in place during the seconds it took for those two men to turn around and take off running, one of them colliding with the skateboarder before disappearing. Patrick had turned around to follow, and had looked straight into the lustful eyes of Marlene Hirtberger.

And the two men must have seen Patrick. They knew he would be there. They knew he could identify them, maybe he even recognized them from Paris. They couldn't let him get away.

They must have had a plan.

Young Jorge had seen one of them head towards Mouraria, the part of town on the other side of the hill.

But what about the other man?

An ordinary man wearing an ordinary suit.

I leaned against the wall and watched the young female artist capturing the tiled rooftops on her sketchpad.

What does Patrick do next? Seconds after the commotion started up on the terrace, all the witnesses are trying to find out what happened. Why are people screaming? Who is dead? But Patrick knows. He doesn't have to follow the others, who are being drawn in horror towards the terrace. He runs in the opposite direction, and he chooses the closest escape route he sees: the long flight of stairs leading down from Largos das Portas do Sol into Alfama's winding lanes. Right there, at the spot where the stairs begin, he encounters an old man walking his dog, a retiree who was born and raised in this neighbourhood and who thinks that a black man running is always the guilty party.

What António Nery, age seventy-two, doesn't notice, is that a white man wearing an ordinary suit is following the black man.

Slowly I started down the steep steps. What was Patrick thinking when he saw his source lying dead at the foot of the stairs? Did he take the time to pause and lean down?

He knew that the men who had killed Yechenko were close by, and there could be others. He must have taken off running, right into the maze of lanes.

I sank down onto the bottom step. No trace of blood remained. I pictured Patrick racing like a doomed soul through the labyrinth of buildings and not finding a way out, like a spirit caught between life and death. I got up and took one last look at the terrace high overhead.

Then I continued on down the lane, just as the inspector had instructed.

Number 62 was located on a small square, or rather an area where the lane was a little wider. A small fountain was built into the wall, with water dripping from a lion's maw. Up above, a woman leaned out of a window to hang laundry on a line. It would have seemed an idyllic setting if a couple of the buildings weren't on the verge of collapsing. Number 62 was one of them.

There were two doorbells, but neither was labelled. I pressed both at once and heard the bells ringing through the blinds covering the windows on the third floor. Through the slats I noticed movement. A moment later the lock clicked and the door opened a few centimetres.

'Who are you?' hissed a woman in heavily accented English. I could see only one eye and part of the full lips of her mouth. The stairwell behind her was in darkness. 'Have you come to get me?'

'Are you Vera Yechenko?' I asked.

'Why?'

'I want to talk about your husband.'

'Is it about the rent?'

A strong scent of perfume wafted towards me.

'My name is Ally Cornwall. It was my husband that Yechenko went to meet when he died.'

'My husband, your husband,' said Vera. 'And who is your husband?'

'His name is Patrick Cornwall. He's an American journalist.'

'Right. So you say.'

'I just want to talk to you.'

'But I don't want to talk to you.' The woman coughed. 'You tell them that. And get out of here before I tell somebody to drag you away.'

'I know that your husband was murdered.'

I thought I heard her draw in a breath, or maybe it was a gust of wind somewhere.

'I think I know who did it,' I said.

The door opened a few more centimetres. She was wearing a bathrobe. On her feet she wore oversize slippers that her husband must have left behind.

'I'm not dressed,' she said, and turned on her heel. Her bathrobe fluttered around her as she climbed the narrow stairs. When I closed the door behind me, everything went black. Slowly my eyes grew accustomed to the dark. I climbed past a door with no lock or handle and continued up yet another steep flight of stairs. The door to Vera Yechenko's apartment stood open, letting light into the stairwell. On the landing outside, a little refrigerator emitted a gurgling sound.

'The police claim that Misha took his own life. But I know him better than that.' Vera stood in the hall with her hands on her hips. Her hair was in curlers. I guessed she was in her sixties. Her skin was stretched tightly around her full lips. She had obviously had a facelift or two.

'So who was it that sent the American? Was it the Slovaks? Or was it the Russians?'

I was still standing in the stairwell, trying to figure out what she meant.

'Patrick was not the one who killed your husband,' I said. 'He was supposed to conduct an interview. They had an agreement.'

'Agreement!' Vera raised her hand as if to deliver a slap, slamming it through the air. 'He was supposed to conclude all his business deals and the tickets would arrive and now here I sit. Like a bird in a cage. And where am I supposed to fly? Answer me that.'

She motioned for me to come in.

'Close the door,' she said.

I stepped inside the front hall. The woman was shorter than me and slightly pudgy. Like a Russian babushka, I thought, picturing in my mind those wooden dolls, those nesting dolls, one inside the other. But I reminded myself that Vera Yechenko was from Ukraine, and she wouldn't like being called Russian.

'I need to get dressed,' she said, crossing her arms. 'But first I want to know why you're running around talking about Misha.'

'I just want to find out what happened to my husband,' I said, taking a quick look around. On the left was the bathroom, in which a tiny shower was squeezed in next to the toilet. Straight ahead was a tiled kitchenette in the corner. The door next to it, probably leading to the bedroom, was ajar. I listened intently but heard nothing to indicate there was anyone else here. Next to it was another door. The living room. All in all, the whole apartment was no bigger than our bedroom in Gramercy.

'Do you know a man named Alain Thery?' I asked.

'You mean the Frenchman?' said Vera. She drew her bathrobe tighter around her waist. She wasn't fat, as I had first thought, but she had enormous breasts.

'I think he's the one behind all of this,' I said. Then I gave her a quick, short version of what I thought had happened.

Vera interrupted me in mid-sentence. 'I told Misha this was going to end badly. Why did he have to make trouble? Business was good. We had a good life.' She went into the living room. The wicker chair creaked as she sat down. 'Where am I supposed to go now? Tell me that if you can.'

I followed her, but stopped in the doorway to the room. 'Did you know he was supposed to meet with Patrick Cornwall?'

'He just said a journalist. An American.' Vera shrugged. 'Then we'd get the tickets and passports. He promised that we'd go to Brazil. What was I supposed to do there? We had a wonderful house. And then he didn't come back. In the evening the police knocked on the door.' She shook her head and looked up at the ceiling. 'Stupid, stupid Misha. He'd written the address on a slip of paper in his pocket. He could never remember numbers and always got lost in the streets.'

She gestured towards the other armchair. I went over and sat down. There was a stack of books on the coffee table, but otherwise it was an impersonal room, furnished by someone who had never lived in it. A lamp spread a yellowish glow that turned skin tones grey.

'My husband was a poet. Do you understand? He had the soul of a poet.'

'OK,' I said, deciding not to comment. *And I thought he was a slave trader.*

'Dostoevsky, Chekhov, Nikolai Gogol. He read them all. Even Pasternak. And Kafka, even though he's not Russian.' She ran her hand over the stack of books. The titles on the spines were printed in the Cyrillic alphabet. She laughed to herself. 'He joked that next time he would be named Pushkin. You know Pushkin, don't you?'

I nodded. A Russian poet, something of a national hero.

261

But I had no clue about his writing style. Probably melancholy and grandiose.

'We're Russian, you know,' she went on. 'It's not easy for us. The Ukrainians want to handle their own affairs, and they'd prefer to get rid of us. Nothing is the way it used to be.'

'Your husband was supposed to give Patrick some documents,' I said. 'Did he take them with him when he left for the meeting on the terrace?'

Vera abruptly got up.

'It was my fault,' she said, fluttering her hands. 'It was my idea for them to meet there.' She tore at her hair, pulling out a curler, which landed on the dirty, faded rug. 'I told him he needed to choose a place that was easy to find. So he wouldn't get lost. My poor Misha. He couldn't even find his way around Kiev. He had no sense for . . . what's it called?'

'A sense of direction.'

Vera shook her head and pointed towards the square outside.

'All you have to do is turn right, I told him. Just walk along the lane, it will take you right there.'

She began to sob as she buried her face in her hands.

'It must have been so awful for you,' I said.

Vera looked up at me.

'What do you know about it?' she said, leaving the room.

'More than you think,' I said quietly to her back.

As she clattered things in the kitchen, I went over to the window. Daylight filtered through the slats in the blinds, making stripes on the floor. It was close to five o'clock. I couldn't see any fire escape outside. There probably wasn't a single one in this whole medieval part of town.

'Is it OK if I pull up the blinds?' I asked when Vera came back.

She was carrying a bottle of port wine and two glasses.

'Sure,' she said. 'I forget to do that. I go out when it gets dark. I sleep in the daytime. It's been like that ever since . . .' She set down the glasses and poured a little into each. 'I'll be right back,' she said, and again left the room.

I pulled up the blinds. The windowsill was grey with soot and pollution. The woman across the way was shouting something to a man walking across the small square. He yelled a reply. A TV was blaring somewhere. Sounds from a soccer game. Why is she still here? I wondered. Why doesn't she leave this city, which will for ever be associated with the place where her husband died on the cobblestones?

'I want the agreement to be fulfilled,' said Vera as she came back. She went straight for her glass and downed the port wine in one gulp. Now that she was dressed, she was transformed into a chic petite woman, as if right out of a tabloid about the rich and famous from England's manors and estates. She had on a stylish suit with a tiny-checked pattern. A jacket and cropped trousers, with a scarf in two colours draped over her shoulders. I could have sworn her hair clip was solid gold.

'I want a hundred thousand dollars. Or euros. It makes no difference.'

She reached for the wine bottle and refilled her glass. The liquor was a deep golden brown, which matched her outfit.

'You've misunderstood.' I took a sip of the wine. A harsh taste on my tongue. A combination of old oak cask and sweetness. 'I have nothing to do with all that. I'm just looking for my husband.'

Vera Yechenko leaned forward and lowered her voice.

'They think we're dead,' she said. 'I can't go back home. You can't fool with death. That's what my poor Misha found out. But I'm going to fool them all. Do you hear me?' She downed her second glass of wine. 'Now that Misha is gone, they're going to dig up everything about him. All the lies they keep in their archives. But let me tell you, he was just doing his job. He was a devoted husband.'

Vera grabbed the bottle and poured herself more wine.

'He wrote everything down. Every number. Names. Everything. They never counted on that. Ha ha.' She set the bottle on the floor. 'He knew how to keep records, my Misha.'

'Did he have the documents with him when he went to meet Patrick?' I asked again.

'Of course he did.' Vera looked at me as if I were a total idiot. 'The journalist wanted the papers. Misha would get the tickets, and we could fly away from here.' She flapped her arms to underscore her words. Then she sank back against her chair. 'And now I'll have to go alone. Do you believe in fate?'

'The police didn't say anything about documents,' I said. 'The men who threw him over the railing must have taken them, unless . . .'

I stopped in mid-thought and looked out of the window again. The sun had begun to set, and the colours deepened. Somewhere down below I could hear a plaintive song, as if someone were trying to force her heart out through her throat.

Unless Yechenko refused to give up the papers, I thought. In my mind I pictured the scene in slow motion. The man plummeting through the air, clutching the documents to his chest, even as he fell to his death. And seconds later, Patrick running down the stairs over to his body. He could have taken the documents. He was obsessed with getting the story. Obsessed enough to tear the papers out of the hands of a dead man?

Then he ran, I thought, as I looked down at the little square where the lane ended and then continued fifteen metres further on, narrowing into yet another set of steps that meandered and disappeared from sight, curving around and becoming entwined with a thousand other lanes covering the mountain slope. They weren't on any map, as the inspector had told me.

They must have followed him.

Faire d'une pierre deux coups.

But Patrick had tricked them. He had taken the documents and fled.

'The police called me,' said Vera. 'They said I can bury my Misha now.' She pressed her hand to her chest. 'Thirty-six years! And they want me to bury him here in foreign soil?'

Earth is earth, I thought.

And my next thought was: A person doesn't just vanish.

If they had killed Patrick here in the neighbourhood, the police would have found his body.

I went over to my bag, which I'd set down next to my chair.

'Patrick fled when your husband . . . He must have come this way,' I said, taking out the photograph. 'Did you see him? Did you let him in?'

'What are you talking about? Nobody ever comes here.' Vera leaned forward and squinted at the picture of Patrick. Then she gasped.

'Are you married to a black man?' The wine sloshed in her glass.

I gritted my teeth and put the picture away.

At least her surprise seemed genuine. Patrick hadn't been here.

'I want my ticket,' said Vera. 'I need to get away from here.' The waning sunlight flashed on a hugely expensive gemstone on her finger as she twirled her glass, looking at the wine as if only now did she notice what she'd been drinking. The label said it was ten-year-old Tawny port. I knew nothing about fortified wines except that you were supposed to drink them in much smaller glasses.

'Anna died and then Misha died. I can never go home again.'

'Anna? Was she his god-daughter?'

Vera stood up and came over to the window. She stood near me, but leaning against the wall. So I won't see her face, I thought.

'Our god-daughter,' she said, closing her eyes. The song from outside rose and fell like a wave between the buildings, wrapping the night in blue sorrow.

'Listen,' she said. 'It's the music of the night. It's the *fado*. They are singing about everything that they've lost.' She fluttered her hands to the music, the tones intertwining in a minor key. 'It's the music of the freed slaves, the conmen and the whores, the music of the alleyways. It speaks to my Russian soul. Misha agreed with me. It's a dirge, he said. They say it took its melody from the waves of the sea. Can you hear it?' She fluttered her scarf, back and forth, swaying her enormous breasts. 'It means fate, you know. The fate that keeps the lovers apart.'

Fate, I thought, in the form of your husband's previous gangster cohorts. And if that was the case, I realized at that moment that it was a fate uniting me with the grieving Vera Yechenko.

'Thirty-six years we are married.' She poked at me with the hand holding the sloshing port wine. 'Don't you think I would know what was in those papers?'

'What?' I said.

'Well, I don't remember. You'll have to read them yourself.'

I stared at her. She must have had too much to drink.

'But you said he took them with him. You said he took the documents along when he went to meet Patrick.'

'Yes, yes, he did.' She smiled, showing all her teeth. 'But not the copies. Ha ha.'

'Are you saying there are copies? And you have them here? Here in this apartment?'

Suddenly I understood why Vera Yechenko didn't want to be seen. Quickly I stepped back into the room, away from the window.

'Misha didn't trust that American. He thought he might take the papers and then run off and take the money for himself.' Vera threw out her hand. 'Americans. All they think about is money.'

She left and went into the bedroom. Don't tell me you've put the papers under the mattress, I thought.

She had.

It was a brown folder. Vera held it pressed to her chest.

'A hundred thousand,' she said, closing her eyes for a moment. 'In euros.'

'I don't have that much money.'

'Then I'll just sell them to someone else.'

'Go ahead,' I said, going out into the front hall. 'I really don't give a shit about those documents.'

That wasn't entirely true.

Vera Yechenko came after me. 'There are plenty of people who would pay for these papers.'

'OK. Just sit here and wait for them to show up. Sit here and rot in the dark and wait for them to come and throw you off some cliff like they did your husband.'

'Fifty thousand,' said Vera.

I reached for the door handle and turned it to open the door.

'I don't give a shit what those papers say,' I told her. 'I want to find my husband, and he's obviously not here.'

Her fingernails bored into my arm.

'Take them for twenty. I don't want them here. I keep dreaming that they'll come and ring the bell and finish me off the way they finished off Misha.'

'Five hundred,' I said. 'And I promise you'll never have to see them again.'

'A thousand.'

I took out ten rolled-up bills from the front pocket of my jeans. I had the rest of the money in my wallet and at the hotel. 'This is all I have,' I said.

Vera muttered something in Russian and reached out to grab the money. At the same time I took the folder and glanced at a few of the pages. Long columns of figures. Some sort of bookkeeping, which was not my forte even though I'd been running a business for eight years. Various transactions recorded, and locations. Names. I leafed through more pages. 2004, 2006, 2008. Names and place names, dates in long columns. Notations such as: Man, Sudan, Woman, Kiev. Number: seven. Number: eight. Money that had changed hands. Several hundred thousand euros for a single transaction. Alain Thery's name screamed at me in black ink. There were other French names, as well as British, German, and Polish names. I closed the folder, clutching it tightly, feeling the heat rise to my face.

No matter what he'd done to Patrick, he was going to pay for it. That bastard.

Vera stuffed the euros into her wallet. She was holding an elegant little purse. I noticed it was a Dior. Genuine. From her wallet she took out a business card and handed it to me. Gilt-edged, with the words printed on linen cardstock.

'The address is no longer valid, of course,' she said. 'But I still have that phone number. In case you need to contact me.'

I stared at the card, uncomprehending. The address was for a perfume shop in Kiev.

'I thought you were claiming to be dead,' I said.

Vera laughed.

'Right! I wonder where they're going to send the bill.'

A mangy dog crossed the lane. The produce vendor dragged the boxes of vegetables into an alcove. I pressed the folder to my chest and looked over my shoulder. No one there. Just as I reached the viewpoint, the sun went down behind the hills, turning the thousands of tiled rooftops a shimmering gold.

On the tram I called Benji. I thought: I'll talk to him the whole way. Then somebody will know who I am when they find me.

'Lisbon? You're kidding,' he hollered. 'Oh, God. That's so romantic. Don't tell me you're listening to *fado*. Amália was a goddess.'

I could almost sense how it hurt him when he bit his tongue.

'Sorry,' he said. 'I forgot. Have you . . .?'

'No,' I said. 'I haven't found him.'

A bend in the road and I almost fell over. I had to scramble to grab the strap hanging from the ceiling. It felt as if I was getting an injection of my old life through the phone, by hearing Benji's voice. I couldn't remember when we'd last talked. It felt like so long ago. Was it only two days? Three? Before I checked out of the hotel in Paris I'd received a bunch of emails from him. Something about a meeting. A job. I couldn't even recall what it was about.

The brakes shrieked as the tram strained to turn and began heading downhill.

'What's all that noise?' asked Benji. His voice sounded

so bright and real. It made me feel grounded. I was Ally, his employer, a friend.

'You wouldn't believe your eyes,' I said. 'This city is a museum, and the maintenance department is no longer operating.'

'Is that why there's no Internet service? I've sent you tons of emails.'

'You should have tried a telegram,' I said. 'What do you need?'

'Oh, nothing really, just a small matter of Cherry Lane Theatre wanting to book you for *Medea* next season, and maybe for a show in the fall too. They need to know this week.'

'Is that all?' I said.

'Should I tell them yes, or do you want to call them yourself?'

The tram made a sharp turn around a cathedral. I longed for straight streets in numerical order. I tried to recall what the head of Cherry Lane Theatre looked like. What his name was. I couldn't remember.

'We'll talk about this later,' I said. 'Do you have a wifi connection right now?'

'Of course.'

'Could you look up the Lisbon post office? I need the address.'

'Sure. What else is a stage designer's assistant good for?' I heard the clatter of his keyboard. 'By the way, they're playing to sold-out crowds at the Joyce. Duncan is threatening to cancel all his future contracts. He's going through some sort of personal crisis. He's never had any commercial success before, so now he thinks he has to go to India to search for a deeper meaning. And Leia has signed a contract with American Ballet. I pity them.'

I let his chatter run through my mind as I looked

around the tram. Tourists with guidebooks and digital cameras, a few young girls out shopping, two very old men — so old that they might have even taken part in building the tram system. A couple of Portuguese citizens who looked as if they were on their way home from work, and a black woman with braids. I felt confident that no one was following me. Had Patrick been equally confident?

The street levelled out and I was now down in Baixa, the flat part of town between the Lisbon hills where all the government offices and international clothing stores were located.

'I assume you want the main post office,' said Benji. 'Praça dos Restauradores, Avenida da Liberdade. Does that sound familiar?'

'Perfect,' I said. 'That's where the Hard Rock Café is. Can you find the opening times?'

'They close at six.'

One of the very old men was winking flirtatiously. I looked at my watch.

'Yikes. When does it open?'

'At nine.'

The document folder was rubbing against my chest. I was going to have to keep the papers at the hotel overnight.

The bell rang for the tram stop where I was supposed to get off. From there it was a ten-minute walk to the hotel. The streets were packed with people. Benji was still talking in my ear as I turned onto Via Augusta, the shopping street through Baixa. Red signs in the windows advertised sales. I thought I must be overdramatizing. Nobody would be following me, since no one knew that there were copies of the documents. And no one except Vera Yechenko knew where they were.

'I'm so jealous,' said Benji.

'Because of the *fado*?' I asked. 'Or because I'm a better set designer?'

'Because of Patrick,' said Benji. 'Because you have someone in your life.'

'He's gone,' I said.

'You'll find him,' Benji told me.

I clutched the phone tightly, lowering it to my chest. I heard Benji continuing to talk, and raised the phone to my ear again in the middle of a sentence.

'. . . never had anyone to lose,' I heard him say. '. . . dare to love and be loved, but I realize that's not much consolation.'

'Just keep talking to me,' I said. 'Just tell me about something that's totally uninteresting.'

'Like my love life?' said Benji.

I laughed and felt tears sting my eyes.

'That would be great.'

Chapter 13

Lisbon
Wednesday, 1 October

I was running through a labyrinth of lanes and dark stairways, carrying the child in my arms. From a bar I heard the song, a plaintive woman who glared at me with her toothless mouth, howling into the night. It's the freed slaves, said a man in the audience. That's who is singing. Then the baby was gone. I ran, and the shadows tore at my clothes. I came out near the river where the boats had come in, loaded down with people hanging over the railings, bound with chains. Then I caught sight of Patrick further along the dock, and I shouted, but my voice was drowned out by rattling carts and screeching steam whistles, and I saw him walking in the opposite direction, and there stood a woman, she was petite and dark and wearing a blue coat, and she joined Patrick, and side by side they disappeared in the swarms of people, and I ran after them, pushing my way forward, wanting to tell him that our child had arrived, and I caught sight of the blue back of the woman, and I grabbed her arm, but when she turned around, it was

Patrick's mother who pressed her face close to mine. 'He doesn't need someone like you,' she said, and at the same time the building behind us collapsed, and I tore myself loose from the sheet that was twisted around my legs, and I realized that the sound was coming through the balcony doors, which stood open, facing the street. Glass shattering. The muted rumble of a garbage truck. Metal striking the cobblestones.

I pulled up the blanket, which had tumbled to the floor, and wrapped it around me. The cool night air filled the room, illuminated by the streetlamps. I had left the balcony doors open so I'd be able to flee quickly, if necessary. No one would enter that way. It would be easier to come in from the hotel corridor.

I'd hidden the folder in the basement when I came back to the hotel and asked to take another look at Patrick's suitcase. Mikail Yechenko's documents were now under a red cashmere sweater. As soon as the post office opened, I was going to put all the papers in an envelope and send them across the Atlantic.

The images from my dream still lingered in my mind: the harbour, which looked like the picture in the bar downstairs, the boats filled with slaves from the past. I abruptly sat up in bed. Stared at the dark windows in the building across the street, and the grimy sign advertising rooms for rent. My heart was pounding.

The boats! The sea and the boats. The people who died and were washed ashore.

That was something I'd seen on my computer screen when I was reading articles about slave trading and illegal immigration.

A sea, a beach.

I got up, not caring whether anyone could see me through the window. I gathered up my clothes from the floor and

274

put them on, noting that it was four in the morning. Downstairs I found the desk clerk asleep on a sofa in the bar.

'Does the hotel have free Wi-Fi?' I asked.

He sat up with a jolt and rubbed his eyes.

'Just a moment,' he said, and disappeared into the office. He came back holding a small card.

'This is the code. Three euros an hour.' He pointed towards a dark wooden table in the far corner of the bar. 'There's the computer,' he said, and then he headed back to his place behind the front desk.

'Excuse me,' I called after him. 'Is it possible to get a cup of coffee this early in the morning? And a sandwich?'

I looked at the little card, and entered the code in the password box. Then I logged onto Google.

I typed in: Illegal immigrant. Boats. Death.

Then I leaned back and waited.

For several days now it had been right in front of my eyes, yet the thought had never occurred to me. I hadn't allowed myself even to consider the idea. I had fooled myself into not seeing. Hope was a lie. A fucking lie.

The first hits were new, all referring to something that had happened over the past few days. Another boat had capsized off the Turkish coast, several bodies had washed ashore in a tourist area on a Greek island. I scrolled down, but didn't find what I was looking for.

The desk clerk set a cup of coffee on the table next to the computer.

'*Obrigada*,' I said. It was the only Portuguese word I'd learned so far.

I typed: man, dead, beach, immigrant. Again I pressed the search button.

I sipped the bitter coffee as the ancient computer searched over a sluggish connection. Aside from the light coming

275

from the partially open door to the kitchen, the screen was the only light source in the closed bar. The windows were covered with velvet drapes that reached four metres, from floor to ceiling.

The third hit was something I instantly recognized.

I clicked on it, and the bar where I was sitting vanished.

I was looking at a beach in Spain, in a town on the Atlantic coast. Tarifa. A Swedish tourist had found a dead man on the beach. The article said he was an African immigrant.

'It was so horrible,' said Terese Wallner, twenty, who had suffered quite a shock. 'He almost looked alive in the water. He had only a tattoo, otherwise he was naked.'

My hand flew up to my left shoulder and squeezed hard. A tattoo. That was what had settled somewhere in the back of my mind, lingering in my subconscious.

I checked the date. The article had been published on Wednesday, 24 September. One week ago. Seven days after Patrick was last seen, up near the terrace look-out in Alfama.

I read the brief article again and again. How did they know he was an African immigrant? That wasn't clarified in the text. On the other hand, more bodies had washed ashore in the areas around Cádiz over the following days. The Spanish police thought they had come from a capsized rubber boat carrying illegal immigrants.

I pulled up a map of Spain on the screen. With my heart hammering, I zoomed in on the southern portion and located Tarifa, at the tip of a promontory, just west of Gibraltar. The distance to the African continent was no bigger than the tip of my chewed fingernail, ten to twenty kilometres tops. And from Tarifa, the Atlantic spread westward, towards the Portuguese border where the earth's crust curved upwards, and the sea was sucked into the estuary where Lisbon was squeezed in, at the mouth of the Tejo river.

It might be possible.

I could hardly breathe.

Dear God in heaven, I thought. *It might be possible*.

My head throbbed as I tried to find out more information about the man on the beach, but the brief article was all I could find. Nothing more about who he was. Nothing more about the tattoo. I went back to the text.

'It was a terrible shock,' said Terese Wallner. 'People go swimming and surfing at that beach all the time.'

I glanced at my watch. Four minutes left of my computer time. I searched 'Sweden, addresses' and then typed in Terese Wallner's name. There seemed to be only one person by that name, with a cell phone registered to an address on Hemmansvägen in a place called Järfälla.

It was 5.03 in the morning. Sweden was much further east, almost all the way to Russia, which definitely meant it was in a different time zone. So it had to be at least six o'clock.

I logged out and went up to my room. In the shower I let the hot water run over my body until my skin felt wrinkled and warm. For a long time I watched the water swirl at my feet until it was sucked down the drain.

When it was six a.m. in Lisbon and possibly seven in Stockholm, I tapped in Terese Wallner's phone number. It rang eight times before anyone answered. The voice sounded groggy with sleep.

'I'm sorry for calling you so early,' I said, hoping that the person spoke English.

'Who is this?' she asked.

'You don't know me, but my name is Ally Cornwall, and I live in New York, although right now I'm in Lisbon.' That was more information than Terese needed to know, but I wanted to give her time to wake up.

277

'What do you want?' she asked.

'You were in Spain a week ago. I read about it on the Internet.'

'Oh, is this about my passport, or something?' She suddenly sounded interested. Then she lowered her voice to a whisper. 'Have you found it?'

'No. But I read that you found a man on the beach. That was you, wasn't it?'

'Yes.' I heard the girl snuffling. 'Sorry. I've got a slight cold,' she said. 'Papa says it's from the wind. Or maybe the shock. I don't know.'

Her English was good, though it had a Swedish lilt to it.

'In the interview you say that the man had a tattoo. Is that right?'

'Where did you say you're calling from?'

'From Lisbon.'

'Do you work for a newspaper or something?'

The girl blew her nose, blasting into the phone.

'What did the tattoo look like?' I asked.

'It was on his shoulder.'

'Which shoulder?'

'On the guy lying there, of course.' She giggled. 'I was sitting on a big rock that stuck out of the water. And it was when I climbed up that . . .' The girl abruptly stopped. 'You don't happen to know Alex, do you?'

I had a tight grip on the phone.

Who the hell was Alex?

'No, I don't know any Alex,' I said, swallowing hard. 'But it's possible that I know the man you found.'

'But he was from Africa.'

'How do you know that?'

'But he was. I've dreamed about him. That he gets up from the water and grabs hold of me. It's scary, and yet it's not. He looks almost alive. Which newspaper do you work for?' Terese was definitely awake now. She seemed happy to have the attention. 'I don't understand why anyone gets a tattoo. It must hurt awfully. I fainted when I got my ears pierced, but I was only thirteen, of course.'

I dug my fingernails into the bedspread.

'What sort of tattoo was it?' I asked.

'It was nice. It really was. Two flowers crossed. Not roses, or anything like that. More like imaginary flowers, a really nice design.'

A really nice design. The words echoed in the room, and the intertwining flowers appeared before my eyes. I could see them curling over a black shoulder and down towards the muscles of the upper arm, and I bit down on the hand that wasn't holding the phone, bit as hard as I could, the pain keeping me in control.

'But the police weren't interested in it. They mostly wanted to know what I was doing on the beach, and stuff like that.' Terese blew her nose again. 'Sorry,' she said, 'but it's hard to talk about this. It brings it all back. Papa thinks it will take time to get over something like this.'

'Did it say anything?' I whispered.

A rustling on the phone. The girl must have changed position.

'What did you say?'

'Did it say anything on the tattoo?' I almost shouted.

'Oh, you mean on his shoulder? Sorry, this is a bad connection. I don't know what it meant. I don't know those languages.'

'So it did say something?' I heard my own voice echo on the line. Everything I said was repeated with a nano-second delay. 'A name?'

Name, name. The word reverberated.

'I have no idea whether it was a name. They said he was

279

from the sub-Sahara, that lots of people have died there in the sea. Just think if I'd gone swimming there the day before. Maybe he was already in the water. But I thought it was too cold and the waves were too big.'

'What did it say on the tattoo?'

'Why do you sound so angry?'

'Sorry, I'm just tired.'

Tired, tired.

'I don't know why I kept looking at that tattoo. First I thought it was an animal he had on his shoulder, but then I realized it was a tattoo. It was like I didn't want to look at his body, he was totally naked, you know, and I didn't dare look at his face . . .'

'What did it say?'

Far away I heard the girl answer.

And I felt my left shoulder burning. From the tattoo I had there. Patrick's name on my skin, a souvenir of that crazy night in Chinatown, the night we got engaged and we'd had each other's names etched into our skin. Much better than rings! It was a permanent commitment, something we would never lose, an insane means of provoking his parents, an impulsive idea of mine when I saw the light shining in the tattoo parlour in a basement across from Mott Street. I hadn't thought he would dare. That he'd so clearly want me. For all eternity. For all eternity.

The girl's voice was forcing its way into my ear.

'It said "alone". Isn't that strange? That's what the word means in Swedish, anyway. "Allena". Although it was spelled with only one "l". Alena. Almost like "alone" in English. It was kind of horrible, because he was actually all alone there in the water. And I was alone too, because Alex . . . But I can't talk about that. It still hurts too much.'

I dropped the phone and the voice was somewhere in the dark all around me. I wanted to scream for it to stop, but it went on and on: 'And then I thought that it must mean something else altogether in his language. Do you know what it means? I've spent a lot of time wondering about that. I don't think anybody ever gets over something like this. My life will never be the same. Hello? Are you there? Is it him? The man you know?'

Chapter 14

Tarifa
Thursday, 2 October

Ahead of me lay the last stretch of road like a lonely pencil line extending straight out to sea. A military warning sign popped up and then disappeared. In a gully stood a partially collapsed sheep shed.

This is the end, I thought. There is no way out of here.

I squirmed on the seat, shifted position. It didn't help. The back of my neck and the base of my spine ached, and my butt was sore after spending the night on various buses, first from Lisbon to the Spanish border, then onward to Seville, where I caught an even older and more ramshackle bus heading for Algeciras, and then this local bus with its hard seats, bringing me the rest of the way. It seemed only right that my body should be hurting. I wanted to feel pain. I paid no attention to any of the places we passed. I had closed my eyes, but hardly slept at all, merely conjuring up one picture of Patrick after another, memories that I had to preserve and hold on to before they were lost to me. The smile tugging at his lips, the warmth in his eyes, and the touch of his hand, the tone of his voice. If I didn't store away every little detail, I would have nothing left.

I felt sick. Nothing but white bread and ham since last night. I imagined the baby wallowing in those swollen carbohydrates, but I didn't care about that either. I hadn't asked for this trespasser inside my body who screamed for food and forced me to go on living.

An old woman got off the bus in the midst of the fading landscape of hills covered with dead grass and scorched bushes. Along the ridge stood a row of wind turbines. They were wildly rotating their wings against the clouds, like drowned men trying to find their way up to the surface.

I closed my eyes and sank back into the images of Patrick. Alive.

When he brought a cup of coffee over to the sofa in the living room. With exactly the right amount of milk in my cup. His lips soft against my forehead. *American Idol* on the TV. A fun little argument about who should be eliminated. Amanda Overmyer was in trouble, and Patrick favoured Carly Smithson. He always voted for the European contestants, while that season I'd had a weakness for that cute David Archuleta, and he'd teased me about starting to show my age and falling for sweet little sixteen-year-olds. We'd eaten take-out from the Chinese place on 19th Street, and then we'd sat at either end of the sofa. I read the newspaper, while Patrick read a book as the TV show kept going, and the votes were counted and there was an infinite amount of time. *And it was supposed to be like that for ever.*

The bus turned and then turned again and braked. And even though I didn't want to, I opened my eyes.

Tarifa.

First there was the wind. It struck me full-blast as I got

out of the bus, practically knocking me over. Dry and hot and relentless, it tore at my hair, tangling it all up, and lashing at my face.

This is the world's end, I thought.

The bus station was a barracks of a building, made from corrugated metal, planted on a windswept heath. I saw a bulldozer, tilting precariously and abandoned among the rocks and thickets. Further away were blocky apartment modules with laundry fluttering from the balconies. I squinted at the glaring sun. Beyond the buildings I caught a glimpse of the sea.

The offices of the Guardia Civil were located in a brown brick complex that occupied an entire block. Behind the buildings, barbed wire reached high above the walls.

Spain had three types of police forces. I'd read that on the web when I was in Lisbon the day before. It was the Guardia Civil that handled security for the border areas, and they were also mentioned in the articles about illegal immigration.

In the waiting room a black-clad woman held a whimpering infant against her shoulder. The child was wrapped in a blanket. Next to her, two men were slumped in their chairs, sound asleep. I was summoned before any of them were called.

'So you're an American citizen?' The police officer sat behind a desk that stood in the middle of the cold room. 'We don't get many American tourists on this side of Gibraltar.'

'I'm not a tourist,' I said, sitting down before being invited to do so.

'I see.' The officer leaned back and looked at me with a slightly insolent expression. On the wall behind him was a picture of the Virgin Mary.

'Last Monday a man was found dead on the beach here in Tarifa,' I said.

'Are you a reporter?' he asked suspiciously.

'No,' I said, struggling to draw a breath. 'I'm his wife.'

The policeman laughed. A loud, hearty laugh that quickly died away.

'No, no, you are mistaken, *señora*. We're talking about an illegal immigrant. A sub-Saharan. They try to get here by boat, you see. Taking hopeless little *pateras* across the straits. We thought we'd put a stop to that sort of traffic here, but there are always people trying to slip through.'

I took the photograph of Patrick out of my bag and placed it on the desk in front of him.

'Is this him?'

The officer leaned down to look at the picture and then glanced up at me. His expression sceptical. Disapproving. He picked up the photo and then tossed it back on the desk.

'Who is this man?'

'His name is Patrick Cornwall. He's an American journalist, living in New York. He's my husband.' I'd carefully considered in advance how to formulate the sentences in Spanish, wanting to use words that were in the dictionary and not just spoken on the streets in Lo-i-saida.

The officer looked me up and down.

'You don't sound like an American.'

'I grew up in the Puerto Rican neighbourhood of New York,' I said. 'A place where we learn a little of everything.'

'And this is supposedly your husband?'

He tapped his pen on the photograph.

'He disappeared from Lisbon two weeks ago. He was murdered.'

'Maybe we'd better slow down a bit,' he said. He got up and nodded at the Virgin Mary's saintly face before he turned to face me again.

'We know that a boat left the coast of Morocco on the night before.' He pointed in the direction of the sea. 'We know that it capsized, or else the people on board jumped into the water. Sometimes they're ordered to do that so the captain can make it back to Morocco and hide before we catch him. Maybe they jumped in too soon this time.' He came around the desk and went over to a map hanging on the wall. 'A body washed ashore here,' he said, jabbing his pen at a spot on the map where the land met the sea. 'The next day we had two more bodies in Cádiz, a man and a woman. She was pregnant, in her sixth or seventh month. During the past week the Guardia Civil and the Moroccan coastguard have recovered a total of seven bodies.'

I took off my jacket.

'He had a tattoo on his shoulder,' I said as I pulled down my shirt from my left shoulder. The man's eyes crept over my skin as I exposed the tattoo. Two flowers intertwined, and the name that was etched there for all eternity. Patrick.

'It says Alena on his tattoo,' I explained. 'I know that's the tattoo that the man on the beach had.'

The officer took a few steps closer. He leaned down. Pressed his finger on my tattoo, stroked it lightly. His breath was close to my ear.

I shivered, but didn't move. He went back to his desk and sat down again.

'Was your husband into water sports?' he said finally.

'What?'

'Tarifa is popular among surfers.' He leaned back, rocking his chair. 'Kitesurfers and windsurfers come here from England, Scandinavia, and all over Europe. They have no respect for the winds or the sea. They think it's a game out there. I'm sure some Americans come here too.'

286

Patrick as a surfer? The idea was so idiotic that at first I couldn't think of a thing to say. If there was one thing he was afraid of, it was deep water. I shook my head.

'He could hardly even swim.'

The officer leaned forward to press a button at the side of his desk. The door opened and a younger man peeked in.

'Bring me the papers on the sub-Saharan from last Monday.'

When the door closed he leaned across his desk, his eyes as penetrating as knives.

'I've been on the force for fourteen years,' he said. 'I know this border. I know what goes on here. New ideas spread as fast as wildfire on the other side. For a time we had overloaded *pateras* entering our territory every week. Then, after we set up radar surveillance, it was popular to hide under car chassis on the ferry from Tangiers. After that it was tankers. I've seen just about everything.' He laughed and leaned back, clasping his hands behind his neck. 'But this is the first time anyone has ever claimed that an American was trying to cross the straits.'

'I didn't say he was trying to cross the straits,' I told him. 'He was murdered.'

The subordinate policeman came in, carrying a folder, which he handed to his boss. Before he left, he cast a glance at me. I straightened my shirt, which was still pulled down to show my left shoulder.

The officer seated at the desk opened the folder and took out several photographs. I felt an icy shiver race through my body and I felt an urge to flee. He shoved three photos across the desk to me.

The first was a full-length picture of Patrick lying on the beach. He was naked. He screamed, I thought. He screamed when they threw him into the sea. The words kept whirling through my mind. I closed my eyes, then opened them again. Forced myself to look, touched the image. A smooth surface. Dead.

The next picture was a close-up. I quickly turned away. I already knew. Didn't want that to be my last image of Patrick, taking over the one of him kissing me before he ran downstairs to get in the cab and ride out to Newark to catch his plane to Paris. I wiped my eyes on my sleeve and forced myself to look at the last photo.

It showed the tattoo on his shoulder, the flowers intertwined around my name, *like something Botticelli might have painted*. It was bright red and green. After our first visit to the Chinese tattoo artist, he'd gone to another one to have the colours filled in. The Chinese artist had only limited experience working with tattoos on black skin. Light colours disappeared against the skin tones, but the deep red showed up nicely, as did the green. Alena in red, the flowers in green.

My stomach turned over. I murmured something as I pressed my hand over my mouth and leaped up, running through the waiting room where the woman and her child flickered past, like something black on the periphery of my vision, as I stumbled my way to the ladies' room.

I bent over the toilet and threw up. White bread and ham and juice. Shaking all over as my stomach turned inside out and the last bit of hope spilled out with everything else.

I spent a long time rinsing my face with cold water. Pressed the palms of my hands to my cheeks. Dried off my face with toilet paper.

The police officer had changed his attitude by the time I came back. He was sitting up straight behind his desk, his expression sombre.

'How are you feeling?'

I merely shook my head. My legs trembled as I sat down.

'We need to identify the body,' he said, gathering up the photographs. I refused to look at them again.

'It's him,' I said, pressing my hands against my thighs to make them stop shaking. 'That's Patrick Cornwall. He's thirty-eight years old. An American citizen.'

The officer scratched his neck. 'This isn't sufficient to pronounce him dead, you understand. There are very specific procedures.'

'What are you talking about?' I fell back on my street Spanish from my childhood.

'Anybody could come in here and say "that's my husband" and then claim the inheritance. I'm not saying you're doing anything like that, but other people might.'

'I'm telling you it's him.'

The officer furrowed his eyebrows. They merged into one above the bridge of his nose.

'We need positive identification,' he said, taking some papers out of the folder.

'What do you mean by that?'

I drew my jacket closer around me.

'If we have a Moroccan immigrant, we contact the Moroccan police and then they take over. When it's an immigrant from south of the Sahara, it's not so easy.'

'But don't you understand anything?' My voice rose to falsetto as my throat closed up. 'He's not some fucking sub-Saharan. He's American, and his family goes back seven generations in the States.'

The officer waved the papers he was holding and then set them down on the desk.

'We can't identify bodies that wash ashore,' he said. 'We don't even know what country they come from. Nigeria, Ghana, Sierra Leone, Sudan . . . Where would we even begin to look?'

I crossed my arms and pressed my hands into my armpits to warm them up.

'We take fingerprints and blood samples. Then the bodies are sent to the morgue. I've never heard of any being identified.'

I stared at him, but he just kept rambling on about his fucking immigrants. It was clear that rational arguments were not going to work, and I realized that Patrick could very well disappear all over again, into some sort of Kafkaesque bureaucracy that handled death. I fixed my eyes on the Virgin Mary and the baby Jesus in her arms. An absurd thought occurred to me: if they'd had DNA testing back in those days, they could have proved who the father was.

'Where is the nearest American consulate?' I asked.

'Seville.'

I don't want to see him, I thought. I don't want to stand in some cold morgue as they lift up the sheet covering his face, and say: 'That's him' and burst into tears. I don't want everything to be so cold the last time I see him.

'Could you send an email with the fingerprints and other information to the American consulate?' I asked.

'No,' said the officer. 'We don't do things like that.'

'Come on . . . where are your *cojones*!' I pounded my fist on the desk and was close to calling him a 'son of a bitch', when the officer opened his mouth and smiled so I could see his gold teeth.

'But we could certainly send a fax.'

Outside the police building I called the number for the consulate in Seville.

A man answered. Tom McNerney. His accent told me he was from the Midwest.

'This has to do with something a little more important than a passport,' I said.

'OK. Tell me what it is and I'll see what I can do.'

I gave him a short version of the story, stating the facts as if they no longer had anything to do with me. As I talked, I stared at the solid walls of the police building. Someone had scrawled an anarchist symbol on the brick.

'All right. I want you to stay calm,' said McNerney when I had finished. 'I'm going to call you back as soon as I get the fax from Tarifa, and then we'll take it from there, one step at a time. OK?'

'OK.' I felt my heart lurch. Finally someone who cared.

'By the way, in Tarifa I can recommend the Café Central in the old town. It's a pleasant place to have a simple lunch. Historic setting and good prices.'

'Thanks,' I said. 'I'll keep that in mind.'

I rounded the corner, and the wind struck me full force. It felt like tiny needles as the sand whipped across my face. Before me was the beach and the sea, a vast horizon extending into infinity.

Somewhere out there was where he'd been found.

I sank down onto a block of cement, looking for the number among the most recent calls on my cell.

She answered on the second ring.

'This is Ally Cornwall again,' I said.

'Oh, it's you,' said Terese. 'You just disappeared the other day. Did you hang up or something?'

I leaned forward, tugging my jacket up to protect me from the wind.

'There's just one more thing I need to know.'

'Papa says I shouldn't talk to journalists. They just distort what you say and slant everything the wrong way.'

'I'm not a journalist.'

'Then what's this about?'

'It's a little hard to explain,' I said, scraping my shoes

291

on the fine-grained sand that had blown up onto the pavement. 'I told you that I might know the man you found on the beach, and now I can tell you that I do. I've seen the photographs of him.'

Terese gasped.

'Really?' she said, and then fell silent for a few seconds. 'I hadn't thought about him that way. That someone would know him, I mean.'

'I need to know where he was lying,' I cut her off. 'The exact location.'

'Why do you want to know that?' asked Terese.

'Please. Just tell me.'

Several seconds of silence. Seagulls circled overhead.

'I haven't been able to talk to anyone about this,' said Terese and then she burst into tears. She snuffled and sobbed. And as the words poured out of her — about how bad she had felt and how she'd gone to the beach that night with a man she'd met only hours earlier, a surfer guy named Alex from some small town in England who had apparently broken her heart — I started walking across the sand dunes. I managed to get a few facts out of the girl on the phone before she surrendered to uncontrolled sobbing.

A dark stone jetty reached several metres out into the sea.

'That's exactly where he was lying,' sobbed Terese. 'Can you believe that I actually stepped on him?'

I climbed up onto the rocks and sat down. The waves raised and lowered the surface of the water, making it seem as if even the ground was pitching, and nothing solid or permanent existed. An orange kite flew over my head with a surfer wearing a wetsuit hanging onto a rope behind it. He bounced on his board and tumbled into the water. The air was salty and hot.

'I don't understand how he could treat me like that,' moaned Terese.

I stared at the phone in my hand. I'd almost forgotten I was holding it.

'Who?' I asked, bewildered.

'Alex. I mean, we had . . .'

The water splashed as a new wave broke against the rocks and then rolled further up the shore. Leaving foam in its wake. Somewhere near this jetty, wedged in among the rocks, was where he'd lain. I couldn't make myself look down.

'I suppose I shouldn't have done it. Right?'

'Done what?'

'Had sex with him, of course.'

'What does that have to do with anything?'

My eyes were stinging from the sand and the glaring light. I squinted at the horizon to the west and couldn't tell where the sea ended and the sky began.

'If only I'd said no,' Terese whimpered. 'Maybe then he would have liked me.'

'Now stop that,' I said, my thoughts flying to that first night when I took Patrick to my place in the East Village, his hand in mine as I led him up the dark stairs where the light bulbs were never changed. 'Sometimes you just have to take a chance.'

I brushed the strands of hair out of my eyes, but the wind blew them right back.

'He stole my passport,' Terese said. 'Can you believe he took it to sell? He just wanted the money. And I actually went back to the Blue Heaven Bar because I wanted to see him again.'

'On which side of the jetty was he lying?'

'I already told you that. On the right side, about halfway out.'

I forced myself to turn my head and look down. Terese was not in the picture I saw. Only the thought of Patrick's body. The chill of the water. A wave breaking in swirling foam, stirring up the sand from the bottom and leaving a few shells behind when the water receded. Then the next wave rushed in, erasing any trace of the one before.

Chapter 15

Tarifa
Friday, 3 October

'How's the weather down on the coast?'

Tom McNerney from the consulate was on the phone. It was just after ten in the morning.

'I assume it's windy,' I said.

I'd eaten a big breakfast and was now sitting at one of the computers behind the front desk. It was a simple *pensión* on a back street, built in the Arabic style, with a rectangular central courtyard and the rooms grouped around it. The walls were covered with blue and white tiles, painted with chubby little cherubs flitting about.

'I'm sitting here with a fax of a set of fingerprints.'

'OK.' I quickly clicked out of the email I was writing to Benji and stood up. I could hear McNerney leafing through papers.

'So now the question is how we should proceed,' he went on. 'First we need another set of fingerprints for comparison.'

It took a few seconds before the meaning of what he'd said sank in. Of course. I hadn't thought that far.

McNerney coughed. 'The alternative is DNA testing, of course, but that's a more complicated matter.'

Not DNA, I thought, sinking down onto a wicker chair. I stared at a group of three life-size pink plastic flamingos that were part of the decor.

Fingerprints were less . . . intimate.

There were fingerprints back home in the apartment, of course. And on his things in Lisbon. I'd left his suitcase in the hotel storage room, giving the desk clerk a 20-euro tip and saying that I'd send for the suitcase later.

'The easiest would be if his prints are already registered somewhere,' McNerney went on.

Registered? Were Patrick's fingerprints in any police records?

Yes, they were! And his father had given him hell for it. The fact that Patrick had ended up with a police record and, according to his father, had ruined his future for the sake of the story he was chasing.

'He was once arrested a couple of years ago,' I said. 'In Maryland.'

'OK,' said McNerney. I noticed a slight shift in his tone of voice. 'Then it's just a matter of contacting the home front . . .'

'He's not a criminal,' I quickly added. 'He was doing research in Prince George police district, working under-cover. Pretending to be a felon, you might say. For a story on racism among the police, how they treat blacks worse than whites. There were rumours of systematic abuse and coerced confessions.'

'That sounds familiar for some reason,' said McNerney.

'He almost got a Pulitzer Prize for the story,' I said. 'Plus a broken rib.'

'So, Maryland, you said?' I heard him tapping on a keyboard, and I imagined Patrick's fingerprints being compared, all the lines matching up perfectly.

'There's something else I was told,' said McNerney.

'What?'

'They have certain routines in cases like this.' His voice sounded scratchy. He cleared his throat and wheezed a bit. 'Well, that is . . . when the first impression is that they're dealing with an immigrant from south of the Sahara.'

He was choosing his words carefully, not wanting to say the wrong thing.

'What do you mean?'

'Well, the thing is, they've buried him.'

'What did you say?'

'Your husband, Patrick Cornwall, was buried a few days ago. On Monday, to be precise.'

My hand holding the phone dropped towards the floor. I closed my eyes and thought about packed-down dirt and the darkness underneath. Layer upon layer of dirt.

'Hello? Are you there?' I heard Tom McNerney saying.

I raised the phone back to my ear.

'They can't do that,' I said. 'They didn't even know who he was.'

'From what I understand, there wasn't enough room,' said McNerney. 'They've had more people over the past few weeks. People who have died, I mean. Some are immigrants, but there are also . . . er . . . ordinary citizens. They die too. Old folks. And it's a small town.'

'He was murdered.'

Silence on the phone. Again he cleared his throat.

'I'm sorry,' he said.

'He's an American citizen,' I said. The words caught in my throat.

'As his next of kin, you can of course request that his remains be sent home as soon as the bureaucratic procedures are taken care of. We'll help you with the paperwork.'

'That's not what this is about,' I said, standing up. 'They

297

killed him. I don't know exactly who did it, but I know who's responsible. A Frenchman who—'

'Calm down. Let's take one thing at a time.'

I paced back and forth in the lobby, listening to Tom McNerney's broad Midwest accent in my ear. Some of what he said sank in.

First, he would see to the identification. He'd learned that no autopsy had been done on Patrick's body. That should be the next step, but it would have to be handled entirely by the Spanish police.

'We don't do anything unless they request our help,' he explained. 'I need to abide by the rules of diplomacy.'

'Can't you just ask them if they'd like your help?'

'That would mean getting involved in the police work in the country where I'm stationed. And we don't want to do that.'

'Right,' I said, rubbing my forehead. I pictured having to pay a return visit to the Guardia Civil and make a big scene in that cold office of theirs. Or would one of the other branches of the police take over now? Maybe the Policía Nacional? I sank down on another chair next to the big pots of plastic flowers, feeling weighted down with fatigue.

'But if we just take one step at a time, it'll all work out. You'll see.'

'Where?' I said then.

'Excuse me?'

'Where is he buried?'

The Catholic cemetery was in a vast field behind a German discount store. Outside the cemetery walls three horses were grazing among the withered grass.

The wind stopped as I entered. Inside the walls the vegetation was lush. It was a leafy oasis in the midst of the arid terrain, as if the very concentration of death had given the earth life. And, as a matter of fact, that was probably the case . . . ashes to ashes, dust to dust . . .

A cemetery worker was putting his gardening tools away in a shed.

'Excuse me,' I said in my most polite Spanish. 'I'm looking for a new grave. A man who was buried here on Monday.'

The man shrugged and shook his head.

'They think he was an illegal immigrant,' I added, and the workman set down his spade. His face was creased, and he was missing most of his teeth. He pointed towards the southern section of the cemetery.

I murmured my thanks and started walking, noting the hierarchy among the dead. First came the rows of neat Catholic *nichos*, crypts with arched roofs, decorated with flowers, and names etched into the stone four feet high, with small statues of Jesus and the Virgin Mary. Then came the ordinary headstones that became plainer the closer I got to the perimeter of the cemetery. The flowers were fewer, and finally even the names disappeared. Several anonymous graves marked with bricks, grass growing up through the cracks. None of them had been dug in the past few weeks.

Finally I came to a small commemorative marker. A simple piece of metal with an inscription and a small bouquet of pink flowers. *En memoria de los inmigrantes caidos en aguas del 'estrecho*. In memory of the immigrants who perished in the waters of the straits — the straits between the African continent and Europe.

The sun was hot on the back of my neck. I turned around. Behind me the field stopped at a wall. A tree cast a wide shadow over the far corner. A rusty wrought-iron fence surrounding an old grave had toppled over. In front of it was a mound of earth, about the size of a coffin. Slowly I approached, bent down, and picked up a fistful of the brown dirt. It was damp, smelling of humus and autumn. I sank to my knees. Placed my hand on the grave.

Emptiness. That's what I felt. A profound, aching silence. Where no sounds could reach. I had never had any god to talk to, neither the Catholic god nor any other. For the first time in my life I felt the lack of something greater, yearning for a solace that I had no clue how to find.

I bowed forward, brushing the earth with my cheek, and whispered: 'Patrick. I'm here, and I just wanted to tell you . . .' My throat closed up and I couldn't say the words.

You're going to be a father.

The shadow from the tree moved slowly across the white wall. Time passed.

When I finally got up, I had a hard time straightening out my legs. I turned one last time to look at the nameless part of the cemetery. And I realized there was a conversation I could not put off any longer.

'It's not true!' she screamed into the phone. I held it away from my ear. Then Patrick's father took over. I could hear Eleanor Cornwall in the background saying: 'My son is not dead. He's not dead!'

Formal and businesslike, Robert Cornwall demanded that I tell him exactly what had happened.

'A Catholic cemetery?' he managed to say, after I'd told him most of the story. 'But you know we're Protestants.'

'It's a Catholic country,' I said. 'And they didn't know who he was.'

Silence. Did I really have to defend this country? As if I were the one who had decided he should be buried here. I sat down on the bed in my hotel room and stared out of the open door to the balcony.

Patrick's parents had never accepted his decision to marry

me. Not when there were so many nice girls from black families among their circle of friends.

'He has to be laid to rest in our cemetery,' said Robert, choking on his words. 'Mother needs a grave she can visit. Our family lawyer will handle all the details.'

And the line went dead. My father-in-law had ended the call. I lay down and stared up at the ceiling, seeing two damp patches that seemed to grow, merging into one another. I hadn't told Patrick's parents that I was expecting his child.

That evening the confirmation came.

I was still lying on the bed and must have fallen asleep, when the phone woke me. My body felt cold and numb.

'I've received word from Maryland,' said Tom McNerney. 'We have a positive ID.'

'I see,' I said.

It felt like nothing could touch me any more. The formalities relating to Patrick's death were something abstract that had nothing to do with the death itself. Bureaucratic procedures, like a school exercise that had to be completed.

'You were right,' said McNerney. 'He was listed in the police records, and the fingerprints match those of the dead man in Tarifa.'

I slid back into a sitting position.

'What happens now?'

'Please accept my sincere apologies. I realize I haven't even offered you my condolences.'

I saw the curtains flutter as a gust of wind came through the window. Outside the light was a matte blue. It would soon be dark.

'The first thing we need to do is arrange for a formal death certificate. We can help you with the paperwork and with contacting the Spanish authorities.'

'And the murder investigation?' I said. 'What about that?'

Tom McNerney inhaled sharply and clucked his tongue.

'That's a little trickier,' he said. 'That would mean getting involved in the internal affairs of the country in which we're stationed and, as you know, I can't do that.'

'But what do the police say about it?'

'From what I understand, they regard the death as an accidental drowning.'

'But it wasn't.'

I got up and paced the small room.

'Patrick would never have gone into waves like that voluntarily,' I said. 'He won't even take the ferry to Staten Island if he can avoid it.'

Wouldn't, I thought. Wouldn't, not won't. Everything is past tense from now on.

'It's my guess that the Spanish police would like to see more solid evidence,' said McNerney. 'If there is any, I'm sure they will open an investigation. I have complete faith in the police of this country nowadays.'

I rubbed my forehead. Evidence?

'They need to talk to the police in Lisbon,' I said. 'An Inspector Ferreira. He knows a lot of the story.'

'As I said, I'm not the man to tell the police of this country what they should do. It would not be regarded kindly, as I'm sure you'll understand.'

I lowered the phone. Solid evidence.

'And I can't—'

'Get involved in their work. I know,' I said, taking a deep breath.

'I'm sorry,' said McNerney.

'Dr Robert Cornwall will be getting in touch with you soon,' I said. 'His lawyer will request that Patrick's body be sent back home to the States.'

I went out onto the little balcony that faced the street

at the back of the hotel. The sounds of another reality rose towards me. The noisy clattering of a moped. Two women loudly gossiping across the street.

An accidental drowning. Was it possible that Patrick's death would be written off that easily?

Not a chance. He had sacrificed his life for this story. There was nothing normal about his death.

I went back into the room, sat down on the bed, and tapped in the phone number for the editorial offices of *The Reporter* in New York.

It took four minutes before I was connected to Richard Evans.

'Ally Cornwall!' the editor shouted on the phone. 'What a coincidence. I'm sitting here with a thick envelope sent from Lisbon.'

Chapter 16

Tarifa
Saturday, 4 October

The first articles appeared in a special Internet edition of *The Reporter*, in the morning, Spanish time.

AMERICAN JOURNALIST MURDERED?

New York journalist Patrick Cornwall was found dead in southern Spain. Indications are that he was murdered.

Patrick Cornwall, 38, is known to readers of The Reporter as a fearless and knowledgeable journalist. Two years ago he was nominated for a Pulitzer Prize for his exposé of racism within the police force.

For more than a month he has been researching present-day slavery in Paris, the heart of Europe and the cradle of the ideals of liberty. He found a dirty world in which human life is not highly valued.

'Patrick was about to expose a criminal network that reaches even to the powerful elite,' says Alena Cornwall, his widow, who has spent the past few weeks

304

in Europe looking for her husband after he disap-
peared.

She finally found him, on a beach in Tarifa, a town
on the Spanish coast. The local police thought it was
a case of yet another refugee who had drowned while
fleeing on a boat from Africa. His body was buried
in an unmarked grave on Monday.

Now Alena Cornwall is demanding that the police
investigate his murder.

'Patrick Cornwall's death is not just a crime against
an individual,' says Senator John Whiteford in a
commentary.

'It is also a crime against the freedom of expression.'

I rubbed my eyes, then I skimmed the rest of the article. I could hardly take in what it said. Black letters flickering on a greyish-white screen. As if it were just any newspaper text that had nothing to do with me. Yet I felt slightly elated, a euphoric sense at finding myself in the centre of the world. I was sitting at the computer behind the front desk in the hotel, clicking back and forth from one article to another. They had worked hard.

There were statistics about slavery in the world, comments from organizations working to abolish slavery, scores of examples of present-day slavery, an article about a hotel fire in which seventeen people had died, a map of immigration routes . . .

It was all there. And yet it wasn't.

Patrick Cornwall was said to have been working on a theory about legitimate enterprises acting as a cover for extensive trading in slave labour for such markets as the construction industry, janitorial services, and agriculture in Western Europe.

A theory? Alain Thery's name was not mentioned

305

anywhere, but Richard Evans had assured me that this was only the beginning.

'At this stage we can't publish any names,' he'd explained. 'Those people could sue our asses off.'

'Patrick is dead,' I said. 'I know that Thery is behind it.'

'You might know that,' said Richard. 'But I'm the one who'd go to prison.'

He had personally stayed on the job and worked half the night, calling in extra staff and taking charge of the whole thing. He'd written the lead article himself.

'I'll be damned if Cornwall wasn't right,' he said when he called me to check on some details. 'This is one hell of a story. A real prize-winning story. It's a shame we won't have his take on it. His eyewitness accounts giving the reader the sense that he dragged this poor immigrant's story out of the blazing inferno.'

From the photo with the by-line of his editorial on the front page, Richard Evans' fierce, pale blue eyes stared back at me.

'The fact that immigrants are exploited as cheap or free labour is the dark side of the global economy,' he wrote, drawing parallels with the slave trade of the past. 'Back then a slave was an investment that was kept for generations. Now he is just one of many use-and-discard types of goods. Let's not debate which is preferable. Instead, let's finish what the abolitionists started almost two centuries ago: let's eradicate slavery from the earth for good.'

The article concluded with a challenge to the politicians. 'Democracies,' he wrote, 'must be able to find better solutions than building walls to keep out the rest of the world.' And then he expressed sorrow at the passing of Patrick Cornwall, and wrote that he was one of the magazine's most valued freelance reporters. His death would leave a real void.

As the hours passed, I watched the news spread over the Internet.

It was mentioned on CNN, and then on one TV channel after another. As the morning progressed in Europe, the story appeared in more and more newspapers in Spain, France, and Great Britain.

Patrick's by-line photo from *The Reporter* was mass-produced in online publications all over the world. Some even ran a photograph of me, taken from the Joyce Theatre home page.

A well-groomed woman wearing light make-up smiled at me from the photo. A woman from another life.

I stopped reading and studied the picture of Patrick. It had been taken about two years ago. His expression was solemn and formal. He looked like a stranger. Frozen in a moment that had swiftly raced past.

Now we just needed to wait.

Richard Evans had promised me that the story would start to take on a life of its own. The demands for a murder investigation would grow until the police would be forced to act. And in the end justice would rise victorious, as he expressed it, out of all the shit.

Chapter 17

Tarifa
Monday, 6 October

On Monday they came to exhume his body.

I watched everything from a distance. It was now out of my hands. The small backhoe turned and manoeuvred until it was next to the grave. The cameras whirred as the first shovelful of dirt was removed. The murmur of voices rose.

I was crouched down between several Catholic graves, my hood pulled up so I wouldn't be recognized.

This section of the cemetery, which had been so desolate before, was now crowded with people. Reporters and TV crews and ordinary spectators. In two days, Patrick's death had become a story capturing worldwide attention. Journalists and TV producers had quickly got hold of my number, and on Saturday the calls had started coming in. I declined all interviews and referred everyone to Richard Evans. I had said everything I was going to say to *The Reporter*. Some had ferreted out my email address. They wanted to know more about our life together, about what Patrick was like as a husband and a human being. They wanted to rip from me every memory that I had left.

I'd walked for miles on the beach. For long stretches I'd taken off my shoes and walked barefoot at the edge of the water with my jeans rolled up. It was too cold to swim, but the sea tempted and tugged at me, and I wished I could have gone in for a swim. To swim the way I used to do long ago, when I was in school. Back then, as I glided through the water, everything around me had disappeared.

On the other side of town, in the east, there were deserted beaches, rocky and inaccessible. There was also a ruin of a fortress filled with broken bottles and used condoms. When the wind got to be too much, I would head up to the old part of town, hidden within medieval ramparts, which had the same meandering Arabic network of lanes as Alfama in Lisbon. I had passed the place called the Blue Heaven Bar, where Terese had met the dirt-bag who had stolen her things. In the restaurant that Tom McNerney had mentioned, the Café Central, I'd eaten a Moroccan salad with tuna and mint for both lunch and dinner.

I'd then slept soundly all night, a slumber without colour or dreams, until I awoke to McNerney's phone call and he told me that the Spanish police had decided to exhume Patrick's body.

The pressure from American and European news agencies had cut through the bureaucratic red tape.

An autopsy was going to be performed. The murder investigation had begun.

Photographs from the exhuming of the grave were quickly posted on the Internet.

I was sitting at my usual computer behind the front desk,

dropping in three euros to pay for an hour of Internet time. It seemed more real and concrete to read about Patrick's death than to experience it myself. The significance hadn't yet settled in the depths of my soul.

Never again.

Retribution, I thought instead. Justice. That's what was important right now. The exhumation order was the first victory, and soon those bastards would be caught, with the whole world watching.

I skimmed through a couple of Spanish newspapers, but it wasn't easy. Spanish was a spoken language for me. So I switched to the New York papers.

The Reporter described the opening of Patrick's grave as a victory for justice. There were several articles about cases of slavery discovered around the world, but nothing new about the fire in Paris, about the death of Mikail Yechenko, or about Alain Thery. His name still hadn't been mentioned. Nor was any of the information from Yechenko's documents reported.

On the other hand, there was a flood of praise for Patrick's work.

You could have bought his articles while he was alive, I thought as I clicked out of the news reports and leaned back. I was starting to think about leaving this godforsaken town. There were buses to Málaga, and from there I could catch a plane.

Home, I thought. Was that possible? To go back, as if nothing had happened? Put on my old clothes, step back into my old life?

I skipped all the emails from journalists, and opened the last two that Benji had sent.

In the first he wrote that he was so terribly, terribly sorry.

That the world was a horrible place in which love never had a chance.

He'd pasted in a poem by W H Auden, the one quoted in *Four Weddings and a Funeral*, and I couldn't avoid the lines about the stars that were put out when a beloved one had died.

He'd also sent three sketches for a stage design for Cherry Lane Theatre. Just some scattered ideas, he wrote, so he'd have something to show them at the next meeting. I couldn't even get myself to look at them. Benji would have to string the clients along until I got home.

'Go with your first impulse,' I wrote. 'Trust your intuition to come up with the right approach.'

I was just about to close the email programme when I discovered an email from Caroline Kearny among the ones that I'd skipped. Her purple-clothed figure appeared in my mind, as if from a different era. Paris seemed so infinitely long ago.

'*Oh, my darling, oh, my dear,*' she wrote. Several more lines expressing sorrow and then a P.S.:

'Meeting Guy de Barreau tomorrow. Have tried to contact Alain Thery, but he's left the city. Rumour has it that he's on one of his yachts, in Saint-Tropez or Puerto Banus.'

I clicked the reply button, but couldn't think of a thing to say, so I switched off the computer. The poem still lingered in my head as the screen went all dark, like a sky without its stars, nor a moon or a sun.

I awoke to a Spanish talk show on the TV. Outside it was still light, with horns blaring. I had stretched out on the bed, zapping through the TV channels. Then I must have fallen asleep. I couldn't remember ever feeling so exhausted.

The remote had fallen to the floor. I picked it up and began searching for a news show.

First a piece on domestic politics in Spain, and then the spotlight shifted to Tarifa. The camera panned over fishing boats and moved on to the statue of the saint that stood at the very end of a pier to bless the shipping lanes. I turned up the volume. A Spanish news anchor was saying: 'It was here in Tarifa that the body of an American journalist . . .' Patrick's face appeared, the photo from his by-line. '. . . now suspect that he was murdered . . .'

A picture of the beach, and then a young black man appeared on screen.

'I didn't know him personally,' said the man, speaking English with a strange accent. In the subtitles, he was identified only as James, an immigrant.

'Patrick Cornwall was on the boat that night. He said he wanted to write about the crossing from Africa for an American magazine.'

All sounds from the street disappeared. What the fuck? A boat? What was the man talking about? Africa?

'It was a terrible trip across the straits,' said the immigrant named James. 'It was stormy, and the boat rocked and took on water and people fell into the sea. I think almost all of them died.'

'But you survived,' said the reporter, whose English was worse than James's.

'I thank my God that I'm alive,' said James, glancing up at the sky. It was Creole English he was speaking, from some former British colony. The interview was subtitled in Spanish.

'You've chosen to step forward, even though you risk being sent back to your homeland,' said the reporter. 'Why do you want to speak out about this?'

'I owe it to God because he rescued me from the sea,' said James.

'And you are quite certain that Patrick Cornwall, the American journalist, was on that same boat?'

'He said he wanted to write about us,' said James. 'I

asked if he could help me get to America. He was a good man.'

Then the immigrant disappeared, and the camera panned across the beach and over to the fortress ruins, where the reporter stood, holding a microphone.

'The death of the American journalist Patrick Cornwall has prompted huge headlines all over the world, turning everyone's eyes to the southern coast of Spain.' He had to shout to be heard over the roaring of the waves. 'Every death is a tragedy, of course, but in this case there doesn't appear to be anything criminal involved, other than the illegal smuggling of people, which still happens here, on our shores.'

A soccer game started up. I had to get up from the bed and go out onto the balcony, letting the lashing of the wind bring me to my senses again.

It wasn't possible. I tried to picture Patrick in a rubber boat on a stormy sea. Wearing chinos and a sport coat, clinging to the gunwale. Could I have been so wrong?

Had he really gone crazy and made his way over the border to commit even bigger stupidities in order to land his story? *I'm headed straight into the darkness.*

In the room behind me my cell was ringing. It was Richard Evans.

'What the hell is this?' he shouted into the phone. 'I'm sitting here with a wire from the AP. Did Patrick go out trying to do some sort of travel report?'

'It can't be true,' I said, closing the balcony doors. 'He would never have gone out on a boat like that.'

'Why not?'

'Patrick wouldn't even take the ferry to—'

Evans interrupted me.

'I'll agree that it sounds like a fantastic story, an amazing eyewitness account, with the waves and the people struggling

313

to get across a merciless sea. But that's not what we wrote in *The Reporter* yesterday. What am I missing? All the lawyers are calling me like crazy.'

I sank down onto the bed. My mind was whirling.

'That man named James must be mistaken,' I said. 'Maybe he's just somebody who wanted to be on TV.'

'They claim he's trustworthy. It's been confirmed that a boat capsized in the Mediterranean that night. Evidently they've found more dead bodies.' Evans put his hand over the phone and murmured something to someone else. I heard a TV on in the background, and other voices. 'We're checking on this, of course, but for the time being we're going to have to pull the story off the web.'

'What do you mean?'

'The other publications have already changed their versions. We can't stand alone against the world and claim that Patrick Cornwall was murdered by a criminal gang. That would completely destroy our credibility. We have to safeguard our integrity, especially since he worked for us.'

'But it's the truth,' I said faintly, not sure whether I believed it myself.

'It's not so much a matter of what's true,' said Evans, 'as what we're able to substantiate.'

There was a rustling on the phone, and I heard the sound become more muted. The background sounds disappeared. He'd had it on speaker.

'I'm just as concerned as you are,' he said in a lower voice. 'But management is after me. They think I'm too personally involved.'

'But everything he was going to write, his whole story, it's all true,' I said.

'We'll keep checking,' said Evans. 'That's all we can do. Check and double-check. Journalistic footwork. That's how it has to be for now.'

Later, when I went down to the lobby and logged onto the Internet, the articles from the front page of *The Reporter* had been removed. All that remained was a discreet reference to a brief article, buried below the news of a planned top meeting between the United States, Israel, and the Palestinian leaders.

Chapter 18

Tarifa
Tuesday, 7 October

The woman was sitting in the lobby, waiting right behind the family of flamingos. She was in her fifties, wearing wide linen trousers and far too many necklaces. Miguel, the clerk at the front desk, had pointed her out with an apologetic gesture. Just like his father, wife, brother, cousins, and everyone else who either worked in the hotel or spent time with their relatives in the bar, he knew by now that I didn't want to talk to journalists. Ever since the news about Patrick had appeared on TV, they had been protecting me. Not even some distant cousin had blabbed to the reporters that I was staying at the hotel.

The woman gave off an unmistakable fragrance of musk and smoke and rose oil. Obviously a dyed-in-the-wool hippie.

I stopped two metres away and crossed my arms.

'I don't give interviews,' I said.

She stood up and reached out to shake my hand. A warm, gaunt hand with many silver rings on her fingers. The woman was nearly six foot five.

316

'My name is Jillian Dunne,' she said with a British accent that spoke of dark boarding schools. 'I'm sorry for your loss.'

'Thanks and goodbye,' I said.

She smiled gently.

'I'm not a reporter,' she said. 'I'm here because there's someone I think you should meet.'

I looked her up and down, noting the sandals she wore with the straps fastened around suntanned ankles, and all the beads strung on chains and cords around her wrists and neck.

'You're not a therapist, are you?' I asked.

The woman laughed.

'No, not really. This has to do with your husband.'

'And?'

'Certain people are saying that he was on a boat that capsized in the Mediterranean about two weeks ago.'

I didn't say anything, just waited for what would come next.

'But the thing is, that boat didn't capsize at all,' said Jillian Dunne. 'And your husband was not on board.'

I stared at her.

'How do you know that?'

With a sweeping gesture, she slung a scarf around her neck.

'Come with me.'

She crossed the street, taking long strides, and turned right, towards the beach. The town had just now awakened from a sound siesta. Cars were parked halfway up on the sidewalks. A man was carrying garbage bags out of the back door of a shop.

'Where are we going?'

I caught up with Jillian, whose thin garments were flapping wildly in the wind.

'Some friends of mine have a café down here.'

'And who am I going to meet?'

She smiled enigmatically. I had a bad feeling that she was going to take me to a tarot reader who would predict my future. Or maybe she would personally read my cards.

'Do you live here in town?' I asked.

'Been here for twenty years.' Jillian slowed down a bit, waving her hand to encompass all of Tarifa. 'It was totally different back then. No tourists. We were bohemians, living for the moment, hitchhiking around. And some of us decided to stay.' She laughed and ran her hand through her hair. There was a hint of sorrow in her voice. 'I would never be able to adapt to British proprieties again.'

We passed a bullring that looked abandoned, with over-grown thickets all around. I had to walk faster to keep up with her.

'Cornwall,' said Jillian, smiling at me. 'That sounds like a British name.'

'A slave name,' I said briefly.

'Oh, right. It's your husband's name, of course. I didn't think of that.' She tugged at her necklaces. 'I didn't know that slaves had last names.'

'It wasn't a last name back then,' I said. 'Some of the slave owners named their slaves after the places they'd come from. Like London or Cornwall. The point was to show who the slaves belonged to. When Patrick's great-great-great-grandfather was freed, Cornwall was listed as his surname. Nobody knows whether it was done by mistake or whether he deliberately chose that name, because a free man always has a last name.'

Jillian stopped next to a series of townhouses on the slope leading down to the sea. She pointed.

'A friend of mine found a woman down there almost two weeks ago,' she said. 'On Monday. She was lying under

318

a footbridge near the shore. You can't really see it from here.'

'On Monday?' I took a deep breath.

The same day Patrick was found.

'I know what you're thinking,' she said. 'Your husband was found about a kilometre from here.'

She didn't have to tell me that. I had walked along the beach so many times over the past few days that I knew it in more detail than an aerial view on Google Earth.

'The woman wasn't dead,' Jillian went on, 'but she was in bad shape and had a high fever. We helped get her to a safe place.' She looked at me. 'I believe in individuals taking responsibility. Inaction is also a form of action.'

'Is it this woman we're going to meet?' I started walking even faster.

'I don't know her name,' said Jillian. 'She didn't say a word, not a single word after we found her. I thought she didn't understand English or that she was in shock. You can't imagine what they go through to get here.'

Jillian stopped outside a terracotta-coloured house. Part of the ground floor was painted turquoise, with flowers sticking out from the facade. The name 'Shangri-La' had been painted in big letters above the door. 'Café-bar-surf-shop.'

'This is where she's hiding?' I asked.

'It's better if you don't know where she's staying.'

Jillian took out a little tube and rubbed cream on her lips as she looked in every direction.

'I brought her breakfast as usual this morning,' she said in a low voice. 'I set down the tray like I always do and poured tea into our cups.'

And then you sat down on the edge of the bed and talked that poor woman to death, I thought. Out of your infinite kindness.

Jillian pressed a hand to her chest.

'And just think, she suddenly started talking. And you know what?'

'I have no idea.'

'She speaks excellent English.'

A bearded guy wearing an earring opened the door to Shangri-La, and Jillian kissed him on both cheeks. He locked the door behind us.

The café was a small room with tables made from old surfboards. The walls were painted with psychedelic patterns. Jillian disappeared behind a beaded curtain at the back of the bar. I followed, passing through a small kitchen and going up a narrow staircase. At the top we entered a room.

On a chair sat a black woman dressed in loose clothing made from green cotton fabric. On her feet she wore a pair of gold-coloured ballet flats that looked too small for her, and completely out-of-place.

I took a step closer and held out my hand.

'My name is Ally Cornwall. Are you the person I'm supposed to meet?'

The woman smiled faintly. She was about thirty, maybe younger.

'I can't tell you my name,' she said, shaking my hand. She spoke Creole English, just like James had on the TV news report.

I sat down on the only other chair in the room. It was a cramped space, a windowless cubbyhole, barely eight square metres. Several crates stood along one wall. It smelled of old ashtrays.

'She risks being sent back if anyone finds out she's here,' said Jillian, who was standing in the doorway. 'That's why the migrants are always so careful about revealing any personal details.'

The woman held my hand in both of hers.

'Don't believe that man,' she said to me. 'He wasn't on the boat.'

'Who do you mean?' I felt my heart pounding.

'That man on TV. He calls himself James.'

'A friend made arrangements so she could have a TV where she's staying,' Jillian explained.

I kept my eyes fixed on the woman.

'He says he was on the boat,' she whispered. 'But he's lying.'

'Are you sure?' I asked, holding my breath.

The woman rubbed her forehead and nodded.

'Not on that boat,' she said firmly.

'You mean the rubber boat that capsized?' I leaned back and studied the woman. There was a slight discoloration in the skin around one eye. Possibly from a blow of some kind. 'Do you know this because you were on that boat yourself?' I asked hesitantly. 'In the early morning hours of Sunday, two weeks ago? Is that when you tried to cross the straits?'

The woman closed her eyes and bowed her head.

'You need to understand how difficult this is for her,' said Jillian, taking a step closer.

'Quiet.' I raised my hand to stop her. The woman's pain only stirred my own; I needed to hear every detail.

A fan could be heard whirring downstairs. The guy with the beard clattered some glasses. And the wind rattled the metal roof and balconies. Those were the only sounds.

'They threw us into the water,' said the woman faintly, her words hardly more than an exhalation. 'They tossed us overboard to die.' She still had her eyes closed, and I imagined what she must be seeing in her mind: the waves and the black sea and people flailing and struggling. My stomach clenched.

321

'But you managed to survive,' I said, trying to keep my voice from quavering. 'You made it ashore.'

The woman opened her eyes, revealing a black abyss.

'A fisherman pulled me out, like a fish from the sea.' I saw her facial muscles tighten.

'And Patrick Cornwall?' I said quietly. 'He wasn't on the boat?'

'No, he wasn't.'

I leaned across the table and took her hands.

'Are you positive about that?'

'For three nights we sat in the shed and waited,' she said, turning to look at the wall. A poster had been tacked up, advertising a concert by some African musicians.

'They told us not to speak,' she said. 'We weren't supposed to say who we were, where we came from, or where we were going. On the first night we did as they said. We sat there in silence. The second night too. A girl started to cry. A woman hit her. I heard the slap. "Quiet," she said. "Crying won't help you get to Europe." On the third night when it was so dark that we almost couldn't see anyone's face, someone whispered his name. "My name is Peter," he said. "Peter Ohenhen." The others hissed at him to be quiet, he would make the smugglers come, he'd be beaten for disobeying the rules, they might beat all of us. But then another person whispered. "My name is Wisdom. Wisdom Okitola." And one by one we all whispered our names, first so quietly that only those sitting closest could hear, but then louder. The names tiptoed like spirits through the room. Teyo, Zaynab, Catherine, Toyin . . . We didn't say where we'd come from, or where we were going. Just our names. A boy began talking about his journey, but the others told him to hush. "We have all travelled far to come here, and your journey is no greater than anyone else's." Nothing more was said, but when that

322

night was over, we all knew each other's names. "My name is Mary Kwara," I whispered.'

She wiped her eyes on her sleeve and turned to look at me, and then at Jillian, who was still standing near the door.

'My name is Mary Kwara.'

'How many of you were in the boat?' I asked quietly.

'Twelve. There were twelve of us besides the crazy men. There were three of them. I've thought about that the whole time. They were only three. They were the ones who should have ended up in the sea.'

The woman drew her knees up to her chin and wrapped her arms around her legs. One leg was bandaged. 'This is how we sat, huddled up like this.' I stared at the gold shoes on her feet. They didn't seem to belong with the rest of her body. 'His name was Taye. Taye Lawal. He was sitting in front of me. Just a boy. I whispered all the names, one after the other, as the boat was tossed by the waves.'

Mary Kwara fell silent and looked up at the ceiling. She lowered her feet back down to the floor.

'No Patrick Cornwall,' she said, meeting my eye. 'There was no American.'

'But it must have been very dark. Could he have used a different name?'

'Eyes grow used to the dark,' she said, in a firm voice. 'I saw his picture on TV. He wasn't there.'

I pounded my hand on the table and got up.

'I knew it,' I said, taking a few steps away in the cramped space and then sitting down again. I fixed my eyes on Mary's face.

'You have to tell this to the police. You realize that, don't you?'

The woman shook her head and pulled back.

'No police,' she said.

I leaned towards her.

'My husband was murdered,' I said. 'He wanted to catch the scumbags like those men who threw all of you into the sea. Don't you want to see them put in prison?'

Mary held up her hands.

'No police,' she said.

Jillian stepped forward and placed her hand on Mary's shoulder.

'That's enough now,' she said.

'Let her speak for herself.' I tried not to snap.

'She's from Nigeria,' said Jillian. 'If she comes forward, they will send her back. She has no right to stay in Spain or any other EU country.'

I tried to look Mary in the eye.

'You're the only one who knows about this,' I said. 'Presumably you're the only passenger from that boat who survived.'

I saw something shut down deep inside those dark eyes of hers.

'You're the only one who can tell this story. Those bastards are going to get away. They murdered Patrick. Don't you understand?'

I looked from the black woman to the white woman, whose hand still rested protectively on Mary's shoulder.

'She doesn't have to say where she's from,' I pleaded with Jillian. 'All she has to say is what she just told me.'

'And who would believe me?' said Mary, standing up. 'If I lie about one thing, who will be able to tell what's true?'

The green clothing she wore looked as if it had come from Jillian's wardrobe. The same scent of musk and roses.

'I've told you as much as I can,' said Mary, bowing her head. 'Seven months ago I left my home. And I haven't yet reached where I'm going.'

I clenched my fists with frustration.

'You can't think only about yourself. This is about thousands of other people. Patrick was going to write about it, but now he's dead.'

The woman stared at the floor.

'I'm sorry.'

'You need to stop pressuring her,' said Jillian, stepping between us. 'She took a big risk just by coming here to meet you.'

I sank back down on the chair.

'Then why did you tell me this?' I said. 'I can't use any of this information. No one will believe me.'

'He was your husband,' said Mary. 'You have a right to know.'

Then Jillian put her arms protectively around her.

'Nico will drive you back,' she told the woman quietly.

As the beaded curtain clattered behind me on my way out, I heard Jillian calling to me.

'And I assume you won't tell anyone about any of this.'

As soon as it was one o'clock in Europe and eight in the morning in New York, I called *The Reporter*. Richard Evans hadn't yet arrived at the office. I bit my knuckles in frustration and then whiled away the time by surfing various newspapers on the Internet.

The articles had diminished and the story was no longer front-page news. The angle had also shifted. James the immigrant was copiously quoted. Patrick's name was not being mentioned as frequently. His death was no longer described as 'a possible homicide'. Instead he was said to have 'died while on assignment'. Now the focus was on the capsized boat and more generally on the traffic across the Mediterranean from Africa. The night before last, two hundred migrants had died in the waters between Somalia and Yemen. Ethiopians and Somalis who had hoped to become guest workers in Saudi Arabia.

The news about Patrick's death was about to fade.

I took my breakfast up to my room. The desk clerk's mother, or maybe she was his mother-in-law or aunt, patted me on the hand and refused to take any payment.

When it was nine-thirty New York time, Evans was finally in his office.

'It's a lie,' I shouted triumphantly, the second he answered the phone. 'Patrick wasn't on that boat at all.'

'Ally Cornwall,' he said, sounding weary. 'I know that you're in mourning, but you need to leave the journalism to me.'

'But I've met a witness. Someone who survived. And neither Patrick nor that James, the immigrant, was in the rubber boat. She's positive about that.'

He sighed loudly.

'Will she come forward? Will she give her name and allow us to photograph her?'

'Of course she won't. She came here illegally. She's in hiding.'

'Now listen here,' I heard a door slamming, and then silence, 'I've sent people halfway around the world to confirm your story, and nothing holds up.'

'What do you mean?' I sank down onto the bed, a rushing sound in my ears. Or maybe it was the damn wind. 'What doesn't hold up?'

'I can't publish an article accusing people of being slave traders and murderers without any proof. You need to understand that. The magazine can't engage in any sort of personal vendetta.'

'But what about Arnaud Rachid?'

'He runs an organization that is trying to rally support

for open borders, but he has never hidden any illegal immigrants.'

'Well, of course he'd say that.'

'And he doesn't know anybody named Nedjma.'

'But the two of them are together, for God's sake.'

I felt everything suddenly start to sway around me. Why was Arnaud lying? Didn't he want this story to get out? Nedjma, I thought. She's gone underground. She's too deeply mixed up in the whole thing, and he's protecting her. I would have done the same for Patrick. Besides, Nedjma had every reason to be furious with me. I'd broken what she considered our agreement. I hadn't sent the documents to her in Paris. Instead, I'd sent them to the magazine in New York. They were part of Patrick's story. He'd given his life for those fucking documents.

'And that lawyer you talked about? Sarah Rachid? She cites client confidentiality and refuses to say a word. We've even spoken to the police inspector who was in charge of investigating the hotel fire. It was clearly caused by faulty electrical wiring.'

'The police are corrupt,' I said weakly.

I could hear how futile my words sounded.

'And that businessman you're accusing of murder?' Evans went on, rustling papers. 'Some organization in Brussels has just named him innovator of the year in the European business world, and . . .' He was still leafing through paperwork. 'It's here somewhere, but never mind. We'll just be fucking lucky if nobody sues us for what we've already posted on the Internet.'

You coward, I thought. Sitting there and worrying about what management is going to say.

'But you didn't even mention any names.'

'No, and that's one hell of a good thing. That lobbyist. What's his name?'

327

'Guy de Barreau.'

'Anyway, he started threatening legal action when our stringer began hinting that he was associated with slave traders.'

'What does Alain Thery say?' I asked. 'Have you contacted him?'

'Yes, we have. Kearny reached him by phone on some yacht in Puerto Banus. He refused to comment. He did meet Patrick Cornwall, but he didn't consider him to be a serious journalist, so he declined to be interviewed again. He said that Cornwall was hounding him. And from what I gather, he's right about that.'

Slowly I stood up, as if in a trance, and threw open the balcony doors to let in more air. The wind shook the hotel sign a few metres away, making it creak. Patrick's story was collapsing like a poorly designed stage set. One truth fell and another appeared, which in an instant changed the old truth into a lie.

'But what about Helder Ferreira?' I said. 'The inspector that I met in Lisbon. He knows that Mikail Yechenko was murdered.'

'There's no proof,' said Evans. 'Yechenko is dead and buried. And those documents you sent me can't speak for themselves.'

'What about Vera Yechenko? His widow.'

'She's dead.'

'What?' I said, giving a start. 'What do you mean?'

As Richard Evans told me what had happened, darkness fell around me, and I was suddenly aware of all the nooks and crannies along the street. The doors opening onto vacant lots, the shadows behind the row of dumpsters a short distance away. Somebody could be watching me. I could be next on the list.

The magazine had sent a reporter from London to Lisbon.

328

He had made his way to the apartment building in Alfama and rung the bell. No one answered. Finally a neighbour came out and offered to let him in. She usually took in the mail for the other tenants if they were out of town.

Vera Yechenko's door was not locked.

They found her on the floor in the living room. Dead from an overdose of sleeping pills, combined with a large amount of alcohol. It seemed clear that she'd committed suicide.

I backed into the room and hid behind the curtains, keeping my gaze on the street below, my legs shaking.

'We've talked to the Spanish police,' said Evans. 'They consider the immigrant's account to be trustworthy. A boat like the one he described did capsize on that particular night, just as the man said. A lot of people died.'

'But that was in all the newspapers,' I replied. 'Anybody could say what he said.'

'He has stepped forward to give his name, and he allowed himself to be photographed, unlike all the others involved in this story. So listen here . . .' Evans paused to speak to somebody else in the room. I heard only 'two minutes' and realized this phone conversation was about to come to an end. 'We've checked up on this James,' he went on. 'The man is in the country illegally. He has now been taken by bus to one of the detention camps, and he's due to be deported within twenty-four hours. He had everything to lose by coming forward.'

'They paid him off,' I said. 'Don't you see that? That's what they do. They gave him more money than he could ever earn by working a whole lifetime in Europe. They paid off that purse vendor too. That guy named Luc, who tricked Patrick. And now they've paid off this guy so the police will stop investigating the murder. My God, can't you see that? You were once a journalist yourself, for Christ's sake.'

329

Not a sound for several seconds. When Evans spoke again, his voice was hard and shiny as steel, like sharp knives.

'This is just what we might have expected from a free-lancer like Cornwall,' he said. 'Always going too far. And so typical of him to get into a boat in such dangerous waters.'

'I'm telling you that's not what he did.'

'Their careers falter, so they go out and risk their lives in some fucking, godforsaken war because they think it will win them prizes.'

I'd made an appointment to meet Tom McNerney on the outdoor terrace of the Café Central. He looked exactly like I'd pictured him. Red-faced and very overweight. Too many cigarettes, too much beer, too comfortable a life. He put his stout arms around me to give me a hug.

Tell me you have something for me, I thought.

I ordered a salad and mineral water. He wanted an omelette and a steak. The waitress with the crew-cut placed bread and olive oil on the table and then disappeared. McNerney cleared his throat.

'OK, well, I only have the preliminary results from the autopsy so far,' he said, wiping his nose on his napkin. 'I had to really push to get them.'

I looked at him, waiting for him to go on. A mangy dog sniffed around under the table, looking for scraps.

'His death was caused by drowning. That much they can say.' McNerney turned away and coughed into the crook of his arm. 'He had a wound here, on the back of his head, but it had healed long before he ended up in the sea.' He touched his fingertips to the back of his own head, on the left.

'They beat him up in Paris,' I said. 'To make him stop digging around in their affairs. They hit him on the head.'

330

The waitress brought our food. McNerney stuck a corner of his napkin in the collar of his shirt, like a bib.

I poked at the salad. 'What else?'

'A few scrapes, but they could have happened in the sea, if he had bumped into a boat or driftwood.'

He tried to salt his steak, but the wind caught the salt as it came out of the shaker, blowing it sideways. Salt was strewn all over the table.

'This damn coast,' said McNerney, setting the shaker down with a thud. 'Did you know that according to legend, the *levante* that's blowing right now can literally drive people mad?'

He shovelled a big bite into his mouth, which temporarily prevented him from saying anything more.

'Two weeks ago, when the body . . . I mean, when your husband washed ashore, it was the *poniente* that was blowing, the Atlantic wind from the west.' He wiped a trickle of gravy from the corner of his mouth. 'But the sea is unpredictable. It's impossible to say where he went into the water.'

'There must be something more,' I said. 'No matter what they say, I know that Patrick was not on that boat.'

McNerney shook his head and gave me a sorrowful look.

'Patrick Cornwall drowned. That's the only thing that can be proved.'

I walked through town, passing the Blue Heaven Bar, and reached the harbour. I sat there for a long time, watching the Tarifa–Tangiers ferry heading for open waters.

If only the woman named Mary Kwara had dared to step forward, then . . . And the next instant it occurred to me that she too could be bought. She had risked her life to come to Europe in order to earn money.

I stood up abruptly and began walking. I had $2,878.

I'd kept a close eye on my expenses, as if the tiny creature inside me were an auditor who would one day hold me accountable. It wasn't enough, but I also had seven or eight hundred left of my salary, and a little more that belonged to my company. And I could sell the apartment. In the worst case, I could borrow money from Patrick's parents. In spite of everything, they would surely want the same thing I did: to catch the murderer.

As I approached the Shangri-La, I saw a light shining in the window, but the door was locked. I peeked inside. A bunch of people were sitting on hassocks around a surfboard table, smoking.

I knocked on the door. The man with the beard, Nico, came to open it. He grimaced when he saw me, his eyes blazing.

'You? What the hell do you want?'

I took a step back. His hostility was completely unexpected.

'I need to get hold of Jillian Dunne,' I said. 'But I don't know where to find her.'

'I don't think she wants to talk to you.'

The surfers inside got up and came over to join Nico.

'I'm sorry, but what . . . I don't understand what you mean.'

Nico leaned forward, his eyes narrow slits.

'They took her. She's gone, thanks to you.'

'Who? Jillian? Mary Kwara? My God!' I leaned against the wall and stared out at the sea. The lighthouse was flashing out on the island, beaming swathes of light through the darkness. No one was safe.

'Jillian is very upset,' he said. 'She did everything she could for that woman.'

I looked at him.

'So she's alive?'

'Jillian? Yes, but . . .'

I grabbed his wrist.

'Take me to her. Please.'

Jillian Dunne lived in a neat little whitewashed row house with violet bougainvillea growing out front. She was sitting on the sofa, her eyes swollen from crying, her expression dejected. She didn't even look up when Nico announced my presence.

'She says she didn't tell anyone,' he said to her. Then he turned on his heel and left.

Jillian stared into space.

'She's gone,' she said. 'You frightened her away.'

I sat down on the very edge of the sofa, forcing myself to remain calm, even though I was screaming inside. They'd found Mary Kwara, the last witness. She'd survived the sea crossing, only to die here, and it was all my fault. Somehow I must have led them to her hiding place, even though I didn't know where it was. I thought about Patrick, Yechenko, Salif. They'd found all of them in the end.

'Tell me what happened,' I whispered.

Jillian fell back against the sofa cushion and stared blankly up at the ceiling.

'She was gone when I came back. Nico drove her home this morning and then I went out to shop for groceries.' Her face contorted as she began crying again. 'I walked around looking in the shops . . . and I bought this for her.' She opened her fist to show me a silver necklace. 'I was gone too long,' she sobbed. 'I just walked around town for several hours, talking to people. I know so many people here.'

'What do you think happened?'

She looked at me, uncomprehending.

'They took her, of course. The police. And now she's

probably sitting out on Isla de las Palomas, or they've taken her to a detention camp, and from there she'll be deported.'

If only that were true, I thought, but I didn't say anything.

Jillian fell forward, sobbing hard, and for several minutes I sat there, looking at her shaking with sorrow and guilt, which was even worse. I tried to think the way they thought — Alain Thery and his men. Ice-cold. In my mind I went through the list of people who'd been killed. There was a certain logic to it. They didn't kill haphazardly. They were businessmen, not psychopaths. They took revenge, wiped away all traces, buried information. They might have gone after Mary, but they had no real reason to threaten Jillian Dunne.

I patted her shoulder. Then I got up and left.

A block before the hotel, a man came up behind me, appearing out of nowhere. I didn't need to turn around to know it was a man. I could tell by the weight of his footsteps and something in the air. Vibrations indicating a threat and approaching danger. You develop an instinctive sense for that sort of thing when you grow up in New York.

I walked faster past the vacant lot. Listened to the rubber soles of my shoes against the asphalt, heard my own breathing. In the surrounding buildings I saw only dark windows, gratings, and closed blinds.

He was no more than ten metres behind me. A black cat scurried past my feet. I saw the hotel sign up ahead and considered running the last part of the way, but that would be risky. Running would reveal my fear. Running was inviting attack.

Instead I told myself to walk quickly and with determination. Just past the row of dumpsters, then I'd reach the intersection where it was a clear shot to the front entrance of the hotel.

The next second someone grabbed my arm from behind. Another man stepped forward to block my way. He must have been hiding behind the dumpsters. The cap he wore kept his eyes in shadow. The man behind me was standing so close that I could hear him breathing against my hair. He was a head taller. I screamed, but he put his hand over my mouth. A glove of stiff leather that smelled of oil. I kicked and struggled to get free, but he just tightened his grip. As I was dragged backwards, I had a dizzying realization that I'd felt the same grip on my arm before, not once but twice. First when I was thrown out of the office in Paris, and then when they threw me out of the Plaza Athénée. That's impossible, I thought. They can't be here. It's just a couple of local crazies. I gritted my teeth. Think clearly. Get ready to strike as soon as you can. Kick them in the balls and run.

They dragged me into the tall grass and thickets in the vacant lot. I saw boards and other junk scattered about. A wall hid the view from the street. The man that I still hadn't seen slammed me against a brick wall and pressed his mouth to my ear.

'So you refuse to give up, you bitch.'

He spoke French, and, in a moment of ice-cold clarity, I realized I was the last one who knew everything. And who could destroy their business.

'Translate so the bitch doesn't miss anything.'

My arm was wrenched upwards, my face pressed against the brick.

'You're going to stop all this fucking around. One more shitty word out of you and . . .' He snarled threats at me, his hand gripping my throat, but I'd stopped listening. It's over now, I thought. This is how it will end. Then my neck was snapped back, and he gave me a hard shove in the back. I landed with my face in a thorny bush and something hard jabbed into my lap. The baby, I thought. Dear God in heaven, he knows I'm pregnant.

'Should we give the fucking American bitch what she wants?'

Branches snapped, and then the man was breathing hard above me.

He yanked on my arm and tossed me onto my back, and only then did I see his face. A wide face, with a nose that looked too small. It really was the same man who had been guarding Thery's office in Paris and who had sat at his table in the Plaza Athénée. A hand unfastened my belt and he panted as he pulled off my jeans. Or maybe it was the other man who did that.

I screamed as he pushed inside me, but the scream was stopped by the glove he shoved into my mouth.

Mama, I thought, as my body was pounded against the ground, and in my head it was her screams that echoed between the brick walls of the house. I'd seen *Monsieur* throw her down on the bed before he locked the door.

You'll survive, I thought, turning my face away. Stared at the thistles and discarded bottles. You can't touch me, because I'm not here.

The man's hands pressed on my throat. 'Look at me, bitch,' he shouted in French, and then he let go of my throat to punch me in the face. I turned to look at him. A patch of bloated red skin with eyes about to pop out and a mouth that was open with sounds coming out of it, 'you fucking cunt,' as he shoved inside me again and again and then he collapsed, heavy as a sack, onto my chest, pressing the air out of my lungs. And I thought, this is the end.

If only they don't break my arms.

But the man got onto his knees and pulled up his pants, grinning. He laughed at his cohort, who was standing in the door facing the street. I curled into a foetal position.

336

'I think the bitch has had enough,' one of them said in French.

The other laughed. 'Maybe she'd like it in the arse too.'

The security guard, or whatever he was, bent down and grabbed my hair, forcing me to look at him.

'Translate what I'm saying so the bitch won't miss anything,' he said to the other man. Then he breathed into my face, a stench of beer and rotting food scraps.

'Go home to America,' he said. 'Otherwise we'll throw you into the sea too. But no one will ever find you.' He yanked my head off the ground. 'Or what do you think?' he said to the other man. 'Should we let her wake up in a bordello in Moldova instead? They'd teach you a few things in that place, you worthless little Yankee whore.'

He twisted my hair around his hand and yanked my head back.

'The boss doesn't want any more American bodies turning up in this hole of a town,' he snarled. Then he spat in my face. 'That's the only reason you're still alive.'

Then he tossed me back on the ground.

'And don't try to hide. We can find you anywhere.'

He kicked me between the legs and I curled up into a little ball, pressing my arm against my stomach. Closed my eyes, waited for the next kick. Waited. Nothing happened.

Branches snapped and then there was silence.

A car started up.

Sounds of an engine driving away.

Only then did I open my eyes and begin fumbling on the ground for my pants.

The sounds disappeared as I left the town behind me. A flock of seagulls shrieked and rose up, but then I was all alone with the sea. The rhythm of the waves. Only darkness existed, and the sand and low plants growing on the shore

337

and scratching at my calves. The black rocks rested like slumbering animals at the water's edge, and all around breathed the sea, raising and lowering its mighty paunch.

I took off my clothes. Placed in a pile my jacket and shirt and jeans, my socks and shoes. The wind lashed the sand against my body. Wearing only panties and bra, I walked into the sea. The waves washed over my feet, ankles, calves. The water was suddenly tepid, almost warm. I thought I heard the sea singing.

Near the black stone jetty, on my right, halfway out, I sat down and lowered my hands into the water, touching the bottom. His body had lain wedged in here. I tried to grab some sand, but it slipped out between my fingers.

I'm sorry, I whispered. I'm sorry I wasn't good enough.

And I lay down in the water and the sand shaped itself around my body. The next wave washed over me so the salt water filled my mouth and nose.

Where are you? I whispered. Is there anything afterwards?

The wave receded and the cold air rushed over me until the next wave came and I felt his hands, warm and soft against my skin, and the sand under me disappeared. I closed my eyes.

Everything for you, I thought. Tell me what to do, because I know nothing any more. Let me know whether you exist or whether everything disappears.

A rushing in my ears, a dull tone increasing in strength. I got up so quickly that the earth turned upside down. I clambered up onto the rocks and lay down, curling up with the cold against my wet skin. The song had grown to a roar, a hurricane of voices. It would have been so easy just to let myself be washed away.

And forget.

In the beam from the lighthouse I saw the furious waves slamming against the rocks in the distance. And I thought about Mary Kwara, who might be lying in the sea now, to be washed ashore today or tomorrow or whenever the sea deigned to give her up.

The wind swept away these last thoughts. My underwear was still damp, but my body had dried and was ice cold. I waded back to the beach, feeling nothing but the lukewarm water swirling around my ankles, enticing and tugging.

Chapter 19

Marbella
Thursday, 9 October

Fifteen minutes left before departure.

In the ladies' room I used a safety pin to fasten the locker key to my panties. I also checked the sock I wore on my right foot. In the ankle I'd stuffed a roll of banknotes. I'd taken the cash out of various ATMs in Tarifa. I had a total of 2,400 euros stowed away in my wallet, my pockets, and my sock. I'd left my passport in the locker. It was a risk, but it was my only option.

At the sink I splashed water on my face and then dried it with a paper towel. I gave a start when I caught sight of the stranger in the mirror. Familiar and yet not. Like a long-forgotten colleague you happen to meet on the street in the wrong part of town, not sure whether you recognize her or not. The bleached hair made me look like a younger version of myself. It smoothed out my face. I could still smell the acrid stink of the hydrogen peroxide.

Buses headed in all directions from the terminal in Marbella. To Seville and Malaga and Madrid and towns

I'd never heard of. I'd chosen the terminal because it was big enough to have seen all sorts of people coming and going. Nobody would pay any attention to me here.

I walked around until I found a mailbox. I took out the padded envelope with the letter for Benji and the keys to my apartment in Gramercy, clutching it in my hand for a few seconds. I wasn't sure whether it was legal, but it would have to do. In the letter I'd written that I was leaving him the company and the apartment. Everything I owned. Patrick's parents might put up a fight, but then he'd just have to fight back if it was important to him. The letter landed inside the mailbox with a faint thud.

At the back of the terminal the bus had pulled in. Exhaust mixed with cigarette smoke as passengers took a few more puffs before going on board.

It was my third bus of the day. At eight in the morning I'd left Tarifa and travelled east, then changed buses in Algeciras and passed Gibraltar where the Atlantic merged with the Mediterranean. The mighty rock faded to a shadow behind me as I continued on towards Marbella.

'Where to?' muttered the driver as I climbed in.

I handed him my ticket.

'Puerto Banus,' I said.

I sat down on a sofa in the Sinatra Bar, with a view of the harbour and all the luxury yachts, which looked grotesquely oversized. Ferraris and Lamborghinis slowly glided past on the street.

Without much interest I studied the menu and ordered a grilled sandwich. Two men with sunburned noses were dozing over their beers, and a woman who wore gold-rimmed glasses was taking a break from her shopping expedition, surrounded by bags from Versace and Armani.

I got out a notepad and pen and drew a sketch of the

harbour while I waited. A stage set for a performance that had to do with success and money. Puerto Banus was built to look like a fishing village in a picturesque setting with whitewashed houses and narrow stairs leading from one street to another, but no fisherman would ever be able to afford to live here.

'Oh God, I'm worn out. What a night,' said a girl with a posh British accent as she dropped onto the sofa closest to the street.

'I don't know when I'm going to get any sleep,' said her friend, beckoning flirtatiously at the bartender, who instantly approached. He wore a gold ring in his ear and a black T-shirt, with the sleeves rolled up over his biceps.

'I'll have a better tomorrow,' said the girl.

'Same here,' said the other one as she sat down opposite her friend. They both stretched out their legs towards the street. One of them took off a shoe and wriggled her toes. Her toenails were painted silver.

The bartender mixed juice and lemons and filled two glasses with ice. A better tomorrow was a non-alcoholic cocktail on the drinks menu.

'These shoes are killing me,' said one of the girls. Both had their hair coloured in nuances that ranged from platinum to light blonde, with the roots deliberately coloured brown. According to the latest trend, the hair style was supposed to look messy and ruffled, as if they hadn't made any effort at all.

'Take a look, but don't turn around,' hissed one of the girls, motioning with her eyes towards the street. A red Maserati glided past for the umpteenth time.

'It's so dreamy,' the other blonde moaned softly.

'He's the guy who picks up young girls. Thirteen-year-olds. He has a rooftop flat here in the harbour. The Jacuzzi is as big as a whole living room.'

'Yes, but that car — it's just so cool.'

'You should see his yacht. It's one of the biggest in the harbour.'

'Have you ever been on it?'

'Twice.' The girl nodded and sipped at her juice cocktail through a straw.

'So, is it bigger than the *Golden Star*? Leeson's yacht? Or the *Athena*? Come on. You're lying. You haven't been on every yacht in the harbour, have you?'

'No, but a lot of them.' The girl tossed her head and turned to look at the cars again.

I put away my sketch of the harbour and leaned forward to speak to them.

'Hey, excuse me. But I was just wondering. Are you models?'

The girls looked at each other and laughed, fluffing their hair.

'Why do you want to know?'

'I work for an American magazine,' I said, feigning an exaggerated New York accent.

'Which one?' The girls smiled, their white teeth gleaming. '*Vogue*? Or what?'

I gave a vague wave of my hand, leaving my reply open to interpretation.

'I'm writing about the glamorous party life on the Spanish sun coast. The jetsetter lifestyle. Do you know anything about it?' I moved closer.

'Do you want to interview us?' The platinum blonde opened her glittery purse and took out a lipstick.

'See, we're a bit tired at the moment. We were partying in the mountains yesterday. We've come straight back from there.'

'The parties are insane. They keep going until eleven in the morning.'

343

The platinum blonde leaned towards me. 'Will there be photographs too?'

'What are your names?' I jotted down their names so they would see I was serious. Emma was the one with the lighter blonde hair. The platinum blonde was named Melanie.

'So you must meet a lot of celebrities at these parties, right?' I said.

'Sure. Of course.' Melanie rolled her eyes. 'There are always plenty of celebrities down here.'

'Sean Connery lives here,' said Emma. 'We haven't met him, but Antonio Banderas goes jogging on the Golden Mile.'

'Yesterday at the party, I met a guy who knows someone who plays with Robbie Williams,' said Melanie. She raised her voice and said, 'He told me Robbie is going to be coming here.'

'What?' said Emma. 'You didn't tell me that.'

'I just heard about it,' said Melanie. She took out a small mirror to touch up her lipstick.

'I've heard there are parties on the boats too.' I motioned towards the docks.

'God, yes. Especially in the autumn, when the owners come here from London and Paris.'

'And the boats just stay moored in the harbour?'

'Sure. Right. Unless they go over to Niki Beach, of course,' said Emma.

'I once saw Princess Madeleine from Sweden over there,' said Melanie. 'And Harry, of course.'

'Harry who?' I jotted down a few notes, just for the sake of appearances.

Emma laughed and slapped her hand to her forehead. 'The prince, of course!' The girls looked at each other and shook their heads, making their blonde curls flutter.

I turned the page in my notepad. The men with the red noses were sitting up straighter now that the girls were here. They were grinning, drinking toasts, and trying to catch the girls' attention.

'There's a super-rich Frenchman who has a yacht down here,' I said. 'I wonder if you happen to know him. His name is Alain Thery.'

Melanie frowned. 'But he's not a celebrity, is he?'

'He's well known in France. And we have lots of readers in Paris.'

Melanie tilted her head to the side, making her long neck more visible. She fiddled with one of her dangling earrings.

'Well, he never goes to Niki Beach,' she said. 'Just takes his yacht out for a short distance.'

'Do you know which boat is his?' I asked.

Emma finished her juice cocktail.

'Would you like something else to drink?' I offered with a smile. 'The magazine will buy.'

'Then I'll have a Cosmopolitan,' Melanie was quick to say.

'A vodka red.'

I waved over the bartender and gave him their orders.

'There was a party over there yesterday,' said Emma.

'Where?' said Melanie.

'On his boat. That guy's boat — Alain.'

'How do you know that?' Melanie grabbed her Cosmopolitan from the tray and took a sip.

'Well, Suze knows the skipper. I told you that before.' Emma turned towards me. 'A lot of girls hang out with the skippers so they can go out on the boats. You have to arrive on a yacht if you want to go out to Niki Beach. Otherwise it's too embarrassing. But later, when the owners are here, the skippers chase the girls off the boats.'

'One of my friends,' said Melanie, 'she once went to a

party on that boat in the spring. There was tons of champagne. Plus anything else you wanted. You know.' She licked her lips and drew her finger under her nose.

'Cocaine?' I whispered.

Melanie pressed her finger to her lips.

'Which boat is it?' I asked, fixing my gaze on the sleek-lined white vessels.

Emma pointed west, towards the edge of the harbour area, where the docks ended. There the artificial fishing village jutted out towards the sea, with shops and restaurants on the ground floors of the buildings. Above were three-room apartments that cost two million euros, according to the sign in a realtor's window that I'd passed on my way from the bus.

'Pier Zero,' she said with awe in her voice.

'That's where the biggest boats are moored.' Melanie clucked her tongue. 'Some people pay up to ten thousand euros a month just to have a boat slip on Pier Zero.'

'Do you know the name of the boat?' I asked. 'I'd like to take a picture of it.'

'Do you have a camera with you?' said Melanie, her eyes widening. 'I'm not ready for a picture yet. I must look a fright.'

'You know, Suze told me about something horrid.' Emma looked from Melanie to me, making sure she had our attention. 'There was a girl who went out there with him. The rich owner, I mean. And she was raped.'

Melanie sniggered. 'That's what everybody says.'

'Well, she asked for it, of course.' Emma took the lemon slice from her glass and licked it. 'I mean, she did go out there with him, didn't she?'

'Some girls are so naïve,' said Melanie. 'They think they can just go out on the boat and drink champagne. And of course he gets cross. It's his boat, after all.'

'What happened to that girl?' I asked.

Emma grabbed her own wrist and held it up in the air. 'Handcuffs. All that kind of stuff. He cuffed her to the bedside lamp. You know what I mean, right? Everything is fastened down when you're on a boat.'

'Lots of people are into that sort of thing,' said Melanie.

Emma sipped her drink. 'But later she wanted to leave, and he wouldn't let her. The boat was only a short way out in the harbour, just beyond the piers. He's known for that.'

I remembered the gossip that Caroline Kearny had mentioned.

'Is that because he can't swim?' I asked.

Melanie and Emma giggled and exchanged looks. It was clear to them that this journalist was clueless. And not very bright either.

'Don't you see? He takes the boat out when there are girls on board, so they can't change their minds.'

'And so nobody can hear them scream.'

'That girl could hardly walk the next day,' said Emma in a low voice. 'It took at least three days, or maybe a week, before she could even come down to the harbour again.'

I glanced over at Pier Zero where the huge yachts bobbed in the calm water, their bows like pointed snouts, their windows like dark narrowed eyes. They looked sinister.

'Is she around here anywhere? That girl?' I asked. 'It would be interesting to interview her.'

'She went back home,' said Emma.

'My God, it's no surprise that things can get wild. That's what parties are all about. You should have seen me this morning.' Melanie leaned down and fluffed her tresses so they billowed even more. 'Well, actually, we were still going at it well past midday.'

'You and that Phil guy?' said Emma. She straightened

347

up when three young Spanish men sat down over near the bar. They wore gold chains around their necks, and had big, flashy watches on their wrists.

'Are you crazy? No. It was Liam. You know — the one who knows that guy who plays with Robbie Williams. I already told you that.'

'But he's so old.' Emma grimaced.

'No, he's not. Robbie is only a little over thirty.'

'I mean Liam. He's got to be forty, at least.'

'But have you seen his house? On the road up to Ronda?'

'It doesn't even belong to him. Suze told me that he's some sort of caretaker. He takes care of the house when the owners are away.'

Melanie put her hand to her mouth and looked away. Then she smoothed down her hair and opened her purse to take out her lipstick again. She pointed the gleaming, blood-red lipstick at Pier Zero.

'It's called the *Epona*, by the way. In case you were wondering.'

'Alain Thery's boat?'

'It's named for the horse goddess,' said Emma.

Melanie and I both stared at her in surprise.

Emma shrugged and turned away. Her gaze seemed to be drawn to a black Porsche driving past at a leisurely pace.

I thanked the girls and took down their phone numbers, telling them a photographer would get in touch with them in about a week. Then I stood up, paid the bill in the bar, and left to stroll along the harbour towards Pier Zero.

The Mediterranean was as calm as a lake, compared with the violent waters off Tarifa. And Africa wasn't nearly as close. The continent was visible only as a thin brushstroke of darker blue on the horizon.

The fifth yacht on the pier was the *Epona*. I walked

slowly past without stopping, giving all the boats an admiring look. The gangway had been pulled up. *No entry, no pasar, ne pas monter à bord* said a sign on the stern next to an opening in the railing where a small companionway led down. The deck was made of some kind of expensive light-coloured wood, the type that was in danger of being wiped out in the rain forests. The doors with darkened windows led to the yacht's interior.

I stopped at the third boat further along, where a man wearing jeans and a navy-blue windbreaker was loading suitcases on board.

'Nice boat,' I said. 'What does something like this cost?'

He glanced at me. 'More than you can afford,' he said, tossing his cigarette into the water.

'I know,' I said. 'That's why I'm more interested in that one.' I pointed at Alain Thery's yacht. 'Do you know what kind it is?'

'The *Epona*?' The man took a step up the gangway and craned his neck. 'It's a Marquis.' He looked me up and down with an insolent expression.

'Is there anyone who sells that type of boat around here?' I asked.

The man pointed behind him, across the piers that stuck out like fingers from the quay. 'Try Marina Banus,' he said.

'Thanks,' I told him, and walked away, cutting across the street.

I took up position next to a little ice cream kiosk, with a good view of the *Epona*. No movement on board. When I bought a bottle of mineral water, I discovered that I'd been short-changed at the Sinatra Bar. I was missing thirty euros. All of a sudden all my anger surged towards the bartender with the gold earring, and I stepped into the street just as a greyish-green Jaguar turned from the quay and parked in front of the *Epona*.

Quickly I backed away, slipping inside a clothing shop, and hid behind a rack of T-shirts.

The driver's door opened and a man got out, wearing a tailored dove-blue suit. He had on aviator sunglasses. His hair was dark blond and cut short. The spark started in the small of my back, crept up my spine, and then burst into flames at the nape of my neck.

It was him.

Alain Thery was in no hurry, just like everyone else in this harbour where no one was going anywhere specific, and most people already had everything they could ever wish for. He turned around and looked towards the row of bars where I'd been sitting, fixing his eyes on a sports car driving away. Then he slammed the door of the Jaguar and pressed the remote. At that instant I noticed movement on the yacht's upper deck. A moment later the doors opened and a man came out. He had dark hair and was casually dressed in white. He raised his hand to wave.

Thery went on board, walking up a gangway that hadn't been there before. The two men exchanged a few words, and then Thery disappeared inside.

I guessed the other man was the skipper. He stayed on deck as the gangway was pulled back through an opening in the stern.

'Can I help you?' said a voice behind me. I turned around. The shop owner gave me a disapproving look as she stood next to a rack of sunglasses. I went over and chose a pair of fake Ray-Bans. When she handed me the receipt, I discovered they were genuine.

On my way back along the quay, I resisted an impulse to go into the Sinatra Bar to demand my thirty euros. That would just cause a ruckus, and an unnecessary number of people would remember seeing me.

350

I stopped at an Armani boutique and went inside.

'I'd like a dress with a matching jacket if you have something like that.'

The snooty woman in the well-tailored suit looked at me as if I were something the fishermen would toss to a cat.

'What colour? What sort of dress were you thinking?'

'Short,' I said. 'And preferably red.'

She offered me three dresses, and I took them into a changing room. The second one fit perfectly. Thigh length and much too tight to move in comfortably. I tried hoisting the skirt up over my butt. It was doable. The dress cost 810 euros.

'I'll take this one,' I said, coming out of the changing room with it on. I caught sight of a jacket on a mannequin and asked to try it on. It fit, so I kept it on too. I stuffed my old jacket into my shoulder bag. It might get cold at night. I rummaged around for the cash to pay for my purchases and realized that I also needed a new purse.

The shop clerk asked me to turn around so she could cut off the price tags. I picked up a wide barrette lying on the counter. 'I'll take this too.'

After leaving the boutique, I stopped in front of another shop window to pin up my hair. I was still startled by the sight of myself as a blonde. The sneakers I wore with the red dress looked odd, as did my worn-out shoulder bag, but I'd have to worry about that later. I put the Armani shopping bag holding my old clothes in a trash can.

A sleepy guard sat slumped in a booth next to the entryway to Marina Banus, nodding to himself. 'Hello,' I said.

He didn't react. I knocked on the windowpane. The guard turned his head and quickly pulled out the earphones he wore.

'I want to look at a boat,' I said. 'My employer will be paying the bill,' I added.

'OK.' The guard pulled himself upright. I was starting to get used to the fact that everyone here looked me up and down, as if I were on display, so I took a step forward. I hoped the guard wouldn't notice my worn-out sneakers, which I'd bought for $15 at the outlet store near Ground Zero a year and a half ago.

The guard picked up his phone. I looked at the piers where the boats for sale were moored. As big as small aircraft carriers, gleaming white and streamlined. I wondered how many millions I would be expected to cough up.

'A salesman is on his way,' said the guard, putting his earphones back in. I looked at my watch. It was 4.45 in the afternoon. I needed to get a different watch too. Everything can be switched, coloured, and changed, I thought. And yet people think they know something about the person standing in front of them.

'Good afternoon,' I said, smiling at the salesman who came hurrying towards me, carrying a briefcase under his arm. 'I'm sorry for coming here without an appointment, but I absolutely must look at a yacht for my employer.'

I pushed my sunglasses on top of my head and put on my best East Coast American accent.

'No problem. Has he purchased anything from us previously?' The salesman gave me a well-rehearsed smile. He was in his thirties, with white teeth and a slack handshake.

'No, but he's in the process of moving here,' I said. 'Richard Evans, a well-known magazine publisher from New York. Perhaps you've heard of him?'

The salesman nodded eagerly as he ushered me through the gate.

'What type of boat does he have in mind?'

'A Marquis,' I said. 'Don't bother showing me anything else. Mr Evans is a Marquis kind of guy.'

'Good choice. Excellent. A lot of people buy American boats when the dollar is low. What size boat are we talking about?'

I placed my hand on his arm.

'Show me what you have,' I said.

I recognized it immediately. Two Marquis boats were moored side by side, rocking gently. They looked like big brother and little brother Marquis, equally arrogant and conceited and with the same sinister look in their dark windows.

'The big one,' I said. 'That one there.'

'The queen,' said the salesman with a tender note to his voice. He stroked the handrail of the gangway as if it were his future wife.

'A 69-foot Marquis,' he said. 'Excellent choice. If he pays in euros, the price is only 1.8 million right now, half a million less than a comparable European boat.'

'Could I take a closer look?'

'Certainly.' The salesman went up the gangway and then held out his hand to help me on board. 'This one is a real beauty, with a grace and elegance no other yacht can match. You'll find that the interior spaces offer more than you usually see even on bigger yachts than this one.'

'My boss wants to know all the details,' I said, stepping on board. 'Could we start with the bedrooms?'

Music was pounding from the centre of Puerto Banus, where the nightclubs would stay open for many more hours, but Pier Zero had started settling in for the night. The restaurants lining the harbour were closed. A couple of girls in high heels wobbled off a yacht named *Ma Petite*. I heard them saying it was a worthless party, but then their voices faded away as they strolled off towards some club.

I was sitting on the ground, leaning against what looked like an old watchtower near the end of Pier Zero. I was tired of wandering from bar to bar, ordering non-alcoholic drinks, and fending off invitations from drunken tourists here on a golf vacation.

The greyish-green Jaguar hadn't moved all night. Twice I'd seen the skipper come down from the upper deck to have a smoke as he surveyed the enticing lights of the harbour. I guessed he must be longing for the owner to leave the boat for the season so he could put the four bedrooms below decks to personal use.

Alain Thery hadn't made an appearance all evening.

I decided to wait another half-hour, and closed my eyes. Sleep pulled me down towards a black emptiness. I gave a start and opened my eyes. The Jaguar was still there. No lights on anywhere. If he wasn't asleep by now, he wasn't going to sleep at all.

I opened the big gold bag that I'd bought for a bargain price and took out my new shoes. I tossed my old sneakers under a bush along with my anorak. The last remnants of my old self. I'd stuffed my shoulder bag into a trash can in the department store ladies' room where I'd completed my outfit by deliberately putting on too much make-up. I'd thrown my phone into the sea when I'd taken a stroll to the end of Pier Zero in order to take a look at the *Epona* from the other direction.

My new shoes had stiletto heels and gold buckles on the sides. They were half a size too small. I'd chosen them that way on purpose, so they'd be tight and wouldn't fall off on the stairs. There was no chance they were going to chafe my feet.

One last time I checked the contents of my bag. I felt

the hard metal between my fingers. The plastic bottles, and the sheet. Then I stood up and shook life back into my legs, pausing to stretch my muscles before I started walking.

Unlike the other piers, there were no gates along Pier Zero to keep out unwanted visitors. The biggest boats all had their own security guards, but it was also customary for the skipper to act as a guard. That's what the salesman at the marina had told me when I expressed concern that the yacht would require too big a staff. I explained that my boss didn't want lots of people running around and getting in the way when he came here to relax.

I stood in front of the *Epona* and called out quietly: 'Hey, hey.' Then I tried whistling and another 'Hey, hey.' Finally I threw a pebble at the low door in the middle of the boat's stern. A moment later the door opened and the skipper stuck his head with the dishevelled dark hair out of the captain's cabin. Behind him was the engine room. The thick orange cable that went down into a hole next to his feet supplied the boat with electricity when it was moored. Silently I repeated every detail from memory.

'What is it?' said the skipper in Spanish, stepping out. He squinted at me, looking groggy with sleep. 'Are you lost?'

I pressed my finger to my mouth, pouted my lips, and motioned for him to come closer. He took several steps across the platform, which could be adjusted up or down, making it a practical vantage point for anyone who wanted to go swimming at sea.

'I'm a present for Alain Thery,' I said in English, running my hand over the elegantly styled silk dress, stopping at the tight curve of my hip. I was not cheap. '*Un regalo*,' I repeated in Spanish, just to make sure he understood.

'Nobody told me anything about this.' He switched to heavily accented English.

'It wouldn't be a surprise if you knew about it,' I said, putting my foot up on the mooring line so my dress slid up and exposed my panties. White, with lace, from the store's lingerie department. There was only a metre and a half of water between me and the boat. On either side of the captain's cabin, stairs led up to the bridge. Four steps. I could glimpse the chrome-plated lid of the diesel tank on the right side of the hull. The gangway was on the left, hidden inside the bottom step. I hoped the skipper had the remote with him.

'Come on. What do you think Alain will say when he hears you let him wait all night for his special treat.'

The skipper tore his eyes away from the white patch between my legs, turned around, and went up the steps on the left. With a sucking sound the hydraulic gangway was lowered.

I went on board. The skipper was leaning against the small gate at the top of the stairs. He made no effort to move aside when I reached him. The fibreglass felt hollow and unsteady under my high heels. His face was close to mine.

I stuck my hand in my bag and closed my fingers around the hard metal. I pulled out the handcuffs and dangled them under his nose.

'It's going to get wild,' I said. 'So don't even think about coming down there and disturbing us while we're having fun.' I let the metal brush his hand.

'When I'm finished with Alain, I'll come up and see you. But first you have to open the gate.'

The skipper grinned and the gate clicked open.

'Good boy,' I said, and pointed up to the bridge. 'After you cast off, go up there and head out of the harbour. Just go straight out. You know the routine.' I pressed my hand against his groin. 'And when you hear me scream, just think about the fact that you'll be next.'

I moved past him across the after-deck where the wood was sun-bleached so as not to absorb too much heat. An excellent spot for breakfast in the sun. I stopped at the doors with the dark panes, waiting for the skipper to open them. His hand cupped my ass as I went in.

The easiest role in the world, I thought. And they fall for it every time.

My heels sank into the thick wall-to-wall carpet, and I had to lean against the wall until my body regained its balance. The recessed spotlights gave off a faint glow that was reflected in the ceiling mirrors. I walked straight ahead, past the concave bar stools and the Italian leather armchairs. A 42-inch TV could be slid out from the wall. The linen drapes in front of the windows were open, and I could see the glittering lights from the harbour bars mirrored in the black surface of the water. No stars in the sky. A night with no wind.

Ahead of me I saw the bridge, the control panel with the radar and GPS and wheel and everything else needed to race across the sea. A stair made of Plexiglas led up to another bridge on the upper deck. I could feel the skipper's presence two metres behind me, and I turned around. His eyes landed on my breasts.

'Wait a moment to start the engine,' I said, lowering my voice. 'So you won't ruin the surprise.'

He scratched the back of his neck and grinned.

'We want to be left alone, so take the controls up there.' I pointed to the stairs leading to the upper deck. 'I'll see you in a couple of hours. OK?'

'You can fucking count on it,' said the skipper, twirling his tongue in his open mouth.

I waited until he'd disappeared above before I went down the narrow wooden stairs leading to the bedrooms.

I held my breath as I cautiously opened the door to the

VIP bedroom. Light fell in from the corridor and ricocheted off the mirror at the other end of the room. The bed was empty. I continued on to the two smaller bedrooms in the middle, designed for children. One had been converted to an office, with a desk and a PC with a large screen. The other room held an empty guest bed. Alain Thery clearly had no children. At least none that came here to visit.

I breathed through my mouth as I went down the two steps to the master bedroom, which was located forward, going over in my mind the details of the interior and hoping it hadn't been altered.

A slight movement, as if the world were shifting. That must mean the boat had been unmoored from the pier.

Slowly I pressed down the handle on the solid wood door. It didn't make a sound as it slid open. There was just a faint change in air pressure, as if the boat were taking a breath.

A king-size bed dominated the room, and I saw the curve of the covers around his body. I heard his steady breathing. He was asleep. I was grateful for the soft rug as I soundlessly stepped inside the room and took in every detail in the faint light coming from the corridor. Cherry-wood cabinets and wardrobes fastened to the bulkheads. The first door on the left was a walk-in closet, the other led to the bathroom and Jacuzzi. The ceiling was a mirror, and along the headboard of the bed stainless steel lamps had been fixed to the wall.

'Time to wake up, Alain.'

At that instant the boat shuddered. I heard the engine and felt my body lurch as the yacht picked up speed. The max speed was 32 knots.

Alain Thery raised his head and opened his narrow eyes, squinting at the light. I hoped all he saw was a shadow. He raised his hand to shade his eyes.

'Hi, Alain,' I said softly. I'd chosen a slight accent for my English.

'What is it?' he said. 'Who's there?'

'I'm a present,' I said and held up the handcuffs, dangling them so he'd see their silhouette.

'What the hell?'

Thery reached for the wall behind him and turned on the bedside lights.

'Who are you? Have we met?'

Yes, in the dim light of a nightclub, I thought, hoping to God that I was too insignificant for him to remember me. And that I'd applied enough of a mask.

'Shall we talk or shall we play?' I said, raising my free hand to loosen the barrette and shaking my head to let my blonde hair fall forward.

He pulled himself into a sitting position and reached for the handcuffs. 'Give them here,' he said. The hair on top of his head was thinning, and his hairline was receding. His face was pallid and looked more bloated now that he wasn't wearing a designer suit. His pale eyes seemed to skewer my body, and I sensed movement under the bed covers.

'You first,' I said. Deliberately swaying my hips, I walked over to the headboard. He pulled up his knees under the covers and let them fall open. I could hear his breathing getting fast and hoarse.

'Whose idea was this?' he said. 'Was it Vincent?'

I reached out and grabbed his wrist. I kept my eyes fixed on his — those pale, almost white eyes looked transparent. With a grin he moved to the middle of the bed and placed his hand between my legs. I clenched my teeth and pulled his arm upwards. Click. His hand was cuffed to the light.

His other hand was on its way down my panties. I twisted away and shoved his arm with my knee. I didn't want him to find the plastic bag I'd hidden in my panties, containing the last of my rolled up banknotes. I gave him a slap on the hand. 'Naughty boy,' I said. 'It's not your turn yet.'

Then I took the other pair of handcuffs out of my bag. Thery emitted a faint moan.

'I'm going to hurt you,' I said as I rounded the bed and grabbed his other hand from that side. 'I'm going to hurt you bad.'

Click.

'So who's the present from?' he said, laughing.

I took a few steps back from the bed so he wouldn't be able to reach me with his feet.

'From Patrick Cornwall,' I said.

It took a few seconds for Thery's brain to process the name, which set off alarm bells, making his eyes widen and his chin drop. He started yanking on the cuffs.

'What the hell?'

I smiled as the next realization fell into place.

'It's you, you fucking bitch! Didn't you get enough in Tarifa? Huh? Didn't they tell you what they're going to do to you next?' He yanked and tugged, but the lamps were securely screwed into the wall. Highest quality, exquisite quality.

'What do you want? This is fucking criminal. Take off these cuffs, or else—'

'Or else, what, Alain? Or else you'll tell your boys to throw me into the sea?' I sat down on a small leather stool and set my gold bag on my lap.

'I don't know what you're talking about,' said Thery. 'You're crazy. Take off these cuffs before things get nasty.'

'Like with Patrick Cornwall?'

'He should never have got in that boat and gone out to sea, for Christ's sake.' Thery tried to wriggle out of the cuffs, but his hands were too big. He had the working-class fists of a man from Pas-de-Calais.

'Wrong, Alain,' I said. 'He was never on that boat.'

He stopped moving, and I saw how he tried to assume an expression that was worthy of a man of his social position.

'I'm a businessman. I know people in the French government, in the EU parliament. Here on the sun coast too. Influential people.'

'I'm sure you do, but they're not here right now, are they?' I looked in all directions. 'It's just you and me at the moment, so let's talk. They took him out to sea, right? After they threw Mikail Yechenko off the terrace in Alfama, they followed Patrick down along the lane. Did they pick him up there, or did they wait until he got back to the hotel? By the way, how did they know where Yechenko and Patrick were going to meet?'

'You're out of your mind.' He yanked and kicked so the covers flew off him, revealing his nakedness. I let my eyes slide over his pale body, and all I could see was Patrick's naked body at the edge of the water. I stuck my hand in my gold bag and took out one of the two big plastic bottles. I unscrewed the top and sniffed at the contents.

'I'm thinking about the fire at the hotel in Saint-Ouen. Seventeen people died, Alain. There was a little boy in there who dreamed of becoming Ronaldo, but he's never going to kick a soccer ball again because you wanted to set an example. That's why you sent your boys to light the fire and make sure nobody got out. Am I right? Because everybody needs to know what will happen if they try to escape from your slave camps.'

'Take off these cuffs. Give me the key, and maybe I'll let you go.'

'How would you do that? We're quite a ways out to sea by now.'

'What the hell?' He looked one way, then the other, fixing

his eyes on the small windows. Outside nothing but darkness. No longer any neighbouring yachts, no glittery nightclubs.

'We could go for a swim,' I said, 'but I've heard you're not a big fan of swimming.'

The boat came to a gentle stop, and the faint vibration from the engine ceased. I stood up and gave the bottle in my hand a slight swirl so that some of the gasoline spilled onto the wall-to-wall carpet. A sharp combustible odour instantly filled the room.

'What the fuck are you up to? What are you going to do? It wasn't me.' His voice rose to a falsetto. 'Those guys — they're insane. They weren't supposed to kill him. I told them to talk to him, pay him off so he'd stop writing all those fucking articles. Wait, stop it, *putain*! You're out of your mind!' Thery thrashed and struggled, kicking and throwing himself to the left, trying to get as far away from the line of gasoline that I slowly poured along the right side of his bed.

I'd bought a spare fuel container at the gas station near the bus stop in Tarifa and then sat down in a vacant lot with a view of the sea. The last thing I did before leaving the town was to empty two big plastic bottles of mineral water and fill them with gasoline. Then I'd thrown the container in the bushes and made it to the bus station just as the bus for Algeciras rolled in.

'Ramón, *merde*, Ramón, come here!' Thery screamed at the top of his lungs. 'I'm going to kill you, you fucking whore. Ramón!'

I took in a deep breath.

'Yes, yesss,' I screamed even louder. 'Kill me, Alain, hit me harder, kill me now!'

Thery stared at me. 'What the hell are you doing?'

I smiled. 'I just want to assure your pal that we're having a good time down here.'

His eyes narrowed into slits.

'Didn't you get enough in Tarifa?' he said. 'Do you want to know what my friends will do to you if they find me like this?'

'When they find you,' I said, 'they won't recognize you at all.' I splashed gasoline on the sheet, and Thery screamed when the fluid struck his leg.

'What the fuck are you doing? I have money. How much do you want?'

'What's it worth?' I said. 'What did you pay James, the immigrant?'

Thery laughed. A sick laugh that echoed, loud and hollow, before falling to the thick carpet and fading away. 'You can have a lot more than that. What the hell.' He gave me a pleading look. 'Everybody knows they lie.'

I held up the plastic bottle so the gasoline gleamed in the light from the bedside lamps. I rolled it against my cheek, feeling the intoxication of the strong smell, the dizziness from breathing in the fumes too deeply.

'What about Mary Kwara?' I said. 'What did you do with her? Did you throw her into the sea too?'

'Who's that?' said Thery. 'I don't know any fucking Mary.'

I walked along the end of the bed, letting the bottle dribble a trail along the carpet. Then I turned and walked along the left side. Thery whimpered. I stopped pouring gasoline and leaned against the wall, looking at the pitiful expression on his face.

'You could have simply denied what he wrote,' I said. 'You could have bought other witnesses, bribed the police, sued the magazine and scared the shit out of their lawyers. But you had to kill him, you couldn't let him go free. Why? Because he interrupted you at dinner?'

'I'm a businessman,' whined Thery. 'I have to think of my business.'

'Don't you have enough money? But it's not just the money, is it? It's the power, right? That's what you're after.' I took aim and splashed some gasoline right between his legs. Thery screamed and tried to protect himself, desperately thrashing and yelling.

'Yes, whip me, kill me!' I shouted towards the ceiling. Thery spat at me, but missed his target by at least a metre.

'*Pute de noir*,' he snarled. 'You bitch, you filthy whore, married to a black man. He thought he was so smart, but that idiot had no idea who he was dealing with. He never even realized they were following him, not even when his cell phone was stolen in the middle of the street in Lisbon. That American. What a fool, letting anyone read his text messages. But he thought he was really something. He thought he was smarter than me.' Thery raised his chin and glared at me, his eyes bloodshot now, and saliva running out of his mouth. I thought he looked like a dog, a chained creature. No longer a human being. I clutched the lighter in my hand.

'I told them to take him far out,' Thery snarled. 'Take him halfway to fucking Africa, I said, and throw him in. They said he screamed like a pig when they dumped him in the sea.'

Slowly I leaned down and picked up a pair of red silk boxers that had been tossed on the carpet. I crumpled them up, took a step forward, and stuffed them in his gaping mouth.

Shut up, you bastard.

He tossed his head from side to side and arched his body to kick, but he couldn't reach me. I studied the man thrashing around on the bed. I looked at his pale skin and wide-open eyes, his stomach sticking out over his shrunken dick. I looked at the watch on his wrist, the expensive wood of the cabin, all the wealth surrounding him.

'What a worthless worm you are, what a disgusting little bastard,' I said. 'What the hell makes you think you're worth more than Patrick, or any of the other people who have died for all this?'

'*Uuuuh*,' he groaned.

I held up the bottle again.

'For Salif,' I said, splashing gasoline on his face. 'For Checkna, for Sambala, for the little boy who played soccer, for Mary Kwara . . .'

I reached out my hand and aimed the stream of gasoline right at the red silk stuffed in his mouth.

'For Patrick.'

For a second I stood there, watching the sheet darken from the fluid. I saw death in his eyes. I felt nothing. Not even a speck of doubt.

I flicked the lighter and held the flame towards him.

'Burn in hell,' I said, and bent down. The flame ignited the gasoline on the carpet and flared up.

Alain Thery uttered stifled screams as the fire raced across the floor. I quickly backed away. The last thing I saw before I slammed the door behind me was a contorted face hanging from the wall, and legs thrashing back and forth as the flames engulfed the bed.

I kicked off my stiletto heels and ran barefoot along the corridor and up the stairs. I glanced towards the Plexiglas steps that led up to the bridge where the skipper sat. The bedroom door would stop the smoke for a short time, but the fire alarm would start wailing any second.

I raced past the galley and through the bar, throwing open the glass door to the black night. In the distance I could see the lights from shore. I tried to orient myself as I went down the stairs on the right. 'Starboard,' said the voice inside me, speaking in the jovial patter of the salesman. 'That's what we yachtsmen call it,' he'd said.

365

Europe must be the continent straight ahead, I decided as I leaned forward and grabbed hold of the lid of the diesel tank, turning it as hard as I could. Thousands of lights glittered along the whole shoreline, the beam from a lighthouse flashed right at me. It was impossible to estimate the exact distance, but it couldn't be more than a kilometre, maybe less. Astern I could see the lights from Africa, further away, like scattered cats' eyes gleaming in the dark. The navigation lights of a boat bobbed and then disappeared. The lid of the tank refused to budge. I grabbed it with both hands. At that instant the fire alarm went off, a screeching wail that sliced right through me and filled the whole space between the sea and the sky.

Now the skipper is running downstairs, I thought. I couldn't see any of the yacht's interior through the black glass in the doors. Maybe he sees the thick smoke seeping under the door. He has to try to put out the fire. The Marquis is equipped with fire extinguishers in every room, but it will take time. At least two minutes. Maybe more, maybe less. Then Ramón will come after me, or both of them will if he's been quick with the extinguisher and also made it to the engine room to find some sort of tool so he can free his boss. Maybe they'll run straight up to the bridge to cut loose the tender, the extra motorboat that's used to take passengers over to Niki Beach or for water skiing. It's probably an inflatable jet boat. Then they'll make their way to shore, and Alain Thery will soon be eating lunch at Taillevent again.

This damned lid. My hands were ice cold. I twisted and turned, but the metal lid still wouldn't budge. That's exactly what happened when I inspected the display model in the marina. The salesman hadn't been able to find the tool that was designed to stick in the two holes to open the lid more easily.

366

The alarm filled the night with its screeching wail. The stars fell towards me.

I threw all my weight against the lid, and finally it released its grip and turned. I lifted it off in my hand. The diesel tank was open. I threw the lid in the sea. Then I took out of my bag the sheet and the second plastic bottle, using my teeth to unscrew the top. My whole arm was shaking, and I had to grip it with my other hand as I drenched the sheet in gasoline. I thought I heard men screaming through the wail of the alarm, but it could merely have been the sound of Thery's stifled screams echoing in my head. With stiff fingers and trembling hands I stuffed one end of the gasoline-soaked sheet into the diesel tank. The salesman had told me that tossing a match into a diesel tank wouldn't have any effect. Diesel oil was not as flammable as gasoline. So he assured me that my boss shouldn't be concerned about safety. We'll see about that, I'd thought as I scrutinized the diesel tanks, which each contained 2,500 litres. An image of a Molotov cocktail had flashed before my eyes, a soaked rag burning inside a bottle of gasoline.

Now I flicked the lighter again and held it to the very end of the sheet. The gasoline flared up, igniting the cloth. A twisting flame that quickly approached the tank.

I jumped down the last step and ran across the yacht's platform, which was supposed to be so great if you wanted to go swimming out at sea. I was positive I could hear screams as I pulled the skirt of my dress up to my waist and dived in.

The water closed around me, ice cold and black, and I slid through a soft nothingness. The silence freed me from all the noise and screams. Only reluctantly did I rise back up to the surface when my lungs demanded air. The sounds instantly descended upon me, and all I could think of was to get away from the wailing, as far away as possible before the shockwave hit. Somehow my body began moving rhyth-mically as my legs found the strength to kick, and I began swimming towards the lights in the distance, swimming as I hadn't swum since the days when I competed in school. Efficient strokes, don't relax, don't give your competitor a chance to get ahead, aim for the goal, pace yourself. The length of a swimming pool was programmed into my body. I was thirty metres from the yacht when the explosion came and turned the water yellow and orange. I dived to avoid the shockwave. I felt it approaching behind me, shooting me forward like a projectile, tumbling me around in an endless whirl. When I had no more air left in my lungs, I rose to the surface and turned around to see the water on fire. The heat reached me like a warm wind blowing across the sea.

The tip of the sleek bow was the only thing still visible of Alain Thery's 69-foot Marquis. The rest was roaring flames and thick black smoke. The alarm had stopped. I heard the sound of boat engines coming from the west, and I could just make out the Rock of Gibraltar in the distance. A motorboat was approaching at high speed. But much more important was the fact that no small rubber boat was moving away from the burning yacht.

I trod water and saw a faint shift in the darkness to the east. In a couple of hours the sun would come up. Ashes would be scattered on the surface of the water, and twisted pieces of fibreglass would wash ashore. Maybe along with the bodies of those who had died at sea.

I turned north, and with steady strokes I began swimming towards shore.

Chapter 20

Öresund
Two weeks later

'Keep quiet now.' He poked his elbow into her side.

She lowered her eyes, thinking that he didn't need to tell her that. She hadn't said a word since they'd crossed the first border, after going through the mountains. Night and day, sitting on the bus. It was a warm bus, with soft seats. She was travelling in comfort. She could lean back and sleep, or think about what was ahead.

'Don't answer any of the questions,' he whispered in her ear. 'You're a woman. You don't speak. They understand that. They know how things are.' He tapped his chest. 'I'll do the talking.'

Then he stuck the earphones back in, and she faintly heard the beat of the music he was listening to. She turned to look out of the window. Never before had she seen so many different variations of grey. The sky was a pale grey, with dark grey clouds scudding past. The pavement was steel grey under the wheels of the bus, and the smoke from the numerous tall chimneys rose up to the clouds, blending the grey of its plumes with the sky. The grass swaying at the side of the road was yellowish grey.

She thought about her new name. The one in the passport.

The picture didn't look much like her. The name felt like chafed feet.

A person is not her name, she thought. When the last people have forgotten me, I will be gone.

And she thought about Sefi, who would soon be married. Sefi would have chattered the whole way. It was a good thing she wasn't the one travelling. Sefi would have settled for a beautiful warm bed to sleep in, and her own room with a view through the narrow slit in the window. She would not have gone to Cádiz, and the family would have been mired in debt for ever. If Sefi had come to Europe, her mother would never have been able to get a house.

Mary Kwara put a hand to her throat as the signs approached. She didn't want the man to see that she was curious. The text rushed past, telling her nothing, but she memorized the names all the same. Some of them she would later forget, just as she'd forgotten Barcelona and Perpignan and Stuttgart as they disappeared behind her. She wondered how far north you would have to go before the earth curved downwards again.

Malmö, she thought. Sweden. København. An aeroplane thundered past, flying low overhead.

She would do what they'd decided. Her mother had made a deal with the men who had lent her money for the trip. They were cousins of someone she knew. 'They'll get you a job. They'll arrange for the proper papers,' her mother had said. Her maternal grandmother had wanted to give her an amulet to wear around her neck to protect her from evil spirits and the infection. 'Witchcraft,' her mother had snapped. 'They don't have that in Europe.' Mary had left the amulet behind, but she'd memorized the address of the man in Cádiz.

She would never tell anyone about the journey. Her mother wouldn't want to know. Sefi would start crying. Her brothers were in South-South and could not find work. They spent their money on *burukutu*, drinking themselves senseless.

But she had told the man in Cádiz about the crooks who had thrown the people in the sea. 'They have nothing to do with us,' he'd told her. 'They were crooks. It's a bad business.'

Last exit in Denmark, it said on a new sign.

The man in Cádiz had locked her in while she waited for her *trolley*. He had shown her the passport. 'Memorize the name,' he snapped. That's how he talked. Snapping like a saucepan that splashed as it boiled over. Mary Kwara had looked at the picture of a woman and wondered who she was. 'Don't ask,' he'd snapped. Then her *trolley* had arrived and taken charge of the passport.

The bus headed into a tunnel. She couldn't see the end, only white walls and rows of lights in the ceiling. The tunnel lasted an eternity. She glanced at the man sitting next to her. He looked like he was asleep, but she couldn't be sure. She would do what he said. The man in Cádiz knew who her parents were.

Finally they emerged from the tunnel, and she could see the water. She huddled in her seat. If only I don't have to get on another boat, she thought, and thousands of lights flashed before her eyes and she couldn't breathe. The road rose up and she saw the bridge, a huge bridge suspended between four tall towers. And far off in the distance, where the bridge ended, she saw a city. She gripped the armrests of her seat. That's where I'm going, she thought. Straight across the sea.

She closed her eyes. Sefi would have stayed with the woman with the many necklaces. She would have settled for having food to eat and a TV to watch. Sefi was lazy. She wouldn't have crept around and found money in the house when the woman was away. She wouldn't have stolen the money to buy a bus ticket.

God has no time for such trivial matters, Mary Kwara had thought, but she had still prayed for forgiveness, just in case. If she didn't go to Cádiz, her parents would have to keep paying back the debt, and then Sefi would have to pay, and Sefi's children as well. And if her brothers ever sent any money home from South-South, they would take that too.

Her heart had pounded hard as she'd sneaked away from that house where she had slept many nights. It had taken several hours for her to find the bus station in Tarifa. It was a small station. She bought a ticket for the bus. When the bus drove up into the mountains, she saw the town far below, like a heap of sugar cubes that someone had spilled out onto the beach. Then the bus turned, and she saw only the countryside all around.

Driving further and further through mountains and fields and forests, passing villages and gas stations, she thought: at least I'm travelling away from the sea. I never want to see it again.

Once, in the night, she'd had a sense that water was all around her, but then she had closed her eyes and decided it was the darkness trying to trick her into seeing something she didn't want to see. Spirits and waves.

But now it was daytime, and she saw the surging grey-green surface on both sides of the bridge. Only a low railing and a railway track separated her from the deep.

She would have to work hard to pay back the debt. Five years. Maybe ten. Then she would be free.

Then she would have a house with white walls. And red flowers growing in the garden. A house with several rooms and a TV and her own bed.

And some day she would travel back home. This was the first time during the entire journey that she'd dare think about that. What if I go back home? Will there be anyone left who remembers me?

The bridge rose up and turned, balanced between those tall towers. A blue and yellow sign flickered past in all the grey. She could feel the bus shuddering in the wind.

My name is Promise, she murmured quietly to herself. My name is Promise Makinwa-Keizer.

Chapter 21

Prague
Two months later

The white wand slid over my stomach, which was smeared with gel. Something moved in the lower portion of the screen, and I saw the outline of a tiny, huddled body floating in slow motion, a quiet pulsing.

'The heart,' said the doctor, pointing with his pen. 'Look how nice and steady it's beating.'

I smiled, because that's what he expected of me, but the only thing I saw was an electronic image. An abstract figure.

'Would you like to hear the heartbeat?'

I nodded, and he placed the stethoscope against my swollen belly, then handed me the earpieces. I heard a rushing, a muffled flowing and thudding. Like when you try to adjust an old radio — the white noise in the space between the channels where no one is sending any signals. He moved the end of the scope. I felt metal against my skin. Suddenly it was there. A rapid and persistent little tapping, and tears rose to my eyes. My whole chest tightened. I pulled out the earpieces and gave the stethoscope back to the doctor. Turned my head away and wiped my eyes.

It was alive. It was really alive in there.

'An alert little sparrow,' said the doctor, tearing off a piece of paper towel and handing it to me. 'Do you want to know what it is?'

I wiped the goop off my stomach. Sparrow?

'I mean, whether it's a boy or a girl?' he said.

I shook my head. It didn't matter. Either one would need food and a place to live. Medical treatment, in the worst case scenario. The months left until the birth felt like an urgent ticking, a demand that everything be resolved.

I hauled myself out of the chair, feeling stiff and clumsy.

'So, I'm going to write down the fourth of May,' he said. 'Which means you're in the twentieth week of your pregnancy.'

I put on my skirt with the elastic waistband and then pulled on the heavy tights.

'So it's not . . . damaged?' I said, casting another glance at the screen. He had paused the image so the foetus was motionless in the moment that had just passed. A printer was spewing out a hard copy of the image.

'Are you worried about that?' He frowned. 'Did something happen to you?'

'I think I'm just nervous,' I said. The memory resurfaced, of bricks and stones pressed against my face, the man lunging above me among the thorny bushes. But I felt nothing. As if it had happened to someone else.

'You look a little pale,' he said, then added something about how I needed to eat this or that, but I didn't understand. I recorded the words in my mind, wanting to look them up in the dictionary that I had in my bag. The language had started coming back to me, but it was barely at the level of a six-year-old.

'Give this to the nurse and she'll set up a time for another appointment,' he said, handing me the black-and-white picture, with the date filled in. 'And let me offer you my congratulations.'

I went straight to the ladies' room and got out my dictionary. *Bílkovina* was protein and *žehlička* meant iron.

Vrabec really did mean sparrow. A bird longing to fly out. Tapping impatiently.

In the reception area the nurse handed me a form to fill in.

'I heard that here it was possible to be . . . invisible,' I said. I was looking for the word meaning anonymous, but I couldn't think of it in Czech. The doctor had tried to speak German with me when he heard my halting accent, but that was even worse.

The nurse peered at me over the top of her glasses.

'I still need a name and date of birth. And we'd like to have a phone number too. Somewhere we can reach you. We won't give out any information if you ask us not to.'

I stared at the form. There was a place for name, date of birth, address, and citizenship, plus an empty space that sneered at me: Name of father.

I quickly scribbled down the information she wanted.

'The phone number . . . I don't have one at the moment,' I said.

The nurse studied what I'd written, alarming me with the amount of time she took.

'Terese Wallner,' she read out loud. 'And you were born in 1978?'

'Mmm,' I said vaguely, hoping I wouldn't have to show her my passport.

According to my passport I was born in 1996 and had turned twenty the year before. Ally Cornwall was in her late thirties when she disappeared. I was short, with a nondescript appearance that could be easily changed. With the right make-up, I could look anywhere between twenty and forty-five. That had worked fine with my landlady, and when I applied for jobs. No one had cared. A passport from an EU country was sufficient. But no one with a medical education would accept that. I was going to have to get a different passport before the birth. I'd have to ask around.

One advantage was that I'd be able to stop dying my hair a Nordic summer-blonde colour, as it said on the package. An unnecessary expense.

I got out my wallet and paid the bill. As the nurse put the money away, I studied the form in front of me.

The father's name.

Sooner or later I might be forced to fill in the space. I would write 'unknown' and claim that I had no idea, but back in the room I'd rented, in the folder in the bottom of my suitcase, I'd stowed away a few small items. My wedding ring. The photo I'd carried with me all over Europe. Some day I would tell my child about Patrick. But only after the child was old enough and had learned to keep quiet about certain matters.

A totally different thought now occurred to me.

'But isn't this information registered somewhere?' I asked.

The word 'registered' was ingrained in my vocabulary, at any rate. It was a word you learned as a three-year-old in a communist bureaucracy.

'No, it's just for us here in the office,' said the nurse. 'So we won't get our patients mixed up.' She gave me a look that said we were all alike, all of us women with the swollen bellies.

'I mean . . . later, at the hospital.'

'If the child is born in the Czech Republic, the birth is registered, of course.'

'The father's name too?'

'Certainly.' The woman stapled the form to the black-and-white ultrasound image. 'Provided you know who he is, of course,' she added.

'How was it done in the past?' I asked, ignoring her remark. 'Under the Communists, I mean. Under Gustáv Husák . . . in the seventies? Was everything registered back then too?'

The nurse burst out laughing.

'Are you kidding? They registered who you met, what you ate for breakfast, and which books you read. So naturally they would register the name of a child's father.'

Just then the little bell rang and a woman came in, her belly huge, her eyes on the floor. She was wearing a veil.

Terese Wallner was given an appointment for the following month.

I came out onto the street outside the doctor's office, which was hidden away in an ordinary apartment building on Malá Strana. December had arrived in Prague with bitter cold. I blew on my hands to warm them up and wrapped my coat more tightly around me. It was a shapeless man's coat made of wool, from a second-hand shop. I figured I'd be able to wear it until the birth. I stuffed my hands in the pockets and began walking rapidly towards the river.

It had worked today too. I was Terese. A young Swedish woman visiting Prague for an unspecified length of time.

I'd practised speaking with a lilting Swedish accent, slowly getting used to sounding like someone from the *Muppet Show*. If anyone asked, I had learned Czech from my maternal grandmother who was born in Bohemia, though I wasn't sure exactly where. We'd lost contact with that side of the family. That was why I was here in Prague. To improve my language skills.

So far I'd been lucky and hadn't met any Swedes. But

a man where I worked had shouted at me one day when he was even drunker than usual, accusing my people of stealing the Silver Bible. I fled before he demanded to have it back.

Alena Cornwall was presumed dead.

From a purely legal point of view, she could not, of course, be declared dead, since her body hadn't been found, but the tragic story had been made public.

Occasionally I would go to an Internet café, though never the same one twice, and read what was being written.

The day after Patrick's funeral, Richard Evans had posted an editorial on the web version of *The Reporter*, in which he heralded Patrick Cornwall's journalistic career. He also wrote about the courage of Patrick's wife, Alena Cornwall, who had disappeared a few weeks after her husband's death. A suicide note, which had been sent to her assistant, indicated that she'd taken her own life, drowning in the fierce sea of sorrow — the same deadly sea that had robbed Patrick Cornwall of his life.

Evans had printed our wedding photo with the editorial, and Benji must have been contacted, since there was a quote from my last letter to him: 'I have no wish to go on living. I hope you find love and if you do, Benji, hold onto it every second.'

A month later Patrick's name appeared in the entertainment sections when George Clooney said that he was involved in producing a film. He had been touched by Patrick Cornwall's passion for justice, and he wanted to tell the true story. After that, only silence.

Alain Thery had slowly vanished from the news feeds. During the first weeks the murder in Puerto Banus had shaken half of Europe and made big headlines. One of the charred bodies had worn handcuffs, which indicated premeditated murder. Although another possibility was a

379

terrorist attack aimed at the jetset culture, so symbolic of the despicable lifestyle in the West.

Alain Thery's body was quickly identified. He was described as a prominent businessman and a well-known figure in social circles in both France and on the Spanish Costa del Sol. Many mourned his passing. Even the French president made a statement, saying that such an attack exhorted Europe to undertake a vigorous effort to counter criminality and terrorism.

But no suspect was found. The terrorist theory was dismissed as weeks passed without anyone stepping forward to claim responsibility. The last article I read said that the murder must have been committed by a lone individual.

I'd never seriously worried that the police would connect the murder to Alena Cornwall. But there were others who might: the man who had raped me in Tarifa, and the network that stretched across all of Europe and even beyond.

I remembered that voice in the vacant lot, as I lay on the ground with my face in the thorny bushes, curled up and waiting to die. '. . . *don't try to hide. We can find you anywhere.*'

So I'd let her die in the sea.

When the steep drop-off ended, and I felt solid ground under my feet — sand and sharp rocks — it was like being born again. I crawled the last part of the way, freezing cold and exhausted, and found myself on a deserted beach outside a tennis club several kilometres from Puerto Banus.

The flames were still visible way out in the water. A couple of boats with searchlights were on the scene, but keeping a safe distance from the burning yacht.

I curled up under some bushes until dawn arrived. And when the tennis club opened, I slipped inside and used a blow dryer in the ladies' room to dry myself off. Then I plucked the plastic bag of banknotes from its hiding place and took out two damp ten-euro bills. I stuck the rest in the waistband of my panties and left the club to head up the road. Barefoot, I kept on walking until I came to a bus stop.

At the bus station in Marbella, I went to the locker where I'd left my belongings, and changed into jeans and a shirt and sneakers. I stuck Terese Wallner's passport in my pocket. I stuffed the Armani clothes in a plastic bag and tossed it into the trash. Then I got on a bus to Madrid and didn't wake up until we were far inland in the Spanish countryside.

Only then did I dare think about where I should go. Definitely not north, in the direction of France. And to the south was the outer border of Europe, where I'd be forced to show my passport. It occurred to me that since I'd already started remembering some French, then probably the Czech language was also buried somewhere in my memory. Being able to speak the language would make it easier to hide in the crowds, and the Czech Republic was both an EU country and in the Schengen zone, with no internal border controls.

'They don't even bother to look at passports,' the man named Alex had told me. I had asked about him at the Blue Heaven Bar, and an hour later he had appeared. Self-confident and attractive in a rumpled sort of way. And yes, he did have a passport for sale. The age wasn't right, of course, and we didn't look much alike, but he said that wouldn't matter. 'Blonde and Swedish and an EU citizen. That's enough. All you have to do is dye your hair, and you can go to any country you like.'

Each time I crossed a border my heart had pounded, but nowhere did anyone ask to see my passport.

I had no sense of coming home when I got off at the station in Prague. I needed a job and a place to live. Everything else was irrelevant.

I spent seven nights sleeping in a youth hostel near the

School of Economics before I heard about a room for rent. The landlady was over seventy and lived alone in a seven-room apartment. I shared a kitchen and bathroom with two students from Dresden. I said 'good morning' and 'goodnight' to them whenever we met. Soon I'd have to find a different place to live, preferably my own apartment, but it was hard to find anything cheap. The landlady had made it clear that she didn't want any baby crying in the apartment. She missed Husák, she said. The old days when order reigned. Back then she hadn't needed to take in lodgers to make ends meet.

I never talked to anyone longer than necessary, not even in the shops. I was always aware of the risk of being discovered. The only solution was solitude.

Sometimes I felt such an urge to call Benji, just for the joy of saying: *Hi, it's me.*

But the network could trace phone calls and find people that I'd known. Under no circumstances could I contact anyone from my old life.

Occasionally I would think: There is one person. If he's alive. Someone that nobody would connect with Alena Cornwall, because even I didn't know his name.

But his name was in the public records.

Not now, I thought, but maybe someday. When I can devote my time to digging through dusty archives. When I can afford to think about myself.

I hurried as fast as I could down the sloping streets of Malá Strana. I hadn't been to this part of town before. In a dingy little bar I bought a hamburger to eat as I walked. *Bílkovina* and *žehlička*. Protein and iron.

Over by the river I stopped abruptly. On the other side Nové Mesto glittered with Christmas decorations. The air stood still in the cold, and the water moved as slowly as sluggish oil.

The buildings on the other side. They looked so familiar. The black water. And a boat gliding along the quay.

It was not the same, and yet I was positive that it was here I'd stood. That time thirty years ago, in one of the only memories I had. When he had put his strong hands around my waist and lifted me high up so I could see the boats better.

I moved a few steps to the side. It was right here. I stared at the dark surface of the water, and all the traffic noise vanished. I heard a sound in my head, a deep voice speaking behind me, as if caressing the back of my neck.

In school they'll tell you that it's the Vltava . . .

His voice! Warm and close to my ear as he held me up so I could see. And the boat down there was very small, with only an old man on board, wearing a cap on his head.

. . . but it's all the rivers of the world. It flows north and merges with the Elbe in Germany, and then they both continue west and absorb smaller rivers and flow into the North Sea and the Atlantic Ocean, and all the oceans and rivers of the world are connected to one another, everything is one body of water.

And I see the vapour curl past my ear, the vapour from his mouth because it's so cold, and I exhale too and laugh when the vapour from my mouth mixes with his.

We are also water, he says. *Above all else, we are water.*

No, I say. *Nijak ne.*

And I laugh at such a silly idea, because I'm certainly not water, and I turn around to tell him that, and then I see him.

I see him.

Slightly crooked teeth and thin lips. He spins me around so I'm looking into his eyes, and they are brown, and the scarf wrapped around his neck is blue. My face is very close to his. A stern glint, a hint of darkness in his eyes.

Don't trust what anyone tells you . . . Alena milenka . . .

Then he laughs and lifts me onto his shoulders. I howl because I want to get down and find out what he means. I don't understand.

But he walks towards the bridge, taking jaunty strides, and he is singing so loudly that people turn around to stare. And I can hear the words in my head so well – about strangers and strange people and faces that come out of the rain – but it's not Jim Morrison I hear. It's my father's voice. A hint of a Czech accent. And I know every word because I've listened to that song so many times, over and over again, not knowing that it was always there, among the memories that I'd lost.

The theatre was located on a nondescript side street to Václavské Náměstí. I noted that the posters for the performance had been put up inside the display case next to the entrance, printed in dirty brown tones, which carried over to the stage set and were meant to make the audience think of the Communist days. It was a week until the opening night.

The girl in the ticket booth hardly raised her eyes. She was deeply immersed in a textbook. Inside, the foyer was deserted. Probably taking a break in the rehearsals. I stopped in front of the stage, quietly murmuring several Czech sentences to myself as I studied the set design.

'There stands an oak on the shore, with golden chains around its trunk.'

I listened as often as I could, trying to bring the rhythm and the poetry into my meagre language. Trying to stop feeling like a child.

There was something that didn't fit. I tilted my head, first one way and then the other, to see what was bothering me about the stage set. There was a symmetry that hadn't been properly accomplished.

The set was pared down and sombre. The director had chosen to move the frame of Chekhov's *Three Sisters* to the Cold War and an unidentified Communist state in which the dream was to go to the United States. It was not an entirely workable interpretation, but the public interest was high, even before the premiere.

It took a few minutes before I saw what was wrong. Quickly I went up the small flight of stairs to the stage and took down the portrait of James Dean that hung on the wall as a symbol of the sisters' longing for the West. I wiggled the hook loose and then licked my thumb before pressing it against the wallpaper so the hole wouldn't be seen.

Then I moved a metre to the left, stuck in the hook, and hung the picture up again. I backed up to the edge of the stage to look at the result.

'What are you doing? Are you crazy?'

I gave a start and turned around. It was one of the stagehands. A guy with blond hair.

'You know you're not supposed to touch the stage set.'

'Sorry.' I clumsily climbed down from the stage. Damned belly. The stagehand held a screwdriver in one hand and was carrying a ladder, on his way to adjust the lighting. I couldn't help casting a glance at the stage set. Now it worked.

'What were you doing on the stage?' He pointed the screwdriver at James Dean. 'Were you thinking of swiping the picture, or what?'

'No, I just wanted to . . . Sorry. It's nothing. You don't need to tell anyone.'

He merely shook his head as he climbed the ladder. I went out through a side door that led backstage. I lowered my eyes when I ran into one of the actors in the corridor. No more blunders.

Back to being invisible.

With my eyes fixed on the floor, I went over to the janitor's closet next to the dressing rooms, opened the door, and took my smock from a hook. It hid the shape of my body and made me look overweight rather than pregnant. I picked up the mops and backed out. Turning the cleaning cart around, I pushed it in front of me as I headed down the hall.

Acknowledgements

Thank you to Julien Bobroff and Sarah Hercule Bobroff for invaluable help with research in Paris. To Ulla Kassius for insight into the profession of set designers, to Richard Reiss for orienting me in the East Village, to Anna Erman for explaining French law, and to Tomas Lindbom for offering analyses of French politics. Thanks to Elizabeth L. Fort at the Joyce Theatre in New York, to Juan Triviño Domínguez at Cruz Roja in Tarifa, and to Johanna Eriksson-Strand at the National Board of Forensic Medicine in Umeå.

Special thanks to Boel Forssell, Claes Forssell Andersson, Kina Alsterdal, Olivia Taghioff, Kicki Linna, Nikolaj Alsterdal, and to all the others who have helped out, answered questions, read the manuscript, and contributed in other ways. To Kristoffer Lind, because you believed in this story, to Kajsa Willén and all the other superb colleagues at the Swedish publishing company.

My thanks to Liza Marklund — as always! For reading and rereading, for encouraging and offering incisive criticism. I couldn't have done it without you.

Finally, my eternal thanks to Elsa Bolin, for everything.

Tove Alsterdal